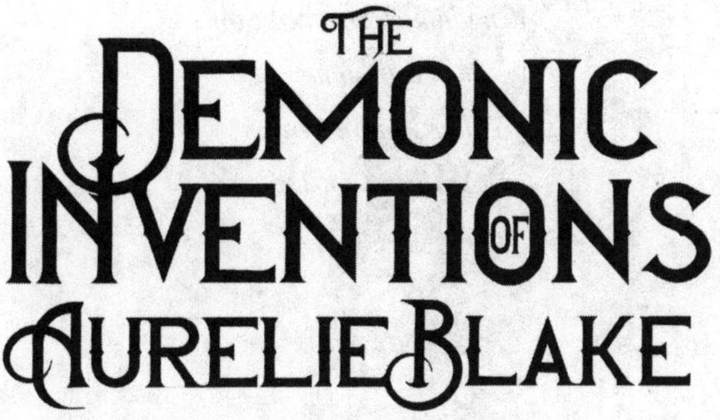
THE
DEMONIC
INVENTIONS
OF
AURELIE BLAKE

ALSO BY MARA RUTHERFORD

Crown of Coral and Pearl

Kingdom of Sea and Stone

Luminous

The Poison Season

A Multitude of Dreams

THE DEMONIC INVENTIONS OF AURELIE BLAKE

MARA RUTHERFORD

HARPER
An Imprint of HarperCollins*Publishers*

HarperCollins Children's Books,
a division of HarperCollins Publishers, 195 Broadway, New York, NY 10007

HarperCollins Publishers,
Macken House, 39/40 Mayor Street Upper, Dublin 1, D01 C9W8, Ireland

The Demonic Inventions of Aurelie Blake

harpercollins.com
Library of Congress Control Number: 2025946580
ISBN 978-1-335-01388-0
Typography by David Curtis
26 27 28 29 30 LBC 5 4 3 2 1
First Edition

Whenever a thing is done for the first time,
it releases a little demon.
—Emily Dickinson

Invention, it must be humbly admitted,
does not consist in creating out of void, but out of chaos.
—Mary Shelley, *Frankenstein*

CHAPTER 1

AURELIE

MONDAYS WERE AN EXCELLENT DAY FOR INVENTING.

After all, they were the first day of the week, and if one were to begin something new, one ought to start at the beginning. Like cracking open a fresh sketchbook or leaving the first footprint on new-fallen snow, there was something about a clean slate that made a young inventor feel alive.

Or at least, it held true for Aurelie. Her sample size was rather limited, considering she'd never met another inventor to ask.

Mondays were also the busiest days at Wisteria University, which meant that her uncle and dean of the college, Dr. Leopold Blake, was far less likely to drop by unannounced. Her best opportunity for unhindered innovation was always late at night, but even Aurelie needed sleep sometimes, and besides, daylight afforded far better visibility. Especially when she was working with fiddly little wires, as she was now.

But the very best thing about Mondays was that they were the day of rest for the kingdom's Iron Guard, also known as demon hunters. And in Wisteria, where there were inventions, there were demons.

Fortunately, Aurelie wasn't overly concerned about this specific invention. She'd been working on a prototype for months, and the subsequent demon had been small and weak, as they always were with undeveloped ideas. She wasn't a risk-taker by nature, but when it came to inventing, she believed the risk was worth the reward. Who could possibly fault Aurelie for solving one of life's greatest difficulties with such a simple creation? Who *wouldn't* want a long, telescoping metal arm to grasp items out of reach? Was there anyone at the university—indeed, in the world—who hadn't stretched for the highest book in the library and found even the tallest ladder wanting?

Three rapid knocks sounded on the door, causing Aurelie to drop the delicate wire she'd bent into the shape of a lopsided question mark. Before she could respond, her best friend entered the room, a large red apple stuffed into her mouth like a pig at a banquet, a stack of old textbooks teetering in her arms. Aurelie wasn't sure how she'd even managed to open the door, to be honest.

"What have I told you about waiting for permission to enter?" Aurelie scolded as Kiara dropped the books onto the overstuffed velvet sofa that served as a makeshift bed, though her tone was light. No one visited her down here besides Kiara and Uncle Leo, but she still felt a jolt of panic every time the door opened suddenly.

Taking a bite of her apple, Kiara tucked her shoulder-length brown hair behind her ears and grinned. "I think what you mean to say is, *'Thank you, Kiki, for being the world's best friend and bringing me all the books I asked for.'*"

"Thank you, Kiki," Aurelie singsonged, her torso now buried in a large wooden wardrobe while she rummaged for the beaker she needed for this afternoon's experiment. She had already checked out her ten-book allotment for the month and often relied on Kiara to help fill in the gaps.

“What are you working on?” Kiara asked, crunching with deliberate vigor while she peered over Aurelie’s shoulder. “The grabby stick?”

Aurelie winced at the ever-infuriating sound of a person chewing and shot a wry look at Kiara. “It’s called the Helping Hand. And I’m currently preparing my new elixir to test on the moss we retrieved from the cemetery wall last month.”

The elixir in question was a clear, viscous fluid gathered from a rare variety of slug that Aurelie had obtained from the zoology department. She had condensed and purified it over the past week in a series of beakers to get it to the right consistency.

“That’s all well and good,” Kiara said, thumbing through one of the books she’d brought from the library, “but our shift starts in fifteen minutes.”

Aurelie glanced at the wall clock and groaned in despair. How was a girl supposed to work twenty hours a week as a bricoleur, tending to the needs of an old and crumbling university and its entitled student body; spend twenty more hours a week working toward her own degree; sleep the recommended eight hours a night; eat the sustenance required by the human body; maintain socially acceptable hygiene; and still find time to change the world?

She wasn’t supposed to, was the obvious answer. But that wouldn’t stop her from trying.

Replacing the elixir in the wardrobe with a weary sigh, Aurelie removed her apron, pulled on the dingy gray coat she used for her repair work, and followed Kiara out into the hall.

“Aren’t you forgetting something?” Kiara asked, just as Aurelie heard a pitiful mew from behind the closed door.

She hurried to open it, nearly squashing one of Mephisto's eight legs in the process. The tiny dragon-like demon scuttled across the floor, its long nails clacking as it ran to its food bowl and blinked up at her with expectant red eyes.

"I'm sorry," she said, bending over to stroke one of its long eyebrows and nearly losing a finger to its sharp teeth in the process. "Ingrate," she muttered as she placed a plump dead cockroach into Mephisto's bowl, patting the demon's head one last time before joining Kiara in the hall.

"Here," Kiara said, handing Aurelie her own apple. She rarely ate breakfast—a waste of time, when there were always so many more important things to do—and would happily have survived on coffee until noon if it weren't for Kiara. The apple wasn't much, but it was portable, and that was a requirement for someone in perpetual motion.

Which reminded her of the paper she needed to write about the theoretical possibility of a perpetual-motion clock. Would it be so much to ask for twenty-*five* hours in a day?

"Where to first?" Aurelie asked as she followed Kiara up the stairs into the main body of Easton Hall. Unlike her laboratory, which was dark and low-ceilinged in a way Aurelie had come to think of as cozy, the halls here were light and lofty, with enormous windows Aurelie had spent far too much time cleaning. The students wouldn't arrive for another hour, but Aurelie tried to do as much work as she could before then. There was nothing worse than having to remove an ink stain from the carpet while some arrogant boy peered down at her as though she were his personal servant.

"Classroom 137. The gas lamps need topping up."

Aurelie sighed. She knew there had to be a better way to light up the university—and the rest of Wisteria, for that matter—but that kind of inventing would produce demons far too large for Aurelie to contain by herself. Inventing was illegal on any scale, so she was forced to keep her creations, and their subsequent demons, as small as possible. If any escaped and came to the notice of the Iron Guard, Aurelie would face a lengthy prison sentence. Worse still, Uncle Leo might also be implicated.

After they finished filling the gas lamps with oil, Kiara and Aurelie went their separate ways. The daughter of the school groundskeeper, Kiara spent nearly as much time at Wisteria University as Aurelie did, though no one else lived on the premises. Uncle Leopold had his own house on campus, an old stone cottage dripping in the kingdom's namesake flower. He still kept Aurelie's room for her, all made up in pink ribbons and flouncy ruffles, the sort of room a childless bachelor might assume a young girl would like. But alas, Aurelie had never been a ruffles-and-ribbons kind of girl.

The rest of the day passed in a blur of classes, but Aurelie's attention lay elsewhere. She was itching to get back to her lab and finish the Helping Hand. She hadn't completed an invention in weeks, and being *this close* to the finish line was exhilarating and maddening in equal measure.

By the time she returned to her laboratory at five o'clock, Aurelie was surviving on adrenaline and the remnants of a slice of pumpkin cake from another student. The cake was delicious, but she could have done without the girl's observation that Aurelie looked "positively dreadful." Passing in front of an ornate mirror, its gilded finish flaking away like autumn leaves, she grimaced at the shadows beneath her green eyes, brought out by the dim glow of the gas lamps. Her long hair was tied back in its usual braid, but wisps had broken free of their velvet ribbon, and there was a stain on her white collar that smelled suspiciously like coffee.

Still, she was determined to finish her invention tonight. She'd be just as tired tomorrow, and exams were fast approaching. She waited by the door for a moment, listening for the familiar clacking of Mephisto's claws, and hissed at it to move back so it wasn't injured.

Inside, the laboratory was even messier than she remembered, with scraps of wire and discarded nuts and bolts littering old, moth-eaten throw rugs. On the wall, diagrams were scrawled on the back side of maps, which made for easy flipping when Uncle Leo visited. Dried herbs and flowers that Aurelie pretended were mere decoration hung from the ceiling, though she often used them in her experiments. A small wall cabinet intended for knickknacks held various specimens behind its doors, which she'd foolishly left ajar. Her job as a handyperson provided her with the perfect cover to keep a toolbox here, though all the tools inside were specialized for her inventing needs.

She was tempted to lie down for a brief nap, but odds were that she wouldn't wake up until morning, and she was expected to eat dinner with her uncle every night at the cottage. She spent less and less time there lately, and though he pretended to understand, she could tell it hurt him. But no matter how hard she tried to stay away, she simply couldn't help it. If she could be anywhere in the entire kingdom, she would choose to be in her laboratory.

Placing her kettle on a small gas stove she'd fashioned for herself—the first and last time Aurelie risked conjuring a fire demon—she prepared herself a pot of coffee and waited for it to boil while she tidied up. Aurelie had spent the last eleven years of her life at the university, and what had once been a dreary and forgotten classroom—back before the "new" annex had been built and classes were relocated aboveground, so students could see the sunlight every now and again—had become her haven when Uncle Leo took her in. At first, the room had hardly been habitable, and Uncle Leo hadn't understood why Aurelie needed more than her perfectly nice bedroom in his cottage.

"It's dingy," he'd said, sniffing. "With a subtle hint of mildew."

But her persistence had won him over, and she'd eventually acquired the discarded library sofa, a desk from another abandoned classroom, and a wardrobe procured from a consignment sale held by a retiring professor. Most importantly, Aurelie had begun to collect items for her laboratory.

Uncle Leo didn't know about Aurelie's inventing. As far as he was concerned, the wardrobe was filled with her spare dresses, shoes, and underthings, rather than beakers, vials, and experiments at various stages of completion. The desk, he no doubt assumed, was where Aurelie wrote correspondence or applied cosmetics, and the sofa . . . well, the sofa was for sitting, to be fair. But it made a surprisingly comfortable bed. Aurelie slept in this room most nights now that she was eighteen.

She poured her coffee into a chipped porcelain bowl and sat at her desk, alternating between inhaling the warm, roasty scent and blowing steam off the surface. Mephisto squeaked from the floor, its claws tangling in her skirt. "Oh dear, is it dinnertime already?"

After feeding it another cockroach, followed by a quick sweep of the few seeds Mephisto left in its wake, she took a sip of her rapidly cooling coffee and settled down again at her desk, where the Helping Hand waited for her.

Despite her excitement, a small worm of apprehension wriggled in her gut. She didn't dread demons the way most Wisterians did—yes, demons could kill people, but those were the sorts of large demons that no one saw much anymore; any that did arise were taken care of by the Iron Guard—but she also didn't like killing them. Mephisto was a demon, after all, and it had never done anything worse than nip her toes or leave seed droppings on her pillow. But even the most benign demons couldn't be allowed to escape. Not if Aurelie wanted to keep inventing.

Perching her magnifying glasses on her nose, she peered down at the fiddly little wire she needed to bend just so in order to fit it into its mooring. One . . . final . . . twist.

"There!" she exclaimed, causing the demon to look up mid-cockroach, a spiny leg dangling from the corner of its mouth. "It's ready, Mephisto. Let's see how it works!"

Removing her glasses, Aurelie pulled the trigger on the device, causing the pincer at the end to open and close. She squealed with delight and reached for one of the books still sitting on her bed from this morning. It took a few tries to get the angle correct, but with a little finesse, the Helping Hand worked like a charm. She pressed the button next to her thumb and the fishing line inside spooled inward, bringing the telescoping arm in with it. And there it was, a book in her lap without her having to move from her desk.

Aurelie hardly had time to enjoy the fruits of her labor before there was a slight shimmer in the air beside her, followed by the smell of brimstone and smoke.

A second later, the demon was upon her.

The rapid appearance of the demon caught Aurelie off guard. Usually it was at least a minute before they came from whatever dimension they originated in, and it was only by luck that her iron dagger was close at hand now.

The demon was larger than she'd anticipated, with seven long arms ending in crablike pincers. Those, she'd been expecting, though perhaps not quite so many; demons always took a form related to the invention they sprang from. It was the fact that it went straight for her books that really threw Aurelie, cramming two into its fang-filled maw before she had even drawn her blade.

Aurelie leapt up, thrusting her chair at the demon and knocking it off-balance to draw its attention to her. As she knew it would, the demon abandoned the books in search of a hot-blooded meal, forcing her to dodge left and right to avoid its deadly pincers. Demons ate whatever living thing they could get their claws on, and some had been known to possess venom strong enough to paralyze or kill their prey.

Diminutive though it was, Mephisto darted between the demon's pincers, confusing it long enough that Aurelie was able to grab the pot of coffee. She flung it at the demon while simultaneously slicing off an arm with her dagger, a claw only millimeters from her nose. Within seconds, the demon began to smoke and crackle, before bursting into green flames that burned out so quickly it was almost as if the creature had never been. All that was left behind were the confetti-like ribbons of pages the demon hadn't yet consumed. That, and her beautiful, wasted coffee.

Aurelie inhaled shakily and dusted off her shoulders, making sure she still had all her appendages. Mephisto, too, seemed unharmed, and she patted its long, bristly tail in thanks. With a sigh, she bent down to retrieve what remained of one of the books. It was an old biology textbook that she would very much have liked to read, and now she'd have to reimburse the library for it.

As Mephisto returned to its unfinished meal, Aurelie picked up the Helping Hand and used it to grasp a glass of water on the side table that served as a nightstand. She drank it all in one long gulp, tidied her hair in the mirror, and mopped up the remaining mess. She was already going to be late for dinner, and as she calculated the cost for two old textbooks—their price inflated, of course, because no new books were being written—she wondered for the first time if this experiment had been worth it.

"Of course it is," she whispered to herself as she locked the door behind her. She knew better than anyone that progress was not a straight path; it featured all the topography of an uncharted world, and all the promise.

And it required a person like Aurelie to brave it.

CHAPTER 2

DES

KEEPING TO THE SHADOWS AS HE STALKED HIS PREY, DEStrier Whitlow wondered why people continued to procreate at all. It was a Monday night, and though he should have been in the barracks with his fellow guards, enjoying his only day of leisure, babies insisted on being born regardless.

The trouble with creating new life was that it also created demons, and particularly unpleasant ones to kill. *Natia*, or natal demons, took the form of young children, indistinguishable from their human counterparts except for the lingering smell of sulfur and ash and their crimson eyes. He gripped the hilt of the iron sword at his hip and continued to follow a girl with blond ringlets hanging to her shoulders, walking with an unnaturally self-assured gait for a child so young.

"Des," his partner hissed from across the street, causing the demon to glance behind her and quicken her pace.

Des pressed a finger to his lips, urging the boy to be quiet before their quarry ran. Demons were fast, and Des was still tired from the two he'd killed yesterday. The commander should have known better than to give him such a green guard as a partner. Then again, Des was being trained for command himself one day, and this was likely a strategic move on Commander Yew's part, not a coincidence.

The boy, Gareth, hurried across the street to where Des stood.

"I told you, never abandon your post unless I give the order," Des hissed.

"I know," Gareth whispered, hovering a little too close to Des. It was a well-known fact among the guards that he didn't like anyone encroaching on his personal space. "But I think we're being followed."

Des glanced over his shoulder, his stomach dropping when he realized Gareth was right.

About a block behind them, a demon peeked out from the side of an abandoned factory, its eyes glowing like hot coals in the darkness. It wasn't a *natia*, at least. He'd need to see it more closely to be sure, but Des was fairly certain this was a *somnia*, produced whenever a person dreamed of something that had never been imagined before. They were common, of course. Invention could be controlled; dreams couldn't. But they were also easy to kill, being somewhat insubstantial themselves.

It was odd, however, that this one was following them. *Somnia* were typically shy, coming out only at night to feast on whatever small nocturnal prey they could find.

Nevertheless, this was a perfect opportunity for Gareth to make his first kill while Des took care of the *natia*, which was getting away from them, no doubt searching for her first victim.

Des whispered the plan to Gareth, who swallowed audibly but nodded, gripping the hilt of his sword as he ducked onto a side street, where he could ambush the *somnia*.

Putting the two of them out of his mind for the moment, Des searched for the girl, who had done exactly as he'd feared: disappeared around a corner while Gareth distracted him. She couldn't have gone far on her child's legs, demon or no. He continued forward on silent feet, moving impressively fast for a man his size.

When he arrived at an alley narrowing to a silent dead end, Des cursed to himself. He'd lost the *natia*, and he'd likely be up the rest of the night looking for her. *Natia* took on the future attributes of their creators, and this girl was going to be clever when she was older. He ran his free hand over his short hair, ruing his own foolishness. He should never have allowed Gareth to take his attention off the *natia*.

He turned and headed back the way he'd come, sheathing his sword as he walked.

Which, naturally, was the perfect opportunity for an ambush.

A passing shadow was Des's only warning before the *natia* leapt on him from above and knocked him off his feet. He grunted at the impact, his head connecting with a cobblestone hard enough that he saw stars. He barely had time to put up one gauntleted arm before the demon's teeth sank into his neck. Instead, she found herself with a mouthful of iron, causing her to screech in fury.

It gave Des enough time to thrust her away while he sprang to his feet. A moment later, the demon had recovered, an unpleasant grin curling her little girl's lips, and Des took a deep breath as he drew his sword.

His body flooded with the familiar rush of adrenaline just seconds before she attacked. The *natia*, though disturbingly intelligent, was inexperienced in combat, and she only managed to escape his blade by inches. He rounded on her quickly and she leapt on top of a pile of refuse, her sharp teeth bared in a snarl.

Why did it have to be a little girl? Des thought as he crouched, waiting for her next attack and keeping a wary eye on her sharp incisors.

The demon's bite wouldn't kill him—probably—but even if she didn't have fully developed venom glands yet, it would hurt like a son of a bitch and could take him out of commission for a week. A demon had scratched him across the hand several months ago and it had gotten so infected, the medic had joked that Des might lose his second-favorite appendage. He couldn't afford any kind of misstep now, not if he wanted to get promoted.

The girl came at him again, and as much as he was dreading what he was about to do, he needed her close in order to kill her. She leapt for his chest, her face contorted in a snarl. With his right hand, he caught the demon by the throat, nearly crushing her windpipe in the process. Wide, watery red eyes stared into his, and not for the first time, he was grateful that her eyes weren't blue or brown or in any way human.

That would have made it much harder to do what was necessary.

Des dropped the demon on the ground, not giving her a moment to recover before his sword flashed, lopping her head off in one clean stroke. Instantly, the body burst into green flames.

It was all over so fast, and yet when Des closed his eyes to catch his breath, he could still see the little girl's face, the blond ringlets and pink cheeks.

Why did it have to be a little girl?

A moment later, Des heard a celebratory whoop as Gareth ran toward him.

"I did it!" he exclaimed, so green he didn't even stop to think that there might be other demons out tonight. If so, he'd scared them away. Des would be sure to search here tomorrow, just in case. "My first kill!"

Des smiled despite himself, remembering his own first kill: the fear, the thrill, the pride. All demon-orphaned children were given to the Iron Guard, and when you were raised with the knowledge that your own parents had been slaughtered by the very creatures you were fighting, you couldn't help but feel that you were righting some wrong, or at least preventing a future one. He clapped Gareth on the back so hard the boy stumbled, but he was still grinning as he recounted the story.

"You did well," Des said, trying to convey the same fraternal pride the older guards had showed him when he made his first kill at age eleven. Gareth was thirteen or fourteen, Des thought, his parents having been killed only a year before. It was easy to forget that each member of the Iron Guard had suffered something terrible, that they weren't all merely involuntary conscripts in service to their kingdom. Or that they'd once had dreams other than fighting monsters.

As they continued their patrol, crossing over the canal and approaching the Iron Fortress in silence, Gareth shook his head, a bemused look on his face. "It was strange, though," he said, glancing up at Des.

"What was?"

"The *somnia.* I understand that they're not known for being threatening, but this one . . . It didn't even try to escape when it saw me coming. It was as though it was waiting for me."

"Waiting for you to what?"

"I don't know, exactly. But it held its hands up, almost like it wanted me to know it wasn't there to hurt me."

Des frowned down at the boy. "That's impossible. Demons don't communicate with humans."

"I know," Gareth said, flushing with embarrassment. "Never mind. It was probably nothing."

"Nice night for it?" the guard in the tower shouted down as they approached the gate.

"Excellent!" Gareth called up. "My first kill!"

The guard whooped in solidarity, raising his sword at Gareth, who hefted his in return. Absently, Des hoisted his into the air as well, following Gareth through the gates. But even as he removed his armor and settled down in his rack, something gnawed at him.

Somnia were easy to kill and trap—oftentimes a sprinkling of salt was enough to paralyze them—but they still fled when they were spotted. They didn't wait for death as though inviting it. And they certainly didn't try to communicate with humans.

He pressed the heels of his palms into his eye sockets. What if he'd been wrong, and it hadn't been a *somnia*? He should never have risked sending Gareth into battle alone, not for his first kill, not ever. Tonight had ended well, but it could have been disastrous for both of them.

There were three rules the Iron Guard upheld above all others: never hunt alone; never act on impulse; never underestimate a demon.

And tonight, he'd disobeyed all three.

CHAPTER 3
AURELIE

AURELIE SAT AT THE FAR END OF THE LONG MAHOGANY dining table, her uncle's expression difficult to read from here. If she was being honest, Uncle Leo was always a bit inscrutable to Aurelie, who had never been very successful at masking her emotions. She wore her heart on her sleeve, according to Kiara, a generous euphemism for saying that if Aurelie was displeased, you knew it.

"How are your studies?" he asked, which was always the first thing he inquired about at dinner.

As always, she smiled and assured him they were going well.

"That's not what I heard from Mr. Viridian," Uncle Leo said, arching a dark brow.

Aurelie winced. Miles Viridian was a history student notable only for his height ("tall to the point of absurdity," as she'd once put it to Kiara) and the fact that he seemed to always be lingering in Aurelie's favorite corner of the library. When he'd asked about her upcoming exams, she may have mentioned that she was feeling a bit overwhelmed, but she certainly hadn't expected him to go running to her uncle as though it were breaking news.

"I'm sorry, Uncle. My studies *are* going well. I simply wanted to avoid a lengthy conversation with Miles."

"Oh? And why is that?" Leo took a delicate bite of fish, chewing methodically. He did everything in the same manner: neat, composed, calculated. His black hair was always slicked back with pomade, his beard trimmed just so. He was her mother's younger brother, only in his mid-thirties, but he came across as older. Where Uncle Leo was reserved and focused, Claudine had been as wild and untamed as her garden.

Even if Aurelie didn't abhor a sycophant, Miles's decision to pursue a degree in history, of all subjects, hinted at a dire lack of imagination. Not that she could ever say as much to her uncle. "I had a lot of work to attend to before classes."

Leo set his fork down and sighed. "I've told you a dozen times that you don't need to continue with your menial labor. We have Mr. Morel and his daughter for that sort of work."

Aurelie bristled, both at the insinuation that such labor was beneath them, and also that two people alone could maintain this entire institution. "They need my help, Uncle. Besides, I enjoy my work." And she *needed* it. It gave her access to tools and parts of the university others didn't enter, and it helped hone her mechanical skills.

"Yes, yes. Your tinkering, as you call it. But if it's interfering with your studies . . ."

"It isn't," Aurelie assured him. "I have plenty of time for both. Besides, I like making my own money."

At this, Uncle Leo crossed his arms and leaned back in his chair. "Aurelie, you are my only living relative. The idea that you would need money of your own is absurd."

For the second time that night, Aurelie winced. When would she learn to think before she spoke? "My apologies, Uncle. I'm extremely grateful for your generosity. I suppose it's that my parents always instilled the value of independence in me. And with them dying so young, I know full well that nothing in life can be taken for granted."

Uncle Leo softened, as Aurelie had known he would. The carriage accident that had resulted in their premature deaths was never far from either of their minds. "Yes, well." He gestured for the servant to clear their dishes. "Old habits can be difficult to break. But Mr. Viridian comes from a good family, and I believe he likes you, Aurelie. He is exactly the kind of young man I hope you'll marry someday," he continued. "After you complete your studies, of course."

She forced a smile and thanked the servant as he cleared her plate, but inside, she felt a familiar twist of dread in her stomach. Every time Uncle Leo mentioned marriage, it was a reminder that the carefree days of her youth were nearly behind her. Leo clearly intended to pass her off to this imaginary husband as soon as she graduated, and no man in Wisteria would tolerate a wife having a secret laboratory.

Her only hope was to find a teaching position at the university herself, where she could remain close to home and her uncle, no husband required. It would be a disappointment to Leo on some level, she knew. He himself had never married, but he was old-fashioned when it came to Aurelie. If he had any idea what she'd just created in her lab only an hour ago, he'd be apoplectic.

In her defense, it wasn't as if she'd sought any of this out. Inventing had been the by-product of loneliness, of not knowing her place in the world anymore. She'd asked Uncle Leo for a pet not long after arriving at Wisteria University, a request it had taken no small amount of courage to make.

"A pet," he'd repeated, voice grave, though there was a twinkle in his dark eyes.

"Yes, Uncle. Any pet will do."

"Hmmm. Dogs aren't ideal at a university," he had mused. "All the barking."

Aurelie nodded sagely. She'd expected as much. "A cat, perhaps?"

"Excellent for libraries, but I'm afraid some of the students might be allergic, and we can't have that."

"Oh." She had prepared for this eventuality, as well. "A hairless cat, then."

Uncle Leo had frowned, leaning closer to whisper, "They look a bit like demons, no?"

Later, Aurelie would not entirely disagree.

Her other proposals—lizard, snail, parrot sworn to a vow of silence—were summarily rejected, so Aurelie had taken matters into her own hands.

A normal plant, she'd known from the start, wouldn't do. Yes, they could grow, shed, and die. But they looked so . . . *planty.* Stealing a chunk of terracotta clay from Mr. Morel's shop, Aurelie had fashioned a pot into the shape of what was supposed to be a dog but came out rather more like a dragon.

Thanks to her parents, Aurelie's knowledge of plants was vast. In one of her earliest memories, she had witnessed a pile of radish seeds left out in the rain develop into a slimy mess that would sprout several days later. *Mucilaginous* was a disgusting and intriguing word, and she happily plastered soggy radish seeds to the sides of her pot, watering it until the true magic began.

Did Aurelie understand the risk of inventing at age seven? She couldn't quite recall. She did know she'd never seen a demon before, and she would never have used the term *invent* regarding her pet-shaped planter, brilliantly named a Planter Pet. In truth, she hadn't fully understood that she had created something entirely new until Mephisto appeared.

It happened the same way it always did: a shimmer, the smell of brimstone, and suddenly, a *something* had appeared out of nothing. The tiny creature had stood blinking at her, seeming as confused and startled as she was, and then it scurried toward her, preparing to take a chunk out of her pinkie finger.

Without thinking, Aurelie had said "No!" in her firmest voice and bopped the demon on the nose. Just then, a cockroach scuttled past, and Mephisto wasted no time in switching its attention to another source of calories. It gobbled the cockroach down with surprising alacrity, crawled into Aurelie's lap, and produced a miniscule seedling dropping a few minutes later. Aurelie had collected an entire jar of them, not knowing what plant they might produce and more than a little afraid to find out.

When Kiara walked in and discovered Aurelie playing with her new "pet," she'd made her first—and only—friend. She'd never felt a need to make others. Not when Kiara was kind, funny, generous, and willing to keep all of Aurelie's secrets without ever asking anything in return.

But even once Aurelie had companionship, it had been too late for her when it came to inventing. She knew the thrill by then, the consuming euphoria of everything falling into place to create something new. She couldn't have stopped herself from loving it if she'd tried. And she had tried.

After dinner, Aurelie and Uncle Leo retired to the parlor, where they sat in what she supposed was meant to be companionable silence. Aurelie would have far preferred to be in her laboratory, where her sketchbook waited for her to draw the demon she'd conjured with the Helping Hand. Aurelie kept meticulous notes on all her demons, despite the risk of discovery. One day, a thousand years from now, someone might want a taxonomy of demons, and who else would provide it but her?

Not to mention her slug elixir was likely evaporating at this very moment. The thought of it made her stomach sour with anxiety. What was the point in doing anything if it wasn't moving toward some better end? Stagnation, Aurelie thought with a sigh, was the most wasteful state of all.

"Aurelie."

She glanced up from the book she had half-heartedly picked up to find her uncle studying her. "Yes?"

"I received some very distressing news today regarding an old friend of mine. I'll be leaving in two days."

Aurelie sat up straighter, now fully alert. "Leaving?"

"I know it must seem very sudden, but he's ill and has asked for me, and I can't refuse his request. I don't know how long I'll be gone, but factoring in travel time, I anticipate it will be at least several weeks."

Aurelie wasn't sure what to say. In her eleven years with Uncle Leo, he'd never left her. "Who will be dean in your stead?" she asked, because at eighteen, she couldn't very well say *Who will keep me out of trouble?*

"Professor Booth, most likely. She has always filled in for me quite capably when I've been ill. I'm certain she's up to the task."

Aurelie nodded. "I see." She liked Professor Booth. She taught literature, which meant Aurelie had little reason to interact with her, but they had known each other since Aurelie first arrived in Wisteria, and Professor Booth had always been kind to her.

The corners of Uncle Leo's eyes wrinkled when he smiled. "Are you worried about me?"

Aurelie huffed an embarrassed laugh. "Not worried, per se. I suppose I've taken your presence for granted. I like knowing you're nearby."

His smile widened. "I must admit, I'm relieved to hear you say that. You've been distant lately. I know that you're getting older and need your independence. But I miss tucking little Aurelie in at night."

She flushed at the memory. When she'd first come to the university, she'd cried every night for months. Afraid of the dark, afraid of forgetting her parents, afraid of everything. Before her parents died, Aurelie hadn't even known she had an uncle. Her mother had mentioned a brother in passing once or twice, but not in a way that suggested he was a part of her life. So in addition to the devastating news that her parents were dead, Aurelie had been stunned to discover she would be living with a man she'd never met.

But Uncle Leo had been unwavering in his patience. He read to her every night, fairy tales that were hundreds of years old, that hinted at a world different from the one she knew. It saddened her to think that by the time her great-grandchildren read the books of her youth, nothing would have changed. Was a fairy tale even a fairy tale if it didn't reveal the mysteries of some bygone era, if it didn't give society a glimpse into its own past?

"But fear not," Uncle Leo continued. "Mr. Viridian has valiantly offered to look in on you occasionally."

Aurelie's eyes shot up to his. "What?"

He held her gaze for a moment. "He's doing me a favor, Aurelie. You will be polite to him."

She looked away before he could see her emotions flaring.

"He'll also be escorting you to dinner next Saturday with my friends, the Applebaums. They have several children around your age I'd like you to socialize with. Their daughter, Lavender, will no doubt be a positive influence."

Aurelie bristled again, knowing full well what he wasn't saying, and about whom. "I'm hardly a *child*, and I'm around my peers every day."

"The other students—"

"I was referring to Kiara."

Her uncle cleared his throat. "Yes, well. It's important you socialize with people *outside* the university grounds. You can't stay here forever, you know."

Aurelie didn't see why not, but for once, she managed to bite her tongue.

Leo sighed and rose, kissing the top of her head as though she were still seven years old. "I won't always be around, Aurelie. It will do my heart good to know that you have other people in your life to rely on when I'm gone."

The words he wouldn't say hung in the air between them: that no matter how intelligent, hard-working, or responsible Aurelie was, he didn't believe she could make it on her own. If only he could see what she was truly capable of, if only the *world* could, he wouldn't try to shoehorn her into a role she'd never wanted for herself.

Somehow, she would find a way to prove Uncle Leo wrong. If she played her cards right, she'd never have to hear the name *Miles Viridian* again.

CHAPTER 4

AURELIE

BETWEEN UNCLE LEO'S URGENT DEPARTURE AND AURELIE'S exams, the week passed like a runaway train, leaving Aurelie flailing to keep up. She'd passed everything—just—and was grateful simply to have survived till Friday afternoon. While sleep was tempting, she could hardly pass up the opportunity for uninterrupted tinkering this weekend. Alas, for perhaps the first time in her life, she was woefully bereft of ideas. Crumpled pieces of paper, each representing a discarded notion, surrounded her wastebin.

Abandoning her lab for the time being, she met up with Kiara to make their afternoon rounds on campus, searching for any fallen branches or crumbling bricks. There was usually plenty to note, as the university hadn't had much in the way of upgrades for the last one hundred years.

"What will you do this weekend?" Kiara asked, plucking a yellowing leaf from a low-hanging branch.

"Besides sleep? That depends. What are you doing?" It was mid-November, a time of year Aurelie enjoyed because it meant the coming of cold weather, when she had every excuse to stay indoors and tinker in her lab. For some reason, people were perplexed when she chose to be a hermit on a warm day.

"I have to visit my grandparents."

Kiara's grandparents lived several hours away by coach. Wardan was a small, quaint town that made the capital city look like a bustling metropolis in comparison. "Well, it has been a while since you visited them."

"A year," she said, nodding. "But I hate it there. They don't even have gas lamps. I'll be forced to read by candlelight every night."

"The horror," Aurelie said, shuddering.

"I'll be back by Monday. Maybe we can go off campus for a change?"

Aurelie eyed her suspiciously. "Did my uncle put you up to this?"

"Maybe . . ."

Kiara lived in an apartment in town, so it was natural for her to do things away from the university. Aurelie hadn't realized quite how narrow her world had become until now, when suddenly everyone seemed to want her horizons to expand.

"Just promise me you won't try to skip out on the dinner with the Applebaums," Kiara said, nudging Aurelie with her elbow.

"Oh, he *definitely* put you up to this."

"Yes, well, he does employ two-thirds of my family."

"I'm going!" Aurelie insisted. "Say hello to your grandparents for me. And try to have fun this weekend."

Kiara rolled her eyes. "I'll try if you will."

Aurelie fished her key out of her collar and headed down the hallway toward her lab, surprised to see an object on the floor outside her door.

It was a book, and a rather old one by the look of things. A handwritten note rested on top:

Aurelie, your uncle thought you might enjoy this book I found in the library. Looking forward to dinner tomorrow. —Miles

Aurelie glanced around the hallway, uncomfortable with the notion that Miles knew where her lab was. That he'd been here, separated from her experiments—not to mention Mephisto—by only a wooden door.

"Great Discoveries and the People Behind Them: A Chronicle of Wisterian Genius," she read aloud. As she opened the book, her eyes slid to the inside cover where a name was scrawled, a serious offense in the eyes of Mrs. Clearwater, the head librarian.

Florian Hawthorn. Aurelie startled. The prince who might have been king, had his twin brother not banished him. Aciano—whose descendants still ruled Wisteria—subsequently had most of his brother's belongings destroyed, but this one must have escaped his notice.

She flipped through the book and nearly squealed with joy when she saw that Prince Florian himself had scribbled notes in the margins, more than a century ago. She clung to the book, her hands sweaty with anticipation, as she unlocked the door and hurried inside. The discoveries in this book were old, but Florian's notes could be a treasure trove of information. If nothing else, they were *new* to Aurelie.

She hardly noticed when Mephisto crawled up her skirt, over her lap, and onto the desk, its long mustache trailing behind it as it sniffed the book. It looked up at her, blinking its shiny red eyes in a way Aurelie might have described as curious. So little was known about demons. As far as she knew, none had ever been around long enough for their behavior to be studied. It was entirely possible that Mephisto was the oldest demon in all of Wisteria. A moment later, it scuttled back into the shadows, hunting insects or mice, most likely. Aurelie turned the cloth-bound cover of the book and began to read.

The first thing she noticed was how well-loved it appeared to be. There were ink smudges on some of the pages, many of which were dog-eared or torn, as if Florian had ripped them in his haste to learn more. Aurelie understood the sentiment—at the time, these discoveries were likely all brand-new.

One hundred years ago, Wisteria had been a hub of culture and innovation. Dignitaries traveled from all over the world to visit the renowned university, which had produced some of the greatest minds ever known. The factories churned with productivity. Inventors were revered for their creations. Demons were mere myths. But when King Yarrow was sickened by a foreign illness, Wisteria was changed forever.

Crown Prince Aciano was cautious and rational, wanting to ensure the safety of Wisteria's citizens above all else, while Prince Florian had been ambitious and curious: enamored with the world and everything in it. He'd spent his youth traveling abroad, returning with unnamed spices and dyes in colors so tantalizing they were reserved solely for the queen. He believed in progress, in moving the kingdom forward through innovation. Aurelie could never admit out loud how much she admired Florian: he was responsible for the demonic curse and was exiled in punishment, while Aciano took the throne.

It was Aciano's grandson, King Gabor, who ruled now, though there was little difference between him and his paternal lineage. All had been anti-progress, anti-development.

That was the second thing she noticed. As she suspected, so

many of the wonderful discoveries described—a new medicine, an improvement on an existing technology, even a new species of insect—were now long-since-taken-for-granted aspects of everyday life. All the excitement these great people must have felt, that Florian punctuated with his own ideas and exclamation points, was gone now. And Aurelie felt the bitter sting of envy every time she turned another page.

A knock on the door startled Aurelie so badly she jumped in her seat. Who could possibly be disturbing her now? Miles would have gone home an hour ago at least. She'd tidied up the lab earlier, so it only took a moment to scan the room and hide any incriminating evidence.

She frowned when she opened the door and found a campus guard standing in the hallway. They never visited her, had never really spoken to her beyond pleasantries. "Is everything all right?" she asked, a tickle of unease brushing the back of her neck.

"Right as rain, Miss Blake. Sorry to disturb you this evening, but there's a man at the front gate asking for you. I told him he'd need to wait till I checked with you first. Your uncle didn't mention anything about visitors tonight."

Aurelie worried her lip with her teeth. "What did he look like?"

"Hard to say, really. He was tall, wearing a long coat. His hat was pulled low, so I couldn't see much of his face. Around your uncle's age, I'd wager."

"Did he give a name?"

The guard nodded. "Everard. Wanted to ask you about a job."

Now Aurelie was utterly lost. She knew of no one named Everard, and she couldn't imagine anyone who would want to ask her about work. She was a bricoleur, for heaven's sake. A handyperson at a university. And eighteen years old, to boot.

"Oh, and he mentioned Mr. Morel," the guard added. "Said he knows him."

At that, Aurelie's shoulders relaxed. If the man was here about a job and knew Mr. Morel, it had to be related to groundskeeping. She would tell him to come back Monday when the Morels returned. "I'll come with you," she said. "I have to be at the cottage for dinner shortly anyhow."

Aurelie pulled on her green wool coat, locked the door, and followed the guard out to the front of the university. True to the guard's description, a tall man in a dark overcoat waited outside the gates, a hat pulled low enough that she couldn't gauge his expression from here. He straightened when he noticed her coming toward him.

"Miss Blake," he said, tipping his hat. "Thank you for meeting with me."

Aurelie could feel the guard's watchful eyes on her as she stepped outside through the small pedestrian gate. The gas lamps were lit, but it was still dark enough that she couldn't make out much beyond what the guard had already told her. "Hello," she said, squinting into the darkness. "I'm sorry to say I wasn't expecting visitors tonight. You're a friend of the Morels?"

Finally, Aurelie was close enough that she could see he was a handsome man a little younger than her uncle, his sharp cheekbones unadorned with whiskers, his eyes an arresting ice blue.

"That's right," he said. "We go far back, Mr. Morel and I. May I come in?"

"I'm afraid Mr. Morel is gone for the weekend. Would you mind coming back on Monday?" Uncle Leo would probably chide her for being rude, but she had learned to trust the small, quiet voice in her head that so very rarely spoke. The one that was whispering now: *Caution.*

"I'm not here to see Mr. Morel," the man said. Then, to Aurelie's surprise, he leaned closer, his face eye-level with hers. "It's regarding an . . ." The word was hardly more than a breath, but it felt like a roar when it hit her. "Invention."

Aurelie gasped, her hand flying to her open mouth.

"Everything all right, Miss Blake?" the guard called from behind her.

She turned to wave at him in reassurance, but her heart was thundering in her chest. Mr. Everard hadn't moved, but when she turned back toward him, he seemed to loom even closer. "I'm sorry, sir." She stepped back until she could feel the cold metal of the gate against her spine. "You must have the wrong person. I don't—"

"Don't worry, Miss Blake. You aren't in any sort of trouble. On the contrary. I'm hoping you can help me. That we can help each other." His eyes, so icy only a moment before, warmed with a smile.

The bells began to toll seven o'clock. The servants would wonder where she was. She should tell this man to go and pray that her rudeness didn't get back to Mr. Morel. But something stopped her.

No one had spoken the word *invention* out loud to her unless it was a warning or a curse. And this man hadn't said it that way. There had been no caution, no vitriol: only an undercurrent of wonder.

Two voices were warring in her head now, each urging the opposite of the other. *Stop. Go. Progress. Stagnation.*

Caution. Invention.

It was no surprise which won out.

"I need to get in for dinner," she said, glancing behind her at the guard. "Perhaps you'd like to join me?" It was a risk inviting this man in, but she wouldn't be alone with him. Her uncle's servants all knew her well and would make sure she was safe. She'd ask the guard to escort them to the cottage. Besides, he was a friend of Mr. Morel. Kiara's family wouldn't have anything to do with someone nefarious.

"Oh, I couldn't impose," Mr. Everard said, placing his hand on his chest. "Another time, perhaps."

"It's no imposition, really. My uncle's cook always makes too much food. I'm sure there will be enough. Please. I'd like to hear more about your . . . proposition." She turned to the guard before Mr. Everard could refuse. "Would you mind escorting us to my uncle's house?" she asked him. "Mr. Everard will be joining me for dinner."

Aurelie sat in her usual place with her back to the window, her gaze focused on the far end of the table. It was the first time she'd ever dined with anyone without her uncle present, and she had a bizarre, unsettled feeling that this was what dinner with her future husband would feel like. Two strangers with eight feet of space between them, forced to make conversation out of thin air.

In the light of the chandelier, Mr. Everard was more of everything he'd appeared to be outside. Tall, with smooth white skin, thick hair the color of copper, and those piercing blue eyes. She doubted he was much above thirty, yet she felt like a child sitting across from him, and not only because she was petite. She had the distinct impression this was a man who had seen things. Who traveled, yes, but who also had experienced so much more of life than she had. He hadn't even spoken since they sat down, but he radiated confidence and purpose. Aurelie wished she could be a little more like that.

The young male servant flashed an uneasy smile as he placed Aurelie's soup before her. She offered a reassuring nod in return.

"So, Mr. Everard," she said when they were alone. "Please, tell me more about why you're here."

He left his soup untouched and folded his hands on the table in front of him. "As I said, I know the Morel family."

Aurelie sat up straighter. "How are you connected?"

"A distant cousin," he said, which was vague enough to be disconcerting. She'd hoped for a more solid connection. "Mr. Morel speaks so highly of you. He said you're an excellent bricoleur, with unique ideas for solving complex issues."

Aurelie felt a wash of pleasure mingled with surprise. Mr. Morel was a kind supervisor, but he'd never complimented her about her work.

"The truth is, Miss Blake, I'm in need of someone like you. A forward thinker. A person not constrained by societal expectations."

The hairs on the back of Aurelie's neck prickled again. Had Kiara told Mr. Morel about her laboratory? Was this man here to blackmail her, or possibly even arrest her?

Everard glanced around the room, as if confirming they were truly alone, and leaned forward, his voice dropping. "I need you to create something for me."

Create. Such a simple word. And yet to bring something into existence out of nothing was a power so vast it was almost godlike. She'd had only a mere taste of that power with her inventions. At one time, she had hoped it would satisfy her. But each invention only left her wanting more.

"Yes?" she breathed.

He rose and approached the chair next to her. "May I?"

A shiver of doubt crawled up her spine, but she nodded, her pulse quickening at the thought that one of the servants could enter at any minute.

"I should warn you, Miss Blake. There will be considerable danger involved in what I'm proposing," he said as he sat down beside her.

She stared straight ahead, afraid that if she met his eyes, she would lose her nerve and ask him to leave. Everything about this conversation was taboo. "The demon, you mean?"

"Yes, of course, though it's more than that." He leaned closer, his mouth just inches from her ear. She inhaled sharply at the sheer brazenness, noticing absently that Everard seemed to have no scent whatsoever.

"This invention will be near impossible," he whispered, his breath tickling the loose strands of her hair. "Many have tried in the past and failed. I know what you're thinking, Miss Blake. Why come to you, when men with far more experience and education have failed time and time again?"

At that, Aurelie bristled. Yes, she was young, but she'd been working for over a decade. She squeezed her hands into fists, prepared to defend herself, but Everard pressed on.

"But the truth is, Miss Blake, it is your youth, your innovation, your potential that have convinced me that *you* are the person I've been seeking. Should it work, should you prove yourself up to the task, my dear . . ." He lowered his voice to a whisper. "You will be ushering in a new world. One where invention is welcomed, not feared."

Her eyes flew open as she turned to face him. "What?"

"That's right," he murmured. "A world where you can invent freely, for all to see. Imagine the opportunities for a young woman like you. Imagine the future you could choose for yourself, *by* yourself."

Aurelie's cheeks burned. She felt as though this stranger was peering directly into her soul and laying bare her secret desires for all to see. "How do you—"

He held a finger to his lips. "No more questions. Not here." He reached into his vest pocket and pulled out a folded piece of paper, his gaze never leaving hers. She suddenly understood why a rabbit froze when it fell under a predator's glare; she could scarcely breathe, let alone move.

"Everything you need to know is written here." He set the paper on the table between them. "When you've had a chance to look it over, you can contact me at this address." He held up a business card and waited for her to take it, his long fingers brushing against hers as he pulled away. They were cold as ice.

"I hope it goes without saying, but don't speak with anyone about this. Even our dear friend Morel. If you decide against it, there's no need to contact me. I'll assume you're uninterested if I haven't heard from you in a week. But, if you are willing to help me, I am prepared to offer you a hefty sum."

He rose then, and Aurelie felt compelled to stand, even though her body felt numb from the waist down. Everard began to walk to the front door, and she trailed him like a puppy, his business card still clutched in her hand. Before she could formulate a response, he was donning his coat and hat.

"What about your dinner?" she asked inanely.

"Alas, I'm afraid I have another appointment I must get to. I do hope I'll be hearing from you shortly." He reached for the door handle himself, as no servants had materialized. "Remember, discuss this with no one, Miss Blake." He flashed that incongruous smile again, flooding Aurelie with a reassuring warmth despite his warning. "After all, not everyone is a visionary like you."

CHAPTER 5
DES

DES HAD BEEN STANDING OUTSIDE THE WISTERIA UNIVERSITY gates for over an hour when the tall man in the black coat finally emerged. Des had followed him here all the way from the other side of the city. Or rather, he had followed a demon here, who'd been trailing the man all evening like a shadow.

Gareth had stood shivering beside him, clearly worried the demon—which had disappeared as soon as the man entered the iron gates—might return. Des had been more focused on the person the man had apparently come to meet: a young woman who had invited the man inside. But as far as Des knew, there weren't any classes over the weekend, and he couldn't understand why she was there in the first place.

When they disappeared into the dean's cottage, her presence began to make sense. He knew of Dr. Blake by reputation; occasionally, the man made visits to the Iron Fortress to extoll the virtues of higher education to the guards, who could choose to leave their service when they turned eighteen. Few did, of course; higher education, for all its supposed glories, didn't pay. Demon hunting did.

Des thought he remembered hearing something about the dean having a niece. He assumed they must be dining together with her uncle. But then the man emerged far too quickly to have eaten, and Des knew then that he was right to have lingered. The guard let the man out through the pedestrian gate, and only moments later, the demon they'd been hunting previously materialized.

It was a true demon, a *verita*, the worst kind because it was intentional. People couldn't control what their subconscious mind did while asleep, and even King Aciano hadn't attempted to outlaw procreation. *Verita*, on the other hand, came from willful disobedience of the law. A person *chose* to compose a new piece of music, or paint a picture, or devise a new solution to a commonplace problem, and a demon was inevitably born.

Des would never be able to understand the selfishness of such people. It was why he was determined to put an end to *verita* entirely. He couldn't eradicate all demons, not so long as they were linked to creation. But he could prevent as many children from being orphaned by demons as possible. He'd tracked down three men in the past year for illegal inventing, though tying them to their *verita* was not easy. One had gotten off on a technicality, but the other two were in prison where they belonged.

Those *verita* had escaped their creators in search of prey, but this demon didn't appear to be hunting. When the man stopped and the demon caught up, Des's muscles tensed in preparation for the attack he knew was coming—but instead, the man leaned down and spoke. A moment later, the demon trotted off in another direction.

Every hair on Des's body stood at attention. This demon hadn't been tracking the tall man at all. It was his thrall. Des had never seen one before—hadn't even been sure they existed—but there was no other explanation for what he'd just witnessed. Demons didn't leave prey. And they certainly didn't take orders. Gareth's mouth hung open in disbelief.

Des turned his gaze back to the dean's cottage, wondering what on earth Dean Blake's niece was doing with a man who consorted with demons.

Des stood ramrod straight before Commander Yew, who was the epitome of what the Iron Guard stood for. His thick salt-and-pepper hair was always kept impossibly short, and his armor fit like a second skin. Even the jagged scar through his left eyebrow looked as though it belonged there, a reminder to everyone he encountered exactly how dangerous it was to be a demon hunter, one who always came out on top.

"Thank you for bringing this to my attention, Whitlow. I'll go to the university tomorrow to speak with Miss Blake."

Des cleared his throat. "Perhaps we should wait, sir. We don't know yet if she was deliberately socializing with a consorter. If so, tipping her off might give this man an opportunity to escape."

Commander Yew's hallmark scowl deepened. "Dean Blake is an upstanding member of Wisterian society. I sincerely doubt that sweet, sheltered girl would do such a thing."

"I understand, sir," Des replied, not wanting to malign a family Commander Yew clearly respected.

After a moment, Yew continued. "But keep an eye on her, just in case. If anything were to happen to her in Dean Blake's absence, I'd never forgive myself."

Des didn't love the idea of babysitting when he should be hunting, but perhaps this was an opportunity. "And the consorter, sir? Would you like me to track him, as well?"

"You'll be plenty busy with your own patrols, not to mention

Miss Blake. I'll put another guard on it."

Des did his best to hide his disappointment, but Yew knew him too well.

"You don't have to take on everything, Whitlow. Your performance has already far surpassed that of your peers."

Des nodded. Commander Yew thought Des wanted what all young guards wanted: glory, recognition, respect. But this went far beyond that for Des.

All hunters had heard old tales of people consorting with the demons they conjured, using dark magic to wield control over them. It was magic, after all, that had created the curse on the kingdom in the first place, and why it had been outlawed along with inventing. But hearing those tales had been nothing compared to seeing, and *feeling*, the very wrongness of a demon under thrall firsthand. It took the fire in Des's chest, the rage that burned at every casual act of negligence that created a demon, and fanned it into an inferno.

Demons were responsible for the fact that every member of the Iron Guard was an orphan. But a controlled demon could be responsible for so much worse. A weapon instead of a rabid animal.

Wisteria kept records of every human-demon encounter, whether it resulted in a human's death or not. There were men at the fort who studied the records for patterns, improving the Iron Guard's capabilities over the years and reducing fatal encounters significantly for humans. When he was fifteen, Des had snuck into the archives and looked for the record of his parents' deaths. He regretted it, sometimes, because what he read had left him with night terrors for months afterward. But it had helped him decide that ending *verita* was his calling.

Des had been four months old at the time of the attack. His father was a farmer, and, per the account pieced together by the Iron Guard, he'd most likely gone out that night to the chicken coop after hearing a commotion. The noise had woken Des, and his mother had gone to rock him back to sleep. But when she went into Des's room, she saw a monster looming over his cradle, its red eyes flashing at her when she opened the door.

According to the records, she had screamed at the demon on purpose to draw it away from Des, and it had worked. It pursued her downstairs and into the parlor, where it caught up with her, tearing her to shreds with its long talons. Hearing her screams, Des's father had returned to the house just in time to watch the life drain out of her. He started to reach for his axe, but the demon would already have been growing after feasting on his mother's flesh. Des's father ran for the alarm bell to alert the town guard, only managing to ring it twice before he was attacked. He lived long enough to tell his neighbor what happened, then bled out on the floor of his house. The demon was eventually caught and killed by a mob of villagers, being too far out of the city to warrant their own platoon of Iron Guards.

There was no time to study the demon once it was pierced with an iron-tipped spear. It had gone up in green flames, like they all did. But the records stated that the demon's talons resembled scythes, and the theory was that a nearby farmer had attempted to create some sort of new blade for more efficient farm work. No one had ever been caught. His parents never received justice.

"You did well tonight, Whitlow," Commander Yew said. "Go get some rest. You look like you need it."

Des saluted and returned to the barracks, where Gareth was telling the rest of the guards what they'd seen. He didn't blame the kid for his excitement; everyone shared stories of their hunting when something unusual occurred. But he didn't like discussing things he didn't yet understand.

"You're telling us you saw an honest-to-gods thrall," a guard around Gareth's age said. She was sitting close to him, her chin propped on her elbow, and Gareth was blushing under the attention.

"If it wasn't a thrall, that man was extremely lucky not to have his face ripped off," Gareth said, glancing across the room to Des for confirmation.

"What about the dean's niece?" the girl asked. "Do you think she knows about the demon?"

"No idea," Gareth replied.

"It's interesting that she waited until her uncle was gone to meet with this man, though," the girl said, and Des nodded in silent agreement. No matter what Commander Yew thought, something stank about the entire thing.

He closed his eyes to rest and grunted as a weight settled on the end of his bunk just a moment later.

"What do you want, Daisy?" he asked without opening his eyes.

"I heard you were spying on the dean's niece tonight," she said in a deliberately teasing voice.

"Hmm."

"I've heard she's very pretty," Daisy pressed.

"It was dark."

"Oh come on, Des. Tell me something! This week has been exceedingly dull."

He forced himself to sit up on his elbows. "I didn't kill anything either, if it makes you feel better."

"I meant in terms of gossip, not demons. Anyway, you saw a *thrall.* That must have been thrilling!" Daisy was cross-legged on the foot of his bed, her chin-length red hair tucked behind her ears. She was scrawny and cheerful and couldn't have been more different from Des if she tried. He'd never understood why she befriended him, but she was his oldest friend in the Guard. He trusted her more than anyone else there.

But he still didn't want her sitting on his bunk.

"Like I said, it was dark. I couldn't make out any details, other than it was about the size and shape of a sheep."

Daisy rubbed at her freckled nose. "Huh. That's not very exciting, is it?"

"I told you."

"But the girl?"

"What about her?"

"She met with this man? With no one else present? What do you make of it?" Daisy's wide blue eyes were staring down at him, and he wished he had the energy to spin a tale like Gareth, to somehow make demon hunting sound like an adventure, rather than duty.

"You already know what I think, Daisy."

"Aw, come on," she said. "I don't think you've used your quota of insults for today."

He sighed in relief when the gas lamps were extinguished, a signal that it was time for everyone to turn in, and for Daisy to return to her own bunk. "I think she's a silly, spoiled fool."

CHAPTER 6
AURELIE

EVERARD'S PROPOSAL KEPT AURELIE TOSSING AND TURNING until well past midnight. She'd raced through dinner so she could get back to her lab and study his notes, but though she hated to admit it, she'd been confused from the moment she sat down.

Everard was asking her to build a door. Not just a regular, run-of-the-mill door, of course. It was intricately constructed, with rather large dimensions. Not exactly something she could hide beneath a sheet or in a cupboard in her laboratory.

The door itself consisted of thirty-six interconnected metal plates. There was no description of how she was to assemble them, just a note that he would provide the plates and that she should not use any other metal in the construction. It seemed to Aurelie that it was more an engineering project than an actual invention, which on its own would be a challenge. But it was the note about the runes that would need to be inscribed in the metal that troubled her most of all.

Aurelie's interest in invention had never extended to the mystical; she was a woman of science, not arcane magic. Why Mr. Everard should think she had any knowledge of runes was beyond her. And not only had he grossly overestimated her capabilities, he'd offered her something far more dangerous than he'd hinted at.

Magic produced demons of a different sort altogether. The kind of demons that slaughtered entire villages. The kind of demons that couldn't be contained by salt or killed with anything as innocuous as an iron blade. Everard had said that if Aurelie *could* complete this project, she'd be ushering in a world where invention was welcomed. What did that mean? Was he referring to the demonic curse in some way? She wasn't sure how demons entered her world, but she was certain they didn't knock politely on a door and wipe their feet on a welcome mat. And if this door wasn't for letting demons *into* Wisteria, was it possible that it was for getting them *out*?

If so, the implications were enormous.

They could also cost Aurelie her life.

Now, in the warm light of morning, as Aurelie half climbed, half rolled off her sofa, she felt no closer to an answer than she had last night. On the one hand, it was as if the universe had heard her plea for an opportunity to prove herself and answered with a resounding *yes.* Here was her chance to prove herself capable of something truly great.

But even if she was able to understand Everard's blueprint and could find somewhere to build it, she'd still need a plan for dealing with the demon it created immediately and efficiently.

Besides, there were still so many other questions left unanswered. She couldn't fathom how a conversation with Mr. Morel could have led Everard to the conclusion she was the person for this job. And who *was* Everard? How had he come by this project, and what did he stand to gain from it? And what, if anything, would he lose if Aurelie failed? Because the stakes were clear for her, but far less so for him.

Then again, if she turned Everard down? He'd find someone else to make the door, surely. She couldn't be the only inventor in all of Wisteria. And the idea of another person building something great because she was too afraid was almost as upsetting as the prospect of death.

She splashed some cold water onto her face, put on one of her school dresses, fed Mephisto, and headed to the cottage for breakfast, Florian's book tucked under her arm with Everard's letter hidden inside. She ended up staying far longer than she'd intended, poring over Everard's proposal and the puzzle of the interlocking plates, when her uncle's maid cleared her throat.

"Begging your pardon, miss, but I believe you need to get ready for your dinner with Mr. Viridian."

Aurelie groaned. "Did you have to remind me, Bonnie? I'm studying."

"I'm sorry, miss, but your uncle gave strict orders."

"I know, I know." Aurelie sighed. "It's not your fault, Bonnie. I'm going."

"Do you need help dressing?" she asked, in a tone that heavily implied Aurelie did.

"I'm perfectly capable of dressing myself."

"But your hair . . ."

"I'll do my hair. I promise."

In her bedroom, Aurelie opened her wardrobe and deflated even further. She only had one dress that still fit her that could be considered appropriate for a formal dinner, and she had no idea if it was in fashion. It wasn't Uncle Leo's fault; he'd offered many times to have new dresses made for her. But she liked her school dresses. They were simple, unfussy, practical. All attributes Aurelie appreciated about herself.

The dress in question was a deep shade of green, with black

velvet trim at the waist and hem. It reminded her of a mossy forest like the one she'd lived next to before her parents died. Her father often went into the forest to collect mushrooms, and he would sometimes take Aurelie with him. They had a large black dog named Raven who accompanied them on their outings, and she loved to sit amid the lichen-furred, gnarled roots of a large tree and watch her father work. They'd return home to find a berry pie cooling on the windowsill, or her mother weaving pine-and-orange garlands for Yule. Aurelie was self-reflective enough to know that inventing filled a hole left behind when her parents died. But she'd give it all up to have them back.

She tied a black velvet choker around her throat, touching the jet beads dangling from it and trying to remember how it had looked on her mother, before tying up half of her hair in a matching ribbon. "Courage, Aurelie," she whispered to her reflection in the mirror. She couldn't remember the last time she'd dined with a family, other than the small, lopsided one she and Uncle Leo had formed.

Miles was waiting for her at the gate in a carriage, presumably his father's. He wore a black dinner suit, and Aurelie had to admit—begrudgingly—that he was not an unattractive young man. He had a clear brow that was mostly obscured by a flop of dark hair, and his round spectacles perched atop a perfectly adequate nose. His eyes were a pleasant shade of hazel, and he didn't have a noticeably offensive odor.

If only he weren't so wretchedly dull.

"Good evening, Aurelie," he said as she settled onto the bench across from him. "You're looking well."

"Thank you, Miles. And thank you for leaving the book for me."

"It was the least I could do for your uncle. What did you make of it?"

She ignored the comment about her uncle and tried to focus on the fact that he was asking for her opinion. It was theoretically possible that Miles shared a hitherto unknown passion for discovery. There had to be at least one other person in Wisteria who believed that innovation, exploration, and creation were the greatest gifts humanity had to offer. Maybe her uncle was more insightful than she'd given him credit for.

"It's fascinating," she said, wishing she'd brought it with her. It was always prudent to have a book on hand. "Though I have to say, I was surprised that it came from you."

His lips twisted in a bemused smile. "I do read, Aurelie."

She blushed. "Of course. I only meant—"

"That history is dry, compared to, say, innovation?"

She searched his face as they rattled over a pothole. He sounded as though he were teasing, but she didn't know him well enough to assume. "*Dry* isn't the word I would use." *Dusty and decrepit, more like.* "I think we must understand our history if we're to progress."

He pushed his spectacles up his nose. "Progress through further innovation, I take it?"

Now Aurelie felt as though she'd been led into a trap. Did *Miles* have something to do with Everard's proposal? Was the book a ploy, part of an elaborate scheme to catch her out?

No, she was being paranoid. Miles wanted Uncle Leo's approval, even if he didn't want hers. "I hardly see how a society can better itself without any change whatsoever."

"You're unsatisfied with the current state of our society, then."

She sighed and looked out the window. While she didn't give a fig what Miles thought of her, she understood that her behavior was a reflection on Uncle Leo, who would undoubtedly hear of how she performed this evening.

She turned back to Miles and attempted what she hoped was a gracious smile. "You can hardly blame a girl for wanting more."

"Hardly," Miles said. "Though as I understand it, life is far worse in other kingdoms, where progress leads to more time spent working, more disease brought in by outsiders, more competition for limited resources."

"But without the demons—"

His brow furrowed in what looked like benevolent concern but felt rather like condescension. "Every time humanity has attempted to progress, there have been terrible consequences that have nothing to do with demons. War, famine, pollution. All horrendous. All the result of wanting more." He leaned forward and looked deep into her eyes, as though he were about to impart some heavy wisdom. "There have always been demons, Aurelie. Some are just more obvious than others."

She was saved from responding by the coach lurching to an abrupt stop, which caused Miles to sit back and steady himself. Her hands had grown clammy, and the air was much too close. She sucked in a deep breath as she dropped onto the sidewalk.

And proceeded to choke on it when she saw the size of the Applebaums' mansion.

Miles leaned in as he offered her his arm. "That's ours," he said, nodding toward a brick monstrosity next door. She'd known Miles's family was well-off, but this was wealth beyond her imagination.

A man greeted them, ushering Aurelie in with more familiarity than formality. "Miss Blake, how delightful to meet you after all these years. Your uncle speaks so highly of you."

Not a butler, then, but Mr. Applebaum. He was short, stout, and mustachioed, giving him the appearance of a kindly gopher.

"Thank you for inviting me tonight," she said. "It means so much to Uncle Leopold. And me, of course."

"We're thrilled to have you. My daughter, Lavender, is particularly excited to meet you. Three brothers, you know. She's always complaining that she's far too outnumbered."

Just then, a girl stepped into the foyer with a smile lighting her face. She grasped Aurelie in an embrace before she had time to formulate a thought.

"Thank *goodness* you're here," the girl said, pressing back to look at Aurelie. "There are so many boys! Miles, why didn't you make your sister come tonight? We're disastrously outnumbered."

Mr. Applebaum raised his eyebrows at Aurelie. "What did I tell you? Lavender, give Miss Blake a moment to breathe, will you?" he asked, laughing.

Aurelie was about to thank him for the intervention when Lavender ignored Mr. Applebaum's request entirely, took Aurelie's hand, and pulled her toward another room.

She hurried after Lavender, who walked at a pace Aurelie would have assumed was not appropriate in polite society, a pace Aurelie had spent most of her life restraining. The girl was rosy-cheeked beneath her mane of dark curls, and her fuchsia long-sleeved dress was perfectly tailored to her curves. Most of the girls at university dressed in somber colors and kept their hair neatly tied back, like Aurelie.

There was nothing restrained about Lavender.

They entered an elegant dining hall, where candlelight reflected off a thousand gleaming surfaces. "Aurelie, these are my brothers, Lawrence, Leonhard, and Lex," Lavender recited, her voice flat with disinterest. "Ignore them, they're all worthless."

Aurelie couldn't help smiling to herself. She'd assumed that a young woman like Lavender would be the pinnacle of propriety, but perhaps she'd been wrong.

They took their seats and soon the room was buzzing with conversation. For once, Aurelie decided to sit back and listen. That was what her uncle would want: for Aurelie to experience what Wisterian society had to offer, to spend a few hours in the life he envisioned for her. And honestly, how hard could that be?

This is how I die, Aurelie thought as she pushed a pea across her plate with a fork. *From extreme and unrelenting boredom.*

Miles and the Applebaum brothers had been arguing about military history for the better part of an hour. Who cared if the Battle of Green Point or the Morning Glory Rebellion had been the more strategic success? All of this had happened two hundred years ago. Why were they deliberating over battles that had taken place at a time when most commoners didn't have running water? Why not discuss the benefits of *running water* instead?

Twice she had attempted to get a word in edgewise at this demons-cursed dinner, and twice she'd had her words trampled over by the herd of young men she found herself surrounded by. Lavender, who to her credit had declared all of them as bland as old porridge, had retired to bed early, complaining of a headache that Aurelie resented because now she couldn't use that as *her* excuse.

One more hour. She could make it one more hour. Then it would be nine o'clock, and she'd be able to tell Uncle Leo that she had truly given it her best attempt with Miles, but they were simply not meant to be. It wasn't because he was boring. It wasn't because he was backward, closed-minded, and an appallingly loud chewer, although those were all perfectly adequate reasons for never spending another moment with the man.

It was that now that they were around other men, he clearly had no interest whatsoever in what Aurelie had to say. She'd tried to ask him to pass the salt at dinner and he'd pinched his thumb and forefinger together in a gesture that indicated she should be quiet. She had the impression that if he could, he'd be doing that to her lips, but as they were in polite company, he restrained himself. In that moment, she'd had to press her hands to her thighs to keep her feet on the ground, because her every fiber was straining to kick him under the table.

"I'm simply saying that the use of the star-cluster formation by Admiral Bittern was the most brilliant example of that tactic in the history of warfare, and anyone who says otherwise is a fool."

Ughhhh.

"Excuse me?"

Aurelie looked up from the poor napkin she'd folded into pleats—it would require a very hot, very firm iron to press them out later—to find all of the men looking at her with expressions of utter contempt on their faces. "Yes?"

"If you find our conversations so terribly tedious, please, illuminate us with your vast wisdom, Miss Blake."

It was Leonhard, the oldest Applebaum brother, who was

speaking, and Aurelie realized that she had actually groaned aloud. Good gravy. She really did need to get a better handle on her internal monologue.

She was of two minds now. The *easy* road would be to apologize, explain that she'd simply remembered something she needed to do back at school and was groaning at her own forgetfulness.

Naturally, Aurelie chose the other road.

"All right. You say that the use of the star-cluster formation was so utterly brilliant. But I would counter that if that's the case, why didn't he use smokeless powder for his cannons?"

Miles flashed a pitying smile that Aurelie wanted to smack off his smug face. "Smokeless powder wasn't invented prior to the First War of Wisteria." His voice was gentle as he shifted a slightly apologetic glance to the men in the room on her behalf.

The other men chuckled behind their fists as though she'd been caught in some humiliating misstep.

"Actually," Aurelie said, hating the way her voice tipped up on the first syllable but unable to stop herself, "smokeless powder was invented two years prior to the start of the First War of Wisteria. It was brought to Admiral Bittern's attention by a scientist named Charlotte Brown, who discovered it while conducting experiments on nitrocellulose. Alas, because she was a woman, Bittern decided not to use her new smokeless powder, thus costing the Wisterians the war. Yes, they won at Green Hill, but they suffered so many losses amid the smoke-filled chaos that they never recovered."

As she spoke, Aurelie had noticed that Miles's face had transmogrified from its usual pale white to a startling shade of purple. Some small, distant part of her had wondered if he might not be choking, but once Aurelie got going on a subject she was passionate about, it would have taken more than an asphyxiating dunderhead to get her to stop.

The other men, who had slowly shrunk in on themselves like an escargatoire of timid snails, exchanged pitying glances with Miles. She knew each one of them would have stated the same misinformation as Miles if they'd only spoken up first, and they were now rather relieved they hadn't. Still, she could feel no pity for Miles, even if she'd humiliated him in front of his friends. One shouldn't state something as fact if one wasn't correct.

"Well, shall we move to the library for some port?" Leonhard said, breaking the tension, and Aurelie watched as Miles stood, his face only starting to fade back to a less unsettling pink, nodded curtly to her, and left the room.

Aurelie rose and stretched, more than ready to head home, as the invitation to drink port had clearly not been extended to her. *Fine,* she thought. *I don't even like port. Probably.*

"You really shouldn't talk to him like that."

Aurelie glanced up to find that the quietest of the Applebaum brothers, Lex, was still lingering in the corner of the room. Aurelie had thought she liked him best. Now she knew it was simply because he talked less than the others.

"Why not?" she asked, finding she didn't care anymore if word got back to Uncle Leo that she'd been rude. She had no idea why he'd ever imagined the Applebaum children would be a good influence. They were arrogant, ignorant, and self-important. A trifecta of exasperation.

"Because he might have married you, before. Now he'll tell everyone some ugly rumor about you, and you'll be ruined."

Aurelie almost laughed. "Who said I wanted to marry Miles Viridian?"

Lex crossed his legs and brought a heretofore hidden glass of whiskey up, raising it to her. "Ah. Well, forgive me for misunderstanding. I thought that's what all you young ladies wanted. My mistake."

Aurelie couldn't tell if he was mocking her, and she found she didn't care about that anymore, either. "Please thank your father for the lovely dinner," she said, and went to the front door without waiting for a response. She would walk back to the university. Miles would probably be relieved she was gone, and though she was sure the Applebaums would provide a carriage if she requested it, the walk would clear her head.

If this was the life Uncle Leo envisioned for Aurelie, then he clearly didn't know her at all. The thought was so demoralizing that by the time she was halfway home, she felt no better about her predicament. Worse still, if she returned early, Bonnie would start asking questions, to which she could hardly provide an honest answer. "I insulted the boys and left without a proper goodbye" would *not* sit well with her maid.

With a desperate glance at her surroundings, Aurelie's eyes landed on a café emitting an inviting glow from its windows. *One drink*, she told herself as she trotted across the street. *One drink, just to clear my head.*

CHAPTER 7
DES

DES WATCHED IN UTTER DISBELIEF AS THE BLAKE GIRL emerged from the large stone mansion she'd disappeared into just two hours ago, alone.

What in the name of Aciano did she think she was doing, walking at night without a chaperone? Had the tall, gangly twig of a boy who escorted her earlier expired from lack of nourishment?

Des receded farther behind the hedge he and Gareth were using for cover, grabbing the younger boy by the collar and yanking him backward just in time to avoid the girl's notice. Not that he should have bothered. She seemed completely oblivious to anything as she sighed and lifted her hair from her neck, clearly relishing the feel of the cool breeze on her skin.

The moon was bright, and there were still plenty of people out and about, but even grown men didn't walk these city streets alone at night. Not when demons were afoot. Had she no sense at all?

"What should we do?" Gareth asked as the Blake girl began to make her way down the street.

"Follow her, of course." He was beginning to think this entire endeavor was a complete waste of time. Whomever the tall man with the thrall was, the Blake girl was not involved. How could she be, when she looked about as threatening as a potted plant? A very small potted plant, wearing a fancy dress. Still, they couldn't very well leave her to be eaten by a demon, not when Commander Yew expected him to keep her safe in her uncle's absence.

Wisteria City, for all its stagnation the past one hundred years, was still considered the crown jewel of the kingdom, which didn't say much for the kingdom as a whole. Along the main boulevard, old shopfronts leaned heavily against their neighbors, leaving corner buildings to jut precariously over their foundations. Here and there, lots stood vacant where a structure had crumbled beyond repair and no replacement could be built in its stead.

Des, who only ever viewed the city from a hunter's eyes, watched as the Blake girl made her way blithely along. Perhaps he shouldn't be surprised that the dean's niece wasn't afraid, considering she spent her entire life behind the university's iron gates.

"What's that?" Gareth said, suddenly gripping Des's arm with surprising strength.

His eyes caught what he should never have missed in the first place: a pair of glowing red eyes in an alley, just feet from where the girl was passing.

His hand went to his sword automatically, but the demon, mostly translucent in the glow of the streetlamps, didn't attack. Instead, it drifted in the girl's wake, maintaining a respectable distance of fifteen feet or so.

"Is it *following* her?" Gareth whispered.

Des grunted an unintelligible response. He'd known there was something off here. He should know better than to discount his own instincts, even if Commander Yew had doubted him.

The girl crossed the boulevard toward Café Dahlia, a common gathering spot for Wisteria's young and wealthy. Des had never set foot inside, and he certainly wasn't going to start now. The demon, perhaps realizing its quarry was unreachable for the moment, drifted into a nearby park.

"Now what?" Gareth asked.

Before Des could answer, he heard someone shout his name from across the street and swore under his breath.

Daisy and her partner, Jasper, sauntered toward them, oblivious to the *somnia* and the girl. "Shift over?" Daisy asked, her wide smile softening Des ever so slightly. "We just finished."

"We're tracking Dean Blake's niece," Gareth replied, pointing toward the café.

Daisy's eyes lit up. "She's in there? Then what are we standing out here for? Let's go meet her!"

As Daisy and Jasper began to cross the street, Gareth looked to Des for instructions. The plan had never been to meet the girl, simply to observe her. Besides, there was a demon loitering somewhere nearby, and he couldn't very well leave it to find a new victim.

Just as he started to turn, the *somnia* came swooping out of the darkness, moving alarmingly fast for a dream demon. He was caught so off guard by the rapid approach that he barely had time to remove his sword from its scabbard before it flew past him, heading straight for the café door.

Des's pulse thundered in his ears as he leapt after it, sure it was going for the girl. But before he could catch up, Jasper had unsheathed his own blade and decapitated the *somnia* in one sweeping arc of iron. The burst of green flame was so close that it nearly singed Des's eyebrows as he reeled backward.

"Aciano's beard!" Daisy gasped. "Where did that come from?"

Des looked past her to the café window, where six or seven patrons stood with their pale faces pressed to the glass, their expressions distorted by shock and alarm.

"For fuck's sake," Des muttered as the owner of the café emerged.

"Well done," the woman said, wiping her hands on a dish towel. "Come inside. Drinks are on me."

The entire night had gone from calm to utter chaos in a matter of minutes. Des dragged a hand down his face as he followed the others in. The café was old but well-kept, with stained-glass skylights overhead, depicting some sort of flower in soft pastels. Most of the patrons had returned to their seats, though some approached hesitantly, hoping to shake the hands of the Iron Guards. A cluster of young people sat at one table, gossiping loudly, while the older patrons sipped their drinks and cast exasperated glances at the youths.

Des's eyes found the Blake girl immediately. She sat on a high-backed stool at the end of the long wooden bar, a purple cocktail sitting in a cut-crystal coupe before her.

"Did you see?" someone hissed nearby. "Cut its head clean off!"

"He didn't even flinch!"

But while Jasper and Gareth clearly relished the praise, and Daisy blushed under the attention, Des hardly heard them. The rush of blood in his ears was too loud. It was the first time he'd seen the dean's niece stationary and in proper lighting. And for reasons he didn't care to examine, the sight of her had taken his breath away.

She was clad in a fine green dress, the square neckline revealing a swath of pale skin interrupted only by a black ribbon around her neck that looked like it would come undone with just the slightest tug.

Des's gaze traveled from the dark chestnut hair framing her heart-shaped face and wide green eyes to her narrow waist, to her slipper-clad feet that dangled a good two feet above the ground, his brow furrowing as he tried to make sense of her. She was smaller than Daisy, which was almost incomprehensible. Daisy, who had sidled up to the bar in her practical training leathers, her red hair tied into a messy ponytail, while this girl looked like she belonged on a shelf in a row of porcelain dolls.

How did a person like Miss Blake survive in a demon-infested world?

A touch on his arm startled him. A young woman had approached and was gazing up at him in a way Des knew most men craved. "Thank you for saving us," she said, batting her thick lashes. His eyes fell on her long, perfectly manicured fingernails against his leather arm brace, and Des felt his stomach turn in disgust.

Girls like Aurelie Blake survived by staying behind the safety of the university's iron gates, he reminded himself bitterly. By idling their days away studying while girls like Daisy risked their lives. Des gripped the hilt of his sword and stepped pointedly away from the girl to move closer to the bar, where his friends were ordering drinks.

And somewhere from across the bar, he heard Aurelie Blake giggle.

His eyes shot up and caught hers, and she blanched under a glare that suggested she was as useless as a demon, something else that needed eradicating but wasn't worth the effort.

"Des, what do you want to drink?" Daisy asked, finally tearing his attention away from the girl. He asked for a pint and tried to clear his head as his fellow guards chattered.

"You really think it was following her?" Daisy asked Gareth, who nodded.

Des grunted his assent. "We need to get back and tell Commander Yew. Something is definitely wrong with that girl."

It took him a moment to realize that the others were staring at him with blank expressions.

"What?" he growled.

"Have you actually looked at her?" Jasper asked. "She's the size of a flea and clearly wouldn't know a demon if it bit her on the—"

"Cheek," Daisy said, cutting him off. "Jasper is right. If the demon really was following her—"

"It was," Des insisted.

"*If* it was, she clearly knew nothing about it."

They all turned their eyes on the girl, who had finished her drink since they entered and was waving her hand politely to get the bartender's attention.

She must have felt the weight of their collective gaze on her, because her eyes darted toward them, and her pale cheeks flushed pink before she looked away.

"I'm going to talk to her," Daisy proclaimed.

"Like hell you are," Des hissed, but she was already halfway down the bar.

"Come on," Jasper said to Gareth, who glanced at Des for permission.

He rolled his eyes and nodded.

By the time he reached Daisy, she was chattering away while the Blake girl stared at her, looking completely baffled by this turn of events. That made two of them.

"I'm Daisy," she said, holding out her hand.

"Erm, it's nice to meet you? I'm Aurelie."

"You're Dean Blake's niece, aren't you?" Daisy asked, as subtle as a sledgehammer, and Des, who had been draining the last of his pint, choked.

Daisy reached around and smacked him hard on the back. "Don't mind Des. He doesn't get out much."

The girl fished in her coin purse pointedly. "No, I expect not."

What was *that* supposed to mean?

"So you are, aren't you? Dean Blake's niece?"

She glanced at Daisy from the corner of her eye. "I am. How did you know?"

"Yes, Daisy," Des said through gritted teeth. "How *did* you know?"

Daisy continued to stare at the Blake girl, ignoring him. "Commander Yew mentioned the dean had a niece named Aurelie. It's a name you don't hear often."

"It's a family name," she said, her eyes drifting to Des, clearly suspicious.

"On which side?" Daisy asked, chin propped in her hand as though she had all the time in the world.

"Um, my mother's. Excuse me, I should be going."

"Where?" Des asked, stepping in front of her as she hopped down from her stool.

Daisy chuckled awkwardly and attempted to sling her arm around

Des's shoulders, found she couldn't reach, and settled for punching him lightly in the bicep. "As I said, he doesn't get out much. Do you need an escort? There's been some unusual demonic activity lately. Better not to walk alone."

"Who said I was alone?" she asked, glancing around as though she might find a friend, or a random stranger, to come to her aid. "I'm only walking back to the university. I'm sure there's nothing to worry about."

"Nevertheless," Des said, thinking of how she'd laughed at him earlier. How she clearly didn't take anything—including her own life—seriously. "We'll walk with you."

"I'll be fine, really." She stepped forward, apparently expecting him to move.

Des folded his arms over his chest. "We insist."

For a moment, he was sure she'd protest again. Des's glower, which had been known to turn grown men to dust, didn't appear to be having its intended effect.

But after a long moment, she let out an exasperated sigh and turned to Daisy. "Well, then, Daisy. After you."

They'd been walking for a quarter of an hour, Daisy babbling nonstop, when the Blake girl stopped in the middle of the sidewalk and turned in a slow circle. Des, with his long strides, caught up to them almost instantly.

"What is it?" he asked, hand subconsciously drifting to his hip. He'd sent Jasper and Gareth back to the fort, and Daisy was clearly distracted.

"No need to panic," the girl said, her eyes tracking his movements, and once again he had the impression she was mocking him. At least she had the sense not to giggle this time. "It's just that I don't know where we are, exactly."

He arched an eyebrow. "Pardon?"

She sighed, crossing her arms over her chest in a gesture he imagined she found intimidating, which was so pathetic it was almost charming. Almost. "I'm afraid I may be turned around. I don't leave campus often."

Des snorted. Just as he thought.

Daisy flashed her easy, reassuring smile, and patted the girl's shoulder. "That's all right. We know the way."

Her lack of fear wasn't just odd; it was unnerving. Des doubted a single person in that café would choose to walk home alone after what they'd witnessed. Commander Yew had told him not to pull on this thread, but his intuition was telling him to pay attention. He'd already made a mistake once by ignoring it.

If she led him to the tall man with the thrall, all the better. No one had captured a demon alive before. If Des managed it, he'd not only be guaranteed a promotion; he'd be one step closer to eradicating *verita.*

When they stopped at an intersection to wait for a passing carriage, Aurelie turned to him, mouth open as though about to say something. Her inquisitive green eyes skimmed his body, top to bottom, sizing him up. He widened his stance and folded his arms across his chest, inviting her to take all the time she needed.

He stared back, smirking at the ink stains on her fingers, which she hid behind her back when she realized he had noticed. His gaze snagged on her mouth, incongruously lush compared to her prim appearance. She bit her lip, her brow furrowing, and Des felt an unexpected stab of desire. He glanced away.

When he finally dragged his eyes back to hers, she was scowling.

Fair enough, he thought as they resumed their walk. He wore the same expression.

"Do you see many demons at the university?" Daisy asked. He wished she wouldn't be so damned obvious. She was going to spook the girl with all her questions.

"No," she responded. "Only a few in all the years I've been there."

"Oh. Interesting. I would have thought with so many intelligent people congregating in one place . . ."

The girl paused to remove a pebble from her slipper, and Des, who'd gained ground on her to eavesdrop, nearly trampled her.

She shot him a withering look when she rose. "The university *is* full of intelligent people. They know better than to risk creating anything that might produce a demon. It's difficult with so many students, but we're all very cautious."

"What do you study?" Daisy asked.

"Science. Chemistry and physics, mostly. I have a keen interest in understanding how things work."

Des scoffed, unable to imagine someone devoting their life to the things that interested them, rather than their duty.

She stopped, probably to glare at him again. He realized belatedly that they'd reached the university.

"Well, it looks like we survived," she said, her voice dripping with sarcasm.

"You would still be spinning in circles if it weren't for Daisy."

The Blake girl raised her chin to meet his gaze, her mouth

twisted in an impudent little smirk. "You're right. There was clearly no alternative, such as, say, *asking someone for directions.*" He glared as she turned to Daisy. "It was nice meeting you."

Daisy smiled, so big all her teeth showed. "You as well, Aurelie. If you need *anything*, you can send word to the Iron Guard."

She cast Des a sidelong glance. "Well, goodbye then," she said, inching toward the street. "Good luck with . . . everything."

A clatter echoed from down the street, and by the time Aurelie had stepped off the curb, a carriage was careening around the corner, the driver wrestling with a broken rein while the horses panicked. Without thinking, Des reached for her, tearing her away from the street a moment before the horses' hooves struck what would have been her head.

The next thing he knew, he was holding her tight to his chest, one hand curled around her wrist and the other wrapping almost fully around her waist, his breathing ragged. Her cheek was pressed against his iron-studded breastplate, her eyelashes fanned against her pale skin.

He didn't hear Daisy over the sound of blood pounding in his head until she tapped his arm.

"Des, let her go," she hissed.

He dropped his arms instantly, but it took a moment for the girl to unfurl herself and step back. "Are you all right?" he asked, afraid to touch her again. He hadn't meant to—

"I'm fine," she said, voice aquiver, and he was relieved to see it was true. She was in one piece, no obvious bruises or scrapes. The wild look in her eyes was the only sign that anything had happened.

“I’m so sorry,” she said, taking a step back. “I don’t know what I was thinking.”

“You weren’t thinking,” Des began, anger replacing the fear he’d felt only a moment before. She had no idea how fortunate she was to be in one piece.

“We distracted you,” Daisy replied, cutting Des off with a sharp look as she tucked the girl under her arm. “Are you sure you’re all right?”

She nodded, avoiding Des’s eyes. “I’m fine. Really.” She allowed Daisy to walk her across the street, said something Des couldn’t hear. And then she slipped through the school gate, never once looking back.

CHAPTER 8

AURELIE

BY THE TIME AURELIE RETURNED TO HER LABORATORY, SHE was exhausted and overwhelmed. Her ribs hurt from where the massive guard with the bad attitude had manhandled her—not that she was ungrateful he had saved her life—and she no longer had the buffer of the lovely violet gin fizz in her system to shield her from the memory of her abysmal dinner with Miles and the Applebaums.

Mephisto emerged from a hole in the wall as she collapsed on her sofa, sporting a wayward piece of lint on one of its eyebrows. Normally, it scuttled immediately to its bowl when she arrived, expecting dinner, but today it sniffed at Aurelie as though she were a stranger.

"What's the matter, little one?" she asked, holding out her hand.

Mephisto inched forward a bit, sniffed at her again, and darted away. She touched her waist with her fingertips, where the hunter's arm had yanked her from the street. Could Mephisto smell him on her? Was that what had the demon acting so squirrely?

She closed her eyes, and suddenly she was back in a pair of muscular arms, the scent of leather and pine flooding her memory. She must have been more frightened than she realized, her senses heightened. Otherwise, why would she remember what the giant smelled like?

Of the four guards, he'd caught her attention immediately. Nearly as tall as Miles, with broad shoulders, tanned skin, piercing gray eyes, and a square jaw, he was the most imposing man she'd ever seen. His light brown hair was cropped unfashionably short, though something about his appearance made her think this was a matter of convenience, not a style choice. The sword that hung at his side was so large that a fully unanticipated and unprecedented giggle had burst out of her. Aurelie Blake did *not* giggle. Certainly not at the sight of a man. It had been nerves and nothing else.

Well, the alcohol might also have had something to do with it.

Shaking her head at the ridiculousness of the entire evening, she stripped out of her dress and hung it up, changing into a simple shift and a cardigan Kiara had knit her for her birthday last year. To her relief, Mephisto approached immediately, skittering right past her to its food bowl. Either it hadn't approved of today's sartorial choices, or the smell of the hunter really had caused a reaction.

She glowered at the memory of the colossus nearly trampling her when she'd stopped to fix her slipper, unable to so much as smile when she teased him about asking for directions. Apparently, there was no room for a sense of humor in all that ridiculously tight armor.

She twisted her hair into her customary braid, her mind returning to Daisy, the sweet redheaded guard who'd approached her first, and the other two boys. She may not know much about how the Iron Guard operated, but it was odd that they had paid her so much attention tonight. Had Uncle Leopold contacted them? Paid them to keep an eye on her in his absence? Yes, he worried, but it would be almost paranoid to reach out to the Iron Guard on her behalf.

Her stomach twisted. Did they somehow know about Everard and his proposal? What if this was part of a *different* elaborate plot to entrap her? Were they already onto Everard and now she'd been brought under suspicion, too?

Impossible, she told herself. It was a mere coincidence that they'd been hunting the *somnia* outside the café. It wasn't as if she'd planned to be there. She glanced around her desk for Everard's proposal, hoping to find some sign that she should accept the commission, and realized with a groan that she'd left it at her uncle's cottage.

Pulling her coat on and trading her slippers for boots, Aurelie cut across the lawn to Leo's house. Bonnie opened the door before Aurelie had a chance to knock, clearly eager for an update. "Good evening, miss. How was your date with Mr. Viridian?"

Aurelie shot her a flat look. "I wouldn't date Miles Viridian for all the cheese in creation. And I assure you, the feeling is entirely mutual."

"Oh, how disappointing," Bonnie said as she ushered Aurelie inside.

"I'm fine, really."

"I meant for your uncle. He seemed to have high hopes for the two of you."

Aurelie waited until Bonnie went to the kitchen to make tea before rolling her eyes. What was Uncle Leo thinking? He knew that Aurelie was introverted and awkward and entirely uninterested in Miles. Had he expected she would spontaneously develop social skills, or a tolerance for pompous windbags, in his absence?

Still shaken from nearly being flattened by a coach, she returned to the library, where she'd left Florian's book with Everard's proposal tucked between the pages. She settled into one of the large armchairs and curled up, examining the diagram again as the same concerns bubbled up. She should say no. It was illegal. It was *dangerous.* Uncle Leopold would never forgive her if he found out what she was doing, and she still had no idea how this door would help rid Wisteria of demons.

But when she closed her eyes, she felt the burning humiliation of Miles speaking over her, the look of horror in the eyes of all the men when she revealed she wasn't a pretty little wallflower but a human being with actual knowledge. The guards' immovable surety that because of her size and gender, she couldn't possibly make it back to the university alone. And the way all of it stretched into an exhausting future of the same doubt and coddling and *stagnation.*

Aurelie couldn't help but imagine it, this thing she wanted so much she was afraid to voice it out loud. Imagine if *she* were the one to eradicate demons. Yes, she'd likely be lauded as a hero, which was all well and good. But far more importantly, she'd be free to invent to her heart's content. She'd prove to Uncle Leo that she could take care of herself. She'd show Miles that innovation was the key to progress, that society could be so much better than his boiled cabbage of a brain could imagine. Bonus points for the fact that she'd put that hulking brute of a guard out of a job.

That final thought filled her with such wicked glee that she was grinning like a madwoman when Bonnie walked in with the tea.

"Erm, everything all right, miss?" she asked.

"What? Oh, of course. I was just . . . thinking about . . ."

"Oh!" Bonnie gasped.

"Wha—"

"No wonder you aren't interested in Mr. Viridian!" She smiled as though she were in on a secret. "You like a different boy, don't you?"

Aurelie began to splutter in protest, then decided it was probably better to let Bonnie believe she was giddy over a crush rather than maniacally planning a man's downfall. "Thank you for the tea," she replied stiffly.

Bonnie winked before exiting.

Sipping her tea, Aurelie forcefully turned her attention back to the proposal. The interlocking metal plates would need to be positioned in a large square, the outer plates carved with runes, the inner plates fitting into recesses when the runes were activated. The runes themselves were engraved into the metal in a specific order. There was no lock or handle. Or rather, the runes themselves appeared to be what opened the door.

She had a good sense of mechanical workings from her job as a bricoleur, but she wasn't an engineer by any means. Everard said he could supply the materials, so mostly this would require understanding and reverse engineering the mechanisms at play here. What she really needed was a mentor in arcane magic. Someone who could guide her without knowing exactly what she was up to. And there was only one professor at the university with the relevant experience who would possibly be willing to work on something this dangerous.

Mostly because he was—as Uncle Leo had once put it—off his rocker. Professor Sheldrake was technically in the science department, but he'd long been relegated to an ancient wing of the oldest hall on campus, near the clock tower, where he worked alone on demons only knew what. He was rumored to be one of the last remaining experts in runic alphabets, though as far as Aurelie was aware, he didn't attend any faculty functions or hold office hours. But he was tenured, and she was fairly certain everyone thought he'd pass on at any moment, so his presence was tolerated.

On Monday, Aurelie would pay him a little visit.

Through the window, she could just make out the lamplighter walking past, relighting an extinguished lamp with his long tool. She smiled wistfully. The tool wasn't unlike the Helping Hand, really. She wondered who had created it, if they'd felt the same thrill she did when it worked. The best inventions were the simplest ones. They made life easier for multitudes of people, didn't require expensive materials, and could be replicated easily. To create something of such purpose . . . Aurelie knew that was *her* purpose. And yet she'd been born into a world that refused to allow her to pursue it.

Except for Everard. He was the first person in her entire life to offer her a chance to do more. *Be* more. She knew it was dangerous, but she also couldn't deny how lit up she felt when she thought about the project. How impossibly tempting the prospect of a genuine challenge was.

She wished she could ask Kiara for advice. She was always able to talk sense into Aurelie without rankling her the way Uncle Leo did. But though Kiara had diligently kept her secret about Mephisto and the lab, she couldn't risk dragging her best friend into something this dangerous. Not when she hadn't even decided if she'd take the commission.

Once the lamplighter passed the cottage's window, Aurelie began to reach for her tea again, but something stopped her. It was little more than a shimmer at the edge of her vision, but . . .

There! A *somnia.* She hurried to the window to observe it. The creature was tall and thin, somewhat humanoid, though its limbs were too long and it had no face, just two glowing red eyes. It didn't appear to be stalking the lamplighter, however. It seemed hesitant, lingering for some unknown reason. A moment later, the demon turned to her, its eyes meeting her own. Aurelie stumbled backward, drawing the curtains closed on instinct.

Her heart pounded in her chest as she collapsed back into her chair, jostling her tea in its saucer. In all her years, Aurelie had seen only a handful of demons aside from the ones she created and killed. And now she'd been within feet of not one, but two *somnia* in a single day.

She'd scoffed when Daisy offered to be of service, but Aurelie wouldn't have minded if she strolled by at that particular moment. Or even the big guard—he was brutish and rude, but she couldn't deny that he looked more than capable of handling a demon. Or twelve.

"Are you all right, miss?" Bonnie said, causing Aurelie to jump halfway out of her seat. "Apologies, miss. I didn't mean to startle you. I thought I heard a noise."

"Yes, fine, all good," Aurelie blurted, her words jumbled together. She risked a glance at the window, but the *somnia* was gone.

As she gathered her belongings, Aurelie tried to convince herself there was no need to sleep in her old bedroom tonight. The walk across campus to her laboratory was short, and there was an iron gate between her and the *somnia,* not to mention the campus guard on duty, but she still contemplated taking the salt cellar with her just in case. It wouldn't kill a demon, but it might buy her some time with a *somnia.*

Finally, unable to put it off any longer, Aurelie thanked Bonnie for the tea and said goodnight. But the moment the door to her uncle's house closed behind her, cutting off her one light source, she knew she'd made a mistake.

She stared across the dark campus, made darker still by the tall buildings and ancient trees that cast sinister shadows over the courtyard. A part of her wanted to turn around and request a lantern from Bonnie, but how could she admit she was afraid to walk such a short distance? Bonnie might even ask the guard to escort her, which would be mortifying. It was only several hundred feet to Easton Hall, and she would walk like the proper lady her uncle expected her to be.

For the first few minutes, everything was fine.

A breeze picked up, tickling the hairs on Aurelie's neck. Somewhere behind her, a branch scraped against a brick, causing goose bumps to erupt on Aurelie's arms.

She squared her shoulders and forced herself to continue walking.

The sound again, closer now.

She was imagining it, surely.

Then why don't you want to turn your head?

She told herself she was being daft. Wisteria City was a safe place. There hadn't been a demon fatality in nearly a year, and she'd never heard of a *somnia* attacking a human. Besides, Daisy and her posse weren't the only members of the Iron Guard patrolling the streets tonight. If there was a demon on the prowl, they would be hunting it.

To her left, the gates stood proud and straight, each spike-tipped iron bar a sentry warding off any would-be intruders. In the distance, she heard a man whistling. One of the campus guards, making his rounds. She forced herself to take a deep breath and winced at the ache in her ribs. Curse the giant and his ridiculous muscles.

Something shimmered in the corner of her vision. Aurelie's back broke out in a cold sweat as sudden certainty swept over her.

She couldn't pretend this wasn't real. A *somnia* was stalking her, and she was still a considerable distance from Easton Hall. Under ordinary circumstances, Aurelie didn't make decisions without conducting research or thinking through each possible outcome and weighing it against the others. Under ordinary circumstances, Aurelie prided herself on her rationality.

Tonight, Aurelie hitched up her skirt and ran.

A scream was rising in her throat, but she pushed it back down, unable to afford the wasted breath. She didn't spend a lot of time running, and her coat, her bruised ribs, her blasted floppy boots, all conspired against her to make it as difficult as possible.

She was imagining the cold draft at her back, she thought as she sprinted for the doors. There was no mournful voice whispering unintelligible words behind her. She was simply panicking, her subconscious taking over and running wild with fear.

Run, Aurelie. Run.

The breathing at your back is not real.

You're imagining the long, sharp fingernails tugging at your braid. None of this is happening.

Run, run, run.

She fumbled the iron key out from under her collar and leapt up the steps. By some miracle, she fitted it into the lock on the first try, turning it and slipping through the door and slamming it shut behind her, her back pressed to it, her breathing ragged.

She'd made it. She was safe. There was nothing behind her.

Aurelie took a deep, steadying breath and turned.

A demon stood on the other side of the glass, staring back at her.

Aurelie squeezed her eyes closed like a small child afraid of the monster in her closet. For a moment she stood there, praying that when she opened them, the red-eyed creature would be gone. She could go to bed and forget about this entire day, preferably forever.

But when she cracked open one eye, then the other, her stomach sank with dread. The demon was still there, its long, thin arms ending in sharp-tipped claws, its glowing eyes boring into hers. Hanging from one claw was a tangle of velvet ribbon. Unconsciously, she reached up and touched her braid, only to find her hair unraveled.

With trembling fingers, she reached into her pocket for her iron blade and met only lint. *Blast.* She didn't carry it on campus. She'd never felt the need to before.

The demon was tall and thin, its face little more than a blur with eyes. If it had a mouth, she couldn't see it. She'd always assumed the shimmering quality of *somnia* had to do with their insubstantiality, but from here, she could see it was covered in iridescent scales. It was very different from the demons she'd conjured in her laboratory. Still frightening, yet incongruously calm.

Why wasn't it leaving? Why was it staring at her as if waiting for something? Surely if it was chasing her, it was with ill intent. But she couldn't shake the feeling that it wanted something from her, beyond her life.

Suddenly, Aurelie heard a deep, resonant voice as though it were in her head.

He wants more.

Was the demon speaking to her? If so, this was an incredible breakthrough, something no one had ever experienced, as far as she knew.

"Who wants more?" she asked, throat dry as sandpaper.

Listen, child. He wants more.

"Miss Aurelie?"

Aurelie let out a yelp and pressed a hand to her chest. A lantern was bobbing toward Easton Hall. The guard was coming. Her eyes met the demon's once more before it disappeared into the shadows.

"I heard the doors slam," the guard said when he reached the stairs, his voice muffled by the glass. He held up his lantern. "Aciano's beard, are you all right?"

She must look a fright, she realized, with all the blood drained from her face and her hair loose and wild. She glanced from the corner of her eyes to confirm that the demon was gone. Cautiously, she opened the doors. "Did you see it?"

"See what, miss?"

She almost said "The *somnia*," but something stopped her. Embarrassment? Doubt? Or was it something else? If she told the guard there'd been a demon on campus, he would alert the Iron Guard. And she couldn't shake the feeling the demon hadn't been trying to hurt her.

"Never mind," she said, shaking her head. "I'm sorry for disturbing you."

"It's no disturbance at all, miss. I was making my rounds. Would you like me to escort you to your uncle's cottage?"

“I just came from there. I’m heading to my la—” She caught herself and smiled. “To my office. Thank you so much for your help.”

The guard, who would have been the age of Aurelie’s grandfather, if she had one, scratched his head uncertainly. “Are you sure, miss? I’d be happy to stay with you for a bit, make sure you’re all right.”

“I’m all right, really. Goodnight. And thank you again.”

It was a relief when Aurelie locked the doors behind her and made her way downstairs to her lab, where she immediately collapsed onto her sofa.

A moment later, she felt the sharp sting of Mephisto’s claws at her ankle. “Hello, little friend.” She bent down and held out her hand, and Mephisto clambered onto it, allowing her to lift it to her lap. The demon curled up in her skirt as she reached for a sketchpad. She needed to draw the *somnia* while it was still fresh in her mind.

As the drawing came to life under her hands, Aurelie could still hear its rusted-door voice, see the way it stared at her with those eerie red eyes. She must have imagined it speaking to her. Mustn’t she? The more she thought of it, the more the adrenaline faded away, the less plausible it seemed. Surely someone would have reported it by now if such a thing were possible.

Skeptically, a little embarrassed, Aurelie leaned down to where Mephisto slept, snoring softly. “Erm, excuse me. Just wondering if you’ve been capable of speech this entire time and I’ve missed it?”

Mephisto, oblivious, slept on.

CHAPTER 9
DES

IN THE SHOWER, DES RAN HIS HAND OVER HIS JAW, SCRATCHY with stubble, and let the water run until it went cold. After all his years of training, his reflexes were so quick he didn't have to think before he acted. But now, in the aftermath, doubt plagued him. What if he hadn't been fast enough? He hadn't even noticed the carriage until it was upon them. The Blake girl would have been flattened right in front of him, and then he'd have one more death on his conscience.

They never should have interfered with her. If Daisy hadn't introduced herself, she would still be none the wiser that the Iron Guard was keeping an eye on her. And he wouldn't be left with the feeling of her in his arms, the way her body had pressed up against his armor, how she'd clung to him for just a moment even after he let go. As if he wasn't the big, scary man who frightened small children, but the person they turned to when the monsters came.

When he'd reported the *somnia* trailing Miss Blake, Commander Yew had commended him for trusting his instincts.

"I want you to keep an eye on the girl, especially until her uncle returns," he'd said. "Leopold Blake is a friend of mine."

"I'd prefer to track down the man with the thrall, sir."

"I put Lieutenant Commander Grayson on the job." Commander

Yew looked up and met Des's eye. "I suggest you take the assignments you're given, Whitlow."

Des had swallowed down the lump in his throat and nodded, but it was with no small amount of bitterness. Grayson hadn't seen the thrall or the tall man, hadn't witnessed a *somnia* deliberately trail a civilian through the city. He would kill first and ask questions later, as all the other guards would. As he himself would have, before. But now . . . he couldn't help thinking that there were larger forces at play here, a bigger picture he didn't yet understand.

Daisy was still awake when he climbed into his bunk, as he'd known she would be. She always waited up for him, though he'd never asked her to. If anything, he'd urged her to get the sleep they all needed. But she said she couldn't rest without knowing he was all right, and though he'd never tell her, it felt nice to know someone was leaving a proverbial light on for him.

"Everything okay?" Daisy whispered from the foot of his bed as he climbed in, weary and exhausted for reasons unknown. It wasn't like it had been physically difficult to follow the girl.

"Mm," he grunted. "Just a long day."

Daisy's silence was so unusual that Des felt the weight of her implied judgment.

"What?"

He could hear the smile in her voice when she whispered, "It's just curious, that's all."

Now it was Des's turn to be silent. *Curious* was a code word for *strange*.

"She rattled you tonight," Daisy continued. "More than I've seen in a long time."

"I'd have reacted the same way if you stepped in front of a runaway carriage." He exhaled. "Like you were a damned fool."

Daisy poked him in the ribs, knowing it was the one vulnerable spot on his body. "Why do you dislike her so much, then?"

He flexed his abdominals, but damn if it didn't still tickle. He batted her hand away. "I don't have any feeling toward her whatsoever. It's all those people who spend their days drinking in cafés while we risk our lives that I can't stand." He sat up, leaning closer to Daisy. "And the *somnia* trailing her, the thrall last night. It doesn't feel like a coincidence."

"Agreed," Daisy said.

"She doesn't seem afraid of demons."

"Or of you."

Des shot Daisy a dark look.

"All right, fine. If you truly believe she's up to no good, what is her motivation?"

Des settled back against his pillow, thinking. Could the *somnia* that had trailed Aurelie be linked to the tall man and his thrall? He didn't see how. Not yet, anyway. "I have no idea. But I do think something about her is attracting demons. Why would that be?"

Daisy bopped him on the nose and climbed off his bunk. "Now you're asking the right questions," she said, and left him twice as confused as before.

As Des cleaned his sword on Monday morning, resigned to spending another wasted day watching the gates of Wisteria University, Commander Yew entered the barracks.

Everyone snapped to attention, clearly unprepared for this unexpected visit. It was their day off, after all. Most of the guards were lounging on their bunks reading or playing cards, and Des heard more than one person groan as they rose, likely hung over from staying up late drinking the night before.

"At ease," Yew said. "I'm here for an update. Don't panic. You'll still get your day off." His mouth curled in a wry grin. "But there were reports of three *verita* last week in the kingdom, three times as many as usual. Starting tomorrow, we'll be extending shifts by one hour to ensure every area of the city is covered."

No one had the audacity to complain, but Des heard more than a few sighs.

"Whitlow," Yew said. "Come with me."

Des followed Yew to his office and waited for the man to settle at his desk.

"I'm assembling a new unit," he said. "The increase in *verita* attacks has King Gabor and his court on edge. To that end, they've asked me to assemble my best guards. I want you to be part of that unit, Whitlow."

Then it wasn't his imagination. There was something strange going on with demons. But the Iron Guard operated almost independently of the monarchy, and it was unusual for the king to interfere this way. Des found himself at a loss for words. "I don't know what to say, sir."

"Say thank you."

"Thank you, sir. I'm honored."

"Good. Part of your new responsibilities will be to investigate attacks throughout the kingdom. For now, you'll stay close to Wisteria City, but whenever possible, I want the creators of these *verita* captured alive and brought to me."

"What about the *verita*?"

Commander Yew arched a brow.

"Should we bring them in alive as well, sir? I feel we could learn far more by studying a living demon—"

"Absolutely not. It's far too dangerous to even attempt something so foolish. You are to kill the demon, as is our founding objective since the days of King Aciano. Do I need to add a history refresher course to your schedule, Whitlow?"

Des's cheeks heated. "No, sir. I'm sorry, sir."

After a moment, Commander Yew continued. "You'll begin training as soon as Dr. Blake returns to the university."

Des struggled not to show his disappointment. He had no idea when Dr. Blake would be back, and in the meantime, other guards would be investigating cases *he* should be on. But he'd clearly pushed Yew's limits enough for one day. "Yes, sir."

"It will mean no more days off, but I don't believe I've seen you rest since the day you were brought here."

Des lowered his gaze. "It's not in my nature, sir."

"No, I suppose not. Go on. I want a full report of Aurelie Blake's comings and goings. If she leaves campus, follow her from a distance. I don't believe any more face-to-face interactions are required, even if she is a lovely young woman."

"Sir, that's not—"

"Dismissed, Whitlow."

Des caught a ghost of a smile curling his commander's lips before he turned to leave.

All the way to campus, he ignored Gareth, who peppered him with questions about the new unit, what Des thought of it, if he'd ever left the city before. He replied with grunts and nods, still ruminating over the fact that he couldn't begin his new duties until Leopold Blake returned. What if it took days, or even weeks? He'd fall behind in his training, and for what?

They stood outside the campus gates for hours, watching other students come and go, but there was no sign of the Blake girl. What good was he doing, standing around here, when she had no reason to leave campus today?

"I'm going to talk to the guard," Des told Gareth. "Keep an eye out for Miss Blake."

The campus guard was an older man with white hair and a belly that strained against his uniform, unlikely to be much use in a demon encounter. But the girl had told him they rarely saw demons on campus, so there was likely little reason for concern.

"Excuse me, sir," Des said politely. "I was wondering if you know when Dean Blake will be returning from his travels."

The guard, taking in Des's armor and stance, straightened a little. "Good afternoon, Lieutenant. We don't know when he'll be back, no. He's visiting an ill friend."

Des stifled a growl. "And in the meantime, who is looking after Miss Blake?"

"Why, we are, of course."

"What if she leaves campus?"

"Oh, that's a rarity. She works away at all hours in her office in Easton Hall, even on weekends."

"Is it normal for a student to have her own office?" Des asked.

The guard smiled with genuine fondness. "There's nothing normal about Miss Blake, Lieutenant. Smart as a whip, she is. She came here when she was just seven years old, orphaned in a terrible carriage accident. Her uncle has raised her here ever since."

Orphaned. He hadn't expected that. He assumed her wealthy parents lived somewhere in Wisteria and she stayed with her uncle while she attended the university. And she may be book smart, but based on his experience, she had very little in the way of street smarts. "Do you know anything about the man who visited on Friday evening?"

The guard scratched his chin, thinking. "Can't say I do. He said he was a friend of our groundskeeper, Mr. Morel. I believe Miss Blake invited him for dinner. But you don't need to worry about Miss Blake, Lieutenant. We take good care of her. I'm off to make my rounds. You boys stay safe."

Des thanked the man and wandered back into the trees across the street, where Gareth waited.

"Learn anything interesting?" Gareth asked.

"Of course not."

"Daisy said you saved Miss Blake from a runaway carriage," Gareth said after a few minutes, earning him a sharp look from Des.

"Why were you talking to Daisy?"

"She's nice," Gareth said with a shrug. "Not many of the other lieutenants will talk to us. It feels good to be treated like a person every now and then."

Des grunted noncommittally. Daisy was too soft on the junior lieutenants. That was why they all flocked to her, and why she'd been partnered with Jasper, who was almost as hard on people as Des.

"So you did save her?" Gareth pressed.

Demons take him, would the boy never learn to shut up? "Yes."

"Daisy said we're to keep an eye on her until the dean returns."

"Blood and bones," Des groaned. "Is there anything Daisy doesn't tell you?"

Gareth ducked his head at Des's tone. "That's all she said."

Des shifted against a tree, grateful the conversation was over.

"What was she like?"

"For fuck's sake, Gareth. Why do you care? She's a young woman. She's short, and soft, and she spends all her time in her office, apparently."

Gareth, far from being disappointed in this information, smiled moonily to himself. "She's like the girls I went to school with before my parents died. They always smelled so good. Unlike the guards. We all smell bad."

Fair enough. That was probably why Des found himself trying to recall the scent of her soap. Not lavender, he knew. It was something floral, but not rose or lilac. Something a little citrusy, almost verdant, but not quite . . .

He realized Gareth was staring at him and cleared his throat. "Yes. Well. She may not smell bad, but she's a waste of my time."

Gareth was about to respond when Des caught the scent of brimstone nearby, chasing away all thoughts of soap. He held up a closed fist to let Gareth know to be quiet.

"What is it?" Gareth whispered after a few minutes.

"I'm not sure. I smelled brimstone."

The sun was setting, and most of the students had left by now. Just when Des was about to give up and step out of the shadows, he saw something trot across the road toward the gates.

It was that same demon they'd seen the other night. The *verita* thrall. It was more like a wolf than a sheep, he realized now, its legs too long and bending the wrong way. It had a pointed snout and horns curling back from its head. Its red eyes glowed in the twilight.

A chill ran up Des's spine. *Was* it a *verita*? It kept its head low to the ground, as though it were tracking something; all the *verita* he'd encountered were in a frenzied state, behaving recklessly in pursuit of a meal. The tall man was nowhere in sight.

Of course, the guard was nowhere in sight either.

A woman's voice called something behind the gates, and Des watched the thrall disappear into the shadows near the guard's hut while none other than Aurelie Blake crossed the courtyard to her uncle's cottage. She waved to an older woman, probably a professor, and stopped to talk for several minutes, unaware of the demon lurking on the other side of the gates.

She really was oblivious, wasn't she?

"Do we attack?" Gareth asked, clearly hoping for a negative.

"Not yet," Des said, but he motioned for Gareth to follow him. Lieutenant Commander Grayson was off duty today. He'd passed the man in the training yard on his way here. Which meant no one was tracking this demon at all.

Once she disappeared into her uncle's cottage, the demon took off into the city.

"Come on," Des said. The demon might lead them to the tall

man, and he knew Commander Yew would want to know where he lived, even if he wouldn't let Des take this case. Aurelie Blake could handle herself for an afternoon.

They kept their distance, not wanting to alert the demon to their presence. Several times it turned down one street, paused, and doubled back, and they were nearly discovered. Fortunately, it seemed singularly focused on whatever it was hunting. After over an hour of darting around the neighborhood, the demon stopped, sat down on its haunches, and let out a long, mournful howl. Des felt goose bumps rise all over his body. Gareth looked like he was about to piss himself.

What *was* this thing? Des had never seen a demon behave in such a strange manner, making him more convinced than ever that it wasn't a *verita*, though it was clearly a thrall. Not of the girl, however; she wouldn't have been able to hide this for so long. And though he knew she was trouble, he couldn't bring himself to believe she could have anything to do with a creature this vile.

Finally, the demon led them to a row of townhouses, trotting up the stairs of a tall, narrow building Des was certain he'd never seen before. In fact, his eyes kept wanting to skim past it, as though the house didn't want to be noticed. He had the strange sense that if he looked away, he wouldn't be able to find it again.

The door opened, and Des only had a momentary glimpse of the tall man before the door closed behind the demon.

Gareth slumped against Des, and for once, he didn't yell at the boy. He sensed that his legs had gone out from under him, and there was nothing else for him to lean on but Des.

"Are you all right?" Des asked, nudging him.

"I don't know why I was so frightened of that thing. There was just something so—so profoundly *wrong* about it."

Des didn't say so, but he was in complete agreement. "It has to be a thrall. At least we know where it lives now. We'll report it to Commander Yew immediately."

"Who do you think the man was?" Gareth asked as they headed back toward the Iron Fortress.

"No idea. And I have no idea why he was visiting the dean's niece last week. Apparently she invited him to dinner."

Gareth shuddered. "I wouldn't dine with that man even if it was for my mother's famous pot roast. He gives me the creeps."

This time, he nodded in agreement. The man was decidedly creepy. And try as Des might to forget Aurelie Blake, he couldn't fight the feeling that he wasn't finished with her yet.

CHAPTER 10

AURELIE

WHEN MONDAY FINALLY ARRIVED, AURELIE HAD NEVER BEEN so grateful for her work and classes. She'd spent Sunday organizing her lab, fiddling with the slug elixir—it had no discernible impact on her moss, but it was tremendously sticky—and puzzling over Everard's door until her head felt ready to explode. Anything that didn't involve thinking about her encounter with the *somnia*, or with a certain demon hunter.

As she and Kiara made their morning rounds, Aurelie wondered how much to tell her friend. Procrastination, she decided, was the best option. "How was your visit with your grandparents?" she asked.

Kiara scrunched her nose, which had gained a few more freckles in the past week. "It was nice, in a provincial sort of way." It was sunnier in the south where her grandparents lived, and she'd spent most of her days outside, helping with their pumpkin harvest. "What did you get up to? See a certain gentleman, perhaps?"

For a heart-stopping moment, Aurelie thought she was referring to the giant, which was not only ridiculous, but impossible. "Oh, Miles," she realized. "Yes, I'm afraid so." She recounted their horrendous dinner, only giving a brief mention of the Iron Guard escort she'd received. But while she couldn't tell Kiara about Everard's proposal, she didn't see the harm in mentioning the *somnia* that had followed her on campus.

"Aurelie! That's terrifying! Why didn't you tell the guard?"

"Because it didn't actually try to hurt me," Aurelie said.

"Aside from yanking your ribbon out of your hair? Maybe it just didn't get close enough to finish the job!"

Aurelie winced as she tightened the screws on a desk that looked about ready to collapse. She prayed someone small sat there for the rest of term. "Maybe."

Kiara sat down on the ground, forcing Aurelie to look at her. "Listen, I know your inventing is important to you. But don't you think it's possible that you've attracted extra attention from these demons by conjuring so many of them?"

"It hasn't been that many. And these weren't *verita.* I've never heard of a *somnia* harming anyone, in fact."

Kiara, who was usually endlessly patient with Aurelie, shook her head. "We wouldn't have an entire Iron Guard if they weren't dangerous."

"Then it was a coincidence. Probably."

Kiara's gaze hardened in a way Aurelie didn't like one bit. "You're thinking of doing something stupid, aren't you?"

Lying to the guards, or even Uncle Leo, was one thing. But lying to Kiara was next to impossible. Aurelie rose from her crouch, moving to another desk. "What gave you that idea?"

Kiara followed. "I don't know. There's something off with you this morning. And with your uncle gone, I could see you doing something you wouldn't dare try with him around."

"Pffft. I have you to keep me in check."

"Not at night!" Kiara crossed her arms over her chest. "Do I need to surround Easton Hall with salt? Or perhaps find this giant of a guard and tell him to keep an eye on you?"

At that, Aurelie's entire face flooded with heat. "No! Absolutely not! I hope I never see that brute again."

When Aurelie finally glanced at her friend, she was grinning. "You like him, don't you?"

"I beg your pardon?" She leaned closer to Kiara, though no one else was around to hear them. "I'm an illegal inventor. I keep a pet demon in my lab, Kiki. Do you really think I could possibly have any interest in a demon hunter?"

"A big, handsome, muscular demon hunter who saved you from a runaway carriage?" She smiled, revealing the gap between her front teeth.

Aurelie gaped. "I never said he was handsome! All that country air has clearly gone straight to your head. You should visit the infirmary."

Kiara trailed Aurelie out of the classroom, still smiling. "You're the one who's lovesick."

"Please be quiet," Aurelie hissed as a pair of students passed them in the hall, giggling.

"Oh, very well. I'm done teasing you for now. My father wants me to help him with the rain gutters."

At the mention of Mr. Morel, Aurelie once again thought of Everard. The least she could do was follow up on his identity.

"Can you ask him if he knows a Mr. Everard?" Aurelie asked, trying her best to sound nonchalant.

Kiara narrowed her eyes. "Why?"

"Just something I've been meaning to ask."

Before Kiara could press her, Aurelie waved goodbye and walked to Professor Booth's office. The acting dean had requested a meeting with Aurelie this morning, though she hadn't said why. She was already planning to head to Professor Sheldrake's tower this afternoon.

"Come in," the professor called when she knocked on the door. Her office was not as orderly as Uncle Leo's, but there was a hominess to it that Aurelie found comforting. Professor Booth's bookshelves were full in a way that looked haphazard at best, though Aurelie had seen her locate books she needed instantly. Whatever system she used worked quite well for her, it seemed.

Professor Booth was at her desk, scribbling notes in a ledger and sipping from a cup of tea. She was a tall, brown-skinned woman with long braids and the warmest smile Aurelie had ever encountered. She could still remember sitting in this office as a child, reading while her uncle and Professor Booth chatted about lesson plans. If she was fortunate enough to become a professor one day, Aurelie would aspire to be like her.

Aurelie sat in the chair across from the large mahogany desk. "You wanted to see me, Professor?"

"Your uncle asked me to check in on you while he's away. It seems you passed all of your exams, though I think we both know you can do better."

Aurelie ducked her head. "Yes, Professor Booth."

"Leo is concerned you're spending too much time working that would be better spent studying. What do you think?"

She couldn't give up her work. And especially not now, when it might be her only cover if she accepted Everard's commission. "It's not my job. I keep to my hours, I promise. But I may spend too much time dithering when I should be studying."

"Dithering? Aurelie, you hardly ever leave campus. You have no social life to speak of, according to Leo."

"I went to dinner with Miles Viridian on Saturday," she said. Never mind that she'd hated every minute of it.

"With the Applebaums, I believe. I don't know the family personally, but I've heard they're a lively bunch."

Aurelie forced a smile. "Indeed."

The professor folded her arms on her desk and leaned forward. "Aurelie, I called you in here because Commander Yew from the Iron Guard sent me a message this morning."

Aurelie's stomach lurched as she felt the color drain from her face. "He . . . he did?"

"He wanted me to know that you'd had some interactions with several of his guards this weekend. He was concerned, since your uncle is gone, that you weren't being properly supervised."

Aurelie felt herself bristling at the implication that she needed to be watched over like a small child. Especially by a certain guard who seemed to have the same opinion, and had gone tattling to his commander as a result. "I assure you, I'm perfectly fine. They were being overly cautious. That's all."

Professor Booth didn't look remotely convinced.

"I *was* thinking of taking on a mentor . . ."

"A mentor? Who did you have in mind?"

Aurelie couldn't help smiling at the prospect of killing two birds with one stone: she could work with Professor Sheldrake *and* keep Professor Booth off her scent until her uncle returned. Not to mention she'd have a wonderful excuse not to socialize. "I've been interested in studying Elder Vansion. I was planning to approach Professor Sheldrake about it today, actually."

Aurelie had tried to sound casual, but the words had fallen out of her in a rush, and Professor Booth narrowed her eyes, clearly skeptical. "Indeed? I must admit, Aurelie, I had no idea you were interested in the runic alphabet. It's not exactly science, is it?"

Aurelie chewed her lip. Faced with someone she respected and admired, it felt wrong to lie. But in for a penny, in for a pound. "I'm interested in the science behind language creation. It's for my biology class."

Professor Booth's smile was still kind, but there was a tinge of suspicion in her voice when she spoke. "There aren't many studies in that area. I hope you're not thinking of doing anything that could get you into trouble. Your uncle would have my head."

Aurelie laughed nervously. "Of course not."

Professor Booth studied her for a moment. "Very well. Professor Sheldrake *is* the foremost expert on Elder Vansion in the kingdom. If anyone can help you, it's him."

Aurelie struggled to keep from cackling in triumph. Things were finally going her way for a change. "Thank you, Professor."

Just as she reached the door, Professor Booth said, "One more thing, Aurelie."

"Yes?"

"Professor Sheldrake's views are a little . . . unorthodox. But he's a wealth of knowledge, obscure though it may be."

"I understand."

"Besides," Professor Booth added, seemingly more to herself than Aurelie, "someone should go and check on the poor dear. Maybe take him something to eat. It must get lonely over there in the old tower."

The "tower" in question belonged to one of the oldest buildings on campus, topped with a turret clock. Built some three hundred years ago, it was always drafty, and it had the smell of decaying wood, wet stone, and a dusty scent Aurelie could only describe as feathers. This was likely due to the vast quantity of pigeons that had made their nests in the holes left behind by fallen bricks. Fortunately, Professor Sheldrake never put in work orders for the place, so Aurelie rarely had reason to visit.

The sky overhead was as gray as iron, portending rain. She crossed the courtyard before the clock tower, clutching a basket of muffins she'd asked Uncle Leo's cook to prepare, hoping something tasty would warm Professor Sheldrake up to her. He only taught one class per semester, an intense seminar on early automatons that students only took when they were desperate for extra credits.

The stairs leading up to his office creaked beneath her slippers. He did have a home, supposedly, and she'd never seen him on campus at night, but she suspected he might stay over from time to time. The fact that he could even make it up and down these stairs was impressive, as Aurelie was winded by the time she reached the top.

She knocked on his door, wondering why he bothered to close it with so few people coming here. She was met with silence that lasted a good three minutes, and she was about to abandon the muffins and head back to her lab when the door inched open, revealing one enormous eyeball.

“Can I help you?” a gruff voice asked. It took Aurelie a moment to realize he was wearing magnifying glasses similar to her own. She’d never considered how ridiculous she must look in them.

She cleared her throat. “I’m Aurelie Blake, Dean Blake’s niece?”

The eye blinked. “Yes?”

“Erm . . . well, I’ve brought you some muffins. I was hoping I could talk to you for a bit.” She held up the basket, hoping to entice him to at least open the door farther.

“I’m quite busy,” he said.

“Of course. It’s just that I’m interested in learning about arcane magic and runes, and Professor Booth thought you might be able to help.”

“Professor Booth?” The old man’s voice brightened considerably. “She mentioned me, specifically?”

Aurelie nodded in encouragement. “She did. She said you’re brilliant. That if anyone could help me, it’s you.”

At that, the door opened wide enough that Aurelie could confirm the professor had two enormous eyeballs. “Do come in,” he said, motioning for Aurelie to step forward. “It’s a bit of a mess, I’m afraid. I don’t often get visitors here.”

“A bit of a mess” was the understatement of the century. Professor Sheldrake’s office made Aurelie’s lab look minimalist by comparison. Every inch of available space here was occupied with books, papers, maps, and tools, but also gadgets and gizmos that Aurelie didn’t have names for. Hanging from the ceiling was what could only be a prototype for a flying machine. A half-assembled automaton in the shape of a man rested in a broken armchair.

Some children dreamed of tables laden with sweets or vaults

full of treasure. Some wandered into a toy shop or a pet store and felt they'd reached the very pinnacle of existence. Up until today, Aurelie had never known that level of joy.

As she turned in a slow circle, her eyes wide with astonishment and glittering with tears, she wondered if she'd finally found what she'd been missing all along.

"Good heavens, Professor Sheldrake," she breathed. "You're an inventor."

Professor Sheldrake shushed Aurelie loudly as he hurried to close the door behind her. "I'm not an *inventor*," he said, back to his gruff self. "I'm a *scientist.* I conduct experiments. And yes, every now and then I create—*inadvertently*, mind—something new. Such is the nature of science."

Aurelie thought about quibbling. What he'd described was an inventor to a T. But she thought better of it, lest he decide he'd had enough of her and force her to leave. Not yet. Not when she'd just discovered this treasure trove of projects and ideas. She could spend hours in this room and not cover everything lining the walls and desks. Yes, desks. She counted three, perhaps four, if one included tables. Which Professor Sheldrake clearly did.

"Professor Booth?" he pressed.

"Yes! She speaks so highly of you." Aurelie was fairly certain Professor Sheldrake was married, and Professor Booth definitely had a wife. "A friend of yours, I take it?"

"Oh, I wouldn't call us friends," he said, almost coyly. "We're colleagues. But she's always been so lovely. She brings me tea from time to time." He glanced at the basket hopefully.

"I'm afraid it's just muffins," she said. "I'll bring tea next time."

"Mm." The tone implied there likely wouldn't be a next time, so Aurelie hurried on.

"What about the demons?" she asked, pressing one gentle fingertip to the flying contraption. She was immediately shooed away by the professor. Now that she could see all of him, she realized he was not as old as he'd been made out to be—eighty, at most—and if his faculties were misplaced, they were likely to be found in close proximity to Aurelie's. Either Professor Sheldrake wasn't truly mad, or Aurelie was. Both seemed equally likely at the moment.

"The demons, if *accidentally* conjured, are dealt with."

She cast him a questioning glance, and he gestured to the corner of the room, where a large barrel of salt sat beside a taxidermied dog the size of a lion.

It blinked.

"Demons take me!" Aurelie gasped. "Is that thing alive?"

"That *thing* is named Alastor, and I'll have you know he's a purebred Wisterian hound. A bit larger than his littermates, to be sure. But still within breed standard."

Aurelie had never seen such an immense animal before. She resolved to give it a wide berth. "That's . . . convenient."

"Hardly. He eats like a horse and has to be walked at least an hour a day or he'll go into a frenzy. But he is excellent with demons." The old man patted the dog on the head. It didn't twitch a whisker. "At any rate," he said, eyeing the basket of muffins, "what was all this about arcane magic?"

Aurelie had nearly forgotten her reason for coming here in the first place. Did she dare to tell Professor Sheldrake about her own inventions? He would likely find them amateur and inane compared to his own work. But the very fact that he was here, creating in secrecy, made her want to embrace him.

"Professor Sheldrake, I was wondering, do you have a protégé at the moment?" She handed him the basket of muffins and watched him make quite a show out of choosing one. "That is, I'm in need of a mentor, and I'm afraid no one else in the science department shares my particular interests."

"Mm," he said, having finally selected his muffin and taken a rather impressive first bite. Small tufts of white hair jutted out above his ears, though the rest of his pate was completely bald. "No one has asked to study under me in years. A decade, perhaps. I doubt your professors would give you any credit for it. They might oppose it altogether."

He set a kettle on a stove Aurelie noticed was very similar to her own and felt another swell of affinity that brought tears to her eyes. Who would have thought that all this time, the person she'd been searching for was the school hermit? And what, exactly, did that say about Aurelie?

"We don't have to tell anyone. I wouldn't be doing it for credit. I'd simply like to glean any wisdom I can from you."

He eyed her over his second muffin, still wearing those ridiculous glasses. "Wisdom, eh."

She reached into her pocket and pulled out the sketch of the door. She'd brought it with her on a whim, really. She'd never actually expected to be able to share it. But this was her chance, possibly her only *real* chance, to learn more about this project. If he told her it was impossible or too dangerous, she'd never speak to Everard again. But if not . . .

With a hope and a prayer and no small amount of fear, she thrust the paper toward him. "Here. I need to build this."

After a long, silent moment, Professor Sheldrake took the paper from Aurelie and carried it over to an orb-shaped lamp, held aloft by a bronze cherub. "What's this? You want to *build* a portal? Using arcane runes? Do you even know what it leads to?"

A *portal*? Why did that word feel so much more ominous than *door*? "Erm, not exactly," she said, her heart in her throat, half expecting him to ring for the guards.

He stared at her, clearly unimpressed.

Aurelie lifted her chin, hoping to portray more confidence than she felt. "It will help eradicate demons."

After a heavy silence, he sighed. "Even if that's true, this is highly illegal. Magic, as I'm sure you know, was outlawed under King Aciano along with inventing. Besides, these metal plates are so intricate that they would require a master's skill. You'd need to enlist a blacksmith's help, and they'd never do it. Far too risky for them."

This was why she needed someone to bounce ideas off of! Imagine the time she could have saved herself in the past if she'd had Professor Sheldrake's knowledge at her disposal. "What if someone else had already agreed to make the plates? I only need to assemble them, and of course etch the runes."

"Mm." Professor Sheldrake had moved on to his fourth muffin. "Still illegal, but you're young. Possibly resourceful." He set the basket of muffins on a table piled with books. "Those runes are a truly archaic form of Elder Vansion, so dated even I may not be able to help with the translation."

"Is a translation necessary?"

He narrowed his eyes at her. "If you would even consider casting a spell you can't read, then I'm sure I can be of no use to you as a mentor. One can't teach common sense."

Aurelie winced. "Of course. It was a foolish question. I will translate them faithfully."

He grunted. "Very well. I'd ask you where these blueprints came from, but I'm fairly certain I don't wish to know. And since everyone around here tells me that I'm as good as dead, I don't suppose I'll have to live with any adverse consequences for long. You may use the empty classroom in the basement. No one ever goes there. Mind you, it's with good reason. It's dark and damp and full of spiders."

Aurelie hadn't heard anything beyond the implied yes. She nodded eagerly. "Spiders. Right. I don't mind spiders." Not true, but Mephisto would clear those out in no time.

"Alastor is not for hire, so don't get any ideas where he's concerned. Your invention, your demon. If anyone asks if I was aware of your work, I'll deny it to the grave."

"I'd expect nothing less."

Finally, he lowered the spectacles to the tip of his nose and sighed. In reality, his eyes were of perfectly average size. It was a wonder he didn't get a headache wearing those glasses all the time. "What is the niece of Dean Blake, arguably the most provincial in the history of this esteemed institution, doing building an illegal invention." It wasn't a question, and Aurelie couldn't have answered it even if it was. He studied her for a moment, the way he might a toad.

"This kingdom, for all its faults, has continued to function because the vast majority of its citizens are law-abiding, rule-following, tax-paying sheep. And thank the seven virtues for that, or we'd be overrun with demons. Until someone breaks the curse on this country of ours, we're doomed to repeat history, year after year, decade after decade. We're no better than these automatons," he said, gesturing to the half-assembled humanoid. "I have no doubt that nothing will change in my lifetime. Likely yours either, if I'm being honest."

Aurelie didn't let herself think that way, and to hear it laid out so starkly by Professor Sheldrake made her feel smaller and more alone than ever. Then again, she was used to disappointment. She always managed to find a way to carry on.

"But," he said, reaching for another muffin, "every now and then, a person comes along who refuses to follow the rules, who decides that the laws don't apply to them, that some things are worth fighting for. We call them criminals," he added flatly.

Aurelie could feel tears welling in her eyes, much to her mortification. "I—"

"I haven't finished, young lady." He replaced his glasses and blinked at her owlishly. "Back in the days of my grandfather, they had a different name for those people. They called them rebels. Radicals. Revolutionaries. They broke societies, started wars. Sometimes they killed in the name of progress. Most people hated them. Very few celebrated them. But they are the ones who changed the world."

A chill ran up the back of Aurelie's neck.

"So, Miss Blake?" Professor Sheldrake asked, handing her back her sketch. "Which one are you?"

CHAPTER 11

DES

AFTER A WEEK OF FOLLOWING HER FROM A DISTANCE, DES had learned very little about Aurelie Blake, though what he did discover surprised him. One afternoon, she'd gone to a carpentry shop tucked off the main boulevard. Des had interrogated the manager after she left, but he insisted that she was only purchasing some nuts and bolts, something she did from time to time. Apparently she worked on campus as a bricoleur, which was odd. She didn't look like someone who was good with her hands.

She carried a little notebook that she scribbled in when no one was watching, and he remembered how she'd said she liked to understand how things worked. It hadn't made sense to him then, but now that he'd observed her, he was beginning to see that she was a genuinely curious person, not so much living in the world as observing it from the outside. He would never have thought he had anything in common with Aurelie, but he felt that way himself, sometimes.

He lay awake at night, still puzzling over the tall man and his thrall. He'd considered that the man might have some sort of obsession with Aurelie, using his demon to track her movements. Perhaps the *somnia* Jasper had killed had been another thrall. But despite the intel he'd passed on to Commander Yew, Lieutenant Commander Grayson hadn't been able to find the narrow townhouse. Worse still, when Des and Gareth had gone back, they couldn't find it again either. It was as if the house had never existed at all.

Commander Yew believed dark magic was afoot and told Des to keep an eye out for either the demon or the man, but he couldn't very well accomplish much while watching Wisteria University. Which was why he had resolved to confront Aurelie himself. If nothing else, he deserved to know when her uncle would return so he could finally get to work with the Iron Swords, the elite group of hunters Yew had assembled.

Around noon on Friday, Gareth, who'd gone into a nearby café for a cup of tea, found Des leaning against a tree, his lids heavy from squinting against the midday sun. "Don't look now," Gareth said, holding out a pastry that Des declined with a shake of his head, "but I believe your quarry is about to flee the coop."

Des glanced over his shoulder at the school gates. Sure enough, there was Aurelie, talking to one of the guards. She wore a leather satchel over one shoulder, indicating she was heading somewhere off campus.

"You can return to base," he told Gareth. "I'll take it from here." She was probably going to the café to sketch, and he didn't want Gareth there when he approached her. The kid would be a distraction. Or worse, a gossip. He didn't need Daisy hearing everything from Gareth.

"Are you sure?" Gareth asked, earning a cold look from Des. "Uh, right. I'll see you back at the fort. Sir."

Des had never been on the university grounds himself. In truth, he'd always found it intimidating, a place not meant for people like him. But for the first time, he felt curious about those large, self-important buildings. What did Aurelie do all day, other than take notes and read? And tighten screws from time to time.

To his amusement, Aurelie looked both ways multiple times before stepping out into the street. His lips quirked in an involuntary grin. At least she'd learned her lesson on that front.

She was wearing a white blouse with a brooch at her collar and a long plaid skirt under her green coat, more like a matron than a young lady. She was so intent on whatever destination she had in mind that she nearly ran into a man who crossed her path. She apologized profusely, earning a charmed and amused smile from the man, who frankly didn't seem at all displeased by the encounter.

His eyes met Des's, and whatever he saw there made him blanch, bow, and scurry away.

Des followed at what was for him a leisurely pace, although Aurelie seemed somewhat harried. She glanced over her shoulder multiple times, and more than once he had to step behind a tree or into an alley to avoid her gaze.

Finally, as Aurelie reached Aciano Square, she approached a crowd standing around a proselytizer on an apple crate surrounded by a circle of salt. He was ranting about demons taking over Wisteria, warning people to repent for their sins before it was too late. It wasn't an uncommon sight. Ever since the demons appeared, a segment of the population had become deeply religious. Before then, Wisteria was a secular kingdom with no official religion or spiritual practice, at least not for several hundred years. Until the question of succession between twin brothers nearly started a war.

Florian wanted radical change in Wisteria. More incentives for exploration and invention, more schools, more immigration to draw the world's most remarkable minds. Aciano, on the other hand, wanted the kingdom to remain as it was. Wisteria was thriving, after all, and bringing in more immigrants would surely mean fewer resources for native Wisterians. When their father chose Aciano as his heir, Florian had unleashed a terrible curse upon the kingdom.

A curse that, according to this proselytizer, stemmed from the kingdom's sins. Des didn't particularly care *where* they came from, only that they be eradicated.

The larger issue was the crowd surrounding the ranting man. Like a mouse among the grass, Aurelie had disappeared almost instantly into the throng of people, and Des found himself forcing his way through to follow her.

It was a mistake. To some, demon hunters were revered as angels doing holy work. Several people began to point out his presence, and then they were touching his armor, pressing toward him until he was entirely surrounded.

It took him another minute to realize Aurelie had done it on purpose.

She glanced over her shoulder once, scanning the horde of people, and this time Des couldn't disappear. Their eyes met, his hard with fury, hers crinkled in the corners with amusement. She'd *known* he was following her.

Shoving aside a man who was clinging to Des's arm, he hurried after her. "Miss Blake," he called, loud enough that he knew she heard him, but she continued on.

"In the name of King Aciano, stop!" he roared in his most authoritative voice. Everyone nearby froze.

Including, he was surprised to see, Aurelie. Her shoulders slumped as she huffed out a sigh and turned to face him.

"Good afternoon, Lieutenant. To what do I owe the pleasure?"

He closed the distance between them while the rest of the crowd buzzed back to life, no doubt relieved he hadn't been speaking to them. "Why did you run away from me?"

She blinked in rapid succession, playing innocent. "I don't know what you mean. I wasn't running, and I didn't know you were here."

"Bollocks. How long have you known I was following you?"

She rolled her eyes. "Since Saturday night, of course."

The whole time? His stomach soured with shame. "Then why did you pretend not to see me?"

She pressed a hand to her chest. "I'm so sorry. I must have misunderstood the rules of the game. I thought you were pretending to stalk me, and I was pretending I didn't know you were there."

"I wasn't pretending," Des growled.

"Then why not speak to me directly?" She hitched the bag on her shoulder, her eyes darting toward the crowd.

"Where are you heading?"

"I hardly see how that's any of your business."

He leaned closer, lowering his voice so the remaining devotees couldn't hear. "My commander tasked me with keeping an eye on you until your uncle returns."

At this, her eyes widened, her lips parting slightly, drawing Des's gaze. Was she merely surprised, or was she concerned that he would glean what she was up to? She schooled her features before he could decide. "That's not necessary. I'm sure you have far more important things to do than follow me."

"Oh, I do. That's why I'm here. I want to know when your uncle will return, so I can get off of babysitting duty and do my actual job."

Her eyes narrowed at the word *babysitting*, but she was distracted by a flurry of activity across the square.

"Your uncle?" he prompted.

"I'm not sure when he's going to return. He's visiting a friend, and I haven't had word from him in the week he's been gone. But you needn't concern yourself with me, sir. I'm perfectly capable of taking care of myself. Consider yourself relieved of duty." With that, she turned on her heel and began to stomp away, realized she was heading in the wrong direction, and abruptly changed course.

Des, who wasn't used to having someone walk away from him without being dismissed, felt his blood begin to boil. Aurelie Blake was impertinent, uppity, and insubordinate as hell. He was preparing to go after her and demand a better answer when he heard a muffled scream nearby.

"Demon!" someone shouted.

Blood and bones, in broad daylight? Things were even worse than he thought if demons were brazen enough to attack during the day.

More screams, the inevitable shoves and flying elbows. Someone stomped on Des's foot. And still, he didn't take his eyes off Aurelie. This was his opportunity to get the true measure of her. She had three options: run, like some people were doing; get behind the demon hunter, as many others had; or take the opportunity to get away from Des. The latter would be a foolish choice if she had nothing to hide. It would be even more foolish if she did.

Aurelie glanced back at him once, smirked, and disappeared for good.

CHAPTER 12
AURELIE

FINALLY, AURELIE THOUGHT AS SHE EMERGED FROM THE crowd and studied the card Everard had given her, thumb stroking the gilded lettering. She almost felt sorry for Des, thinking she didn't know he was there. As if the man could easily hide. It was like an elephant trying to crouch behind a rosebush. All week at dinner, she'd spotted him from her uncle's window, leaning against a tree and looking as though he'd rather be anywhere else. The day he'd trailed her to the carpentry shop, she'd been tempted to lead him on a wild-goose chase, just for the fun of it.

But as smug as she felt about Des's terrible sleuthing skills, she knew he had far better things to do than trail her. This was a waste of his time and effort, and if she'd thought he might actually listen to her, she'd have told him so herself.

It was easier than expected to lose him in the crowd. Truth be told, she had no idea people made such a fuss over the Iron Guard. But she couldn't have Des following her all the way to Everard's house. If she accepted this commission, a demon was inevitable. And Des needed to be well clear of Wisteria University when that happened.

She'd spent the week drawing a detailed schematic of the interlocking plates, reading up on engraving, and even scouring the library for books on runic magic. Unfortunately, the card catalog revealed a rather gaping hole on the subject. Someone, perhaps her uncle, maybe the king himself, had ordered all the books removed. Professor Sheldrake had only a few old tomes on Elder Vansion, which he'd lent to Aurelie under the strict proviso that she keep them well hidden.

"I hope you know what you're getting into, girl," he'd said as he handed them over.

"Not at all," she replied. To her relief, he had laughed.

Aurelie knew little of the world, but she was sure of one thing: she was put on this planet to create. To accept otherwise was to believe she was as adrift as dandelion fluff, as pointless as the young aristocrats who spent their days gossiping in cafés. Her parents had shown her that a life well-lived included fulfilling work, joyful pastimes, and loving relationships.

But what if life, what if joy, what if *love* didn't exist for Aurelie outside of Wisteria University? She knew Uncle Leo wanted what was best for her, but if he truly believed a man like Miles Viridian could make her happy, then he didn't know her at all. She knew beyond a shadow of a doubt that she couldn't make Miles happy. She couldn't even make it through a single dinner with him.

This past week, her thoughts had returned again and again to her parents. If she didn't accept this project, if she didn't at least *try* to create something great, she would be denying the gifts they had given her. She would be dishonoring their memories by settling for a life she didn't love.

More than death, more than social ostracization, Aurelie feared inertia. That she would never move forward *or* backward, but that she would spin in circles, finding herself trapped by the walls society had built around her. She wanted what Professor Sheldrake had said. She wanted the earth-shaking creation that would change her world. She didn't want to open a door—she wanted to bring the walls down entirely.

Despite her conviction, she quailed when she reached Everard's tall, narrow townhouse. Located on Marigold Street, the house was wedged in like an afterthought, tucked between two homes several times wider. Painted black with a decorative gabled roof, it had the appearance of an old grandfather clock warped from age. She checked the address again. This was definitely it. Now all she had to do was knock.

Aurelie couldn't help feeling that at least one other human should know where she was. If she went into this house and never came out, Uncle Leo wouldn't know to look here. And now that she'd lost Des, even he wouldn't know what had become of her.

But that was the point, wasn't it? Because Des *couldn't* know she was here. Mustering her courage, Aurelie walked up the steep staircase to the front door and clapped the knocker three times. It wasn't until after she'd released it that she recognized the shape: a leering demon.

"I can't tell you how happy I am to hear you're willing to work with me," Everard said as they sat down for tea in his drawing room. The house had the peculiar aspect of seeming much larger on the inside than it was on the outside, which was a relief, as Aurelie had worried she might feel claustrophobic in such a narrow building. "I admit, I was afraid you might not accept."

"I haven't *fully* decided yet," Aurelie said, taking a sip of tea from a fine porcelain teacup, though it was mismatched from its saucer, as was the cup Everard held. It looked almost like a miniature in his long fingers. "I have a few questions I wanted to ask in person."

He swirled a silver spoon in the cup, though he hadn't added any sugar or cream. In fact, Aurelie hadn't seen him take a single sip, and she glanced down at her own tea with the same sense of unease she'd felt since she arrived. "I see," Everard said.

"I've drafted some schematics on the interconnecting plates, and I think the needed pattern has to do with the runes themselves . . ." She broke off as Everard raised his free hand.

"No need to go into the details, Miss Blake. *You're* the inventor, after all."

Aurelie flushed, at once pleased and embarrassed. Did she really have the right to be called an inventor? She was nothing compared to the great minds of the past who had created clocks and steam engines and all the miraculous innovations of bygone centuries. Aurelie's crowning achievement was a small lift operated by a pulley that allowed her to send supplies up an old chimney shaft to the upper floor of the university, which she called the Load Lightener. Of course, she could only use it at night when no one else would discover it, but she found it quite useful and had no doubt others would as well, if she were ever allowed to share it.

Still, it wasn't exactly the stuff revolutions were built on.

"Simply tell me what supplies you'll need, and they'll be sent to the university at your convenience." Everard sat back in his chair, watching Aurelie with his unnerving pale eyes. "You know, it's a shame you weren't born one hundred years ago. I have no doubt you'd have changed the world."

Something in Aurelie's chest clenched. Something dangerously close to her heart. She'd never had her own feelings mirrored back to her so directly in her entire life. Smiling, she picked up her teacup again and took a slow sip. "Well, who knows," she said. "I might yet."

Everard smiled back. "I believe you just might."

Blushing, Aurelie let her eyes take in the rest of the sitting room. There were shelves on either side of the lit fireplace, holding dozens of old books with well-placed curiosities and objets d'art interspersed among them. Above the mantel was a large oil painting, a still life of a bouquet of colorful tulips and peonies, studded with insects so realistic Aurelie felt they might crawl right off the edge of the ornate gold frame. In an unseen hallway, she heard the click of a dog's nails as it trotted across the wooden floors. It was all rather cozier than she would have given Everard credit for.

"How long have you lived here?" she asked, because the silence had stretched on far too long and she could still feel Everard's eyes on her.

"Oh, ages," he said, crossing one long leg over the other. "Sometimes it feels like it's been a century."

She nodded for lack of anything else to say. After another uncomfortable lull, she cleared her throat. "Pardon my bluntness, but what exactly will this portal do?" She'd been afraid to ask, partly because she was afraid of Everard's reaction, but also because she wasn't entirely sure she wanted to know the answer.

"*Do,* Miss Blake?"

"Portals have to open *something,* to lead *somewhere.* Don't they?" She hated how her voice grew weaker with every word under the weight of his cold gaze.

His lips curled as he tapped a finger against his chin. "Tell me, Miss Blake. Why do you create?"

Aurelie once again felt as though this were some kind of trap, though she couldn't imagine what it would be. If he wanted to arrest her for illegal activity, this seemed an awfully convoluted way of doing it. "I feel it's what I was made for," she said. "It's my life's purpose."

"Do you believe every person has a purpose, then?"

"Of course I do." Uncle Leo's purpose was to help others learn. A farmer's was to feed people. The Iron Guard existed to protect them. "Everyone needs to be *useful*, surely."

"I agree," Everard said. "And I believe my purpose is to help facilitate change. I know that's not what our king wants, or even very many of our citizens. But since I was born, it's been a calling. I may lack the imagination of people like you, but I have the means. This is how *I* can be useful, Aurelie."

"But what do you plan to do, exactly?" The *what* mattered as much as the *how*. All Everard had given her were vague assurances, and Aurelie was a scientist: she could never be satisfied with incomplete data.

He sighed and rose, strolling to his bookshelf. "If there was a great conspiracy in this kingdom, would you want to know?" he asked over his shoulder.

"Of course," Aurelie said.

"Even if that knowledge created a terrible upheaval in our society?"

She blinked and sat back. She didn't put much stock in conspiracy theories, and while she wanted progress, she wasn't sure "terrible upheaval" was what she had in mind. "I don't know," she answered truthfully.

He turned to face her, a book in his hands, a slight frown on his lips. "Then perhaps I underestimated you. I thought we had similar worldviews. I thought we both valued the truth."

"I do value the truth," she said, a spark of indignation burning in her chest. "But if that knowledge hurts a lot of people . . ."

"So you only value truth when it's convenient. I see." He shook his head, clearly disappointed in her. "I was afraid going to someone so young was a mistake."

Aurelie's cheeks burned. "I don't think this is a matter of age," she managed.

He was still facing her, the book cradled against his chest. "Perhaps not. Still, I may have overestimated your capabilities. When I heard there was a young woman in Wisteria crafting brilliant creations, I was so excited I leapt at the opportunity to speak with you. Rash, in hindsight."

She rose from her chair, so caught up by the need to defend herself she didn't stop to question who, exactly, was talking about Aurelie and her "brilliant creations."

"It has nothing to do with my capabilities, Mr. Everard, and everything to do with my sensibilities. Humans should care about each other. That's the very definition of a functioning society."

"And yet you invent, Miss Blake. You risk the lives of all your fellow humans when you create for yourself, do you not?"

"That's not—"

"So which is it?" he continued. "Is our loyalty to the truth, or to each other? Do we protect one another at the expense of everything else, or do we pursue knowledge for knowledge's sake, even if what we find might shatter our collective comfort?"

Aurelie found she was breathing heavily, as though she'd just run up a flight of stairs. She had never felt so defensive before, and now she was humiliated as well, because she didn't know the answer. Worse still, she didn't know how to go about finding it.

"I don't know," she finally admitted, deflating.

Mr. Everard looked so sad that Aurelie found she wanted to comfort him now. "That's a pity, Miss Blake. I had hoped I'd found the person I was looking for." He returned the book to the shelf. "You should get back to your university. It seems that's the perfect place for you. After all, one can't get into too much trouble by reading."

Aurelie could only nod and follow him toward the front door. A distant voice in her head asked how this man knew so much about her—she very much doubted he knew *everything*, but he knew far more than he should—but she was too disappointed in herself to hear it. All this time, she'd believed she was dedicated to the pursuit of knowledge, but Everard had revealed something deeper. Something she had never looked at very closely before.

Did Aurelie want progress? Or was Miles right? If the status quo was good enough, was it worth upsetting it for progress' sake? At what point did morality factor in? Did a true scientist abandon their experiment because they might not like the answers they found?

No. No, of course they didn't. And neither could Aurelie.

She stopped before the open door and turned to face Everard. "I'll do it."

His lips twitched. “Do what, Miss Blake?”

“I’ll make your portal. I don’t know what is happening out there in the rest of the world, but I know what it was like in this kingdom prior to Aciano’s curse. History has proven that progress is a good thing. I believe that, with all my heart.”

His smile spread, revealing sharp eyeteeth that reminded Aurelie of a wolf from a fairy tale. “As do I, Miss Blake. Now, we haven’t discussed payment.”

“I haven’t done anything yet,” she replied, slipping into her coat. “Let’s see if I’m actually capable of this before we worry about the money.”

“We also haven’t discussed a deadline.” Everard had positioned himself between her and the door.

“Oh. Right. Well, I suppose I’ll need a year, at least. I have my studies, and I’ve barely begun to grasp the runic alphabet, let alone ancient runes. Then there’s my uncle to think about . . .”

Everard frowned again, and all the bravado Aurelie had felt just one minute before withered like a spent bloom. “Aurelie, I’m afraid I can’t wait a year. Time is of the essence. Surely you can manage this by spring.”

She hated the way she fidgeted in Everard’s presence. It must make her seem very young to him. “Less than six months? I have a job, and my studies.”

“Yes, you mentioned that already.”

“Right.” Aurelie pulled at a loose thread on her sleeve and instantly regretted it. A hole had opened up along the seam, and this was her very favorite coat. Her mother’s coat, in fact. Her mother had been petite, like her, but she had very little of her mother’s clothing. She hadn't had the foresight at seven to ask to keep it. What child could imagine being as large as their parents, taking up the same amount of space as the people who were her entire world?

"Let's take it day by day for now, shall we?" Everard said gently. "I'll check in with you from time to time to see how you're getting on."

"All right." Aurelie hoped he meant by letter, because if he showed up at the university while her uncle was there, she'd have more explaining to do than she could possibly manage. She was an expert in the small, mostly benign lie, but a cover-up of this magnitude would require a level of deception she didn't think she was capable of.

That she *hoped* she wasn't capable of.

Finally, Everard opened the door, and Aurelie was in such a hurry to take in a lungful of fresh air that she forgot to thank him. By the time she was at the bottom of the stairs and looked up, the door was already closed, the demon knocker staring down at her like a bad omen.

CHAPTER 13

DES

DES BARELY HAD TIME TO CURSE AURELIE BEFORE THE CROWD dispersed enough to reveal the demon in question.

To his shock and horror, it was the thrall from the university, the one he'd trailed to the tall man's house. And worse, it was already upon its victim, razor-sharp teeth tearing at the man's throat. As his screams choked off into a bloody gurgle, Des heard the sound of someone vomiting behind him.

Des slipped into the focused, trancelike state of battle. It was what he'd been trained to do from infancy: Don't question, don't think. React.

His sword was already drawn, his head down as he charged the demon. Every other *verita* he'd encountered would have stayed to enjoy its meal after going through the trouble of killing it. But not the thrall. It fled the scene immediately, impossibly fast on its long legs, and Des faced the split-second decision between treating the victim or going after it.

Des glanced at the man, blinking in surprise when he realized it was the one Aurelie had bumped into earlier. Unfortunately, it was too late to save him. The thrall had torn out his jugular, and there was no physician in Wisteria who could heal that. It couldn't be a coincidence that this demon had showed up within ten feet of Aurelie Blake, *again.* He started to turn.

Someone tugged on Des's arm, pulling him back.

"Help him!" a woman cried, gesturing toward the victim. "He's my husband! We have two children and one on the way." She cradled her stomach as tears spilled over her cheeks.

"I'm so sorry, madam. It's too late."

She began to wail as the crowd dispersed around them, no longer concerned now that they weren't in danger.

Des glanced back toward the direction of the thrall and cursed. The demon was gone. A man was dead.

And Aurelie Blake was going to rue the day she'd crossed Destrier Whitlow.

By the time Des returned to the barracks to report to Commander Yew, his tail tucked between his legs as he admitted that he—a big, strong, scary demon hunter—had lost a notebook-wielding university student, Aurelie could have gone anywhere.

Commander Yew, to his credit, didn't admonish Des, probably sensing that his shame was punishment enough. "There's no question dark magic is involved, Whitlow. We've put our best senior guards on the case. Your responsibility was Miss Blake, and as I understand it, she's come to no harm."

"Sir, with all due respect, she's been spotted near this thrall multiple times now. I believe she may have been visiting the thrall's master when the attack occurred. She evaded me. Again."

"Maybe she just doesn't like you," Yew replied, the only indication he was teasing Des a slight twinkle in his dark brown eyes.

"Oh, I've no doubt she doesn't like me," Des said. "But if she has nothing to hide, why not make that abundantly clear so I'll stop following her?"

"Take a seat, Whitlow."

Des swallowed, doing as instructed. A man had died, and if he hadn't allowed himself to be distracted by Aurelie, he would have saved his life. He deserved whatever punishment was coming.

"You're my best lieutenant. You know it and so does everyone else here. To be frank, I only let you follow the Blake girl because I thought you needed a break. I should have known you'd take this as seriously as all your other duties."

Des lowered his gaze, humiliated. "I see."

"It's not all bad," Yew said, with more softness than Des had ever heard from him. "I've been trying to decide when to promote you, and I think the time has come."

Des's eyes shot up. He'd been a lieutenant for so long, he'd started to wonder if he'd die one. It wasn't unlikely; most guards who died in service did so as lieutenants. Younger guards, like Gareth, came on as junior lieutenants and were generally watched closely by their seniors. If a guard made it to the rank of lieutenant commander, they'd survived enough demon encounters that they were likely to survive their service. It was those middle years one had to watch out for.

"Thank you, sir." Des wondered if he was supposed to stand, what the proper protocol was.

"We'll have a ceremony for you soon. By the end of the year, certainly. I'm relieving you of watching Miss Blake."

"Sir, I'm convinced she has something to do with this surge in demon activity."

"And I'm not. There have been more attacks throughout the whole kingdom recently, including in the provinces. Sightings of day-walkers are becoming more common. Whatever Aurelie Blake is doing here, she can't possibly be responsible for all of it. Part of the reason I'm promoting you is because I want you on equal footing with the other members of the Iron Swords. Tracking and killing *verita* is where you belong."

Two days ago, Des would have agreed wholeheartedly. It was all he'd ever wanted. But now, knowing that Aurelie Blake had been onto him all week, that she clearly didn't fear demons the way any normal citizen would, that they seemed to appear whenever she left campus, Des couldn't help thinking that he had work to do right here in Wisteria City.

"I don't know what to say, sir."

"Say thank you. And go get in a solid training session. You look like you have some energy to burn."

"Thank you. I won't let you down, sir." Des saluted and left the commander's office, heading across the dirt training yard where other guards sparred and drilled. But despite the good news of the long-awaited promotion, there was an underlying sense of foreboding he couldn't deny.

Was it the promotion itself? Was a part of him afraid of what this meant? To be promoted to lieutenant commander put him in the top 10 percent of the Iron Guard. In that, he could take a great deal of pride, especially considering he was significantly younger than the other lieutenant commanders.

But it also unofficially meant he was accepting that this was going to be the rest of his life. Not that he'd ever expected anything more, but it suddenly felt like a very serious commitment for someone to make at nineteen.

Perhaps it was that, for the first time in his entire life, he'd seen firsthand this week what other Wisterians his age did. Namely, talk, flirt, drink, flirt, eat, shop, and flirt. Their futures were wide open, and no one was asking them to commit to anything for the rest of their lives, except perhaps marriage. That was the privilege of money. Your time was truly your own to do with as you pleased. Des couldn't remember the last time he'd done something for pleasure.

His thoughts, to his annoyance, turned to Aurelie. She had a purpose, a vocation, and still seemed to find time for recreational pursuits. Des didn't know how someone achieved that sort of balance, but it was nice to know that such a middle ground *could* exist in theory.

And yet here she was, wandering blithely through the city, demons trailing in her wake, wreaking havoc, all while batting her pretty green eyes. The audacity. The selfishness.

Promotion or no, if he found out that she was knowingly doing something to attract these demons, he was going to relish grinding Aurelie's perfectly balanced life into dust.

By the time Des completed his run, showered, and changed, it was time for the evening meal. He went to the mess hall to find Daisy had saved his usual seat. Somehow, she always managed to get there early enough to secure one of the few two-person tables that weren't reserved for senior staff.

"Where have you been?" she asked, all eyes and freckles, buzzing with barely contained curiosity.

Des didn't want to admit that he'd lost Aurelie. "I had a meeting with the commander. I'm officially off babysitting duty."

A small furrow formed between Daisy's pale brows. "Why?"

"He's determined she's not a threat."

Daisy rolled her eyes and gnawed on a corner of a chunk of bread. "Of course she's not a threat. What about the threat *to* her?"

Des speared a steamed potato on the tines of his fork. "Believe me, she can handle herself."

"What about the attack today? Jasper said she was there when it happened."

"How does Jasper know about it?"

"You know how quickly word travels here, Des. Are you all right?"

Blood and bones, everyone must know about his failure now. He took a breath in through his nose, releasing it slowly, willing his pulse back down to its normal fifty beats per minute. "I'm fine. If I hadn't been distracted by that little hellion, I'd have gotten to the victim in time and killed that damned thrall."

"If it's any consolation, that thrall might have done us all a favor. The victim was a . . ." She lowered her voice. "Barley, his name was. He was a wanted criminal. Assaulted several women, apparently."

Des stewed on this new information for a moment. Just because the man was a criminal didn't mean he deserved to die that way. He'd had a wife and children. And an attack in broad daylight meant something worse: Commander Yew was right. Demons were getting bolder.

Des knew better than most how arbitrary death was, and how little demons cared about their victim's identity. Next time, it could easily be an innocent under a *verita*'s claws, instead of someone vile like Barley. Something was wrong here, and deep down he felt it was going to get worse.

Daisy leaned closer. "I'm glad you're all right, but we need to keep this quiet. Otherwise we're going to start even more rumors spreading among the junior lieutenants, and right now we need cooler heads to prevail."

She was right. Des took a deep, steadying breath, stabbing a green bean because it was his only outlet at the moment.

"So," she said after a few minutes, "what about the girl?"

"What about her?"

"Don't you think you should warn her that she won't have protection going forward?"

He snorted. "I don't think she saw me as protection, Daisy."

"Regardless. She's alone, and she deserves an explanation. After dinner, we're going to pay her a visit."

"We?"

"Yes, *we.* I don't trust you to go alone."

He sighed, resigned. The truth was, he didn't trust himself either. Not when it came to Aurelie Blake.

They waited outside the gates for fifteen minutes while the guard went to fetch her, returning with a clearly exasperated Aurelie. She'd changed since this afternoon. Her coat was too large, dangling well past her fingertips, and the hem of what appeared to be a nightgown pooled around her feet. It was only nine o'clock. Had he woken her?

She stepped outside the gates and approached them. "Daisy. Lieutenant. To what do I owe the pleasure?"

"I'm following up on your little excursion this afternoon," Des said.

She folded her arm over her chest, which only accentuated the floppiness of her sleeves. "Why? I'm not a child."

"Really? You certainly look like one. What did you do, raid your father's closet?"

Aurelie blinked, glancing down at herself. "Actually, yes. This was my father's coat." Something akin to sorrow passed over her features, only for a moment, and he felt a stab of guilt after remembering she was an orphan. "Not that it's any of your damn business."

Guilt officially revoked. "You made it my business when you decided to go consorting with . . . demon consorters!"

Aurelie scoffed. "*Demon consorters*? What in the name of Aciano are you talking about?"

A shout rang out in the distance, causing them all to turn their heads. "I'm going to check on things," Daisy said. "Behave yourself." She shot Des a warning look, and he sucked a breath in through his teeth. He had to maintain control of himself, even if Aurelie was disproportionately infuriating for someone of her size.

"You have no right to be following me."

He blinked as if he couldn't possibly have heard her right. "No *right*? I'm a member of the Iron Guard. It's my sworn duty to protect the citizens of Wisteria from demons."

"I don't see any demons," she said, tapping her foot in annoyance. "*Just you.*"

He couldn't help himself. A groan of sheer, unadulterated exasperation slipped out of him.

"Did my uncle put you up to this?"

His eyes bulged in disbelief. "Your—" He shook his head. "Of course not. I followed a demon to the university last Friday night, only to discover it was trailing a man you were . . ." He waved his hand in the air vaguely. "With."

Aurelie's mouth dropped open in outrage. "We weren't . . ." She made the same gesture. "He came for *dinner.* And what do you mean, a demon was trailing him?"

"Don't tell me I have to explain the term *trailing* to you."

Her nostrils flared. "No, you absolute clod. If there was a demon trailing him, why didn't you *kill it*?"

It was bad enough that this irritating gnat of a woman was taking him away from his actual work, but turning this around on him? "You're unbelievable. Someone died today because of you, and you have the nerve to ask why *I'm* not doing more to stop demons?"

Aurelie blinked and took a step back. "What?"

Much to his relief, Daisy hadn't returned yet, because she'd no doubt be throttling Des by now. He looked back at Aurelie's pale face. He'd clearly stunned her with his outburst. He gestured to a nearby bench. "Sit."

"I beg your pa—"

"Would you please sit?" he ground out.

Aurelie rolled her eyes and sat, her arms still folded over her chest. Her coat gaped open, revealing the lacy collar of what was definitely a nightgown, and his thoughts stuttered to a halt. Clearing his throat, he shifted his gaze to the crown of her head.

"Why did you run today?" he asked.

Aurelie sighed. "Is that what this is about?"

"No. But indulge me anyway."

She brought her eyes up to his. "I had something personal to attend to. I don't have to explain what it was. In fact, it's rather rude to expect me to."

Personal? Was she visiting the apothecary? Meeting a lover? He could feel the tips of his ears going pink and straightened a little. "In that case, I apologize."

"There's no need. Now tell me why you're so sure this attack—which I'm the first to admit is a tragedy—has anything to do with me."

"There has been an unusual amount of demonic activity this past week, and geographically, it all leads back to you."

"A coincidence," Aurelie said with a dismissive wave of her hand, though he thought he saw her shift uncomfortably.

"Multiple demons have appeared within feet of you in one week. I don't believe it's a coincidence."

She rose then, as if that would somehow put them on equal footing. Even if she stood on the bench, she'd still be shorter than him. "What do you think *coincidence* means, exactly?"

"Excuse me?"

"A coincidence is a remarkable concurrence without causal link. The very fact that it's unlikely, even unbelievable, is what makes it a coincidence." She started to pace up and down the sidewalk, her chin in her fist. "If it was hunting me, then why did it kill someone else?" she continued. "You assume that because I lost *you* in a crowd, I was also capable of losing a demon, which is a lot of credit to give a person you didn't think could walk home from a café alone."

"I—"

"Besides, even if I'm somehow inadvertently attracting unusual demonic activity, which is a very big *if* by the way, it in no way makes me accountable for that man's death. I can't control what demons do. You of all people should know that."

Aurelie was so focused on her ranting, her eyes trained on her pacing feet, that she failed to notice she was headed straight for Des. As much as he would have liked to watch her run headlong into his iron-studded breastplate, he put his hand out.

A moment later, Aurelie's forehead butted up against his palm. She blinked and jumped back, blushing profusely. "Do you mind?"

Des snorted and stepped aside. "Begging your pardon, *my lady.*"

"My—what? What exactly was that supposed to be?" she asked, flapping her hand at his attempt at a bow.

He hooded his gaze, refusing to let her get the better of him. "I assume that's how you like to be treated by men."

"You have no idea what I like, least of all in men." Their eyes met, hers blazing in challenge. He couldn't have said what his conveyed, because his thoughts were jumbled at the sight of Aurelie, fists on her hips, the implication of her words hanging between them.

Why was he letting this slip of a girl rattle him? He'd stared down *verita* with nothing more than an iron switchblade in his fist. He'd killed two *natia* in one night. He'd put up with Daisy for *years.* And yet five minutes with this creature, and all his composure and reason fell to pieces.

He leaned in close, his voice lowered to a rasp, his finger thrust in her face like she was a child in need of scolding. "I know you're a consorter. I've known it since the first night I laid eyes on you. That demon was a thrall, wasn't it? That's why you had to ditch me. So you could send the demon to do your dirty work for you, while you flit around like a pixie, all wide-eyed and innocent, and—and leave the rest of us to clean up your mess!"

"Des!"

They both turned to see Daisy stomping toward them, and Des realized he hadn't been quiet at all. He'd been shouting at full volume. Daisy reached up to punch Des in the arm, thought better of it, and slapped his cheek instead. It was about as punishing as a smack from a wet towelette.

She tutted in disgust and turned away from him toward Aurelie. "Are you all right?"

Instead of answering her, Aurelie rounded back to Des. "How *dare* you?" she snarled. "I've done nothing to you since the day you met me, and you've turned your bizarre hunch into this . . . this . . . obsession!"

Des was caught between astonishment and indignation. "I am *not* obsessed with—"

"I'm not finished! Why can't you just admit that someone got hurt and you didn't stop it? That you're being crushed by your own guilt. That it's easier for you to take it out on a woman than to accept the truth!"

From the corner of his eye, Des saw Daisy dig her hands into her hair and turn away, but his blood was pumping so loudly in his head he couldn't hear what she was muttering under her breath. Aurelie had no idea how many lives he'd saved, how many children he'd kept from being orphaned. She didn't know that every time he failed a mission, he punished himself for days with grueling workouts on little sleep and less food. She could never understand what it was like to devote his life to a cause that didn't allow for a single misstep, where every day was life or death.

He'd never allow a subordinate to speak to him this way if they were back at the Iron Fortress.

But they weren't at the fort, and she wasn't a guard, and she wasn't worth his wasted breath.

Des's gaze shuttered, and whatever Aurelie saw on his face, she must have realized she'd touched a nerve, because she closed her mouth and stepped back.

"You really don't need to worry about me," she said softly, deflating. "I promise I won't go out alone this weekend. I'll be back at the university, safe and sound."

His eyes narrowed, his fists clenching at his sides. He stepped closer, Daisy momentarily forgotten, his entire world tunneled to Aurelie's pale face, her wide eyes and flushed cheeks, and that vicious, beautiful mouth. "I'm not *worried* about you. I'm *warning* you. My job is to eliminate threats in this city. And as far as I'm concerned, that includes frivolous, self-absorbed, dangerously irresponsible menaces like you."

Almost as soon as the words were out, a part of him wanted to take them back, because he knew she was right. He was taking out his own guilt on her. He was the one who was supposed to be watching Aurelie. And he was the one who had failed to save that man. But a strong leader didn't back down; he *doubled* down. And so he closed his lips and said nothing.

Tears welled in Aurelie's eyes, sending a stab of regret straight to his chest. Wrapping her coat tighter around herself, she murmured goodnight to Daisy and turned on her heel, Des's gaze boring into the space between her shoulder blades until she was finally, blessedly, out of sight.

CHAPTER 14
AURELIE

ALL NIGHT, AURELIE TOSSED AND TURNED IN HER BED AT her uncle's cottage. For the first time in as long as she could remember, she hadn't wanted to return to her laboratory, hadn't wanted to be alone. Though she knew Bonnie and the other servants were paid to be kind to her, she also needed to be reminded that not everyone found her unbearable.

The nightgown she'd been wearing was damp with sweat from her altercation with Des. She still had a few old things in her wardrobe here, and she changed into one with silly pink ribbons at the cuffs and collar, inhaling the scent of the lavender sprigs sprinkled in every drawer. Frivolous, he'd called her. And perhaps he was right. She snuggled under her ruffled comforter, still trying to ward off the chill the giant had left her with.

She hated the way being near him made her feel weak and small, how his presence forced her to confront her physical limitations. Most people would have been relieved to have a member of the Iron Guard watching over them, but she hated knowing that all week, she'd been spied on by that overgrown flatiron of a man. He'd said the first time he saw her was the night she met with Everard, which meant he'd seen her before the café, doing heaven only knew what.

Who did he think he was, telling her what to do and where to go? When he'd stuck his finger in her face, she'd had an almost overwhelming urge to bite it clean off.

Perhaps she'd been spending too much time with Mephisto lately.

Was the universe trying to give her a sign? Trailed by demon hunters. Stalked by *somnia.* She had taken a commission from a stranger to do something she *knew* would create more demons, and while she had spent the greater part of the last ten years pretending that demons were not all that dangerous in today's Wisteria, she now knew how wrong that notion was.

She believed the lieutenant was mistaken about the man's death, for the record. He had said a thrall was following Everard, but she'd seen no sign of it herself. Besides, this portal was going to create the greatest good possible, and rid Wisteria of demons forever! She and the giant were working toward the same goal, even if he couldn't see it.

She may be dangerously irresponsible, but she wasn't the only one who knew the necessity of taking risks. Professor Sheldrake had all but encouraged her to take this project on. To change the world, because clearly stagnation hadn't made things better.

At the university, all that mattered was the strength of her mind, the stamina of her intellect. Her curiosity. Her ambition. She nestled deeper into her pillow, comforted by the fact that she could now begin Everard's project in earnest. Uncle Leopold would return soon, and Aurelie would be tucked safely behind the university gates.

And the giant would be back where he belonged.

Aurelie's first order of business the next morning was to take a proper bath. Uncle Leo had a lovely claw-foot tub in his room with a view over the tops of the campus's many trees to the clock tower, and she allowed herself to wallow in it until the water went cold. She changed into one of the few dresses she kept here—a little risqué for her tastes, considering it showed a hint of clavicle—and combed out her hair, pretending not to see the haunted look in her own eyes in the mirror. Yes, last night had rattled her. She would recover.

With her hair still wet, she went down to the library and started a fire in Leo's fireplace, the one thing she was missing in her lab. She ran her fingers along the familiar spines of books she'd once thought boring but now found profoundly comforting. She made herself tea and curled up in an armchair with the spare sketchpad and pencils she kept in her room.

The tingle she felt every time she started to work on a new project traveled from the tips of her ears to her pinkie toes. Everard's schematic for the door was more sketch than blueprint. From what she could tell, each metal plate fitted to its neighbor via a series of grooves and notches that needed to be lined up just so, but there were no clear instructions on how to achieve this.

With her growing—albeit slowly—understanding of Elder Vansion, she skimmed the runes again, but she could barely recognize a single one. Elder Vansion was known for its fickleness: one wrongly placed accent or overly curved flourish would change the meaning of the rune entirely. A symbol resembling a quaint little cottage represented safety, prosperity, and good fortune, but it became the rune for eternal damnation if the "chimney" was placed on the wrong side. It was no wonder Dr. Sheldrake insisted Aurelie translate the runes before she carved them.

The overall dimensions of the portal were quite large, almost as tall as the ceiling and just as wide. She would need engraving tools, scaffolding materials, and a lot of coffee to get through this project by spring.

Bonnie's chirpy hello startled her so badly that Aurelie spilled tea all over herself. "Dash it!"

"Begging your pardon, miss. There's someone here to see you."

"Oh, for heaven's sa—"

"It's *not* Mr. Viridian," Bonnie said.

Aurelie stopped mopping at the wet spot on her skirt—luckily it was dark blue and wouldn't be visibly stained—and met Bonnie's suspiciously twinkling eyes. "Then who is it?"

"A Lieutenant Whitlow, he says."

"Who?"

Before Bonnie could respond, a man walked into the room, and Aurelie's heart stuttered beneath her ribs.

"Apologies," he said, his massive frame taking up most of the doorway. "I wasn't sure if I was meant to come in or wait in the hall."

Bonnie's eyes flicked to Lieutenant Whitlow, her round face flushed pink. She bobbed a curtsy and disappeared before Aurelie could formulate a coherent thought.

He wasn't wearing his armor or his sword, and while he was still enormous, Aurelie felt almost as though she were seeing a turtle without its shell. There was something vulnerable about the open collar of his tunic, which revealed a sliver of smooth, suntanned skin.

Aurelie rose, praying Des couldn't see that she'd spilled tea all over herself. "What are you . . ." She pushed a lock of wavy hair behind her ear, realized that her hair was wet and unbound, and wondered if it would be possible to melt into the floorboards. "I mean, can I help you with something, Lieutenant Whitlow?"

He raised his brows slightly at her polite tone. "I hope I'm not disturbing you."

"Not at all. I . . . My uncle still isn't at home."

"I'm aware."

Aurelie watched in a daze as Des entered the library, which now felt almost claustrophobically small, given how much space he took up. She gestured to a wingback chair, then bent down to where her spilled teacup was still resting on the carpet. She set it on its saucer, hoping he didn't notice the rattling caused by her shaky hands. "I'm sorry. I wasn't expecting anyone."

He studied her for a minute, clearly relishing the fact that he'd caught her off guard. Fortunately, the fire had died down to kindling, because Aurelie was flushed all over. Why didn't he say something?

His lips twitched in an almost-smile as they took their seats in the two armchairs. The difference between how much space they took up seemed suddenly impossible to ignore. Aurelie was often described as petite, but the truth was, she was short, barely five feet tall on a good day. It made Des's size feel even more ridiculous. She was acutely aware that her feet dangled several inches above the ground, and while there was nothing wrong with being little, there was a certain indignity in having to perch at the end of the armchair or sit back fully and have her feet hover above the floor. She had the peculiar feeling of having no earthly idea what to do with her own hands and somehow concluded that sitting on them was her best course of action.

She'd never been alone with this man before.

This man, who had humiliated her and accused her of horrible things. This man, who had also saved her life.

Now she was in such a state that she honestly didn't know what to feel. Aurelie looked up to find Des watching her intently.

She shook her head to clear it. "I apologize. I'm not myself today. This week has been . . . Well, you know how this week has been."

He nodded but remained quiet.

"At the risk of sounding self-absorbed," she said, trying and failing to keep her tone neutral, "is there something I can do for you?"

He scratched the back of his neck, looking more sheepish than Aurelie would have thought possible. He inhaled and released his breath slowly. "I came to apologize, Miss Blake. The way I behaved last night, how I spoke to you." He shook his head. "It was uncalled-for."

Aurelie hadn't expected an apology, and now she found she didn't want it, either. It was easier to believe that he was a callous, unfeeling ogre than a human being who made mistakes. "Oh, please don't—"

"What you said, that I was accusing you because of my own guilt? You were right. My duty is to protect the people of Wisteria from demonic activity, and someone died because of my own failure. Mr. Barley . . ." He broke off when he saw the confused look on Aurelie's face. "The man who died. You should know, he was not a good person."

Aurelie had no idea what to say to this. To any of this. Every single word out of the giant's mouth was anathema to every feeling she'd had for him up until this moment. "I don't understand."

"He was a criminal. The worst kind, in my opinion. If someone had to die at the hands of a demon, I suppose we should be grateful it was him."

Aurelie wasn't sure if this made her feel better, but she decided it didn't make it any worse. "I see. Thank you for letting me know."

He cleared his throat and shifted in his seat, as if he were waiting for Aurelie to say something more. For a brief moment, the image of the *somnia* on the other side of Easton Hall's doors came back to her. She'd tried not to think about it, because every time she did, she became a little less certain about accepting Everard's proposal. A little less certain that she *wasn't* consorting with demons, considering she had one sleeping in her laboratory at that very moment. Right now, Lieutenant Whitlow believed he was mistaken about her. But what if he was right? Should she tell him about the *somnia* that spoke to her? Was she putting others at risk by *not* telling him?

If she did, that would be the end of her inventing, at least for the foreseeable future. The Iron Guard would probably put more guards on duty at Wisteria University, and she'd be under particular scrutiny. Mephisto would have to be kept hidden, which would not be easy. Though she often thought of the little creature as more companion than demon, she knew no one else would see it that way. Except for Kiara, and even she refused to touch it.

Before she could make sense of her jumbled thoughts, Des leaned forward with his hand outstretched and Aurelie froze, her mind a complete blank as to what was happening. He swiped his thumb against her forehead, sweeping her fringe aside, and she only managed to stifle her gasp by biting her lip. His face was inches from hers, but his eyes were focused on her forehead.

"Are you hurt?" he asked softly.

Aurelie had stopped breathing. Des had lifted out of his seat slightly and was bracing himself against the wing of the chair with his left hand, caging her in, while his right continued to gently probe her forehead. She could feel the soft puff of his exhalations on her skin, a stark contrast to the roughness of his hands. She'd never been this close to a person since her parents died, let alone a man.

She told herself he was a guard, that this sort of proximity between men and women was perfectly normal in his world. He and Daisy regarded each other as equals, likely doing everything together, from eating to training to sleeping.

The thought made her blush, and yet she didn't move. He lowered his right hand. His eyes, which had been fixated on her forehead, suddenly flicked down to hers.

Warmth flooded Aurelie, her blood rushing in her ears. Her stomach, or something just below it, did an odd swooping thing that she'd heard Kiara describe as butterflies.

Oh, she thought, with all the surprise of a scientist realizing, suddenly, that their hypothesis had been entirely incorrect. *Oh, my.*

He was so close that she noticed his eyes were not gray or blue, but something in between that reminded her of the soft silver-green of lamb's ears. There were several small scars scattered across his face, as though from shattered glass. She felt the strangest urge to touch them. Ten minutes ago she would have described his mouth as stern, but now—

He glanced at his thumb. "Ah, just charcoal. I thought it was a bruise," he murmured.

She blinked, recovering herself, and was grateful when he sat back all the way. A few more seconds and who knew what she might have done. "That happens a lot."

"A hazard of the job," he said.

She breathed a laugh, not entirely sure if he was mocking her. A part of her wished he would leave so she could refill her teacup and ponder what in the world had just happened to her. And another part of her wanted to test the hypothesis further.

"So you're all right, Miss Blake?" he asked.

"I . . . What?" She shook her head to clear it. "I'm fine. And please, call me Aurelie." Her shoulders lifted in a small shrug. "If you'd like."

"Then call me Des. It's less of a mouthful than Lieutenant Whitlow."

"Des." It was the first time she'd said his name out loud. "Is it a nickname?"

His eyes flicked down to his hands, which were braced against his knees. "My full name is Destrier. But again—"

"Destrier? As in a warhorse?"

He tilted his head in an offhand manner. "The Iron Guard took me in when I was an infant. What can I say, they had high hopes for me even then."

"An infant?"

"Yes."

She studied her ink-stained fingers for a moment. "Is it true that all guards were orphaned by demons?" She'd heard the rumor before, but it seemed impossible that so many children could have been affected in that way, considering how uncommon demonic deaths were these days.

His nostrils flared as he gave a tight nod. "Yes. We're brought from all over Wisteria."

A wash of shame came over her. "I didn't realize."

"Few do."

"My own parents died when I was seven." She hadn't planned to say it, but it felt wrong to leave him alone in his vulnerability. "A carriage accident. I don't remember much of it, fortunately."

"You were there?"

Aurelie nodded. "We were coming to the university that day. Just for a visit. I didn't realize my uncle worked here. I certainly didn't expect that I'd never go home again." She swallowed the knot forming in her throat. "The only thing I remember was my mother screaming my father's name."

Des was quiet for a long moment. Judging her, she imagined. His parents died and he found himself being raised by the Iron Guard, while she ended up in relative luxury.

He surprised her when he said, "I'm sorry. I suppose I'm fortunate not to remember my parents' deaths."

She exhaled. "I've never found it particularly useful to search for blessings in misfortune. Terrible things happen to good people. Good things happen to terrible people. Trying to make sense of it all could drive a person mad."

What was she blathering on about? Des was staring at her as though she truly were mad, and she felt her cheeks go hot. "I'm sorry. I—"

His words were so soft she scarcely heard them. "I know exactly what you mean."

Their eyes met. Aurelie felt as electrified as a raw nerve under his gaze. Her lips parted, though she had no idea what she wanted to say. Except, perhaps, that she was grateful for his honesty. The moment stretched on, the butterflies in Aurelie's stomach migrating south as she fought the urge to . . .

He rose, breaking the tension she'd been nearly consumed by. "I should get back to the fort."

"Yes, of course." She nodded and rose, her legs as unsteady as a newborn foal's. She couldn't understand why her body would react to Des this way, when she was attracted to intelligence and ingenuity, not burliness and brawn.

Wasn't she?

"I suppose I won't see you again," she said when they reached the door, finding herself oddly disappointed by the thought. "That is, I have no plans to leave the grounds in the near future."

He gazed down at her. "Who knows. You must get demons here from time to time."

She licked her lips, her mouth suddenly dry. "Not lately."

He arched a brow as he turned on the threshold, and for a moment she was sure he could tell she was lying. She wasn't even sure why she *had* lied. Two seconds in the presence of a man and she'd lost control of her faculties. It was a good thing she'd dedicated her life to scholarly pursuits and eventual spinsterhood.

"In that case, goodbye, Miss Blake. Aurelie," he corrected himself, before she could. "Good luck with your studies."

"Good luck with your hunting, Des."

She waved and closed the door behind him, still feeling a little floaty and lightheaded. It wasn't until she had returned to her seat and taken several deep breaths, trying to decide if she was still certain she hated Destrier Whitlow, that she reached for her sketchbook.

The top page was gone.

CHAPTER 15
AURELIE

THE MOMENT AURELIE NOTICED THAT DES HAD STOLEN HER drawing, she did the only sensible thing she could: panic.

It took over an hour of pacing the halls of her uncle's cottage before she calmed down enough to think things through.

"It's all right," she said to herself, because without Kiara there to act as the voice of reason, it was the best she could do. "He found a drawing of a door, not the Helping Hand or any of my inventions. It wasn't labeled or particularly good. Even if he turns it in to his commander, they can't prove anything. Perhaps I just like drawing doors. It's not a crime!"

Truthfully, it could have been far worse. She could only thank her lucky stars this was a new sketchbook, because normally they were filled with portraits of demons. If he'd torn off the top page to find a drawing of a crab-pincered *verita* shoving books into its maw, Aurelie would be in serious trouble.

She froze in front of the hall mirror. Her hair had finally dried into dark waves, and for a moment, she tried to see herself as Des saw her. Wide green eyes, pale skin, a full lower lip that she'd used to good effect on Uncle Leo when she was little. He'd been defenseless in the face of Aurelie's pout for years.

She'd seen what most female Iron Guard members looked like: strong, somber, severe. All the things Aurelie had been told not to be.

And for a moment, she wished she could be like those women, who wouldn't cower in the face of one of Des's temper tantrums, who would chase him down and demand their property back. He'd likely never created anything in his entire life, only torn things apart, leaving demons—and people—in his wake like refuse. He should be called Destroyer, not Destrier, she thought bitterly.

She took a deep breath. She may not have inherited large muscles or nerves of steel, but she'd been given a brilliant mind and the vision to imagine a future different from the world she knew. She didn't need the approval of Destrier Whitlow. She only needed herself.

Aurelie returned to her lab and made herself a cup of coffee, starting on a new schematic while she sipped. If—when, more likely—the Iron Guard came to question her, she would be ready with an explanation. She would confuse them with academic jargon about physics, how the portal wasn't a portal at all but rather a sophisticated demon-trapping device. Or perhaps she'd claim it was something she'd found while perusing Florian's book. Everyone hated him anyway; she might as well capitalize on that.

Or, if she was truly desperate, she could claim it was something she'd seen in a dream. No one could prove otherwise.

Mephisto was gone for most of the day, and it was quiet aside from the ticking of the clock and the scratch of her pencil. She had to re-create her work from this morning, but fortunately she remembered most of it. Tucked away in her favorite place, it was easy to lose herself in the work and ignore the fact that she could be arrested at any moment.

Hours later, she'd only managed to string together three runes: awakening; energy; shadow.

She had no idea what it meant.

She fell asleep at some point, her cheek pressed to a sketchbook, her fourth cup of coffee slowly growing cold beside her, only to be awoken by a rather troubling dream.

Aurelie sometimes dreamt about her parents, occasionally about Uncle Leo or Kiara, but most of her dreams were not connected to any real person or place that she could name. Which was why this particular dream had been so disturbing. She'd been back in Uncle Leo's study with Des. She swore she could smell the spilled tea on her dress and the clean, masculine scent on Des's tunic.

Only he hadn't been wearing the tunic, and she hadn't been wearing her dress, and the hand that had braced itself beside her head was somewhere else entirely.

Recalling it made her blush so profusely she had to open her window to let in some cool air. What was the matter with her? Des had deliberately played her for a fool so he could steal her drawing, and she was *dreaming* about him? To think, she'd believed they were connecting in some way! It was all too mortifying to bear.

She walked to her washbasin to splash some cold sense into herself and caught her reflection. The ghost of a charcoal rune was slashed against her cheek from where she'd slept on her notebook: *shadow.*

She scowled as she scrubbed it away. Des had been like a shadow this past week. A looming storm cloud following her wherever she went. But she wasn't going to sit here and wait for Des to make a move. Forward momentum had kept her going all these years, ever since her parents died.

From that day forward, Aurelie had never let anything stop her. And she wasn't about to start with Destroyer Sodding Whitlow.

CHAPTER 16

DES

DES WALKED BACK TOWARD THE IRON FORTRESS WITH AURElie's sketch clutched in his hand. He hadn't taken the time to study it, hadn't even really thought it through when he took it. But the moment he saw it resting on a tea tray, he'd known it was something dangerous, the same way he knew when a shadow contained a hidden demon. It had been far too easy to confiscate it while he pretended to inspect the smudge on her forehead.

A small, distant part of him felt some guilt for using her naivete against her. He knew she'd likely never been that close to a man before, and while physical proximity was not something Des sought out, he was also used to it.

But his touch had clearly elicited a reaction in Aurelie. Her pupils had dilated to take up nearly all of her green irises, and a flush had crept up her exposed neck all the way to her hairline. No wonder she kept it covered most of the time. Only a few bared inches and she was no longer the persnickety schoolmarm, but something softer, compliant. He had a feeling she'd never let him get that close to her if she were dressed in her usual armor.

Or perhaps it was simply that he'd caught her off guard. He could still feel the softness of her skin beneath his calloused fingers, the silkiness of her damp hair. The scent of her soap lingering in the air between them, pulling him closer. He imagined the inviting gap between her parted lips, the temptation to fill it with his own almost overwhelming.

He despised her for all of it.

Des admired strength, integrity, loyalty. He would never marry as a member of the Iron Guard, but if he were to find a companion, she would be everything Aurelie was not. Disciplined and self-sacrificing, not idle and self-indulgent. Someone who wouldn't spend their time doodling by the fire with a porcelain tea service at their side.

And so what if Aurelie's scent and softness had triggered a response in him as well? True, it was unusual for Des to feel . . . well, anything. But novelty could illicit arousal. It wasn't any sort of indication that he was *attracted* to her.

And even if he *was*, physical desire was a need to be met as efficiently as hunger or exhaustion. Aurelie likely wanted the same things as all the tittering civilian girls: romance; chivalry; love letters; flowers. All things that Des had neither the time for, nor the interest in pursuing.

To think he'd gone there with the sincere intention of apologizing. He should have trusted his instincts all along. He'd pass this drawing over to Commander Yew and get back to work, like he kept saying he would.

He swore when he saw Daisy leaning against his bunk. He hadn't told her where he was going, which was an error in hindsight. If he'd told her he was going to train, she wouldn't have questioned it.

"Where have you been?" she asked, glancing at the sketch still clutched in his hand. He'd meant to go straight to Yew's office, but his feet had taken him to the barracks instead. Odd.

Des knew he could lie, and he also knew that Daisy would know he was lying and then pester him for the truth for the rest of the day. "I went to visit Aurelie Blake."

Daisy's eyes went wider. "Again? My word, Des, two visits in less than twenty-four hours. You've got it worse than I thought."

He shouldered her away from his bunk, where he pretended to remake the corners of his already perfectly made bed. "I went to apologize."

Daisy barked a disbelieving laugh. "Hell froze over and I *missed* it?"

"Har-har. I threatened her last night. It was wrong. I wanted to make it right."

"And did you?"

Des collapsed on his bed, undoing all his tucking and straightening. "I doubt it. But it did get more interesting." He handed the paper to Daisy, still staring at the bunk above him. "I stole this from her."

Daisy was quiet as she perused the sketch. "What is it?"

"No idea. But she was drawing it when I got there. She seemed . . . rattled by my presence."

"Rattled? *Impossible.* Why would she be nervous around the enormous member of the Iron Guard who threatened her last night?"

Des ignored the jab. "What do we know about her, Daisy?"

Daisy settled down next to him, holding the paper up so they could both look at it. "She's a scientist. She likes understanding how things work."

That was a generous assessment. "She rarely leaves the university, but when she does, demons follow. She's not afraid of them, or of us. She's clearly hiding something."

They turned their heads toward each other. "Is she . . . ?" Daisy began.

Des felt his stomach drop. "She wouldn't be *that* foolish. Would she?"

Daisy's mouth twisted to the side, implying that she just might be.

Demons take him, was the girl inventing?

Commander Yew said the demon problem was worse all over Wisteria, not just in the capital. Even if Aurelie was making minor inventions in her office, it couldn't explain everything. But what if there were more people like Aurelie scattered throughout the kingdom: intelligent but naïve, far enough removed from the days of demon slaughter to forget it ever existed? People with far too much time on their hands?

Des tore the paper from Daisy's fingers, studying the sketch closer, but he couldn't make sense of the door-like structure, or the illegible scribbles in the margins. "I need to take this to Commander Yew." He turned to her again, a sliver of doubt worming through his gut. "Don't I?"

"He'll know you went to see her again, even though he took you off Aurelie duty."

"But this—"

Daisy took the drawing from him gently. "I'll turn it in for you, Des. He won't care that I went to see her. He hardly knows I exist."

Des ground his molars together. Aurelie had been his responsibility, and he should see this through. Finish this assignment, one way or another. Put an end to what would someday be a footnote in the story of his life.

He closed his eyes, which was a mistake. All he could see were shrewd green eyes, a pert nose, a mouth that made him lose his senses. He should have kissed her while he had the chance, because she'd been right: they were never going to see each other again.

Once Commander Yew knew the truth about Aurelie Blake, she wouldn't be seeing anything but the inside of a prison cell for a very long time.

He rose, unable to meet Daisy's questioning gaze.

"Do it," he said, and left like the coward he was.

CHAPTER 17

DES

BY EARLY DECEMBER, THINGS FELT ALMOST NORMAL IN Wisteria, though it was a quiet he wasn't sure he could trust. Yule was in just a few weeks, and with it, Des's promotion ceremony. Nothing changed at the Iron Fortress, but the city proper was festive, with families strolling the streets to buy wooden toys, roasted chestnuts, or glass baubles from vendors' carts. There were no more day-walking demon sightings, Gareth had moved on to working with Jasper, and Daisy was training a new guard (a girl far too timid for this line of work; Des didn't give her more than a month before she was moved to clerical).

Most of Des's days were spent training with the Iron Swords. He had thought himself in peak physical condition, but he quickly learned that there was another level to him. What little fat he carried was whittled off his muscles. He was sore everywhere.

In the evenings, he studied all the available texts on *verita*, none of which were particularly helpful, since they were mostly witness statements and crude renderings. Des and his nine squad-mates, all older and more experienced than him, were becoming a well-oiled machine, however. Shifts were clean and straightforward. He'd never slept better in his life. Everything was going as it should.

And if every now and then he caught the scent of Aurelie's

soap, or he found himself remembering the way her braid swayed between her shoulder blades as she walked, or how green her eyes were up close, he quickly put her out of his head. Daisy had never told him what her punishment was, and he'd never asked, though he no longer relished the thought of her languishing in a prison cell. Perhaps her uncle had returned and spoken with Commander Yew on her behalf. So long as she wasn't causing trouble, he didn't care what happened to her.

Des was in the armory cleaning his weapons one evening when Aspen, another of the Iron Swords, appeared in the doorway.

"Whitlow. Gear up. There's been a *verita* sighting near the university."

Des lowered his rag to his lap. "Any injuries?"

"Not yet. But the campus guard raised the alarm. Meet me at the front gate in five."

It took Des less than three minutes to get fully suited in his armor and meet Aspen. He willed his racing pulse to slow down, telling himself he was just excited because tonight he might finally have a chance to catch a *verita* alive.

"You seem tense," Aspen said as they crossed the street toward the university's iron gates.

She was almost as reserved as Des, only communicating when necessary, which meant she must be concerned about his behavior if she was bringing it up. Des forced his shoulders to relax and took a few deep breaths. The dean had to be back by now. It was well past dinnertime, and the lights were off at the cottage. Aurelie would be in bed, not creating demons, if she were here at all.

“There you are,” the guard said, lifting his lantern up so that it shone directly in their eyes.

Des raised his hand to block out the glare. “Where’s the demon?”

“Still on campus, far as I know. I lost sight of it out near the cemetery.”

“Who else is on campus tonight?” Des asked, earning an arched eyebrow from Aspen.

“Just Miss Blake.” Des was beginning to grumble when the guard continued. “And one of her professors. Sheldrake, I think. He’s been known to conjure the odd demon or two; by accident, of course. It’s been years, though.”

This was no accident. Des was going to murder Aurelie, if she wasn’t already dead. And then he was going to tell Daisy off for clearly not handling the problem like she’d promised.

“What’s that?” Aspen asked, pointing to a light in a tall tower.

“Professor Sheldrake’s office. But like I said, the demon was near the—”

“Cemetery, got it.” Des stalked past the guard onto campus, wishing he’d seen it in daylight so he had a better sense of the place.

“Where are we going?” Aspen asked.

“To the tower. I think we should question the people who conjured the demon and find out what we’re dealing with first.” It wouldn’t get far with the iron gates surrounding the campus, and he didn’t want to give Aurelie a chance to cover her tracks.

Aspen nodded. They were quiet as they approached the old building housing the tower, which listed precariously to one side. It should have been condemned years ago.

A popping sound split the silence, followed by a shout.

Without thinking, Des broke into a run . . .

And skidded to a stop the moment he reached the courtyard in front of the tower.

"My word," a man said. "That was a bit more than I bargained for."

"It was incredible, Professor Sheldrake. I've never seen anything like it!"

Des's stomach did something strange. It was too dark to see anything, but he'd know that voice anywhere. It was bright and confident, educated without coming across as stuck-up. Just so long as it wasn't directed at him.

Aurelie had the audacity to laugh then, a sound he'd never heard before. It was, to his utter annoyance, adorable.

A moment later, a massive creature leapt on Aurelie. On its hind legs, it was nearly as tall as she was. Sure she was being attacked, Des drew his sword and rushed forward into the courtyard.

Then, as if the entire universe was conspiring to humiliate him, the clouds shrouding the moon parted. Silver light bathed the courtyard and everything in it: a little old man wearing thick spectacles, presumably the professor, and Aurelie, struggling to push off the snarling beast . . .

Which was, in fact, an overgrown Wisterian hound. And it was licking Aurelie's cheek.

Des's sword arm dropped as the two turned to look at him and he became acutely aware of the cold sweat on his brow. Aspen caught up to him just in time to see Aurelie and Professor Sheldrake standing side by side, the hound now seated beside them, docile as could be.

“Who are you?” Professor Sheldrake asked, sounding more curious than alarmed.

Aurelie, clearly not planning to be of any use whatsoever, only folded her arms across her chest and cocked her head.

“We’re the Iron Guard,” Aspen responded, saving Des from further humiliation. “We were told a demon was spotted on campus.”

The professor and Aurelie exchanged a look and burst into laughter. “Who told you that?” the old man asked, wiping tears of mirth from his eyes.

“The campus guard. Said it was near the cemetery.” Aspen stepped forward and leaned over to pat the hound on its broad head. “Fine-looking specimen you have here. I haven’t seen one this size since I was a child.”

Des, finally gaining control of his faculties, gestured to the iron-spiked collar around its neck. “I imagine it comes in handy for fighting demons as well.”

“Who, Alastor?” Professor Sheldrake shook his head. “He looks far fiercer than he is.”

“He’s a big softie, aren’t you, Alastor?” Aurelie kissed the top of the hound’s head, her eyes never leaving Des’s. He hadn’t seen her in weeks, but it was clear she hadn’t spent any of that time in a prison cell. She was as vibrant as ever, cheeks rosy, eyes sparkling. Nothing had changed for her, and he should be furious.

But he wasn’t. He wasn’t happy about it, but he wasn’t angry, either. The only emotion he could pinpoint was *relief.*

“So there’s no demon?” Aspen asked.

“Highly unlikely. We’re the only ones on campus, and I can assure you, we aren’t conjuring anything but a little smoke. The guard must have seen Alastor out for his nightly constitutional and become confused," Professor Sheldrake explained.

Des was about to protest when Aspen nodded. "Glad to hear it. Sound the alarm should anything change. We won't be far off campus."

Des, once again at a loss for words, could only nod and follow her.

"That was strange, wasn't it?" Aspen asked when they were on the other side of the gate, seemingly unfazed by Des's inane behavior.

"She's the dean's niece," he said, his voice gruffer than he'd intended. Aurelie *was* a science student. It wasn't any of his business what experiments she conducted, just so long as she wasn't inventing anything new. Sheldrake seemed like the sort of bumbling professor who could accidentally conjure a demon, foreign as the idea was to Des. And the dog was just a dog, albeit overgrown. He should be glad Aurelie had supervision of some sort while her uncle was away.

Scratch that. He should be indifferent to all of it.

Des groaned and ran his hands through his hair, which was in dire need of a cut. It was so long he'd actually had to brush it this morning, which annoyed him to no end.

"Everything okay?" Aspen asked.

"Fine. Just tired."

Aspen, bless her, said nothing.

When they reached the barracks, they went their separate ways to shower and sleep. Daisy, as usual, was waiting up for him, reading a book that she'd purchased from one of the Yule vendors. It was ancient and missing half its pages, but that was all she could afford. Unlike many of the other guards, she did have remaining family. She sent most of her earnings to her cousin, who had three children of her own. Des worried they were taking advantage of her and had started putting part of his own salary aside for her. When she got out of here next year—and Des was confident she'd leave at eighteen, if only to be with family—she'd have something to show for it.

"Not tonight, Daisy," he said as he collapsed on his bunk. Just a few hours ago he'd been feeling optimistic about his life. Well, not optimistic. But close enough. Now he felt tired and out of sorts, and he wanted to close his eyes and not replay the sound of Aurelie's laugh in his mind.

"Of course tonight," she said, settling down so her feet were next to his head.

"You stink," he told her.

"So do you."

He arched an eyebrow but said nothing.

"Heard you went to the university with Aspen."

He sat up on his elbows. "When you say you 'heard,' what does that mean exactly?"

"Fine. I asked the duty officer where you were."

He collapsed back again. "And?"

"And I was wondering if you saw our friend."

Des sighed heavily. "She's not our friend, Daisy. Which reminds me, why isn't she in jail where she belongs? I thought you were going to turn the sketch over to Commander Yew."

Daisy at least had the decency to look chastened. "I *was* going to. But then I got a letter from her . . ."

"What letter?"

She sat up, pulled something out of her pocket, and dropped it in Des's lap.

He stared down at a folded piece of ivory-colored parchment. "What is that?"

"I already told you what it is."

"She actually wrote to you?"

Daisy nodded, looking mighty smug for someone with two short pigtails sticking off her head like turnip greens. "She wanted to thank me for all my help last month. She has excellent penmanship."

Des kept his hands at his sides, avoiding the paper that rested in his lap like a live grenade.

"Go on. Read it. She mentions you." Daisy waggled her eyebrows as she said it.

He would never admit that he was curious. "Not sure why you think I care."

Daisy sighed and snatched the paper out of his lap. "'Dear Daisy.' That's right, she called me *dear*. Like I said. Friend." She cleared her throat. "'I wanted to thank you for your help during what was a rather difficult week. I realize that someone of your rank and capability has far more important duties than escorting a university student around the city, and it touched me deeply that you went through such an effort to keep me safe.'"

Des made a gagging sound. "Aciano's beard, is she long-winded. I've never heard such a wordy—"

"I'm not finished. Ahem. 'To be honest, I've never given much thought to the Iron Guard. Living on campus as I do, we rarely see your work, and what encounters I've had have given me a rather different impression of your fellow guards. Frankly, I expected them all to be of Lieutenant Whitlow's character. Imagine my delighted surprise, then, to meet someone as kind, intelligent, and thoughtful as yourself.'"

Des reached for the paper. "She did not say that."

Daisy managed to evade him and continued reading. "'I understand that your work keeps you busy, but should you ever find yourself with a few free hours on a Monday afternoon, please don't hesitate to reach out. I would love to buy you a cup of tea, or perhaps a hot chocolate, as thanks. Yours, Aurelie.'"

Daisy sighed and folded the note back up. "Isn't that the most beautiful letter you've ever heard?"

"It's a load of absolute bollocks."

Daisy's mouth opened in mock offense. "How dare you speak about my friend Aurelie that way! I've already asked for permission to leave for a few hours on Monday evening to meet with her."

Des was speechless. Well, nearly. "Daisy, you can't be serious."

"I am."

"She wrote that entire letter to get to *me*. Even you must see that."

Daisy was quiet, and for a moment, Des was afraid he'd gone too far. He was sure Aurelie did like Daisy. She was a thoroughly likable person. But anyone could see that she was fishing to find out if Des was going to turn her in. She'd deliberately insulted Des, knowing that Daisy would share it with him. Had she no shame at all?

"My, you certainly think highly of yourself," Daisy said, punching him lightly on the shoulder. She was smiling, but there was genuine hurt there, and Des hated that he'd caused it.

"I'm sorry, Daisy. I didn't mean it like that. It's just clear that—"

"That what, Des? That no one like Aurelie could possibly want to be friends with someone like me?"

"Daisy." He reached for her hand, but she was already climbing off his bunk.

"I suppose I'll be able to ask her on Monday when we meet. If she can talk about anything other than *you*, of course."

"Daisy, I didn't mean it like that."

She didn't respond, but a moment later, he felt her settle back down next to him.

"I did see her tonight," he said gently. He felt like he owed it to her, somehow. "I think she blew something up."

"Aw," Daisy said, patting his forehead. "See, you two *are* more alike than you want to admit."

Des shoved his pillow over his face, hoping he might suffocate by morning.

CHAPTER 18
AURELIE

AURELIE READ THE LETTER FROM UNCLE LEO AGAIN, PRAYing that the words would rearrange themselves and tell her something different. That he wasn't remaining with his friend until after Yule. That she wasn't going to spend the rest of the year on her own.

Uncle Leo was profusely apologetic, but that didn't change the fact that he couldn't leave his friend's side. In fact, he spoke about him so tenderly that Aurelie knew they must be more than friends. Uncle Leo loved this man, deeply. And while she felt quite sorry for herself at the moment, all she could do was write to him and tell him that she understood entirely. She'd spend the holiday with the Morels. She'd be perfectly fine without him.

For the most part, it was the truth. She'd fallen into a routine these past weeks, spending less and less time in her lab as she began working on Everard's portal in earnest. She was exhausted from staying up later than usual, and she had to be extra vigilant when Mr. Willoughby, the guard who'd checked on Aurelie the night the *somnia* chased her, was on duty. He'd made it his personal mission to ensure she was safe, and his spontaneous visits kept her from falling into complacency. The knowledge that someone could walk in on her at any moment forced her to take all necessary precautions, ones she'd have to continue with when Uncle Leo did eventually return.

But building the portal was exhilarating in ways she couldn't have predicted. She had never faced such a large challenge, and between the runes and the puzzle of the metal plates, she went through dozens of pieces of parchment working on her schematics.

Before the metal plates arrived, she procured wooden blocks of a similar size and attempted to connect them without using any other metal, as instructed. She'd considered that if the frame were perfectly sized, she may be able to slot them into place without any additional means of connecting them, but one slight shove and they all collapsed onto the floor. It would have to be an adhesive, then, but one that could work on metal, which opened up an entire other world of research.

When the metal plates were finally delivered in several large wooden crates, Aurelie nearly squealed with joy. She pried one of the crates open with a crowbar as Mephisto peered over the rim next to her, then promptly left when it realized there were no cockroaches inside. She lifted one plate reverently. It was as bright and shiny as polished gold, without a single scratch or blemish. As she turned it on its side, she noticed that there were already engravings there, smooth lines and notches that must be the key to connecting the plates, though they weren't provided in any particular order.

Another puzzle for Aurelie to obsess over. It felt like she'd tried a thousand different combinations before she finally discovered that there was a complex pattern at play. She had cackled maniacally at the discovery, startling even herself.

It was Professor Sheldrake's tacit approval that helped buoy her when she began to question herself, or worse, when Kiara did. And though he never worked with her directly on the door, he was indeed mentoring her, aiding her with her studies when she was falling behind. She'd slept through one class for the first time in her life, but her professor had allowed her to complete the experiment with Professor Sheldrake instead.

Yes, they'd accidentally conjured a small *verita* when Professor Sheldrake decided to change the experiment around, just for fun, and she'd been convinced they were done for when it got loose and was spotted by the campus guard.

But Alastor had quickly chased it down, puncturing it with his iron-spiked collar. Seeing Des so publicly humiliated was a nice perk, although the sight of him had caught her off guard. She'd nearly forgotten how imposing he was, how his physical presence did strange things to her body.

After he had stolen the drawing, she had spent an entire week in terror, waiting for him to come in and arrest her. Then, when no arrest came, she'd decided to fish for information instead, or provoke it, if necessary. If Des hadn't turned her in, she needed to know why. And if he had, she needed to know why no one had acted on it yet. Daisy had responded to her letter right away, proposing they meet at a small café close to the university today at five o'clock.

Now, she set the letter from Uncle Leo on her desk and sighed. It was early in the winter for snow, but snow it had, for three days. Aurelie pulled on thick wool tights under her dress and swathed herself in a knit cardigan before bundling herself in her coat. She let Willoughby know where she was heading and when to expect her back, then let herself out of the university gates.

It was just ten days until Yule, and the streets were more crowded than ever. Children sledded down any slope they could find, including the middle of the road. Aurelie couldn't help smiling at a boy pulling his sister on a toboggan while she threw snowballs at his back, urging him to move faster. A dog sporting a full-body snowsuit with fluffy white trim trotted after them.

The café was just several blocks away, tucked onto a side street that Aurelie had never noticed. She entered to find Daisy already sitting at a small table at the back, where she waved to Aurelie.

"It's so nice to see you again," Daisy said as Aurelie removed her coat and hung it on a nearby hook. "How are things at the university? Nearly finished with your studies?"

"It's always busy this time of year," Aurelie said, perusing the menu. "I have a few papers to write before the term ends. And you? It seems that things have calmed down, demon-wise."

A man approached their table, asking to use the third, empty chair. Aurelie was about to give him permission when Daisy replied, "Sorry, we're waiting for a friend."

Aurelie's stomach did an odd maneuver that felt similar to a cartwheel, though she hadn't moved. "We are?"

Daisy grinned in what Aurelie suspected was meant to be a sheepish way, but she looked more mischievous than sorry. "I invited Des."

"What? Why?" Aurelie glanced over her shoulder just in time to see the giant in question enter the café, looking as miserable and uncomfortable as ever.

"Over here," Daisy called, though he was already walking toward them.

"Why would you invite him?" Aurelie hissed. "He probably hates hot chocolate as much as he hates people."

Daisy didn't respond. Instead, she rose to greet Des, and Aurelie felt obligated to do the same.

"Hello, Aurelie," he said, and all at once she was back in Uncle Leo's office, with Des's hand on her forehead and her heart in her throat.

"Hello, Des," she squeaked, then immediately regretted it. They shouldn't be on a first-name basis. Not after what he'd done to her.

"I read your letter to him, and he *insisted* on joining us," Daisy explained.

"That's not . . ." Des trailed off, apparently accepting that there was no use arguing with Daisy. "Hello, Aurelie," he said again.

Aurelie found herself at a loss for words. How was she going to ask Daisy about the drawing now? Was that why he'd come? So that Daisy couldn't reveal his plans? He had a lot of nerve showing up here as though he hadn't attempted to seduce and then rob her, the lousy thief. She especially hated that he looked so nice with longer hair, which was dark and curling from the melted snow.

He removed his coat and hung it next to Aurelie's. She almost laughed at the difference in size.

Des took the seat between the two of them, his legs so long they nearly brushed Aurelie's. He murmured an apology, and Aurelie wasn't sure if his cheeks were rosy from cold or embarrassment. She selfishly hoped it was the latter. He *should* be embarrassed, for using his masculine wiles against her.

"Let's order," Daisy said, waving a waiter over. "Three hot chocolates, extra whipped cream and chocolate buttons, please." She winked at Aurelie. "Trust me. Can we also get some of those lovely cream biscuits? Ooh, and lemon curd, if you have it. That should do for now. Thank you!"

"Daisy's sweet tooth rears its ugly head," Des muttered, attempting to sink lower in his chair. Aurelie glanced around and noticed that he'd caught the attention of several patrons, who whispered behind their hands and giggled.

"What?" Daisy asked, all innocence and cheer. Aurelie wanted to smack her on the back of the head. "It's not like we get sweets at the barracks. I have to make up for it whenever I get the opportunity."

Aurelie rolled her eyes and turned so she couldn't see the people fawning over Des. Yes, he was handsome, but there were plenty of handsome men in the world. Why must people make such a fuss?

She shook off her annoyance and focused on Daisy. "Do you come here often?" she asked. She knew the Iron Guard had Mondays off, for the most part, but she had expected them to spend the time resting or visiting friends, not eating chocolate buttons.

"Oh, once a month or so. Des prefers to spend his days off moping around the fort, but I like to remind myself there's a world outside the walls." Daisy drummed her fingers on the table, seemingly unable to sit still. "So, Aurelie. Tell us what you've been studying lately."

"Chemistry," she said, her eyes sliding to Des, only to find him staring at her. She immediately looked away. "I've been working with a new mentor. Professor Sheldrake. He's a bit unusual. We nearly blew up his lab the other night," she added with a laugh. "But I'm enjoying it."

She turned even farther toward Daisy, deliberately knocking Des's knees with her own. "And you, Daisy?"

"I'm training a new recruit. She's not particularly good at demon hunting, I'm afraid. But that's what happens when all orphans have to become demon hunters."

"Not all orphans," Des said, his eyes once again skating to Aurelie.

Now he'd gone too far. "Yes. How fortunate that my parents died in an accident," she said through gritted teeth. "They were so badly mangled I wasn't allowed to view their bodies, but I suppose that's a blessing, too."

There was a long, awkward silence, and then Daisy slapped her hand on the table, startling Aurelie and Des. "There has been one bit of good news! Des is getting a promotion next week," she said, nudging him with her elbow. "You're looking at Lieutenant Commander Whitlow. Or you will be, soon."

"Congratulations," Aurelie said stiffly. What was he *doing* here? She was certain he hadn't come for the hot chocolate or the company. Was this his excuse to check up on her, or was he intending to arrest her here, tonight? If so, she wouldn't go down without a fight. Or at least a very long-winded speech.

He grunted what she supposed was meant to be a thank-you. Fortunately, the waiter arrived then with their order, and soon Daisy was telling them excitedly about the hot chocolate, and Des and Aurelie found there was no need for either of them to speak.

Several times, while Daisy chattered on about her cousin and her children and how she'd be going to live with them next year, Aurelie glanced at Des to find him watching her. The first two times, she looked away immediately, her cheeks reddening. But the third time, she forced herself to meet his gaze.

This time, he looked away first, brow furrowed, and stared into the dregs of his hot chocolate. Aurelie smiled as though she'd won a battle, though she wasn't exactly sure what she'd gained. At least if he planned to arrest her, she'd gotten to drink her hot chocolate, which was admittedly delicious.

When they were finished, Aurelie reached for her purse to pay. She flinched when Des placed his hand over hers, just for a moment.

"I'll get this," he said. "No one should be responsible for Daisy's insatiable sugar addiction."

"But I invited her," Aurelie protested, her hand aflame where he'd touched her. Who was this Des? she wondered. The first few times she'd encountered him, she'd thought him as one-dimensional as a blank sheet of paper. But each meeting revealed that there was more to him than she'd originally given him credit for.

"There's no use arguing," Daisy said, already standing and pulling on her gray Iron Guard peacoat. "Des always insists."

"She's right," Des said with a shrug, pulling on the same coat, albeit considerably larger. "There's no use arguing."

Aurelie followed them outside, feeling more than a little unhinged. It was probably all the sugar, she told herself. Perhaps the cold air would help clear her head. The streets had emptied out a bit by now, and she was looking forward to getting back to her laboratory. She had more runes to interpret, which was proving challenging. Professor Sheldrake had been impressed with her progress, but Aurelie had never felt so lost in a subject. Fortunately, engraving the runes was the final task, so she had time yet.

Aurelie sighed, ready to be on her way. "It was nice seeing you, Daisy. And thank you again for the hot chocolate, Des." She wasn't entirely sure how she'd gone from vowing to despise this man until the end of time to thanking him, but here they were.

"We'll walk you back," Daisy said, already linking arms with Aurelie. "And again, there's no use arguing," she said out of the corner of her mouth. "Des will insist."

"I will," he agreed from behind them.

Aurelie rolled her eyes but acquiesced. Perhaps he'd wait till she was back at campus to arrest her. She almost wished Daisy would leave them alone so she could confront him directly. At the same time, the thought of being alone with him again terrified her, given how absurdly she'd behaved the last time.

"How have things been on the demon front?" Aurelie asked. The gates loomed up ahead, representing safety in more ways than Aurelie could count. "Quieter?"

"Much," Des answered from behind her. "I assume that has nothing to do with you staying behind the gates of late."

She turned to scowl at him, and just as she was about to turn back, she caught a flash of red eyes in the dark.

Aurelie didn't have time to scream or even think. Instinct kicked in, her hand reaching into her pocket for her iron blade as she placed herself squarely between Des and the demon.

"Aurelie, what are you—" Des cut himself off when he saw the creature for himself. It was a *natia,* crouching in the snow not twenty feet away.

From the corner of her eye, Aurelie saw Des reach for his sword, realize he didn't have it, and swear before pulling his own blade from his coat. "What the hell is going on?" he asked as he stepped in front of her, much to her annoyance.

"You tell me," Aurelie said, peeking out from behind Des. The demon was a boy, about seven years old, with dark hair and skin so pale it seemed to glow in the darkness. She knew *natia* were hungry, but to attempt to take on three adults was brazen in the extreme.

Daisy had deliberately separated herself from Aurelie and Des, hoping to draw the demon's attention, but it was focused squarely on Aurelie. She could feel its eyes tracking her, the pointed red gaze impossible to read. For a moment, she had the terrible thought that it might attempt to speak to her.

"Aurelie, get behind the gates," Des hissed, his stance low and wide. He was preparing to attack.

Normally, Aurelie would have argued for the sake of it, but something about this demon, the first *natia* she'd ever encountered, was frightening in a way the *somnia* hadn't been. Demons should look like monsters, not this eerie approximation of human children. And with those red eyes fixed on her right now, there was nothing she wanted more than to be behind the safety of iron. She turned and sprinted for the gates.

She screamed as a different *natia* leapt into her path, a girl that looked quite similar to the boy. Twins, perhaps. She heard Daisy call her name, but she didn't have time to respond before the girl came for her, her sharp teeth bared behind her curled, snarling lips.

Aurelie was suddenly grateful for all her prior interactions with demons. Without them, she might not have anticipated how fast demons were. But all she needed was one cut. She ducked left, the demon missing her by inches, and whirled. Somewhere behind her she could hear Des and Daisy struggling with the boy, but she couldn't afford to be distracted.

The girl leapt at her again, and Aurelie struck out with her blade, narrowly missing the demon's shoulder. It seemed to rattle her, because she paused for a moment, head cocked to the side.

A soft, oddly resonant voice in her head said, *It's you.*

And then something slammed into Aurelie, sending her sprawling into the snow.

Aurelie couldn't breathe, and for a moment she was afraid she'd been attacked by some other unseen demon. She struggled to lift her knife and found her hands pinned at her sides. "Get off of me!" she screamed. Or tried to. Her lungs were being crushed under the weight of—

She opened her eyes to see Des looking down at her, seemingly as stunned as she was. His wide eyes were just inches from hers, and the fear she saw in them was almost as shocking as the feeling of his weight on top of her. She was fortunate she was on snow and had sunk down a couple of inches, or she might have been flattened.

For a moment, time stretched into something endless. Des's eyes roamed her face, though she had no idea what he was searching for.

"I'm all right," she whispered finally, and he scrambled off of her, lifting her to her feet before she could process what had happened.

"The girl is dead," Daisy panted behind them. "The boy got away."

She was speaking to Des, but he was still focused on Aurelie, his hands on her shoulders, his eyes scanning her body as though he couldn't believe she was in one piece. She still held her iron blade in her right hand, though it hung limp at her side. It was a wonder she could even stand.

"I'm all right," she repeated, and that seemed to bring him back to himself.

"What the hell just happened?" he asked no one in particular, running his free hand through his hair.

Aurelie took a deep, shuddering breath. "I believe they were twins. They looked very similar, and it would explain them appearing in the same place at the same time."

Daisy nodded. "Thank goodness you're okay," she said, patting Des on the shoulder. "I was afraid the giant here had squished you."

"That would have been quite the headline," Aurelie said with a surprised laugh. "'Destroyer Whitlow Crushes University Student to Death.'"

Daisy let out her own puff of laughter. "Destroyer?"

Aurelie shrugged. "It fits."

Des shook his head. "I don't understand."

"It's a play on Destrier," Aurelie replied.

His eyes hooded in annoyance. "Thank you, Aurelie. I understand the play on words. I meant the demons. They attacked simultaneously. I've never seen two demons coordinate an attack before."

"The connection between twins is extremely strong," Aurelie explained, sheathing her blade and starting for the gates. She hoped her knees wouldn't give out before she reached them.

"But to take on three adults like that?" Daisy shook her head in a similar disbelieving manner to Des. "We should get back and tell Commander Yew. Someone needs to track the male."

"Redding and Bowie are on duty tonight," Des said. "I'll find them."

Aurelie fumbled for her key in her collar with shaking fingers. All she wanted was to get to her lab and change into her softest nightgown and go to sleep. The runes could wait till morning.

"No," Daisy said. "We're going back, Des. We're not properly armed. If Aurelie hadn't had her own blade to defend herself . . ." She trailed off, and suddenly both Des and Daisy were staring at Aurelie in a way she didn't care for at all.

"What?" she asked. "The guard gave it to me. He thought it would be a good idea for when I leave campus, after the attack last month." It was a good lie, all things considered. Aurelie was rather proud of it.

"Whitlow? Shaw?" A pair of guards was coming toward them from across the street. "What are you doing out here?"

"I'll explain," Daisy said, sharing a look with Des.

Dash it. Aurelie finally fished her key out from her collar and held it aloft. "I should get back. It's late and I have more studying tonight."

"Not so fast," Des said, stepping between her and the gate. "You're telling me you just got that blade tonight?"

"Yes . . ."

"And you're that comfortable wielding it."

"It's not that hard," Aurelie said with feigned offense, skirting around him. "Handle in hand, pointy end in demon."

His eyebrows lowered in what Aurelie now knew was not a good sign. "Aurelie."

"Des."

"What aren't you telling me?"

She turned away from him, inserting her key in the lock. "I've told you everything. Go home." She gasped when he slammed his hand against the gate, holding it closed.

"Aurelie."

She groaned and turned back to him, once again finding herself caged by him. She could easily duck under his arm and leave, but considering the gate was behind her, that wouldn't get her any closer to her lab. "What do you want, Des?"

"I know you know I took the drawing."

She sighed in annoyance. "Of course I know."

He leaned closer. "I know you wrote that letter to Daisy to get to me."

She shrugged. "That was merely an added bonus."

He placed his other hand against the gate, right next to her head. "Where did you learn how to fight a demon, Aurelie? What are you doing in that building?" He jerked his head toward Easton Hall. "Why are demons following you around Wisteria?"

"I don't know!" She hadn't meant to lose her temper, but she was cornered and tired, and without adrenaline coursing through her anymore, she was afraid she might actually collapse. She was leaning heavily against the gate now, the iron bars pressing into her spine. She shivered as the snow that had made its way inside her collar melted down her back.

The truth was, demons *were* following her. There was no denying it. No denying that the *somnia* had spoken to her before, that the demon tonight had, too. No denying that she was in completely over her head.

"I don't know," she whispered, her vision tunneling.

Des's furrowed brow was the last thing she saw before she fainted.

CHAPTER 19

DES

"I CAN TAKE HER FROM HERE, SIR," THE SERVANT SAID TO DES as he reached for Aurelie, who was currently lying unconscious in Des's arms.

It had all happened so fast. One minute she'd been shouting at him, and the next, her eyes had rolled back, and she'd started to fall. Des caught her without thinking. It had been easy, given that he'd had his arms on either side of her already, though he couldn't remember placing them there. Even as dead weight, she was almost laughably light. He had turned to find Daisy staring at him, her mouth open in shock.

Now, Des found himself drawing Aurelie closer to his chest as he stepped around the young male servant and into the cottage. Des was grateful he'd been in the dean's house once before. He knew exactly where the nearest sofa was, and he intended to make sure she was at least placed somewhere comfortable. Daisy followed him inside, apologizing on his behalf, as two maids clustered in the hallway.

In the dean's sitting room, Des ignored the armchairs he'd sat in with Aurelie and went straight to the settee, laying her gently on its plush brocade surface. Unconscious, she looked like a doll, her long lashes resting on her porcelain cheeks. Her lips, which Des had gotten a good look at the other day when he was stealing her sketch, were parted slightly. He had the strangest urge to press his finger to her full lower lip, to know if it was as soft as it looked.

"Is she awake?" Daisy asked, peering over his shoulder.

Des rose. "Not yet. Maybe we should send for a doctor."

"She's unconscious, not ill." Daisy turned to the maid. "Can you fetch a glass of water and some smelling salts, if you have any?"

The maid nodded and hurried off, while the young valet hovered worthlessly in the doorway. "Is Miss Blake going to be all right?" he asked.

"She'll be fine," Daisy assured him, but Des could hear the concern in her voice. "The best thing you can do right now is give her some space."

The boy nodded and left.

"Thank you," Des said to Daisy. "I was getting ready to remove him myself."

"I could tell." She eyed him meaningfully. "You all right there? You were looking a little pale for a minute."

Des sat in one of the armchairs and pressed the heels of his hands to his eyes, suddenly exhausted. "Did I cause this, Daisy?"

"You mean by yelling at her?" Daisy smiled to let him know she was teasing and sat across from him. "She was overwhelmed, Des. She'll be fine."

He ran his hands down his face, unable to get the image of Aurelie lying against the snow beneath him out of his head every time he closed his eyes. All that lovely dark hair spread around her, mouth open in a small *o* of shock. It had been pure instinct to knock her to the ground and out of harm's way, leaving Daisy to go after the female *natia*. He glanced at her now, unable to reconcile the bookish, sheltered girl he thought he knew with the woman who had so naturally stepped in front of him to confront the demon, knife clenched in her fist, boots planted firmly in the snow. She had fought demons before. There was no doubt in his mind.

Why did she insist on lying?

The answer was obvious, even if it infuriated him. If she admitted she'd faced demons, she'd have to admit to whatever illicit activity she was participating in. And how could she when the truth would land her in jail?

None of that mattered now, though. He *had* to turn her over to the Iron Guard. It wasn't just her on the line anymore—maybe it never was. He'd be culpable if she was caught, right alongside Daisy. They'd let the other guards know there was a male *natia* on the loose, but Commander Yew would need a full debriefing as soon as possible. Des had been right to take that drawing, to tail this girl from the first night he met her. She was dangerous. All the more so for looking like she did. Small. Scholarly. Beautiful.

Brave.

"I know what you're thinking," Daisy said, forcing him to look at her.

Before he could respond, a maid returned with the smelling salts and water. Daisy took them and asked her to fetch some tea, which Des was fairly certain was another excuse to get her out of the room, though the fact that she'd asked for sugar didn't bode well.

Daisy opened the tiny vial of smelling salts but didn't immediately move to Aurelie's side. "We're going to hear her out before we make any decisions. Do you understand me?"

Normally, Des would have argued, but not tonight. Not when

he'd almost gotten Aurelie killed. He found himself saying a silent prayer that she had a perfectly good explanation for all of this, but his stomach twisted with doubt. What explanation could there possibly be?

Aurelie regained consciousness the moment the salts were placed under her nose. She gave a strangled little gasp, trying to sit up. Daisy pressed her back against the pillow gently.

"Easy, now," she murmured. "You fainted outside the gates. Des carried you to your house. You're safe."

Aurelie's eyes skittered to Des, and he remembered the way she'd looked at him at the café, finally meeting his gaze and daring him to look away first.

He'd never backed down from a confrontation in his life, but he had surrendered to Aurelie Blake. Staring back was too vulnerable when faced with her sharp, indecipherable stare. Did she despise him, as he had been so sure he did her? Or did she, too, feel an inexplicable pull between them?

"You carried me here?" she asked, then covered her face with her forearm. "Blood and bones, this is mortifying."

Des couldn't help the smile that curled his lips. There had been nothing mortifying about her fainting. He had seen grown men faint dead away in front of demons, *without* fighting them first—let alone stepping in front of an Iron Guard. Something in him kept returning to that moment. Was it pure instinct, or was she truly trying to protect him?

Daisy helped Aurelie sit up, though she insisted she was fine. "I just need some sleep," she said, turning so that she was facing Des. "Thank you for bringing me home."

Had she forgotten all the explaining she had to do? What they had been speaking about less than ten minutes ago? "Aurelie—" he started, but Daisy cut him off with a glare as the maid bustled into the room with a tea tray.

"Oh, thank heavens, Miss Blake. I'll tell the others. We were all so concerned about you." The maid glanced at Des beneath her lashes and blushed. "How fortunate Lieutenant Whitlow was here to help."

Aurelie's mouth slanted in a wry smirk at Des when the maid left. "Fortunate, indeed."

"We do need to talk," Des said.

"I know," she replied. "But surely there's time for tea. And then . . . I'll tell you everything." Aurelie glanced up at him, all lashes and pouty lip, and in that moment, he had the terrible, sinking feeling that he would do anything she asked. That he'd find time for tea and whatever else this brazen creature had in mind.

He'd never been more afraid in his life.

Thirty minutes later, after a lackluster explanation that Aurelie had been taking demon defense classes, they had put on their coats and stepped back out into the snow. Aurelie led them across the campus to the hall Des had seen her disappear into before, ostensibly to prove that she truly had nothing to hide.

It was surreal to be on this side of the gates, to walk in the literal footsteps of a girl whose life was impossibly different from his.

Their only similarity was that they were both orphans. But even in that, their circumstances couldn't be farther apart. Even if he'd had a wealthy uncle like Aurelie did, he still would have come to the Guard, given the circumstances of his parents' death. The king's decree made it seem like an honor for a demon-orphaned child to have the opportunity to avenge their parents' deaths, but he knew plenty of guards who would have preferred to be raised by civilian relatives or friends.

"What is this place?" Daisy asked as they entered the building. It was old, that much was clear, with imposing stone columns and gilt-framed oil portraits of stern-faced men and women lining the hall.

"This is Easton Hall. One of the oldest on campus. I don't spend much time at my uncle's cottage anymore. Not since I turned eighteen. My office is this way."

This was where Aurelie belonged, with her tidy notebooks and prim dresses, not flitting around noisy cafés with the elite. Yes, she was smug and self-satisfied to a profoundly obnoxious degree, but at least she was occupying her time with more than flirting and day-drinking.

She led them to a stairwell and they descended two floors. Only a few of the gas lamps were lit here, and the hall had an abandoned feeling. He couldn't imagine choosing this over her uncle's house. For just one moment when they'd been sitting there the other day, surrounded by books, a fire crackling in the hearth, he'd felt as though he had stepped into someone else's life. Someone who talked to his wife over tea and looked after her when she was injured. Someone who had a lovely home to return to at the end of a day.

Someone who had a home.

"I need a moment to tidy up," Aurelie said when they reached a doorway that looked no different from the others lining the long hallway. Before Des could say anything, she had smiled, unlocked the door, and disappeared inside.

While she'd sipped her tea—strong and black—Des had insisted she show them where she studied. Daisy, whose cup was filled with more sugar than tea, had elbowed him and asked Aurelie politely. Des knew she wanted to believe Aurelie was innocent, perhaps more than he did.

Aurelie opened the door a minute later and motioned for them to step inside. It was a large, rectangular room with one high, narrow window above the desk. Des had to duck his head to keep from running into the dried herbs and flowers hanging from the low ceiling. The room was full but not untidy, with rows of bookshelves lining the walls, holding more scientific objects than books. Des noted a small collection of skulls and blinked in surprise.

"As you can see," Aurelie said, taking a seat on the sofa, "it's more or less a study. I spend most of my time here when I'm not in class or working. I'm afraid it's all rather dull. I read, I take notes, I memorize formulas. I work here at the university as a handyperson. That takes up a good deal of my time. Occasionally I sleep." She patted the sofa. "It's more comfortable than it looks."

Daisy walked to a large wooden wardrobe. "May I?" she asked, gesturing to the door.

"Of course."

Des wasn't sure what he'd expected when Daisy opened the doors—clothing, perhaps, or more skeletons—but it wasn't a series of vials and beakers, some filled with unidentifiable objects floating in fluid. Aurelie was even stranger than he'd given her credit for, but he didn't see anything that would indicate illegal activity. Certainly nothing akin to the sketch he'd taken. Could it simply have been an assignment for one of her classes, some sort of hypothetical exercise? After all, he had no idea what university students did, and he doubted Commander Yew did, either.

"What do you use all this for?" Daisy asked over her shoulder. She looked as out of place here as Des felt.

"Scientific study," Aurelie explained, joining them at the wardrobe. "Not novel experiments, of course. Nothing that could produce demons. But part of learning how things work is observing the processes for ourselves." She lifted out a small dish containing a jagged lump of crystals. "I'm growing these to learn about the crystallization process. These were made with water and alum."

"And this?" Des asked, pointing to a jar full of cockroaches.

"Food for the amphibians in the zoology department. I catch so many around here that I figured I may as well do something useful with them."

Daisy seemed to accept all of Aurelie's explanations at face value, but Des kept his eyes on Aurelie. There was a bead of sweat at her temple, though it wasn't warm down here. If anything, it was quite cold. There was no fireplace. The thought of her sleeping down here by herself troubled him for some reason. Perhaps he was too used to sleeping in a room with dozens of other people.

"All right," Des said, sitting at the desk. "So if you're not doing anything here to produce demons, what's *your* explanation for what we've been seeing lately?"

Aurelie shrugged and returned to the sofa, where Daisy sat next to her. "I don't have an explanation, Des." She turned to him, eyes suddenly sharp. "I suppose one could ask if there isn't some other common denominator at these demon sightings."

"Meaning?"

"Meaning *you.* You have also been at every one of these encounters. How do we know you're not the one attracting the demons?"

Des glanced at Daisy, who shook her head unhelpfully. "Because it hasn't been happening when you're not around," he said, though he wasn't sure. Commander Yew said there were more encounters elsewhere in the kingdom. Des had read the reports himself.

Aurelie untied the ribbon at her neck, exposing the pale hollow of her throat, and shook out the remnants of her disheveled braid, as if she no longer cared to keep up her student persona. And why should she? She was obviously exhausted, and both Des and Daisy had already seen under the guise of the dean's perfect niece.

"Tell me one more thing and we'll let you get some sleep," Des said.

She sighed and met his eyes again. "What?"

"Who was the tall man who came here to visit you?"

"Everard? He's a friend of my uncle's."

"And yet he came when your uncle was away."

Aurelie blinked slowly, as if she was fighting sleep. "He wasn't aware my uncle would be traveling. It was a last-minute trip to visit a dying friend."

"And you invited him to stay for dinner?"

"I did. But he wasn't able to stay long. We had a glass of wine and then he left."

Fair enough. That did explain why the visit was so short. "What else do you know about him?"

"Very little. I'd never met him before that night."

"Have you seen him since?"

A small scratching noise from across the room caught Aurelie's attention. Des followed her gaze to the far corner near the floorboard.

"Mice," Aurelie explained with a light laugh. "They're nearly as bad as the cockroaches."

"Your uncle's friend?" Des asked, doing his best to keep his tone curious.

"I haven't seen him since, no."

Des rose. "Very well. We have to report tonight's incident to Commander Yew, of course. But since you've shown us that you have nothing to hide, you shouldn't expect to hear from us again."

"Oh." Aurelie followed Des and Daisy to the door. Did he detect a hint of disappointment in her voice, or was she simply surprised they were leaving so abruptly? "Would you like me to see you out?"

"There's no need," Daisy said, placing her hand on Aurelie's shoulder for a moment. Physical touch came so easily to her, something Des had never understood. Then again, she was small and gentle, not a giant like him. A destroyer, as Aurelie had called him. "You should get some rest."

"I will," Aurelie said. "Thank you again for the hot chocolate."

Des managed a tight smile. "You're welcome."

Aurelie shut the door behind them. He heard the scrape of the key in the lock a moment later, and he wondered if she always locked herself inside. Some part of him hoped she did.

His eyes met Daisy's. They knew each other well enough now that they could communicate volumes with a single glance.

The guard was waiting for them at the gates. "Thank you for taking care of our Miss Blake," the man said as he opened the gate for them. "Her uncle has been gone longer than expected, and he's all she has in this world. If anything were to happen to her . . ."

"She's fine," Daisy assured him. "She's stronger than she looks."

Des waited until they were halfway down the block before he turned to Daisy. "You saw it too, didn't you?"

Daisy nodded. "I did."

"You know we have to turn her in."

Daisy sighed, a look of genuine sorrow passing over her features. It pained Des to see her so sad. Even on her darkest days, Daisy could find something to smile about. She genuinely cared about Aurelie. "I do."

Des clenched his jaw and looked away. "I was right about her, Daisy. You know I was."

After a long moment, Daisy said, "I know."

They were silent for the remainder of the walk back to the Iron Fortress. His stomach was in knots, his mind racing with the knowledge that if Daisy hadn't also seen it, he might have actually let the whole matter go. Just as he had done with her sketch, perhaps even knowing on some level that Daisy wouldn't have the heart to turn the girl in.

Before he met Aurelie, he would never have considered such deception. All he had was his honor, his vows. Before last week, he believed with his entire being that the only thing worse than a demon was a person who chose to create them.

But that was before he'd held someone in his arms for the first time, had felt their heartbeat against his own. Before he'd watched a person, the very kind he was sworn to protect, step between him and danger. Before he'd known that a demon summoner could also be curious and thoughtful and brave. Before he'd stared at a girl's mouth and wondered how it would feel against his. If it was as soft as he feared and hoped it might be. If it would taste as good as it looked.

He curled his hands into fists, his entire body burning with self-loathing.

Whatever Aurelie was up to, he simply couldn't bring himself to believe she was evil. But she *knew* who Des and Daisy were. She *knew* how they'd ended up in the guard. Aciano's beard, a demon had killed a man only feet from her, in broad daylight!

His body knew what he had to do, even if his mind wouldn't allow himself to accept it. It had known since the moment he saw the "mouse" in Aurelie's laboratory, the one she had tried to gloss over with a nervous laugh.

The one with the pair of glowing red eyes.

CHAPTER 20

AURELIE

"DAMN. DAMN, DAMN, DAMN!" AURELIE PACED UP AND DOWN the room, her hands fisted in her hair, her mind racing at a million miles a minute. Why had Mephisto chosen that moment to come out from hiding? As soon as she'd entered her lab, she'd hidden the few pieces of incriminating evidence, including her sketchbooks, in the Load Lightener, but Mephisto had been nowhere to be found. She'd even scattered salt near its hidey-holes, hoping that would prevent it from making an unwanted appearance. She had been almost certain she was going to put Des and Daisy off her scent for good, to draw a close to this wretched evening and go to sleep. Almost certain she had actually gotten away with everything.

Until she'd heard Mephisto's telltale scuttle on the floorboards.

She couldn't be sure Des had seen its eyes in the dark, but she strongly suspected he had. The change had been subtle, but the tone of his voice had shifted, and his hands had clenched in his lap. Mephisto had left again immediately, clearly sensing that it was in danger, but the damage was likely done. Aurelie would either have to get rid of Mephisto or leave the university, which was impossible. It wasn't as if she had somewhere else to go. But Des and Daisy would be back. Soon. Likely with Commander Yew.

When she'd exhausted every possible scenario, she sat down on her sofa, put her head in her hands, and cried. She knew it was foolish, that she never should have let herself get so attached to a demon, but it had been a part of her life for eleven years. She'd been a child when she conjured it, a lonely, orphaned girl with no friends. She'd never deliberately killed anything in her life up to that point. Not even a fly, thanks to her mother, who had explained the necessity of pollinating insects to Aurelie at an early age. There had never been any possibility of her harming Mephisto.

And now what? If she released it off the university grounds, she had no idea if it would survive. How could she have been so stupid, allowing any of this to happen? She didn't understand why demons were following her any more than Des did, but she couldn't deny that he was right. And now she'd as good as killed her friend.

A small squeak near her feet caused Aurelie to wipe her tears and look down. Mephisto was there, staring up at her with its cursed red eyes. She held her cupped hands out, not knowing if the creature would bite her or climb aboard. Tonight, fortunately, it seemed to understand that something was amiss, because it clambered onto her hands and spun in a little circle before settling on her palms. Its long, slender body was covered in bristly white fur, its pink flesh visible beneath them. It released a sigh through its nostrils and closed its eyes, and Aurelie felt a fresh wave of hot tears slide down her cheeks.

She laid it in her lap, hardly daring to run her fingers over its long back, feeling the delicate movement of its breath. Mephisto may be a demon, but it was far from evil. Anyone would see that, if they bothered to look.

"I'm sorry," she whispered against its head, earning a small growl and a squeaky yawn.

Aurelie sniffled and set the demon on its pillow. For this week, at least, it would get all the cockroaches it could eat.

On Tuesday morning, Aurelie did what she should have done from the start. She told Kiara everything.

"I know it's all completely mad," she said when she'd finished. "And I should have come to you sooner," she added, before Kiara could say so herself. "But I'm terrified, and I don't know what to do. I need your help, Kiki."

Kiara, who was sitting on Aurelie's sofa with Mephisto curled up next to her, hadn't said a word for the entirety of Aurelie's speech. She blinked a few times, chewing on her lip. "I don't . . . I can't . . ." She leaned forward so abruptly Mephisto bolted from the sofa. "What the hell were you thinking?!"

Not once in the eleven years of their friendship had Kiara yelled at her. Hot tears sprang into Aurelie's eyes, which was completely ridiculous. She deserved to be yelled at for what she'd done.

"I wasn't thinking," she cried. "At least not with my scientist's brain."

"Well, whose brain were you using, then? Because they are an utter pillock!"

"I know!" Aurelie rose and began to pace around her office. Some part of her had been hoping for reassurance that things weren't as bad as she feared. But the rest of her had known they were worse. Otherwise she would never have dragged her best friend into this. "I'm done for, aren't I? No matter what I do from this point on, I'm going to prison, and Uncle Leo will never speak to me again, and Mephisto is going to die."

She collapsed onto the floor, somehow finding a reserve of tears despite all her crying last night. Thank goodness it was only seven o'clock in the morning and the students wouldn't be here for at least an hour.

She felt Kiara sit next to her and wrap an arm around her shoulders. "I'm sorry I shouted. I'm just worried for you, that's all. Besides, I'm partly to blame."

"What do you mean?"

"I meant to ask my father ages ago about this Everard, but I only just remembered this weekend. Father has never heard of him, Aurelie. Which means not only did that man lie to you, but we also have no idea how he learned of you in the first place."

Aurelie's back prickled with a cold sweat. Some part of her had known that all along, hadn't it?

"But let's remove one concern from your plate. I'll take Mephisto to my grandparents' house. I'll release it into the countryside, where it will have all the grasshoppers and field mice it can eat."

"Really?"

"Really. In the meantime, it can live in your other workshop. No one goes in that building."

"That's a good idea." Why hadn't she spoken with Kiara sooner? She would never have let Aurelie get so wrapped up in this mess.

"As far as the Iron Guard is concerned . . . Well, they haven't turned you in yet. Maybe they're not planning to. But either way, you *have* to tell this Everard person you can't build his portal. It's far too dangerous. And I love you too much to let you lose everything over this."

"But—"

Kiara leveled her with a flat gaze. "Aurelie, if you don't, I won't help you with anything ever again."

Aurelie lowered her head. She knew Kiara was right. She should never have accepted in the first place. Her life had been a disaster ever since Uncle Leo left and Everard showed up at the university. Before then, everything had been going well. Her grades were fine, her relationship with Uncle Leo was changing but not in a bad way, and she was keeping her inventing manageable.

She'd let her pride take over these past weeks, when she had always been so logical, so practical. For heaven's sake, she still didn't know what the portal was truly *for*, only a vague idea of what it might be meant to do. Still, all that hard work for nothing. The schematics, the hours wasted on Elder Vansion. Not to mention the risks she'd taken and the people she'd endangered, with nothing to show for it in the end.

She took a deep breath. This was the right decision. Everard would be disappointed, but he'd find someone else to do the job. At least Aurelie wouldn't have to see it. And at least she'd know she had tried.

"All right," she conceded as Kiara pulled her into her arms. "I'll tell him by the end of the week. I promise."

Aurelie spent the rest of the week constructing a cage for Mephisto in whatever time she could spare, one that was portable but large enough that it wouldn't feel too restrictive. She crafted a shoddy cover for the cage—sewing was not her strong suit—and concocted a lie that she'd captured a juvenile least weasel and was keeping it for the zoology department until after Yule. No one would mistake an eight-legged demon for a weasel, but at least the color and size were close.

By Thursday, she was breathing a little easier. There was no sign of the Iron Guard, Miles Viridian had a boil the size of a small kingdom on his nose, and her professors were all in good moods because of the upcoming holiday. She even managed to get an extension on a paper for her requisite philosophy class, which she'd hardly paid attention to all semester.

There was just one loose thread hanging over her. At some point during the chaos of the other night, she'd lost the key to the front gate. Mr. Morel had a new one made for her, but she didn't like knowing the other was still out there somewhere.

After speaking with Kiara, Aurelie had sent a letter to Everard to let him know she'd be coming with an update. It felt like it was something she ought to do in person, and besides, she needed to tell him that she'd return the metal plates as soon as possible. She had balked at taking most of the money she'd earned this year from her locked safe, but she couldn't very well tell Everard that she was canceling his project without paying him for lost time.

On Friday, with her money in a satchel and a scarf wrapped around the lower half of her face, Aurelie stepped out of the gates into the city. It had snowed nearly a foot this week, and the temperature had dropped to a low usually reserved for January. The few people who were willing to brave the cold were bundled up almost beyond recognition, looking more like walking duvets than humans.

Everard's house was even narrower than Aurelie remembered it, as though the cold had caused some kind of shrinkage. She forced herself to walk straight up the stairs and grip the demon-head knocker, ignoring the twisting in her stomach. This was the right thing to do. And it would all be over soon.

"Miss Blake," Everard said when he opened the door. "I'm impressed you made it here today. Come in, come in. You must be freezing."

Aurelie was, indeed, half frozen. It took several minutes sitting by the fire for her teeth to stop chattering. "Thank you for meeting with me," she said when she'd recovered. "I know it was a bit last-minute."

"That's all right. I'm looking forward to hearing of your progress."

Aurelie glanced around the room nervously, her eyes landing on a book that looked rather old. "Where did your collection come from?" she asked, stalling even though she'd vowed not to.

"Here and there." Everard sat across from her, one long leg folded over the other. "I have a great love of books."

Aurelie wished she had tea, just so she'd have something to occupy herself with. The more time she spent around Everard, with his vague answers and bizarre habits, the more resolved she was to end this relationship. And there was no time like the present.

"Mr. Everard, I came here today because I am unable to complete your project." She paused, not sure what sort of reaction to expect, but he merely arched an eyebrow. "You see, I have become far too busy with my schoolwork to take on what is clearly a very important project to you. It's not fair of me to hold you up further. I will have your supplies delivered here as soon as possible, and I'm prepared to pay you for all the time I've wasted. It was arrogant of me to take on the project in the first place, and you have my most sincere apology." She began to reach for her coin purse, but Everard held up a hand, silencing her.

"It's only been a few weeks, Aurelie. Surely you aren't going to give up so easily."

She forced herself to meet his gaze. "I think part of being successful in life is being able to admit when you're in over your head. And I'm afraid that's where I have found myself."

"I see." Everard uncrossed his legs and leaned forward. "And there's nothing I can say that will change your mind? More money, or more time perhaps."

"I'm afraid not. As I said, I let my ambition and my pride get away from me. I hope you can forgive me."

Everard rose and went to the bookshelf that Aurelie had been looking at. He trailed his fingers over the spines of the books. Aurelie once again heard the clicking of dog paws on the hardwood floor and wondered where the animal was. It sounded large, larger even than Sheldrake's hound.

"Aurelie, I chose you for this for a reason. As I mentioned before, I know a great deal about you." He turned back toward her. "Beyond what I learned from Mr. Morel."

She could confront Everard about this lie, but she'd already done what she came to do. She didn't want a lecture, and she certainly didn't want him to offer her something more. She wanted to leave this place and never return. "There's very little to know."

He huffed a wry laugh. "Oh, I don't know about that. Your inventions, for example. The Helping Hand and the Load Lightener? Hardly 'little,' I'm sure you'd agree."

Aurelie blanched. "How could you possibly know about those?"

"Because I know about all the demons in Wisteria. I even know about your little pet. Mephisto, isn't it? One of the oldest specimens in this world, and certainly one of the most benign. It's no wonder you kept it around."

He knew about Mephisto. He knew Mephisto's *name.* It wasn't possible, and yet there was no one who could have told him. Aurelie wanted to run, but fear had her rooted in her chair. "Mephisto is innocent, Mr. Everard."

"Of course it is. All demons are. They don't choose to be conjured, and they only act on the instincts they're born with. Unless, of course, they're controlled by someone else." Everard didn't make any discernible movement, but suddenly the clicking sound started up again. It was growing closer and closer, until at last, the "dog" appeared.

Even without its enormous red eyes, no one would mistake it for anything other than a demon. Wolflike, with a long, pointed snout crowded with teeth, it had two massive horns curling back from its skull. Its legs were long and bent in a strange way, ending in claws the length of Everard's fingers. Seated, the demon reached above Everard's waist. On its hind legs, it would be taller than a grown man, even one as tall as Everard.

Aurelie shrank back in her chair, hand instinctively reaching for her dagger.

"Not to worry," Everard said, patting the creature's back. "Kobal is entirely within my control. It won't hurt you unless I tell it to. In fact, it has saved your life."

"What?"

"The man who died in Aciano Square? He was a predator, and he was hunting *you*, Aurelie. Kobal killed him at *my* command."

The implicit threat was enough to make Aurelie's limbs go

watery. She would have collapsed if she hadn't been sitting. Now she understood why Des believed her to be a demon consorter. This must have been the creature following Everard the night she met him. And Des had seen the attack Everard was referring to.

"I don't understand," Aurelie said, shaking her head, even as her heart began to drum wildly in her chest. "How can you know that about the man who died? How do you know about my demons?"

Everard sat down again, with Kobal by his side in some macabre version of master and companion. "Do you remember how I mentioned that there was a great conspiracy in this kingdom?"

Aurelie swallowed. "Yes."

"I am a descendant of Prince Florian, who was exiled by his brother, Prince Aciano. I assume you know the history."

Aurelie nodded.

"Most of what you've learned is true, although there are lies that were spread by Aciano after Florian was exiled. Namely, that Florian attempted to murder his brother. In fact, it was the other way around."

Despite the tacit air of danger that had descended around her, Aurelie couldn't help but latch on to what Everard was saying. She'd always believed there had to be more to Florian's story.

"When Florian cursed this kingdom, he did so by thinning the veil between our world and the demonic world through the use of dark magic. Why do you suppose no one ever lifted the curse, Aurelie?"

She shook her head. "I don't—I assume because it was extremely difficult or dangerous." What else *could* it be? What other possible reason could justify keeping such a curse in place?

Everard, keenly aware of Aurelie's rapt attention, lowered his voice, almost forcing her to lean closer. "It is both of those things, but there is a far more sinister force at play. The curse hasn't been lifted because those in power don't *want* it to be lifted. Wisteria has stayed exactly as it is, preserved like an insect in amber, because of a choice made by Prince Aciano and his father. A choice that has been perpetuated by every generation since. Fear of progress has become so ingrained in our society that there is no longer a will to eradicate demons. And so everything remains the same."

Aurelie spoke without thinking, so eager to believe what he was saying. "What would it take to undo the curse?"

Everard smiled. "I was hoping you would ask me that, Aurelie. Because it's where you come into play in all of this."

Despite her fear, Aurelie couldn't help feeling a surge of hope. There was still a chance that she hadn't made a terrible mistake. Still a chance for redemption. "But creating this portal will spawn a *terrible* demon. How is that meant to close the veil between worlds?"

"This portal is a mirror image of one originally created by the court mage, Revenin, which opened the doorway to the demonic realm. *This* portal will send demons back from whence they came, and once Wisteria is free of all demons, we will destroy the portal and end the curse for good." His tone turned almost chiding. "Surely even you can see that one final demon, no matter how powerful, is a sacrifice worth making."

Aurelie had the distinct impression that *she* was also a sacrifice worth making to him. Perhaps she was. If Everard was telling the truth, and a single invention could end demonic activity once and for all, then her life meant little in comparison.

But would that be enough to save the people around her? If Everard was correct and the Crown wanted the curse to stay in place, then anyone defying that order would face severe consequences. There was no possible way Uncle Leo wouldn't be punished for this, even if Aurelie could find a way to contain the demon.

A terrible certainty stole over her. That her act of rebellion, of finding purpose, had spiraled into something dark and treacherous. No matter how much a part of her longed for a world that could progress without the threat of demons, she couldn't shake the feeling that this path would lead to something she couldn't yet comprehend.

Aurelie finally managed to stand, though her eyes never left Kobal. "I am not saying I disagree with your cause, Mr. Everard. If anyone in this kingdom would agree with you, it is me. But I don't exist in a vacuum. I have people around me who deserve to be safe. I can't endanger my uncle. I won't."

Everard rose, towering over her in much the same way Miles did. She hated it.

"I was afraid you might say that. You're principled in your rebellion, Miss Blake. I'll give you that."

She couldn't help lifting her chin.

Everard grinned, his eyes colder than ever. "Which is why I suspected I might need some collateral to help you see things my way. Nothing like a little familial loyalty to force the hand."

CHAPTER 21
AURELIE

AURELIE DIDN'T BEG. SHE DIDN'T EVEN CRY. INSTEAD, SHE locked her knees to keep them from trembling. "What have you done to my uncle?"

Even now, even after admitting how cruel he was, Everard wore what she imagined he considered a pleasant smile. "He's quite well. I can take you to him now, if you'd like."

He showed her to a locked door leading down to a basement, Kobal's rancid breath hot on her back. Aurelie gasped when they reached the bottom. Uncle Leopold was trapped in a cage like a wild animal. He was bound and gagged, though—to her enormous relief—he didn't appear injured.

"Uncle Leo!" She started forward but was stopped by Kobal's low growl.

"He's fine," Everard said over the muffled cries of her uncle. "And he will be released as soon as you do what I've asked."

Uncle Leopold was trying to say something to her, but she couldn't understand him around the gag or the sound of her own blood rushing in her ears. Hot tears coursed down her cheeks. What a useful idiot she'd proven, so eager for the praise of a stranger that she'd allowed herself to be manipulated, allowed her own uncle to be kidnapped.

"I'm so sorry," she managed. "I'll get you out of there, Uncle Leo. I promise."

He shook his head no, tears making his dark eyes glimmer in the dim room, but before she could respond, Everard was shoving her back toward the stairs. "I'm afraid our timeline has been accelerated a bit, given the rising suspicions of the Iron Guard. You have until the end of next week to complete the portal," he said as he sat her down in the armchair again. "All but the final rune, the one that looks vaguely like an open eye."

Aurelie, still blotting at her tears, was at an utter loss. "I'll never have it finished in time. What you're asking is impossible."

"Now, now. You know what they say. Necessity is the mother of invention. I think you'll find having a deadline keeps you far more focused on the task at hand."

Aurelie felt paralyzed by her fear in a way she'd never experienced before. "I'm supposed to go to the Morels' for Yule," she said weakly. "What am I meant to tell them?"

"Tell them whatever you like. You'll stay on campus and work until the job is done. That's what you've been hired for. That's what I require if you wish to see your uncle again."

At the renewed threat to her uncle, Aurelie felt a bit of her nerve return. If she couldn't be brave for herself, she would be brave for him. "Tell me why," Aurelie demanded. "Tell me why you chose *me* for this, when it could have been anyone."

Everard's lips curled in that now-familiar grin. "Anyone? Come now, my dear. You must give yourself more credit than that. Who else could I manipulate so easily? Who else but a young, headstrong girl would be so willing to go against her own morals for her vanity? People think the best victims are the ones with the most to lose, but they're wrong, Miss Blake. The best victims are the ones with very little to lose, because they know how dear that little is."

Aurelie's fear and sorrow crystallized into sheer hatred, and she would have lunged for Everard's throat if Kobal hadn't emitted a low snarl then, baring all its sharp teeth. "I'll make your portal," she ground out. "And you will let my uncle go."

"I do believe that's what I said." Everard rose, clearly finished with her. "Bundle up, Miss Blake. You'll need all your extremities if you plan to finish your work in time. And don't forget to save the final rune."

Cold with shock and utterly lost, Aurelie stumbled out into the snow. Somehow, she made her way to the café she'd been to with Daisy and Des, seeking comfort in the company of other humans.

She ordered a hot chocolate with extra whipped cream and chocolate buttons, though it tasted like ash on her tongue. As hopeless as everything felt, she had no choice but to try to finish the portal, which meant she was about to spend an entire week alone. Even the campus guards had lighter shifts this week. There would be no one to protect her from Everard if he returned, no one to help her when she encountered difficulties, as she no doubt would.

Around her, parents laughed as children guessed what they'd get as their Yule present. Young people with boxes and parcels huddled around tables, none of them eager to get back to the cold walk home. She wouldn't even have Mephisto this week. Before she knew it, she was sobbing into her hot chocolate.

"Are you all right, Miss Blake?"

Aurelie looked up to see one of the demon hunters from the first night she'd met Des, a boy who seemed far too young to be part of the Iron Guard. She took the napkin he held out to her and dabbed her eyes, humiliated to be seen crying in public. "I'm all right, thanks. Just a bad grade on a term paper," she lied. "It was Gareth, wasn't it?"

"That's right." He smiled, pleased she'd remembered him. "I have today off for the holiday. We each get an extra day off this week." His smile faltered. "Except for Des. He insisted on filling in for Daisy."

"Of course he did," she muttered, still wiping her tears.

"Would you like me to walk you home? Daisy told us about the attack near the university last week."

Aurelie hadn't confirmed it, but she was fairly certain she was in no imminent danger from the demons who had been following her. They likely worked for Everard as well. He hadn't explained to her how he had enthralled Kobal, or why he had a connection to the demons he so badly wished to eradicate, because he hadn't needed to. Everard was well aware that once she knew her uncle's life was at stake, she'd do anything Everard commanded. But she also knew today was the last contact she'd have with another kind person for some time.

"That would be nice," she said. She paid for her drink and bundled back into her coat, following Gareth outside. The snow had started to fall again, obscuring nearly everything. There were no coaches out with such poor visibility, so people walked down the middle of the street, appearing out of the swirling white like ghosts.

"Where will you spend Yule?" Aurelie asked as they neared the gates of Wisteria University. Gareth was bigger than Aurelie—nearly everyone was—but his arm felt insubstantial compared to Des's. Des, who was tall like Everard and Miles, but who used his strength to protect people. No wonder he despised her. She'd been making the world less safe for everyone, including him, all these years, and she hadn't even had the wherewithal to realize it.

"A friend of my parents has invited me to spend it with his family, but I'll be working on Yule itself. No rest for the weary, I'm afraid."

Aurelie didn't tell him that she, too, would be working on Yule. She should have been at the Morels', laughing with Kiara about how annoying the other students could be, helping to decorate the family tree.

No. She should have been with Uncle Leopold. She should have known he'd never stay away for so long. Not from the university, and not from her.

"If you see Daisy, wish her a happy Yule for me," she said as they arrived at the gates.

"I will. Have a happy holiday, Miss Blake."

"You as well, Gareth."

He'd almost disappeared into the swirling snow when Aurelie called after him. "And wish Des a happy Yule as well!"

He turned, his smile fading into the white. "I will!"

"I'm not leaving you," Kiara said as she sat on Aurelie's sofa. "I'll tell my father I want to spend Yule here, with you."

"Absolutely not." Aurelie was attempting to coax Mephisto into its cage with a cockroach. So far, nothing was working. "This is your favorite holiday."

"Which I won't be able to enjoy knowing you're here all alone being forced to build the damn portal."

Aurelie gave up on Mephisto and sat down next to Kiara, dropping her head into her hands. "It's no use. Mephisto knows I'm trying to abandon it." The demon, sensing victory, darted into the cage, stole the cockroach, and disappeared into a hole in the wall within seconds.

Kiara spread her hands apologetically. "To be honest, I'm not sure I would have been comfortable handling Mephisto on my own this week."

"I know. It was too much to ask. I'm sorry."

Kiara patted her on the back. "Maybe it's safe here. If Des or Daisy had seen it, surely they would have turned you in by now."

"Maybe, but the Iron Guard has been patrolling frequently around here ever since the attempted attack near the gates." The male *natia* that escaped had been tracked down and killed before anyone was hurt, but Wisteria was on alert once again. She'd seen demon hunters patrolling the area more than usual, though blessedly never Des or Daisy.

"I can be a lookout, then," Kiara said. "Besides, I can help you with the portal. Another set of hands can't hurt, right?"

Another set of hands would be ideal. But she'd already gotten Kiara far too involved in her mess. "I just . . . I can't risk it," she said finally. "I don't have a lot of people in my life, Kiara. But the ones I do mean everything to me."

Kiara looked at her for a long moment as though she were going to argue, but finally she tucked her hair behind her ears and managed a tight smile. "All right, then. I suppose my parents will simply have to put up with me this week, without the cultured Aurelie Blake to buffer me."

Aurelie managed a laugh. "Ah yes, I'm the pinnacle of proper womanhood."

"At least you wear your hair tied back," she said, pressing a quick kiss to Aurelie's cheek. "Be careful while I'm away. And if at any point you change your mind . . ."

Aurelie nodded. "I know where to find you."

When Kiara was gone, Aurelie moved to her desk. All her sketches and work on the portal were in her other workspace, and the thought of making the trek across campus to that old, lonely building made her want to cry again. But none of this was about her. It was about Uncle Leo. She changed into suitable work clothing, including her dingy gray bricoleur coat, and made her way through the snow. She had just entered the building when she heard a clanging from overhead.

Campus had cleared out last night. There was no reason for Professor Sheldrake to still be here. She climbed the stairs to his office and knocked on the closed door.

"Just a minute!" he called.

He opened the door wearing his magnifying glasses, which Aurelie now thought of as part of his face. It was almost jarring when he removed them, his eyes as small and blinky as a mole's when emerging from the earth. "Aurelie! What a pleasant surprise. What are you doing here?"

"I could ask you the same thing," she said as she entered the room. It was slightly less cluttered than usual, to her surprise.

"Oh, just packing up. I'm taking my wife to the country for a few weeks."

"A few weeks?" Aurelie couldn't disguise the panic in her voice. Professor Sheldrake was the only one who could help her with the runes, and with her new, impossible deadline looming, the thought of him being out of reach made her stomach churn.

"Not to worry. I'll be back in mid-January to help you with your project. I expect you'll have made good progress by then."

By mid-January, Aurelie would either have completed the portal and freed her uncle, or she'd be dead. Once again, she felt a confession rising in her throat. She swallowed it before she could drag another innocent down with her.

"I do have one question before you go," she said, sitting on the edge of one of the desks because the chair was covered in books. "What do you know about the demonic curse Florian put on Wisteria?" Sheldrake knew the history as well as anyone, and he was far more willing to talk. If there was any wisdom she could glean, any hole in Everard's story that she could use to her advantage, she needed to hear it.

"Well, as I said, my grandfather was alive during Aciano's reign, but I was still a child when he died. The curse has been as much a part of my life as it has yours."

"What became of Revenin, the court mage?"

"Beheaded, if I recall correctly." He scratched at his bald pate thoughtfully. "Or was it burned at the stake?"

Aurelie almost growled in frustration. "Was there no one else who could remove the curse?"

At that, Professor Sheldrake set down the pliers he was holding and looked up at Aurelie. "Curses aren't so easily broken, young lady. And dark magic is nothing to mess with. Which reminds me. Have you finished your translation?"

"Nearly," she said, trying to keep her tone light. "But surely *someone* must want it removed. Someone with a vested interest in progress."

He shrugged, lifting the pliers again before setting them in the same exact place. "Mages aren't kept at court anymore. Unfashionable, you know." He winked at Aurelie, as though the fashion amongst royalty was ridiculous. "No, no. Magic is all but dead, like my poor runic languages. I know little of curses, Miss Blake. I'm a man of science, not mysticism. My research in magic is purely from an outsider's point of view. At any rate, it's not something I'd go poking too deeply at. Some things are best left buried."

Aurelie nodded. If only she still had that luxury.

"If you need me while I'm away, you can write to me at the Ivy Cottage in Bodlin."

"That's kind. Thank you. I hope you have a lovely holiday, Professor Sheldrake."

"You as well. And I hope you'll take some time to rest this week, child. You've been quite busy, by the look of things."

Aurelie winced. She knew how terrible she looked, with dark circles under her eyes and her work coat covered in oil and coffee stains. "No rest for the weary," she said, thinking of Gareth.

"The weary are the very ones who should rest, my dear. Burn the candle at both ends, and you'll soon find you've run clean out of wax."

CHAPTER 22

DES

REPORTING AURELIE'S DEMON TO COMMANDER YEW WAS one of the hardest things Des had ever forced himself to do, and that was truly saying something. But even if he had been willing to risk his own safety, he couldn't jeopardize Daisy's—nor that of the civilians who would suffer if Aurelie's inventing wasn't stopped. He had been the one to discover her in the first place, the one who had been tasked with watching her, and that meant this was his responsibility. He cursed her uncle for not returning when he was supposed to, for not keeping an eye on her himself. For putting Des in an impossible situation with a girl he was afraid he cared too much for.

It had been late Monday night by the time he made it to Commander Yew's office, but the man seemed to be awake at all hours, writing in files that no one else ever saw, because they were kept locked up.

"Whitlow," he said when Des knocked on his open door. "It's late. What are you doing up?"

"I just came from the university, sir. I need to report a demon consorter."

Yew placed his quill down and leveled Des with his stony gaze. "If this is about Miss Blake—"

"Sir, I saw it myself. Inside her secret laboratory, where she . . ."

He had to swallow before he could say the word. "Where I have cause to believe she *invents* things. She and her professor are working together to create demons, and while they seem to eradicate most of them, there is one living on the Wisteria campus. She needs to be stopped."

There. He'd done it. He'd turned her in. And now he could stop thinking about her and focus on what really mattered.

Unfortunately, there was no immediate relief. Only an awful, sinking dread.

Yew remained silent, that iron gaze never wavering. Finally, he sighed and said, "Take a seat, son."

Des did as he was told, though a strange sensation washed over him. Yew had never called him that before. No one ever had. And he realized in that moment he'd been waiting to hear that word for his entire fucking life.

"Whitlow, you're an excellent guard. I've told you this, again and again, because I've known you since you were a child. You've always needed reassurance that you were doing the right thing, even though I've never met a more diligent and dedicated soldier. So tonight, I'm going to reiterate that you've done the right thing."

Des felt the tension in his shoulders subside a fraction. "Thank you, sir."

"I'm sending you out with the Iron Swords for your first mission. You'll be back in plenty of time for your promotion. In the meantime, stay away from the university. I don't want you feeling the need to check up on that girl. I'll handle her myself."

Des nodded. Aurelie was not his problem any longer. He'd done his duty, the way he always had. Perhaps she'd been put in his life as a test. And if that were the case, he had passed. He was a good man. A good soldier.

So why did he still feel so awful?

He hoped that for once in her life, Daisy wouldn't wait up for him, that he wouldn't have to confront what he'd done. It was easier to pretend that Aurelie would always be in her lab, tinkering with her beakers and hanging up bundles of herbs to dry, writing in her silly notebooks and tying ribbons around her throat. A throat he desperately wanted to kiss. Because apparently he'd lost his mind entirely.

But Daisy was there, as always, curled up and dozing on his bed. In that moment, he wished he loved her as more than a friend. It was impossible now. They knew each other too well, had spent too much time filthy and angry and afraid to allow any sort of romantic feelings to blossom. But life would have been much simpler if they could.

"Hey," he said, nudging her gently. "You're in the wrong bunk, Shaw."

She blinked and curled away from him, clearly not intending to move. With a sigh, he crawled in next to her, wincing as something cold and hard dug into his ribs.

"What is this?" he asked, lifting an iron key from the sheets.

"It's Aurelie's key to the university," Daisy murmured. "I stole it."

"You *what*?"

"Quiet. You'll wake everyone." Daisy finally rolled back toward him. "I took it off of her when she fainted, remember? To let us into the gates?"

"I remember," Des said, voice strained. "I thought you gave it back to her."

"I was going to." She shrugged sheepishly. "Then we saw the demon in her laboratory, and I thought it might be handy to hang on to this."

"Why? Were you expecting me to break onto campus?"

"Probably not. But you never know." Daisy sat up, apparently realizing she wasn't going to get any sleep without an explanation. "Look. Aurelie may have a demon living in her lab, but we don't know what it was doing there. She attempted to kill a *natia*, which means she's not a demon sympathizer."

"Even being sympathetic to one demon is enough," Des said. They both knew the law, both knew the consequences. So did Aurelie.

"But what if her knowledge could be helpful?"

Aurelie was a lot of things, but helpful wasn't one of them. "What do you mean?"

"She has experience with demons, right?"

"She says she doesn't."

Daisy rolled her eyes. "A lie, obviously. But how many civilians do you know of who've encountered demons and lived to tell about it?"

Des thought for a moment. A few, maybe, but none who hadn't been severely injured in the attack. "Point taken. She has knowledge of demons that even we may not." Including *verita*, it seemed. "Nonviolent encounters haven't been studied."

"Right. Because we didn't think they were *possible.* And Aurelie has been living with a demon! She's a scientist, Des. She's smart, and insightful, and we know she's faced demons before, based on her behavior tonight. Isn't there a chance that if she's studying demons, she knows things we don't? Things that might actually help us make Wisteria safer for everyone?"

Des inhaled deeply, trying to quell a rising sense of doom, and let it out slowly. "Yes, Daisy, it's possible. But it's too late. I already turned her in." He held out the key.

Daisy patted his shoulder and climbed out of the bed, ignoring his outstretched hand. "I'm sure if you went to the university first thing tomorrow, you could catch her. But it's entirely up to you, Des. Get rid of it, if you don't think it could be useful. If you don't think there's some chance Aurelie Blake isn't as useless as you claim she is."

"Daisy—"

"Goodnight, Destroyer."

"*Daisy*," Des hissed, but she had already disappeared in the dark.

Thanks to Daisy, Des got no sleep that night, and by mid-morning, he was on his way out of the city with the Iron Swords, no time to visit Aurelie even if he'd wanted to. They were on horseback, which Des, despite his name, had never been truly comfortable with. Even these destriers—black and gray stallions with the hooves of draft horses and withers higher than Des's head—shouldn't have to bear so much weight, though they did it admirably.

He rode next to Aspen, his thoughts returning again and again to Aurelie as he tightened his grip on the iron key tied to a leather thong around his neck, unable to use it but equally unable to leave it behind.

By the time they reached the village, it was dusk, and Des was afraid that they might be too late. If the demon had fed on human flesh already, it could be even larger than when they'd departed that morning. The village, which lay directly between Wisteria City and Hellebore, another large city, didn't have its own Iron Guard, and the platoon in Hellebore was already stretched thin, covering several other outlying villages.

They went directly to the creator's house, where his newly widowed wife and their three children waited. There would be no catching this inventor alive; his illegal activity had cost him the ultimate price.

"If it's all right, I'd like to help question the family," Des said, earning an odd look from Aspen. "I've never collected a witness statement," he explained. The other Iron Swords agreed to wait outside, not wanting to overwhelm the family.

"Be quick. And take notes." The order came from Lieutenant Commander Thorne, a man Des bore grudging respect for but had never liked. Thorne was short and stocky, with a neck nearly as thick as his head. He had the most kills of any hunter in the Iron Guard, and the ego to go along with it.

The young widow, a Mrs. Piper, and her children were huddled together on a sofa, looking as afraid of Des as though he were a demon himself. "It's all right," Des said as he sat in a chair across from them. "We're just here to ask a few questions."

The widow nodded, quietly asking her oldest son to take the other two children upstairs.

"I'll make some tea," Aspen offered, heading off toward the kitchen.

"Can you tell me what happened, Mrs. Piper?" Des said, trying to be as gentle as possible. "Did your husband make something illegal?" Seeing the concern on the woman's face, he tried for a soft smile. "You're not in any trouble. We just need to know for our records, to help prevent things like this from happening again."

"Our well was contaminated," she said, her voice raspy from crying. "Something must have died in it, or . . . I don't know. But we couldn't dig a new well, and we were desperate for clean water."

Unease twisted Des's gut. "So your husband . . . ?"

"He created a filter using sand. I didn't understand how it worked, just that it did. We finally had clean water again. But he decided to tinker with it, to see if he could make it more effective." She broke off in sobs. "He didn't know he'd invented anything. He just wanted to keep us safe!"

"Why didn't you ask for assistance from your local magistrate?"

She released a watery sigh. "This isn't the city, Lieutenant. The local government doesn't have that kind of money. We're on our own."

Des was relieved when Aspen returned with the tea and sat next to the woman, offering her a cloth napkin to dry her tears. He thought of all the vials and jars in Aurelie's laboratory, how he'd assumed everything she worked on was for her own amusement. But Mr. Piper, even the person whose *verita* killed Des's parents . . . who was to say what pushed them to invent. Was it really so terrible to want a better life? If there really was no help from the government, how were people expected to survive hardship?

Another Iron Sword poked his head in the doorway. "Demon's been spotted just south of here. We're going after it."

"Come on," Aspen said to Des, and before he knew what was

happening, they were all back on their horses, heading south at a breakneck speed that allowed for no conversation.

They reached a fenced pasture and dismounted as soon as they saw what they were looking for, the horses balking at the gruesome sound of flesh being torn from bones. The *verita* was in the pasture, stooped over a sheep's carcass, while the rest of the flock was bleating frantically, huddled in a mass as far from the demon as the fence would allow.

Des began to draw his sword but was held back by one of Thorne's gauntleted fists. "Let it pick off a few more before you kill it."

Des, sure he'd heard incorrectly, could only stare at the man blankly.

Aspen stepped up to the fence next to him and waited for Thorne to walk away before leaning toward him. "It's protocol."

"*What's* protocol?"

"To let the demons cause a little extra damage before we kill them."

"What are you talking about? *Why?*"

Aspen stared out at the pasture, where the demon was now loping toward the flock, which broke apart in panic at its approach. Her short hair was ruffled by the passing breeze, her brown eyes seeming untroubled as the demon leapt on its next victim. "It's the Crown," she said, voice low, as though someone might overhear them. "The demons are useful, you see."

Des took a step back.

"Don't look so shocked, Whitlow. If demons didn't damage property every now and again, people would be tempted to start inventing more."

"You mean the king allows this to happen?"

She turned to face him. "Where do you think Commander Yew's orders come from?"

A cold, sinking sensation washed over Des, and he steadied himself against the fence. "And the people?"

"What people?"

"The ones who get slaughtered by demons. Does the king allow that, too?"

She shrugged. "Maybe, every now and then. Better than the entire population of Wisteria, though."

Des gripped the fence so hard the wood splintered.

At that, the demon raised its head and sniffed the wind, as if realizing there was human flesh nearby for the first time. Its large red eyes were like two torches glowing in the darkness.

"Well, no waiting around now. Come on," Aspen said, reaching for her sword. "Time to put all that anger to good use."

That night, after the demon was killed by Lieutenant Commander Thorne and everyone went to a nearby inn to celebrate with beer and war stories, Des made some excuse about feeling ill and headed upstairs.

The truth was, he *did* feel ill, and while a drink may have helped, pretending everything was fine wouldn't. A man had lost his life simply for trying to take care of his family. A woman was trembling in her bed, wondering what it would mean for her family that her husband had died a traitor, perhaps not yet aware that she would get no government assistance because of it. And meanwhile, another farmer had lost half his flock to a demon that could have been killed far sooner.

Was no one else in the Iron Guard bothered by the fact that they risked their lives every day for something their government seemed to *want* to perpetuate? That the Crown found convenient because it kept its citizens in line? He knew it was no coincidence he was learning all this now that he was going to be promoted. No doubt he'd be expected to keep this information to himself, as his superiors did. Just as the king was exerting control over his subjects, Commander Yew was exerting control over the junior guards, who all believed their cause was righteous, if not downright holy.

He fell into a fitful sleep, his dreams dark and disturbing, morphing into a nightmare of the wolflike thrall chasing him down, as defenseless as the sheep in their pasture.

When it finally had him pinned on his back beneath it, Des stared up into two massive red eyes, its hot, putrid breath steaming onto his skin. Just as it was about to sink its teeth into his throat, he reached for Aurelie's key and lashed out, as if that tiny piece of iron could somehow save him.

He woke screaming, the key clenched in his fist, his heart hammering beneath it.

Commander Yew had said he'd take care of Aurelie Blake. But what if she was just another useful tool in his arsenal? What if he knew all along that she was surrounded by demons?

What if he knew, and he was going to let her die anyway?

CHAPTER 23
AURELIE

DESPITE PROFESSOR SHELDRAKE'S WARNING, AURELIE worked herself until she collapsed with exhaustion. With only her and a single guard on campus, she had free rein at the university, which meant more hours to spend on the portal. Even her uncle's servants had been dismissed, unaware that Aurelie was staying behind. Because she hadn't told them. A part of her was relieved: if she created any demons this week, she would endanger no one but herself.

At this point, the portal was little more than a wooden frame, the metal plates at last arranged in the correct pattern before it. Thirty-six large stone blocks were stacked in the corner, though Aurelie couldn't lift a single one on her own. When they'd been delivered by four strong men, she'd had to lie to the guard that they were for Mr. Morel, who was replacing a stone wall near the cemetery. She would need to build a pulley system to get them in the frame, but that alone could take days. What Everard was asking of her was impossible, and perhaps that was the point. Perhaps he wanted to torture her, to prove to her how insignificant her creations were. How insignificant *she* was.

She knew what Kiara would say: that it was time to involve the authorities. But Everard had warned her that if she went to the police, her uncle would die. She had briefly considered telling Daisy, who might be willing to help her. But she would inevitably tell Des, who would kill *her* if he knew the truth. He'd never understand all her lies and deception, not considering demons had murdered his parents. But Aurelie was alone in this world, too, and she couldn't let Uncle Leo die because of her own foolish pride.

Yule was coming in just five days, and Everard, in all his magnanimity, had set her deadline for the day after. She'd spent all of this morning working on the runes, her eyes swimming from staring at old books yellowed with age. More than once, as the hours ticked by with so little progress, she considered inscribing the runes without translating them—but something stopped her every time. She couldn't forget Sheldrake's sharp rebuke when she'd suggested it: *One can't teach common sense.* She was desperate, but she wouldn't give in to panic.

So far, she had put together the following meanings: ancient; thorn; balance; rebirth; shadow; renewal, soul; transformation; portal; broken. Still, every one of those runes had two or three meanings, and she could be translating them entirely wrong, for all she knew.

When her stomach rumbled so loudly she could no longer ignore it, she threw a sheet half-heartedly over the portal and locked up, heading back to her laboratory. She collapsed into her desk chair for a moment, only planning to catch her breath before heading to her uncle's cottage for sustenance, but she'd carelessly left her sketchbook open earlier, and the drawing of the dream demon stared up at her with its awful, blank face.

The *somnia* had been trying to warn her about something; of that, she had no doubt. And given Everard's connection to demons, was it possible it had been trying to warn her about *him*? Everard did want more from her, after all. Had it known about Uncle Leo somehow? The portal?

She closed her eyes and remembered the face of the little female *natia*, the way she'd said, *It's you.* What would have happened if Des hadn't slammed into her then?

She had nearly fallen asleep when she startled at the sound of breaking glass. Mephisto stood at the foot of her desk, next to the now-shattered jar of its seed droppings, blinking innocently.

"Mephisto!"

It scuttled away, tipping over its water bowl in the process.

This was the last thing she had time for. The seeds were tiny, as small as the radish seeds she'd used in Mephisto's creation. She'd started collecting them at the time, afraid to throw them away for fear they might germinate somewhere and sprout into an unknown plant that would reveal what Aurelie had done. Now, it was more habit than anything else that kept her from discarding them.

With a sigh, she carefully picked up the pieces of glass and put them in her waste bin, then scooped up the seeds and placed them in a beaker. She took in the messy room, as disorganized as her own addled brain. Books and sketches were strewn haphazardly over every surface. A pile of dirty laundry nearly to her waist was heaped in one corner. She only had one clean dress left, and her remaining shift was so small it hardly reached her knees.

With another hearty sigh, she tossed her laundry into a basket and made the trek back across campus to her uncle's cottage. The snow was already a foot deep and showed no signs of stopping. She hoped Willoughby was keeping warm in his guardhouse.

Aurelie wasted another hour she didn't have scrubbing her clothing in the large washtub in the servants' work area, then pinned it up on the lines there, stoking the small furnace to dry them. Her underthings and stockings hung at wonky angles, likely to dry as wrinkled as they'd been before she washed them, but at least she wouldn't smell.

Afterward, she rummaged in the pantry and fashioned herself a meal of bread, cheese, and dried sausage, grateful the servants had left the larder somewhat stocked. Sitting in the library, she debated starting a fire but decided it wasn't worth the firewood, considering she couldn't stay and enjoy it. For a moment, she had an overwhelming surge of self-pity, her eyes welling with tears.

Miles and the Applebaum brothers had been right about her. Des, too. She was silly and self-important. She should have listened to Uncle Leo, made herself meek and pliant and married the first man to ask for her hand. She had brought pain and misery to the person she most loved, all because she wanted to prove herself right. And the cruelest irony was that Uncle Leo was the one who had been right all along: she *couldn't* take care of herself. A few weeks unsupervised, and she'd destroyed everything.

But even as she had these thoughts, they rang hollow in her mind. Marrying Miles would only have made both of them miserable for eternity. And now that she'd messed everything up, the least she could do was make it right. She dried her tears on her sleeve and steeled herself for another cold journey across campus. She would have liked to curl up in her bedroom here, but she had too much work to do.

Wrapping her coat tighter around herself as she stepped into the snowy night, Aurelie realized how different it was to be alone by circumstance instead of choice. She enjoyed peace and quiet, but that was only because she was generally surrounded by people and noise. In the absence of those things, Wisteria University no longer felt like the home she'd grown up in. It felt more like a graveyard, the buildings massive tombstones that loomed above her, a tiny mouse in a dangerous world.

Aurelie was nearing Easton Hall when she heard the sound of a man's cheerful whistle. She smiled to herself. Willoughby, making his rounds. He couldn't know she was still on campus; otherwise he'd insist on calling back the servants. But it helped that he was here, too, that she wasn't entirely on her own. Across town, Kiara was cozied up with her family, preparing for Yule. It wasn't too late to fix everything. Not yet.

As she neared her lab, she noticed that one of the other doors on the long hallway was ajar. She hadn't bothered to go in these old, forgotten classrooms for years, having long since plundered them for her own needs. But as she went to close the door, she decided to poke her head in for a minute. It was possible there was something here that could help her, something useful that she hadn't needed previously.

All of the old classrooms were dingy and eerie. They were mostly used for storage now, and in the light of her lamp, furniture hulked under dusty sheets like the ghosts of strange beasts. She heard a scuttling nearby that she attributed to Mephisto or rats; presumably one of them had squeaked through the door at some point in the last day or two.

At the back of the room, she discovered a box of old iron charms that would have been handed out to graduating students at one point. She sifted through them by the light of her oil lamp, smiling at the various shapes: an owl for wisdom, a key for knowledge, a pillar for fortitude. If only they were weapons instead, she thought with a sigh. Still, iron was always handy, especially if one were conjuring demons.

In another box she found small bags of salt, also a graduation gift for seniors back in her parents' days. She didn't use salt on her own demons usually, since she never knew where they'd appear. But it wouldn't hurt to have a little extra on hand.

As she began to unlock the door to her laboratory, she paused at the noises coming from the other side. There was none of Mephisto's scuttling, but clattering and banging, as though someone were ransacking the place. It sounded far larger than anything Mephisto could do, and the demon had no reason to go rummaging around her lab, anyway.

Aurelie racked her brain for what could possibly have gotten into the lab with the door and window locked. There wasn't a rat in the world large enough to make this much commotion, and she couldn't imagine a demon would have gotten in without—

Aurelie gasped and clapped her hand to her mouth as the clattering stopped. She'd been harried when she swept up the seeds Mephisto had scattered, and she couldn't be certain she'd gotten all of them. What if one had landed in the spilled water and germinated?

What if they weren't seeds at all, but eggs?

There was a heavy thud, as though something had leapt down from a height onto the floor. Aurelie frantically scanned herself, looking for anything she could use. Her iron blade was on her desk, of absolutely no use to her. And she was almost certain she was going to need it. Whatever had come from Mephisto's seed was very likely causing this clatter, and from the sound of things, it was far bigger than its creator.

CHAPTER 24

DES

BY THE TIME THEY RETURNED TO THE IRON FORTRESS, DES was exhausted. They'd killed two other *verita* in the three days they'd been gone, both the result of inventions gone awry, when typically they saw only a handful in a month. The third inventor was a woman in her fifties. Unlike the other two, her creation was no accident. She had set fire to her laboratory before they arrived in an attempt to hide the evidence, but what remained was damning. She had been arrested and brought back with them and was now awaiting trial.

Every night when he tried to sleep, Des's thoughts turned to Aurelie. Had she been arrested, like this woman? Or was she still working alone in her laboratory, producing demons? Or was she innocent, as Daisy believed she was? The questions gnawed at him like rats as he tossed and turned in unfamiliar beds.

Now, just a few days before his promotion, Des had been told to take some time off. It was customary for the guards to get an extra day to themselves during Yule week, but Des typically gave his day to Daisy so she could spend more time with her family. This year, she insisted he keep it. As the two caught up, Des tried to casually bring up Aurelie. Daisy, as per usual, wasn't fooled.

"Go check on her," she said as she packed her bag. Her aunt was coming to pick her up soon, and night was already falling.

"Commander Yew told me to stay away from the university," he said as he cleaned his boots, muddy from riding in the country. "Anyway, I thought I might do some research tomorrow."

"All day?"

He grunted in response.

"All right, then after you do this vital research, you could perhaps get yourself a hot chocolate. And if you happen to pass by the university on your way home . . ."

He set his boots down and gave Daisy a kiss on her cheek.

"What was that for?" she asked, touching the spot where he'd kissed her. "In case I haven't been clear, I'm not interested in you that way."

He huffed in indignation. "Don't flatter yourself, Shaw. I was just saying goodbye. I'm looking forward to having you off my back for the next twenty-four hours."

"Don't get too excited. I'll be back for your promotion."

"You'd better be."

He went back to cleaning his boots, then bent over to tuck them into his trunk. As he did so, the iron key slipped out of his collar, dangling before his eyes in what felt like a pointed manner. The key had become something of a talisman the past few days. He found himself squeezing it before bed each night, praying to something he didn't believe in that Aurelie was safe.

The next evening, after exercising, studying, and making a trip to the library, he found himself with hours left before Daisy returned and nothing to fill them. Cursing his friend for putting the idea into his head, he headed for the café with the disgusting hot chocolate.

The entire walk, he told himself he had no plans to visit anyone. He was merely killing time, since he had nothing better to do. But he was struck by how quiet the city was. It had snowed over a foot, and in the still night, the only sounds were the occasional crack of a branch collapsing under the weight of its snowy shroud, or a bark of laughter from one of the nearby pubs.

The café was busy, though not quite as busy as the last time he'd come. He perused the menu, ignoring the stares of the other patrons. A wave of melancholy washed over him, and he ordered Daisy's ridiculous concoction, then proceeded to hardly touch it. It was so sweet it was practically inedible. He left ten minutes later, pretending, as Daisy had suggested, that he just happened to pass by the university, but he couldn't lie to himself. He needed to know what had become of Aurelie. Otherwise, he'd wonder for the rest of his life.

He approached the guardhouse in what he hoped was a casual manner. Perhaps the grandfatherly guard was on duty and would remember him. He could find out where she was without ever alerting her to his presence.

A scream cut through the night, raising all the hairs on Des's body.

It was coming from campus.

Without thinking, Des yanked the leather thong off his neck and unlocked the gate, letting himself inside. He listened intently but could hear no other sounds of distress. He checked the guard tower only to find it cold and empty, before setting off through the campus.

Des froze when the cottage came into view. There wasn't a single light on there, or anywhere else on campus that he could see. Without the aid of the moonlight, he would be in total darkness. Perhaps no one was here this week. Aurelie could have gone somewhere with her uncle for the holiday. They might have given the guards the week off.

Another scream, this one garbled and guttural, coming from near the hall where Aurelie had her laboratory.

Des broke into a run, noting the small sets of footprints leading toward the building. Someone had been here within the past few hours, at least. Someone with tiny feet. And only one person he knew had feet that absurdly small.

He froze when he saw something lying on the steps leading up to the stone building. There was a creature hunched over it, moving in a way that made Des's stomach roil. He'd rarely seen a demon feed, and only once on a human. For a split second, he was sure it was Aurelie lying on the steps, but the body was too large, and he felt a brief wash of relief. The demon raised its head, a dark silhouette in the moonlight, and sniffed the air.

Des ducked behind a statue, slowly pulling his sword from its scabbard. Where the hell had this thing come from? If Aurelie had been foolish enough to summon another demon, he was going to kill her himself. He peeked out again and swore when he realized the demon was gone.

Des approached the body carefully in case the creature decided to come back, his sword raised. He was still several yards away when he realized that it was the kindly older man who spoke so fondly of Aurelie. His stomach had been torn open, his entrails steaming in the night. Des swallowed down the burning sting of bile and tried to piece together what had happened.

Then he saw the shattered glass near the base of the building, and he remembered that Aurelie's basement lab had one single, high window. He cursed again as the pieces began to fall into place.

The demon he and Daisy had seen must have escaped and killed the guard. Now it would grow larger and more dangerous. He could only hope the iron bars were enough to keep it trapped on campus, where presumably there was no one else it could hurt. Aside from him, of course. He should get back to base and round up more guards. He took a step toward the gates and froze.

He could have sworn he'd heard a whimper.

There was no light coming from the shattered window, but he ran to it anyway, calling down. "Is someone there?"

"Des?" It was a plaintive voice, tinged with a mixture of fear and relief.

Something clenched in Des's chest at his name being spoken like that. "Aurelie?"

"It's me. I'm . . . I'm injured."

Demons take him. "How badly?"

"I don't know." A long silence followed.

"Aurelie?"

"I think I need help."

Of course she did. And *he* needed to track down the demon. "Is there anyone else on campus?" he asked.

"No. Just the guard and me."

"Are the grounds completely encircled by iron?"

"Yes."

Good. The demon wouldn't get far, then. "Stay there. I'm coming." Des ran past the guard's body and entered the hall, retracing the steps he'd taken with Daisy and Aurelie. By the time he reached her laboratory, she was sitting outside in the hallway, the shoulder of her dress torn open to reveal several bloody gashes. "What happened?" he asked, crouching beside her, fighting to keep his voice calm.

She shook her head and closed her eyes, releasing a stream of tears. "He's dead, isn't he?"

"The guard?" Des asked. "I'm afraid so."

Aurelie put her hand over her face and sobbed silently. "It's all my fault."

Des's own hands hovered worthlessly near Aurelie's shoulder. The wound looked painful and angry, seeping blood onto the white shift beneath her dress. "We should clean you up," he said, though he knew he was wasting time here. This was why they worked in twos, dammit.

"I'm sorry," she said, wiping her nose on her sleeve. "I tried to stop it when it went for the window, but it was so strong."

"How did a demon get in here, Aurelie?" Des was still hoping there was some miracle explanation, that she hadn't deliberately been conjuring demons.

"A seed," she said nonsensically. "It came from Mephisto."

"Who's Mephisto? What seed?"

Aurelie attempted to push to her feet and immediately slid back down the wall. Was she hurt somewhere else? If she'd been a guard, she'd know to report immediately where she was injured, but Aurelie wasn't a trained soldier. Her face was bloodless, her hands trembling. She was going into shock.

"I'm going to pick you up," Des said, then proceeded to scoop Aurelie into his arms without waiting for a response. Her wound brushed his armor, and she made a small, feeble noise that he wanted to hate, but he found himself readjusting her anyway. He shouldered his way into her destroyed lab and laid her down on the sofa, then glanced around the room for something to clean and bind the wound with.

"There," she said, pointing to a basin and ewer with her good arm. "There are washcloths in the cupboard."

Des rummaged around, trying not to touch any of Aurelie's equipment. For all he knew, there were combustible materials in here, like whatever had caused that explosion.

When he returned to her side with the washcloths and a pitcher of clean water, she had turned toward him slightly. He tried not to stare at where she'd untied the ribbon at her neck, pulling her clothing aside to reveal more of the wound, which ran from the base of her throat to the skin where her chest met her shoulder. Her throat had been mere inches from being torn out.

Des was used to seeing bodies unclothed, though male guards had separate showers from females. Sometimes they changed in front of each other if they were in a hurry, and some people were comfortable enough to walk around naked even if the situation didn't warrant it. But the bodies Des had grown up around were scarred and battle-worn, hardened from training and lean from a controlled diet. He was used to skin tanned from the sun, calloused and blistered from wielding weapons.

Aurelie's body was nothing like that. This was skin that had never seen sunlight, flesh that was soft and unblemished. Even the severe lines of her school dresses couldn't hide the delicate curves beneath. Des swallowed. If Daisy were here, she'd know what to do. But she wasn't, and Des couldn't leave Aurelie bleeding out on her velvet sofa.

He took a washcloth and touched it as gently as he could to the wound, though a part of him felt that she didn't deserve his care.

Aurelie sucked in a breath, catching her lip with her teeth, and Des froze, dragging his gaze up to hers. Her wide green eyes were staring into his, so close he could see the threads of gold in them, the individual droplets of tears on her lashes.

"Is this okay?" he asked, feeling foolish and embarrassed but also as though every part of his body were on fire. Damn her and her ability to disarm him.

She nodded, her lower lip still bearing the dents from where her teeth had dug into it, and Des forced himself to look back at the wound, which he cleaned as best he could, knowing how closely she watched him, how she held her breath against the pain.

When he finished, he helped her sit up. "We should bandage this," he said, unable to explain that she'd need to remove her clothing. When had he become such a damn fool? "I don't think it will need stitches, but we should get you to a doctor anyway."

She shook her head. "No doctors. I have antiseptic. Just give me a moment."

He nodded and she moved past him to her wardrobe, removing a clean shift and another simple dress before disappearing behind a wooden screen. He turned to face away, his hands twisted around the bloodied cloth. "I need to get back out there," he said. "The demon could be anywhere on campus by now."

Aurelie emerged a minute later. She held her unfastened bodice to her chest, her arms only partly in her sleeves. "I can't wrap it myself," she explained, her gaze fixed on the floor. Her cheeks were flushed scarlet against the pallor of shock. "I'm sorry."

He found himself murmuring some sort of acceptance, which

was not what he'd meant to do. He should be berating her for her reckless behavior, should be making it abundantly clear that this time, she *had* killed a man.

Instead, Des took a deep, steadying breath, and approached the chair she was sitting in, as she drew her braid over one slender shoulder and did her best to raise her arm so he could wrap the bandage beneath. He told himself it was like caring for any other wounded guard member, even as the scent of her soap hit him. Orange blossom, he realized, though he had no idea where the knowledge came from.

As he worked, winding the bandage under her arm and across her chest, his knuckles grazed skin he was sure had never been touched by another human before. Not judging by the way Aurelie shuddered, her eyes fluttering closed, though she didn't pull away. It was the most intimate thing Des had ever done, and he wasn't a virgin.

When she turned to look up at him, her face framed by tendrils of dark hair, her eyes still glittering with tears, Des had to stop for a moment to recover himself. Why did he feel so protective of this girl, when she was the one endangering everyone around her?

"What?" he growled, more disgusted with himself than with her.

"How did you get on campus?" she asked.

He'd thought she might properly apologize, or at the very least thank him. But instead, she was asking about logistics. Lucky for her he had been nearby, had been carrying Daisy's stolen key around his neck. Lucky for her he didn't just leave her to bleed out on her own. The audacity she had, to question his actions when he'd saved her life. Twice.

He pulled the bandage tight to stanch the bleeding. Aurelie gave a small whimper that he felt in his soul. He cleared his throat. "Finish getting dressed. Then you can tell me everything that happened while we are on our way back to the fort."

Aurelie rose, fumbling for her bodice as it began to fall. "Our?"

Des turned around again, but not before catching a glimpse of even more of her. Far more than any man should see. It crossed his mind that one day, a man would get to see all of her, and he hated this imaginary man almost as much he hated Aurelie.

"Yes, *our*. I'm going to get backup to kill this demon. And you're going to turn yourself in."

CHAPTER 25
AURELIE

DESPITE THE FURIOUS TONE IN DES'S VOICE, HE HAD THE decency to shield Aurelie's view of Willoughby's body as he escorted her down the steps of Easton Hall. Even still, he couldn't shield her from the stench of his innards, or the sight of blood in the snow. She had worn a scarf around her neck to cover her wound, and she ducked her face into it now, obscuring what she could, though she knew she'd never recover from the guilt of what she'd done.

Des had his sword in one hand, the other slung around Aurelie's waist as he hurried her toward the gate. The demon was still on campus, but she wasn't afraid of it attacking her. Not when it had the opportunity before and went after Willoughby.

When she'd opened the door to her lab with an iron doorstop in one hand and a bag of salt in the other, she'd screamed at the sight. Not only of the demon itself, which was a squat, hunched horror that reminded her of the gargoyles on the clock tower, but also of the absolute destruction it had wrought. There was broken glass everywhere. Books and papers were scattered across the floor, and trampled herbs and flowers littered it like faded confetti. The demon was on her desk, rummaging around as though searching for something, and its red eyes had fixed on her the moment she entered.

But rather than come for her, it had turned its head at some sound Aurelie couldn't hear, its focus on something outside the little window. Her stomach dropped when she heard Willoughby's familiar whistle.

She flew at the demon the same moment it leapt for her window. She managed to grab one of its muscular legs, but it kicked out at her as it punched through the glass, catching her in the chest with its talons. She reeled back at the force of the kick, not realizing at first that it had torn through her dress before it disappeared through the window into the snow. By the time she scrambled onto her desk, one hand pressed to her wound, Willoughby was already screaming.

She'd never erase that sound from her head, she thought as fresh tears stung her eyes. They'd reached the gates, and Des ushered her through with the key she realized now was the one she'd lost the night of the *natia* attack. All this time, he'd kept it, and for what? Why had he come here tonight? Was it mere coincidence that a demon attack occurred when he was close by, or was it as she'd thought before, that *his* presence was also part of the equation? If she could have taken the time to think, she knew she could make sense of all this chaos. But Des was pressing her forward, it was snowing again, and Aurelie could feel the wound in her chest seeping through the bandage.

"Stop," she said finally, when she felt she might faint. "I need to rest."

"There's no time to rest. Not while a demon is loose on the campus."

"All right. I need time to *think*. Surely even demon hunters take a moment to strategize. Or do you just rush in without thinking every time?"

His lip raised in a snarl, but he allowed her to sit down on a bench beneath a streetlamp. She checked under her scarf to be sure the wound wasn't bleeding onto her coat. "What do you need to think about?" he asked. "The story you're going to tell the commander?"

He wasn't entirely wrong, but she felt as though there were puzzle pieces jumbling about in her head, and she needed to fit them together to make sense of all this, just like the pieces of the blasted portal. "Can I at least explain where that demon came from?"

"I'm assuming it's the one that was living in your laboratory," he said.

Aurelie shook her head, horrified at the thought. "No. At least, Mephisto isn't the one who did this. But it was its seed that produced the demon that killed Willoughby."

"What is Mephisto?"

"Mephisto is the demon you saw in my lab, but it's tiny and wouldn't hurt anything larger than a cockroach." Aurelie tilted her head up to look at Des, who was standing in front of her, all traces of the gentle man who had cleaned her wound gone. "I have so much to explain, but I can't do it out here where I'm frozen and bleeding." Indeed, her teeth were chattering audibly, and it was a challenge even to hold still.

"Where do you propose we go?" he asked, his voice strained. She knew he was desperate to get back to the Iron Fortress, to pass her off to someone else. But she couldn't let him do that. Not until he knew the risk to her uncle.

"A pub, a café. Anywhere loud enough for us to speak without being overheard."

Des glanced up the street to a pub. "Fine. You have thirty minutes."

They weren't quite as inconspicuous as Aurelie had hoped. It wasn't entirely Des's fault that he was the largest man in every room he entered, or even that he was wearing his Iron Guard uniform. But he could have at least attempted not to look so angry all the time.

They managed to squeeze onto the end of a long bench side by side, with Aurelie pressed between Des and a drunken man who kept spilling his beer into Aurelie's lap. Eventually, Des's furious glares cut through the man's haze, and he stumbled off somewhere, giving them slightly more room to themselves.

"We should order something," Aurelie said.

"I'm not hungry."

"Fine." She caught the attention of a serving girl, who batted her eyelashes prettily at an oblivious Des.

"Can I get you anything?" she asked him, ignoring Aurelie entirely.

"Two coffees, please," Aurelie said. "And a plate of whatever greasy food you serve here." She noticed Des staring at her. "What? I haven't eaten in hours."

The serving girl rolled her eyes as she walked away. Aurelie shrugged out of her coat and Des took it from her without a word. She kept the scarf around her neck, though it was hotter than a witch's cauldron in there. The wound on her chest ached, and she still hadn't figured out how she was going to convince Des not to turn her in.

"Start talking," Des said when their coffee arrived.

Aurelie noted with disgust that hers had been diluted with milk and sugar. She swapped it for Des's black coffee silently and ignored his arched brow. "I made Mephisto by accident when I was a child," she began, but he stopped her with a look. "What?"

"I don't have time for your life story. Quit stalling."

"It's relevant," she hissed. "Now be quiet and let me speak." She hadn't meant to be quite so bossy, but sheer agony was wreaking havoc on her self-control, always in short supply in Des's presence anyhow. As Aurelie launched into the story of Mephisto's creation, then her history of inventing, Des tried to cut her off several times. But the words were spilling out of her now, and she couldn't stop even if she wanted to. They were surrounded by people, but they'd all eventually lost interest in the demon hunter and his companion. The more she spoke, the more riveted Des became, his coffee untouched. When she finally reached the part about Everard, he stopped her with a hand on her thigh. The unexpected contact made her flinch.

"What?" she asked, then followed his gaze to the door. Aurelie felt herself blanch when she realized that the man himself had just entered the pub. It couldn't be a coincidence. "What's he doing here?" she whispered, unconsciously shrinking closer to Des. Everard would think she had gone to the authorities, she realized. She couldn't let him see her with Des.

Without thinking, she pulled her scarf over her hair and scrambled off the bench. They were in the back of the pub, giving her only a precious few moments to leave unnoticed.

"Where are you going?" Des asked, but she'd already donned her coat and was darting for the back door.

The cold night air sobered her instantly. She let out a strangled gasp when she saw Kobal's silhouette skulking down the street. Before she could back into the pub, she felt Des's presence behind her.

"That's the demon that killed Barley," Des whispered, sending a shiver up Aurelie's spine.

"It's Everard's thrall," she whispered back. "He must have posted it back here in case I tried to leave." She turned to face him. "We can't be seen together, Des. He can't know I told you the truth, or he'll kill my uncle."

"Your uncle?"

She hadn't gotten to Leo yet, hadn't explained that she was being blackmailed to finish an invention. "Just listen to me. You have to go back inside. I'll talk to Everard, throw him off my scent for a few minutes."

"I'm not leaving you alone with that monster."

She wasn't sure if he meant Kobal or Everard, and she felt a strange surge of warmth even as she wanted to throttle him for not listening to her. When the demon turned back toward them, she turned and shoved him into the shadow of the doorway. He must not have been expecting it, because he grabbed her as he stumbled back.

Once again, she found herself pressed against him. She looked up. The confusion on his face was bizarrely endearing. "Just stay here."

Aurelie didn't wait for a response before she made her way into the alley behind the pub. Kobal turned instantly, scenting the air, and began to trot toward her. She walked out to meet it, anything to get it away from where Des was hiding.

She knew it wasn't going to kill her, but Des didn't. She could practically feel him tensing behind her, preparing to follow. But Everard must have been alerted the moment Kobal scented her, because he came around the side of the building just seconds later.

"What are you doing here?" Everard demanded. Aurelie fought the urge to look toward Des, to make sure he was properly hidden.

"I came for dinner," she said, taking a few more steps down the alley away from Des.

"Dinner? Does that mean you've finished your work?"

"Not yet," she said. "But I still need to eat. My uncle's staff left for Yule. There's nothing edible at his cottage."

"If you're not finished, how did you summon the demon?"

Aurelie's brain scrambled to understand. "You know about the demon?"

Everard, perhaps realizing that he'd said too much, grabbed her by the injured shoulder. Aurelie cried out in pain, earning a strange look from Everard.

"It wounded you?" he asked.

Why was this surprising to him? What link could Everard have to these creatures, that he knew when they were summoned? "Not on purpose," Aurelie said. "I don't think so, anyhow. I was trying to stop it from going after the guard."

Everard swore under his breath. "All right. You'll need to come with me."

"What? Why?" This time, Aurelie couldn't keep her eyes from darting to the pub. Everard followed her gaze, but he must have assumed she was only searching for the safety of other people, because he didn't pursue it.

"Demons often have low levels of venom in their teeth and claws, and only I have the antivenom to treat it."

Perhaps that explained why the wound was throbbing so badly. It hadn't been that deep, though she'd noticed angry red streaks radiating from it when she changed earlier. "Can't you bring it to me?" she asked, thinking that Des was never going to allow her to leave with Everard. Not when he was planning to turn her in.

"There's no time for that. You're small. The venom will work quickly on you." Without waiting for her response, he placed his hand on the small of her back and began pressing her away from the pub. Away from Des.

Aurelie had no choice but to go with him. Kobal had moved past them toward the pub, still sniffing the air, and Aurelie was afraid it had picked up Des's scent. Without thought, she pitched herself forward as though she'd stumbled and collapsed into the snow, landing on her bad shoulder and sending shooting pains throughout her chest.

"Foolish girl," Everard muttered. He scooped her up, and despite the fact that she was dizzy from the pain in her shoulder, Aurelie couldn't help noticing how rough he was compared to Des, despite not being as strong. Which meant Des must have taken extra care with her.

The thought warmed her, even as her vision faded to black.

CHAPTER 26
AURELIE

BEFORE EVEN OPENING HER EYES, AURELIE KNEW SHE WASN'T at home. The room smelled of burnt feathers and spicy incense, a strange and utterly revolting combination. She sat up, then immediately regretted it. Her head ached and her shoulder was still throbbing, though the pain had dulled somewhat.

"Ah. You're awake."

Aurelie collapsed back at the sound of Everard's voice, as the past few hours came rushing back in. A part of her wished she had died earlier, or that it had been a bad dream at the very least.

"I'm awake," she said to the ceiling, which, along with the rest of the room, was painted a shade of green so dark it was nearly black.

"Good. That means the antivenom did the trick. That wound was rather nasty."

Aurelie's hand flew to her chest, which was bandaged in thick linen. She glanced down and recoiled in horror when she realized she was clad in only her shift.

"Oh, calm down," Everard said, as if it were truly nothing that she was near-naked in a strange man's house. "I have no interest in women. Or men, for that matter. It was all rather perfunctory."

Aurelie's stomach twisted at the thought of Everard handling her unconscious body. It had unsettled her in an entirely different way to have Des touching her bare skin, one she would prefer to contemplate more when she was alone, not in Everard's creepy, narrow house in her shift.

She sat up again, slower this time. "I'd like to go home now."

"Yes, I imagine you would. But you'll stay here until I'm sure you're not going to die. And until you've explained to me how you happened to conjure a demon without finishing your project."

Aurelie reached for a glass of water on the nightstand, her mouth suddenly parched. "I'm not going to die," she said.

"Not tonight, perhaps."

She cast Everard a glare. "Is my uncle safe?"

"Why wouldn't he be? Your deadline hasn't passed yet. But if you don't start revealing the source of your demon, I can't guarantee that either of you will live to see morning."

Aurelie wondered what had become of Des, if he'd followed her here or gone back to the fortress. She wasn't about to mention him to Everard, though a part of her feared she'd endangered him tonight without ever meaning to.

"It was an accident," she said. "My demon, Mephisto, produces seeds. I've never planted them. I suppose I must have known on some level that they could be dangerous. But one germinated by accident, and when I returned to my laboratory, the demon was loose, destroying everything it could get its claws on."

"Yes, they'll do that. Especially *tenebra* like the one you conjured."

"*Tenebra*?" Aurelie said, rubbing at her temples.

"Demons of darkness, conjured without intention. They are the rarest of demons, and arguably the worst."

"Why didn't it go after me?" Aurelie asked. "It could have killed me, but it went straight for Willoughby." Why had *none* of the demons she'd encountered recently tried to kill her?

"I can't say for certain. Perhaps it didn't see you as a threat."

She couldn't be satisfied with that answer. Not when Willoughby hardly posed more of a threat than she did. She needed to think, which was almost impossible with Everard so close and her head pounding and Kobal somewhere in the house.

"Like you, I've been studying demons for many years, Aurelie. And like you, I understand that they are not inherently evil. Impulsive and destructive, yes, but that is their nature. It's possible this demon only wanted freedom, and the guard was in his way."

"If you believe demons aren't evil, then why go to all this trouble to build the portal?"

"My goal is to break the curse. To allow this kingdom to flourish once again."

Aurelie didn't respond. She didn't believe him anymore.

"I need to know how you conjured that demon, Aurelie."

"It was an *accident*," she repeated.

"But the seeds. There are more of them, surely?"

Aurelie shook her head, hoping he didn't see through the lie. The fact that Everard seemed to know so much about demons, to perhaps have some sort of connection to them, but didn't know how she'd managed to create the *tenebra*, was information worth squirreling away. "I've always discarded them."

"Then this demon, Mephisto. It's still at the university?"

"It lives in my laboratory."

"Then you'll bring it to me."

Aurelie took another sip of water to disguise her fear. What could a man who controlled a demon like Kobal want with her tiny companion? "Mephisto is my friend," she said.

His lips curled in a pitying frown. "I know it seems that way, but believe me, your demon doesn't think of you as a friend. You are a means to an end for Mephisto."

And what end could that possibly be? It had never demanded anything from her, other than cockroaches. There was no loyalty from it, the way one might expect from a dog. It was more like a cat, choosing affection when it wanted to and just as capriciously rejecting her. Even knocking over the jar of seeds felt like something a cat would do, casually causing chaos just for the sake of it.

"I can see the wheels in your head turning, Aurelie," Everard said. "Don't forget about your uncle. Surely he means more to you than a demon."

In that moment, Aurelie had never despised someone the way she did Everard, his callousness, his willingness to treat people as disposable for his own aims. Aurelie had made terrible mistakes, but she would never deliberately hurt someone.

A lump rose in her throat. Just beneath her disgust for Everard was a pit of shame, knowing that she had allowed herself to be used so easily. That she had gone against her better judgment under the foolhardy belief that she could change the world.

She clenched her jaw, pushing down the tears and humiliation. Now was hardly the time to wallow in self-pity. Everard was a despicable human being, but he was also the only person she'd ever met who knew more about demons than she did. If there was anything useful she could glean from him that could help save her uncle, or at least convince Des not to turn her in, she had to learn it.

"I've never understood the connection between demons and invention," she said truthfully, neatly changing the subject. "The way it's always been explained to me, Florian's curse *caused* the link. But if he wanted more innovation, why connect it to demons? It's completely counterintuitive."

Everard gestured to the foot of Aurelie's bed, as though asking permission to sit down. She drew her knees all the way up to her chest, earning a look from Everard that suggested she was being overly dramatic. "Invention has always been linked to something . . . otherworldly, shall we say. From the simplest contraption to the grandest marvel, innovation can't exist without a fragment of untamed potential, a spark of chaotic energy."

Aurelie couldn't help but smile at this. She had always thought of the tingling sensation in her body that came with a new idea as something that came from outside of her, though she wouldn't have called it "otherworldly." Just . . . special.

"When human minds shape this potential into reality, they unknowingly invite the attention of that other realm, separated from us by what many refer to as a veil, though of course it can't be touched or even seen."

"Like the atmosphere?"

Everard nodded. "Exactly. When the veil is fully intact, humans are entirely unaware of this other realm. Their hopes, their dreams, their ideas all feel as though they are organic manifestations of their own minds."

Aurelie wondered what it must be like to live in that world, where people simply had an idea and then acted upon it. On the one hand, it sounded like unbridled freedom to her stifled imagination. On the other, if no one had to think of the immediate consequences of their actions, it could lead to a lot of unanticipated destruction down the road.

"But," Everard continued, "when the veil is thinned to the point of near absence, the dark entities themselves—known to us as demons—are physically able to enter our world."

"So Florian didn't know he was thinning the veil?"

"Ah, now we get to the heart of the matter. Aciano, as the first-born, was always assumed to be the future king, and he was raised accordingly. His father, though never admitting it, secretly blamed Florian for his wife's death during his delivery, and the resentment he had for his second son never wavered. When the twins were twenty-five, Aciano and the king fell ill with a disease brought back to Wisteria by a trader, and there was speculation that Florian was behind it."

Aurelie couldn't help scoffing. That wasn't how diseases worked.

Everard inclined his head, as though acknowledging her unspoken words. "Those who knew Florian were skeptical; he'd never shown any interest in ruling, and he spent as little time at home as possible. But his father had also begun to pressure him to stay closer to Wisteria, knowing Aciano would need his brother's council when he became king.

"With both Aciano and the king near death, Florian had no choice but to step in and help run the kingdom, and he proved an insightful ruler. Having traveled abroad, Florian knew of the war brewing outside Wisteria between two neighboring kingdoms, Callerya and Samara. Callerya had invested heavily in its military, and many believed it would invade Samara. Samara, a small kingdom between Callerya and Wisteria, would likely fall easily, and Wisteria could be next.

"Florian wanted to go on a diplomatic mission to Callerya to try to stop the war, but Aciano, who knew little of what went on beyond his kingdom's borders, refused to allow it. Soon after, the king died, and Aciano made a slow but steady recovery. At his coronation, he named Florian his chief advisor. When Callerya eventually did invade Samara and all hope of a diplomatic solution fizzled, Florian begged his brother to invest in their defenses. There was a risk, of course. Weapons have always been the most dangerous of inventions. Demons are naturally drawn to chaos and destruction, and nothing pushes against the veil more than war.

"But instead of meeting Callerya in combat, Aciano constructed a wall to protect the kingdom, not only keeping enemy forces out, but keeping Wisterian citizens within. Furious at his brother's weakness, Florian began to work on his own inventions, including the weapons he believed could save Wisteria."

"So he did commit treason?"

"Not at first. It was Revenin, the court mage, who came to Florian with a proposal. Aciano despised magic as much as he hated innovation, and he was in the process of decreeing magic illegal. But Revenin had a proposition, one that could save magic *and* Wisteria: Florian's soul in exchange for access to the power trapped on the other side of the veil."

At that, Aurelie's heart sank.

"Then Florian *is* the reason we have demons, the reason Wisterians are isolated and unable to progress," she said bitterly. "Aciano was right to ban magic. If he'd done it sooner, none of this would have happened."

"A closed-minded person might believe that, I suppose."

"That kind of reasoning might have worked on me before. But I can't pretend that being open-minded is all that matters anymore. Not when it's led me to this."

Everard placed his hand on Aurelie's leg, causing her to shrink back farther. "Aurelie, by building this portal, you can right all the wrongs caused by Florian and Aciano. Please don't tell me that no longer matters to you."

She shook her head, desperate to be back in her lab, away from this horrible place. "I don't understand. You claim to want to rid this world of demons, and yet you're obviously linked to them somehow. You have a *thrall.* How can you even be sure Kobal is under your control?"

"A thrall is linked to its master. Anything it might do to hurt me would ultimately hurt itself."

Aurelie lowered her gaze. That was certainly information worth holding on to. "You never finished telling me about the curse."

"Ah, yes. Aciano, alerted to his brother's plans by the council, decreed that all inventing would be banned in Wisteria, hoping to stop Florian before he could start. He was too late—Revenin had already opened the portal, thinning the veil enough that each invention would bring a new demon through, and Florian's soul had already been bartered. But access to the power on the other side of the veil never came. Aciano had the portal destroyed, murdered Revenin, and attempted to have his brother tried for treason. But

Florian escaped, and all Aciano could do was uphold the ban on invention and magic, in the hopes that the veil would hold."

"What happened with Callerya?"

Everard spread his hands in a shrug. "They no longer wanted a kingdom cursed with demons."

"You told me before that the king won't put an end to the curse because he uses it to control people."

Everard nodded. "Yes."

"And this new portal will strengthen the veil again, so that demons remain on the other side."

"Correct."

"Then why are you suddenly in such a hurry? If this is so important to you, shouldn't you want it done correctly, not haphazardly?"

"I do, Aurelie. But every new invention spawns another demon, and every new demon thins the veil that much more. In the past few months, it has grown increasingly weak. Wisterians are suffering, which has caused them to invent more than ever before. If we don't do this now, it will be too late. Once the veil is broken entirely, it cannot be restored."

The words were like a physical blow. Aurelie fell back against the pillows, suddenly exhausted in every way. "Blood and bones," she murmured.

"Indeed. So you see now why we can't afford to lose any time? And why Mephisto must be contained, before it produces more demons?"

Aurelie nodded.

"You should get home," Everard said, rising. "I'd offer to escort you back, but something tells me you'd prefer to go alone."

"Just tell me one more thing."

"Yes?"

"What does a person lose when they offer up their soul?"

Everard's smile was almost sad. "Their humanity. Their mortality. They lose the ability to love or be loved, to show mercy or compassion. I know some people would see those as weaknesses. They might think the deal is worth the making in the end."

"And was it?" Aurelie asked, realizing that she hadn't understood Florian at all. That whatever they had in common was far less important than their differences.

Everard sighed, his blue eyes focused on something invisible, or perhaps on nothing. "I suppose we can't know for sure."

"Why not?" she whispered.

He brought his gaze to hers, and the absence of any emotion there was more chilling than anything she had seen in him before. "Because we have not yet reached the end."

CHAPTER 27
DES

DES WATCHED IN HORROR AS EVERARD SCOOPED AURELIE off the ground, leaving behind a bloody streak on the white snow. He was torn between following her to a townhouse he would never find again on his own, returning to the campus to eliminate the demon, and going back to the fortress for reinforcements.

He couldn't tell Commander Yew what he'd seen tonight, not without risking Aurelie's life. Even if they could find the townhouse, any attack on Everard could result in her death—and her uncle's, apparently. But he was fairly certain that whatever Everard wanted from her now, he wasn't going to kill her unless he felt threatened. Not when she was clearly useful to him.

With no good options, he clenched his jaw and set out for the fortress. He wrestled with telling Daisy the entire way back, and yet he shouldn't have. She was already waiting on his bed when he returned, excited to tell him about her trip to visit her cousin. But her mood shifted immediately when she saw the look on Des's face, the blood staining his tunic.

"We need backup," she said after he had quickly explained. Everyone else was asleep, but Des knew she was right. He woke Jasper, but it was Daisy who insisted they tell Gareth.

"He's just a kid," Des argued.

"Yeah, one who cares about Aurelie."

Des didn't like it, but he didn't know who else he could trust. They met at the obstacle course, armed and buzzing with adrenaline.

"Where do we go first?" Daisy asked. "Should we split up?"

Des shook his head. "The demon is contained, but it's already fed on human flesh. We need to stay together until it's taken care of."

"What about Aurelie?" Gareth asked.

"I think she's as safe as she can be right now. Everard seemed to know how to treat her wound. For now, we need to focus on the demon." Having seen what this demon did to the guard, he knew this was not going to be an easy dispatch. All the more reason they couldn't let this monster loose in the city.

Des let himself on campus first, followed by Jasper. "We're going to see if we can find any sign of the demon," he said to Daisy through the iron bars. "You two stay here and watch the gates. Whistle if you see anything."

Daisy nodded, and Des spared a moment to worry that he'd endangered the only person in the world he cared about by bringing her into this. At the same time, she never would have let him come without her.

Des and Jasper made their way back toward Easton Hall with their swords drawn. The guard's body was still on the stairs, and a set of clawed footprints in the snow trailed away from it toward the back of campus, where Des and Aspen had encountered Aurelie and Professor Sheldrake.

As the old clock tower came into view, Des held up a closed fist, sure he'd caught a whiff of brimstone. They ducked behind a tree and peered out. Sure enough, the demon was near the door leading into the building. It had grown considerably since Des first saw it, though it retained its same ghoulish shape.

Des motioned to Jasper to stay put while he went after the demon. It wouldn't do any good for them both to become cornered or trapped. Inside, the building was dark and dank. He followed the demon's trail of brimstone up a winding, narrow staircase, his sword raised in front of him.

He reached the top floor without seeing any evidence of the demon. Afraid it may have doubled back behind him, he decided to do a quick sweep of the floor. Then he'd find a window and warn Jasper that it was heading his way.

He entered what appeared to be a professor's office, though it was far messier than Aurelie's lab. Des bumped his head on a contraption hanging from the ceiling and flinched. This had to be Professor Sheldrake's office, and based on the oddities here, it certainly looked like he was producing demons. But he didn't have time to worry about that now. He felt a cold breeze reach him and noted that the window was open, a pair of yellowing curtains flapping noisily. He had a feeling it hadn't been open before.

Des hurried across the room to the window and looked down. For a moment, he didn't see Jasper, and his heart rate began to tick up. Then he located him, standing near an old well in the courtyard below. He was waving somewhat madly at Des.

He looked up.

At first, he thought it was one of the gargoyles adorning the older buildings on campus. Then the creature moved, so swiftly Des shouted an obscenity and ducked back into the room, knocking his head against the windowsill.

The demon burst in after him. Des stumbled backward into a desk, sending paperwork flying. The creature was enormous, the size of a full-grown man, its muscular frame a near match for Des's. During their demonic studies classes, Des had heard of all types of demons, but this had to be among the largest. If it fed on Des, it might become a record setter. He couldn't allow this thing to escape.

Des charged, hoping to catch it off guard, but the demon was smarter than it looked. It leaped sideways, knocking over a mirror. Glass shattered, littering the floor, but the demon crunched over it without flinching. It growled at Des, its fangs smeared with blood and gore. Des's stomach turned. The remnants of the guard's intestines.

He charged again, this time nearly catching the demon's shoulder, but it managed to scramble away on all fours, rushing back out the door. Des grunted and hurtled after it, praying he could get to it before it reached the stairwell.

He was too slow. The demon ricocheted off the walls, making far better time than Des could on two legs.

"Jasper! Get ready!" He doubted his partner could hear him, but he had to give some kind of warning. Des was breathless as he reached the bottom of the stairwell, his legs burning from the effort.

By the time he reached the snowy courtyard, the demon was perched on top of the old well, Jasper only a few yards away.

"This thing is huge!" he shouted at Des, who could only nod wordlessly. "Any ideas?"

Des joined Jasper, wishing they could regroup but too afraid to let this thing out of his sight. "It's not interested in fighting, from what I can tell," Des panted. "It keeps running away, not toward."

"Maybe it's full," Jasper deadpanned.

"We can't get to it while it's on that damn well," Des said. "I'm going to climb up toward it. When it jumps down, try to hit it with whatever you can." He wished he'd brought some iron-tipped arrows, but they weren't typically necessary for close-range combat.

Jasper nodded, assuming a fighting stance, and Des approached the well, his eyes trained on the red glare of the demon. It bared its teeth again, emitting a foul stench Des hadn't noticed in the commotion upstairs. Its skin was gray and warty, like a toad's, its hands and feet almost humanlike, aside from its claws. If he had more time, he'd capture this thing and study it. It was unlike any other *verita* he'd encountered. He couldn't guess at any invention it might be related to, and a horrified part of him wondered if it even *was* a *verita*.

As Des got closer, the demon did as he expected: it leapt over him, heading for Jasper, or at least for the path behind him.

Des dove with his sword, missing the demon by centimeters. When he hit the snow, the wind left him in a rush, and he could only wheeze for Jasper to run.

Someone shouted. Des staggered to his feet in time to see the demon rounding on him. He reached for his sword, realized he'd dropped it when he fell, and braced himself for impact.

A blade whizzed through the air and hit the demon between the shoulder blades. It was a killing blow. Or at least it should have been.

The demon roared in fury, but instead of going for Des, it turned to the person who'd thrown the blade.

Aurelie. Her arm was still outstretched, as if she couldn't quite believe what she'd done, but she yelped in fear as the demon rounded on her.

What the hell was she doing here? Why was she *always* in the midst of danger?

Des scrambled to his feet and grabbed his sword, unable to understand what he was seeing. The demon, still snarling, was circling Aurelie. But it should be *dead*. Des had never known a demon to survive direct contact with iron before. Jasper looked to Des as if he had some idea what to do next, but he was at a loss. The demon would attack Aurelie far faster than he could reach it.

As if things weren't dire enough, Daisy and Gareth came running into the courtyard then, distracting the demon momentarily.

"Why did you abandon your post?" Des demanded as he waved them over to his side, never taking his eyes off Aurelie.

"We tried to stop Aurelie from coming in, but she wouldn't listen," Daisy said.

"She hit it with that blade," Jasper said, joining them. "It should be dead."

Meanwhile, Aurelie and the demon were doing a strange dance. She was unarmed. The demon should have finished her by now. But it seemed to be warring with itself, taking a step forward and then backing off again.

"A little help here?" Aurelie said out of the side of her mouth.

If an iron blade wasn't enough to kill this thing, what would be? He was going to have to decapitate it, and the only way to do that was to approach and risk Aurelie in the process.

"What do we do?" Daisy asked, her voice tinged with a slight edge of fear. She was a good soldier, but she obviously cared about Aurelie.

"The well is filled with salt water," Aurelie said, still slowly turning as the demon moved around her. "I'm going to try to lure it there."

“Aurelie, I am ordering you not to—”

“Do you have a better idea?” she hissed at Des. To his dismay, she was already moving toward the well, the demon keeping pace.

It was a ludicrous idea, but if Aurelie could at least get the well between the demon and herself, he might have a shot of getting to it before it got her. He began to make his own slow movements in their direction. As he got closer, he could hear Aurelie saying something under her breath, though he couldn’t make out the words. The demon, as though somehow understanding her, was cocking its hideous head from side to side. As she skirted the well, the demon approached, placing its forelegs on the edge as though to leap over it toward her.

It was now or never. Des rushed forward with his sword raised. By the time the demon realized what he was doing, he was upon it. He drove his sword up through the demon’s chin, releasing a spray of green blood that hissed and steamed as it landed in the snow. Caught off-balance—though still not disappearing like it fucking should—the demon toppled over into the well with an ear-splitting screech.

They knew the moment it hit the water, because a massive green cloud of toxic air rose out of the well, causing Des and Aurelie to reel backward.

Before he’d even had a chance to process, he was running toward her. “Are you all right?” he asked, his eyes skimming every inch of her for signs of damage.

“I’m okay,” she said, taking a step back, and he realized that he was crowding her.

He forced himself to move away. Somehow, she appeared perfectly fine. It was a miracle she'd been able to throw a blade at all, considering the shape she'd been in earlier.

Which begged the question, where the hell had she learned to throw a blade like that?

Then Gareth, Jasper, and Daisy were all there, crowding around them, Gareth peering into the well and noting that the demon was gone. As if that hadn't been obvious already.

Jasper was patting Des on the arm, and Daisy was doing her own assessment of Aurelie, but her eyes never left his.

"Come on," Des said when his heart rate had returned to normal. "You have more explaining to do. And this time we're doing it in your uncle's cottage. I'm guessing he has a bottle of something a little stronger than tea."

While Aurelie went to turn on a few gas lamps in the otherwise dark cottage, Daisy started a fire in the sitting room. Jasper and Gareth went to find something to eat, and Des glowered into the kindling flames.

"You could at least look a little relieved," Daisy said as she joined him on the settee. "The demon is dead and Aurelie is alive. And at the moment, no one knows what happened here besides us."

"A guard is also dead, Daisy. We're going to have to report it. He probably has a family, maybe even children or grandchildren." It was never easy to pass along such news. He dragged his hand down his face. "What if he has grandchildren?"

Daisy patted him on the back. "Well, at least I found this." She pulled a bottle of amber-colored liquid off a nearby bar cart.

"First good news I've heard all day." Des yanked out the crystal stopper while Daisy fetched two glasses. "What are we going to tell Commander Yew?"

"Why do we have to tell him anything? Can't Aurelie do it?" Daisy asked, though her tone lacked conviction.

"Aurelie must decline that particular suggestion."

Des looked up to find Aurelie standing in the doorway, at least having the decency to appear contrite for a change. Gareth and Jasper still hadn't returned. "And why's that?"

Aurelie glanced at Daisy.

"Whatever you have to say to me can be said in front of Daisy, as well as the others. They know everything I learned tonight."

"And do they know about my uncle?" she asked, taking a seat in one of the armchairs. Daisy handed her a glass of whiskey, which she took wordlessly.

"As much as I know. Everard has him, I take it."

Aurelie nodded, took a sip of the whiskey, and instantly began to cough. Des suspected she'd never tasted hard alcohol before. "Yes," she said when she'd regained her composure. Jasper and Gareth entered and sat down on the floor, and Des felt a stab of affection for his fellow guards. The Iron Guard might be viewed as a form of imprisonment to some, but for Des, it was family.

"Everard asked me to build something for him," Aurelie explained. "At first, I thought he wanted it for political reasons."

"And you were willing to help him?" Des asked, not sure why he still found her actions so appalling. He'd known from the moment he laid eyes on her that she was trouble.

Aurelie glanced away, taking another sip of whiskey, wincing at the burn. "I was. I didn't know what he was like, then. But yes,

I'm an inventor, and I let my pride get the best of me. I wanted the opportunity to create something great, to change the world."

Des shook his head, disgusted with Aurelie, and even more with himself. She was the antithesis of what the Iron Guard stood for. She had put her own individual desires above the safety of everyone in Wisteria, all for grandeur and recognition. And he had helped her.

"I know what you think of me," Aurelie murmured. She said it directly to Des, making him feel as though they were the only two people in the room, especially when her eyes locked with his. He couldn't help remembering the feeling of her soft flesh beneath his hands, the way he wanted to sink his fingers into her. How could he desire someone so selfish?

Why would someone so selfish risk her life for someone she clearly despised?

"You have no idea what I think of you," he rasped.

"For what it's worth, Everard told me it would be the end of demons in Wisteria. I would never have taken the job if I didn't think it would do some good."

Des wanted to hate her. What kind of naïve fool would believe such an obvious lie? But it wasn't entirely her fault she was so gullible. She'd been shut off from reality her entire life. All she knew was what she'd read in books. Her only real experience with demons was a small, rodent-like creature that had never tried to hurt her.

He remembered how she'd thrown the blade and knew he was lying to himself. She'd definitely encountered her share of demons.

"How could an invention be the end of demons?" Gareth asked. "I didn't think that was even possible."

"That's because it's not," Des muttered. "Everard lied to her, obviously. And now he has her uncle, which means that Aurelie is going to go through with this madness no matter the cost."

"That's not—"

"It's a nice thought," Jasper said, cutting Aurelie off. "But the Iron Guard exists precisely for this reason. *We* keep Wisteria safe. And it sounds like if we get rid of this Everard, your uncle will be safe, too."

Aurelie tipped her head back and groaned in exasperation. "Do you know how many demons are currently in Wisteria? Because Everard does. Do you know that demons have venom, and that there's an antidote? Everard has it. Do you know what *tenebra* are, or that the king could lift the curse on the kingdom but chooses not to?"

Doubt twisted in Des's gut. He'd never have believed her before. But after what Aspen had told him . . .

"The only thing Everard doesn't know is that I have more of Mephisto's seeds, which I'll destroy tonight." Aurelie took an impressive gulp of whiskey and met Des's eyes. "And if you help me finish the portal, then whatever monster it unleashes could be the very last demon any of us ever has to face again."

CHAPTER 28
AURELIE

AURELIE FOUND MEPHISTO CURLED UP ON AN OCHRE VELVET pillow on her sofa when she returned to her lab, looking rather pitiful and bedraggled. Fortunately, it perked up at her arrival, running to greet her with its funny, snakelike gait, legs akimbo, mustache and eyebrows trailing behind it like minute streamers.

Breathing in the familiar scent of her lab—lavender and rosemary, old wood, the various tinctures and tonics she'd created—Aurelie wished she could stay here forever. Wherever she ended up, she would miss sleeping on her forest-green sofa, the way the light slanted through the single high window, how quiet it was in the basement. She would miss her books and her shabby rugs, her solitude.

It was close to midnight, and Aurelie was simultaneously exhausted and restless. While the others had eaten the food Gareth and Jasper scrounged up, she tried to convince Des, the last hold-out, why they needed to keep all of this a secret from Commander Yew. Why if they helped her finish the portal in the next few days, they'd all survive whatever punishment Commander Yew could dream up, because there would be no more need for an Iron Guard at that point.

In the end, they'd agreed to continue the conversation tomorrow, because the guards were all expected to be present during morning roll call. Aurelie had no idea if she'd done enough to save her uncle, but she now believed Everard that the veil was thinner than ever. There was no other way to explain why the *tenebra* hadn't been killed by *two* iron blades. That, at least, had seemed to rattle Des.

She spent over an hour cleaning the mess the demon had left, sweeping up glass and salvaging whatever she could. She put a wooden board in front of the shattered window to keep out as much draft as possible. Finally, she came to her last task. Aurelie lit her stove, then unceremoniously dumped all of Mephisto's seeds into the flames.

The demon watched with unblinking red eyes. If the seeds were eggs, did Mephisto know? Had it deliberately germinated one? If so, why? It had never shown any proclivity for evil before. Could it even have known what its seeds would produce? It didn't try to stop her from destroying these ones, but there were more where they had come from. All she needed to do was feed Mephisto a few more cockroaches.

She thought back to how the *tenebra* had circled her instead of killing her. She'd tried to reason with it, but unlike the *somnia* and the *natia*, it didn't seem capable of communicating with her mentally. Still, it hadn't wanted to hurt her, that much was clear.

Aurelie stripped out of her dress, which was bloodstained and reeked of Everard's bedsheets. She wasn't sure any amount of washing could undo the damage, and she shoved it into the Load Lightener for now, where at least she wouldn't have to smell it.

Padding across the laboratory, she caught her reflection in her standing mirror and sighed. Her shift hung loosely off her injured shoulder, revealing Everard's bandage. At least the wound had stopped bleeding, and any exhaustion she now felt was unrelated to demon venom. But her hair was a mass of tangles and there were smears of blood on her arm. She washed herself brusquely and changed into her last clean shift, though it was agony to raise her left arm higher than her shoulder. Finally, she reached for her hairbrush and pulled it through the tangles, ready to succumb to the siren song of her sofa, when she heard a light knock on her door.

Aurelie was so startled she dropped the brush, which clattered on the wooden floorboards. There wasn't anyone left on campus. She'd seen the Iron Guard members leave. Kiara would never be out this late at night. And the only campus guard was dead. A lump formed in her throat. She didn't believe in ghosts, but she had the sudden horrible thought that Willoughby was on the other side of that door, his intestines pooled at his feet, his eyes full of accusation and betrayal.

"Open up, Aurelie. It's me," Des called from the hallway.

Blood and bones, he still hadn't given back her blasted key! "What are you doing here?" she replied, reaching for her robe. Her shift was indecently short, and he'd seen more than enough of her earlier. The last thing she needed was one of Des's lectures, but she had a feeling that was exactly what he was here for.

When she opened the door, Des was leaning against the frame, looking as shattered as she felt. She knew she'd put him through hell tonight. What she didn't understand was why he wasn't in bed, asleep. "I needed to speak to you."

"I thought we agreed to continue the conversation in the morning," she said as he shuffled past her, collapsing onto her sofa as she had done mere minutes ago. He was so large there was no room for her to sit down, so she perched on her desk chair, hoping this would be quick.

"This isn't about Everard," he said, glancing with half-hearted interest around the room. When he flinched and pushed himself back against the sofa cushions, Aurelie's gaze followed his to the corner.

The corner where Mephisto was nosing around in its empty bowl, searching for cockroach remnants. Would the dratted demon never learn when to make itself scarce?

"It's all right," Aurelie said, stooping to pick up Mephisto, which snarled as she attempted to wrangle all its legs. "As long as I feed it and don't try to cage it, it's perfectly harmless."

Des looked horrified as she approached, almost as squeamish as the boy she'd had to "rescue" from a mouse in one of the classrooms several months ago. "Keep it away from me."

Aurelie couldn't help the grin that quirked her lips as she dangled Mephisto in Des's face. "Aw, come on. A big, strong almost–lieutenant commander can't possibly be afraid of a little demon."

Des scowled at her, but she'd learned that he was more bark than bite. Even if he despised her for getting him into this mess, she was confident he would never hurt her. Not after saving her life twice.

"Oh, very well." She set Mephisto down and it scuttled off through a crack in the wall. "Better?" she asked.

Des nodded stiffly, a faint blush staining his cheeks. She knew she shouldn't embarrass him like this, not when she needed him on her side, but it was so tempting. When he wasn't being an insufferable ass, he was almost charming. Almost.

"If you're finished fooling around, I have something serious to talk to you about."

Aurelie returned to her desk and sat down, doing her best to look as solemn as Des.

"First off, I wanted to thank you for what you did earlier."

She arched an eyebrow in question.

"I don't think I could have killed that demon on my own."

The compliment was so unexpected Aurelie could only blush and murmur, "You're welcome."

His mouth twitched in a half grin. "Someday you'll have to explain how you learned to throw like that."

"Of course. Just as soon as I come up with an answer." Their eyes met for a moment, something unspoken passing between them. His jaw was shadowed with stubble, his hair mussed, and there was something in his gaze that made her want to comfort him. He looked lost, so young and yet so weary at the same time.

He blinked first, as though the prolonged eye contact was as difficult for him as it was for her.

"What did you want to tell me?" she asked.

"I had some free time earlier, so I went to the archives in the Iron Fortress to do some research." He noticed her raised eyebrows and scowled. "Yes, Aurelie, even clods like me can do research."

"For the record, I don't think you're a clod," she said. "I tend to get a little carried away with my words when I'm upset."

"Go on. You can say it. You're not the first person to tell me I'm stu—"

Aurelie rose again and stepped closer to Des. "I do *not* think that," she said, more vehemently than she intended.

"No?"

She shook her head, reeling a bit. She told herself it was the whiskey, though it had been hours since she consumed it. "No. I'm not so sheltered and naïve as to think there is only one kind of intelligence in this world, Des. Besides, there are *plenty* of clods at this institution."

He stared at her for a minute, his expression inscrutable. "At any rate, I felt—what I said at the café, about being an orphan . . ."

She waved a dismissive hand. "It's fine. I overreacted."

". . . it led me to look at the demon-related deaths from the year you were born." He sighed and held out a piece of paper. "I found this."

The parchment was scrawled with handwritten names and dates. Aurelie skimmed it, wondering what could possibly interest her about this, when her gaze snagged on the name *Blake.* It was written twice.

Once for each of her parents.

Dr. Claudine Blake; Dr. Liam Blake. Cause of death: verita *attack.*

Aurelie scanned the paper over and over, as if some other explanation would materialize. "I don't understand," she said finally. "My parents died in a carriage accident. I was there." True, she had been unconscious for much of it, but she would have remembered a demon. Besides, Uncle Leo had confirmed it when he picked her up from the police station that evening. It was what everyone had said at the funeral. *A tragic accident. A broken harness, a frenzied horse. There was nothing anyone could have done.*

"I don't know for certain what happened," Des said, his voice gentle in a way Aurelie wouldn't have expected. "But my guess is that your uncle didn't want you to end up in the Iron Guard, so he bribed someone to let you stay with him. It's happened before."

Aurelie tried to swallow down the tears clogging her throat, not wanting to cry in front of Des. He already thought the worst of her; what must he think now that he knew she'd dodged her duty to Wisteria? She handed the paper back to him, her hand trembling. "I don't know what to say."

"There's nothing to say. I just wanted you to have all the information before you decide what to do next."

"What to do next? From what you're saying, my uncle has done far more for me than I could have ever imagined. I have to save him, Des."

Instead of responding, he ran his hands through his hair, which had grown long enough that he looked a little less like a soldier. He had gone back to the barracks and changed into a tunic and breeches, though he still had his sword with him, and Aurelie had the impression that no matter what Des did, even if they somehow managed to eradicate demons, he would always be this way. He'd been a guard since he could walk. Perhaps he didn't *want* anything else. "I just thought I should be the one to tell you. I thought you had a right to know the truth."

She nodded. "Thank you."

He shrugged. "Who knows. Maybe you'll decide to join the Iron Guard after all. You know more about demons than anyone I've ever met."

She winced, guilty as charged. "I'm hoping that won't be an issue, once I complete the portal."

Des's brow furrowed. "I don't understand. How can you trust that Everard is who he says he is? What if he's lying to you? He's obviously using dark magic. He can make his house disappear at will. He has a *thrall*, for Aciano's sake."

"A thrall that could very well be his weakness. Everard said—"

"Another lie!"

Aurelie dropped her head into her hands. She couldn't go over all this again. Not without a lot of sleep and even more coffee. "I don't know, Des. But he has my uncle, and the only way you'll stop me from trying to save him is by locking me up. So if that's what you have to do . . ." She took another step toward him, holding her arms out in front of her. "Arrest me now."

Des exhaled through his nostrils. "You know I'm not going to do that. I don't even have the authority to do that." He rose, towering over her, reminding her once again how much bigger he was. "I should get back. It's been a long day and tomorrow will be no different."

She planned to walk to the door and let him out, but her feet weren't cooperating. She craned her neck to look up at him, suddenly unsure if she even wanted him to go. Ever since her uncle left, Aurelie had been in a heightened state of awareness, subconsciously vigilant for danger. But when Des was nearby, she could relax, if only a little. If there was any danger, he would handle it.

She thought she hated how small she felt around him, but she wasn't so sure now. Perhaps she felt a pull toward him not in spite of his size, but because of it. He had the power to ruin her life, and yet she felt so safe with him. It made no sense. In a laboratory experiment, she would never be able to duplicate these results. And yet here they were.

"Thank you," she said again. "I know you didn't want any of this, that I've made your life worse in innumerable ways. It was never my intention."

"So you're *unintentionally* a huge pain in my ass? Is that supposed to make me feel better?"

Aurelie glanced up to see that he was smiling down at her, and something about his kindness made tears well in her eyes. Tears she hadn't even seen coming. Before she could murmur an apology, Des's hand rose, tentatively.

"Hey," he said, one calloused finger sliding against her cheek, catching her tears as they fell. "Don't cry."

"I didn't mean to," she said, laughing at her own foolishness, hardly able to process the fact that he was comforting her. "I think it's all just been too much lately. And now my uncle, the only person who cares whether I live or die, is in danger . . ." She broke down completely, her entire body racked with unanticipated sobs. She turned away in embarrassment. "I'm so sorry. I'm a blubbering mess. You should go."

"I'm not leaving you alone like this," Des said, and even though she was humiliated for appearing this weak in front of him, the words were exactly what she wanted to hear. She found a handkerchief and wiped her face, still turned away from him.

"I'm alone all the time, Des. Honestly, it's my preferred state."

"I don't believe that," he said, so close behind her that she felt his breath on the crown of her head. "If it was, you wouldn't keep company with demons."

"Maybe it's for the best. Maybe demons like me better than people," she whispered.

Another laugh, a soft puff of air. And then, in a voice like honey, "Impossible. Not when I like you so damn much."

CHAPTER 29
DES

DES WASN'T SURE WHERE THE WORDS HAD COME FROM. HE felt as though he were in some strange dream, and that dream-Des had wrested control from real-Des, doing and saying things he never would in the waking world.

It wasn't as if he had never comforted a woman before; Daisy's tears came as easily as her smiles. But that was akin to reassuring a sister, a best friend. Until tonight, he would have called Aurelie more nemesis than friend, and yet the more he learned about her, the stronger their connection grew. From her single-minded determination—wrong-headed though it may be—to her loyalty to her ability to take even the worst news in stride, he recognized himself in her in a way he could never have expected.

The fact that she was, without a doubt, the most beautiful woman he'd ever seen didn't hurt.

Aurelie stood with her back to him, her hair hanging in dark waves down to where the robe was tied around her waist. Tied up like a damned present, just waiting to be unwrapped. He was desperate to see more of her, and he was also painfully aware that if he did, he might lose his voice entirely.

She turned, tilting her chin up to look him in the eye. Her pale cheeks gleamed with tears, and hell if her skin wasn't the softest thing he'd ever touched. Aurelie didn't seem surprised by his nearness, though he'd approached her silently. And even more surprising, she didn't back away.

"You can't possibly like me, Des. Not knowing how our parents died, not knowing what I do in this very room."

There was a challenge in her green eyes, but Des couldn't keep his gaze from her mouth. Was this the real reason he'd come here tonight? Was it because some part of him knew that when he turned her in a second time, she'd never forgive him? That he'd never have the opportunity to do what he'd been dreaming of for weeks? He'd certainly never be alone with her again, because he wouldn't be foolish enough to give in to the temptation a second time. Not now that he knew how weak his defenses really were when there was no one else around to stop him.

He *should* hate her for what she'd done. But he didn't.

For once, he gave in to his basest, most selfish desires and pressed his thumb against that lush lower lip that had been tormenting him for weeks, eliciting a small gasp.

Startled at his own daring, he started to pull his hand away, but she caught him, pinning his thumb in place. Her fingers were much too small to wrap all the way around his wrist. They stared at each other for a moment, both willing the other to step away first.

Was it possible she wanted him, too? *No.* She was turning his weakness to her advantage, more likely. Perhaps she believed she was manipulating him into agreeing to her absurd scheme.

But if that were the case, he was no longer sure he cared.

With his free hand, he reached for a strand of her hair, twining it around his fingers. He was at the brink of his self-control. If she moved at all, he was going to wrap her hair around his fist and never let go.

She stayed perfectly still, as if she knew his thoughts. But then, ever so slowly, she took the pad of his thumb between her teeth, nipping it.

Des closed his eyes against the sensation. It was such a small point of contact, and yet he felt it everywhere. Instead of pulling away from him, she stepped closer, releasing his wrist to place her hands on his shoulders. She had to stand on her tiptoes to do so.

Feeling as unsteady as a colt, he brought his hands to her waist, circling it easily. The silky fabric glided over the bare skin beneath, causing all sorts of inappropriate thoughts to flood his mind. No, he could never do the things he desired with Aurelie. She wasn't a guard. She wasn't even a typical civilian. She was a woman who would marry someone proper, educated. She would dedicate herself to one man for the rest of her life. A man like Miles Viridian, that spineless scarecrow, who wouldn't know how to please Aurelie if his life depended on it.

But instead of shrinking from his touch, she leaned into it. She moved one hand to his neck, tugging him down in a silent entreaty.

It was so easy to lift her and set her down on the edge of the desk, bringing her face closer to his as he moved toward her. And then those soft lips were pressed against his, and Des's hands were tangled in her long hair, and she was making breathless noises that made him nearly crazy with longing.

It took all of his training as a guard, every last shred of self-control, to pull away and step back. "Aurelie," he said, voice strained.

She looked up at him, her robe slipping off one pale shoulder, revealing the bandage covering the raw wounds on her otherwise flawless skin. He wanted to kill someone for allowing this to happen to her, though he knew it was her fault as much as anyone else's. How could she be so careless with herself? Didn't she realize how precious she was? The space between her thighs was empty, as if she was waiting for him to fill it, and yet he couldn't bring himself to step forward.

"We can't," he managed. The words he was *supposed* to say, though he'd had to tear them out of his own throat. At least he'd caught himself before it was too late.

"Why not?" she asked, looking genuinely bewildered.

Des had never been more flummoxed by a question in all his life. "You're a lady?" he said weakly.

She tipped her head to the side and smiled. "Am I."

"In theory," he said, unable to fight the grin on his own face.

In response, she untied the sash around her waist, letting her robe slip off her shoulders onto the desk. Des dropped his head back and groaned, forcing himself to look away from her. Laughing at the absurdity of this situation, of how easily he could be undone by a beautiful woman in a silk shift. An obscenely short shift, he now realized.

She tucked her legs underneath herself until she was on her knees, bringing them nearly eye to eye. "Des. Look at me."

He complied too easily, drinking her in, exposing himself to the shameful knowledge of how defenseless he was when it came to Aurelie. Her shift was just transparent enough to hint at everything underneath, and something about that was even more intoxicating than her bare skin.

"I am a grown woman. I am capable of deciding what I can and cannot do. So if you don't want me, you simply need to say so. But don't fall back on some vague notion of what's proper or appropriate. *We* can do whatever *we* wa—"

He caught her mouth with his, his hands cupping her face, and he felt her smile against him. It faded as he pulled her to him, her legs wrapping around his waist. He walked backward to the sofa until it hit his calves, sitting as gently as he could, bringing her with him so that she straddled his lap. She giggled, reminding him of the first time they'd met.

"What's so funny?" he asked, pressing back to meet her eyes, suddenly insecure.

"It's nothing," she said, catching her bottom lip in her teeth.

He somehow resisted the urge to claim that lip for himself. "You giggled at me like that once before, the first time we met. What is it?"

Her cheeks flushed crimson. "Your . . . sword. It's just . . . larger than I expected."

Now it was Des's turn to laugh.

"I like you like this," she said, cupping one hand to his jaw. "I like you so much more than I thought I could." She seemed as stunned to be saying the words as he was to hear them.

"I like you, too."

She leaned forward, her lips barely skimming his ear. "Are you certain?" she whispered, and though he thought the answer was rather obvious, he could hear the fear in her voice.

He smiled, adjusting her on his lap, and she gasped. "Does that answer your question, Aurelie?"

She replied with another kiss, bolder this time, her tongue darting past his lips to taste him. He sensed she'd never done this before, but she wasn't shy and timid like he might have expected. She was curious, studying him, her hands skimming over his muscles, her own body reacting in response to his. If he had all the time in the world, he might have allowed her to explore him forever, because it felt so fucking good.

When she rocked against him, he inhaled sharply, already at the brink of his self-control. She smiled as she repeated the motion, and though he was trying his very hardest to be a gentleman, he couldn't stop himself from touching her, too. "Is this okay?" he whispered as his hand skimmed up her side.

She nodded, her own breath hitching at the sensation. She was exquisite, soft and pliant, and yet somehow in complete control. He buried his face in the crook of her neck, inhaling her orange-blossom scent as if he could memorize it.

And for once in his life, there was no one there to make fun of him later, to tease him for falling for the prim and proper bookish girl. The girl who had risked her life for his. The one who made friends with demons.

The thought was like a bucket of ice water on his entire body, freezing him involuntarily.

Aurelie sensed the change immediately and sat back, her eyes searching his. "What happened? Am I doing this wrong?"

He laughed at the absurdity of her question. A few more minutes, and he might have lost himself entirely without even removing his trousers. *Not* that he was going to remove his trousers. "You're perfect," he murmured, his stomach already clenched against the thought of leaving her. "But I really do need to get back to the barracks. And you need to rest." He slid the strap of her shift back into place. "This wound won't heal otherwise."

She studied him for another moment, clearly distrustful, but finally she nodded and scooted herself off his lap. He closed his eyes and took in a shaky breath, willing his body into submission before he rose again.

She bent to retrieve her robe, and he was grateful when she put it back on. Otherwise he wasn't sure he'd make it out the door. "Can you do one thing for me, Des?"

In that moment, he would have said yes to almost anything.

"Tomorrow, can you train me how to use a sword? Whatever ends up happening with the portal, it's going to create one hell of a demon. And I need to know how to fight it."

She was too brave for her own good, he thought, and she'd never be able to lift a sword with her injured shoulder. "You need to rest and heal. Get some sleep. I'll see you tomorrow."

She opened the door for him, then stopped him with a hesitant hand. "Des, what's going to happen now?"

Did she mean with the portal, or with him? Either way, he had no idea what the answer was. And because he was as much a coward as she was brave, he bent down and kissed her beautiful lips one last time. It was exquisitely bittersweet, knowing he'd never be satisfied by anything less ever again. "Goodnight, Aurelie Blake."

"Goodnight, Destroyer Whitlow."

He returned her smile, but inside, he felt a twist of dread. Because she wasn't wrong. Des was going to destroy this girl, one way or another. And he was going to destroy himself in the process.

CHAPTER 30
AURELIE

THE SOUND OF DES'S FOOTSTEPS DISAPPEARING DOWN THE hall echoed the beating of Aurelie's heart. She couldn't reconcile the Des who'd just left her with the man she'd met weeks ago in a café. Stranger still, she couldn't reconcile *herself.*

How, in a matter of days, had she gone from serious, studious Aurelie to a woman who willingly disrobed in front of a man? Where had she gotten the nerve to kiss him, never mind the gumption to proclaim her right to do so? She became a different person around Des, and the thought was both intriguing and terrifying. Aurelie had always known she contained multitudes, but this particular one had shown up out of nowhere, with rather shocking notions.

She placed a finger to her lower lip where Des had touched her, and smiled.

Mephisto had been smart enough to remain scarce until now, but it emerged cautiously from a crack in the baseboard and snuggled into its favorite pillow. Aurelie, suddenly exhausted, joined it on the sofa.

But though her body ached nearly everywhere now that it was devoid of adrenaline, she couldn't fall asleep. They still only had days to finish the portal, and while Des and Jasper would certainly come in handy when it came to moving the stone slabs, she hadn't finished with the runes. She had assured them that this project would solve all of their problems, but she didn't know that for certain. Des was right: it would be foolish to trust Everard, a man who consorted with demons and knew things no one else seemed to. The possibility of him being *right* haunted her. What if this was all it took—one final invention to rid their society of demons. What if she could save more than her uncle? What if no other child had to lose their parents the way she and Des had?

Aurelie actively avoided recalling the worst day of her life, but now when she closed her eyes, she allowed herself to travel back in time to the seat of a carriage she shared with her mother and father. They didn't leave their village often, and there was an undercurrent of excitement all that morning. Aurelie had been wearing her favorite dress, plaid with a white collar and a smart bow at her throat. It had belonged to her mother when she was a little girl, carefully preserved over the years in tissue paper. Aurelie could still remember when her mother presented it to her the week before.

"This was my favorite when I was your age," she'd said as she held it up to Aurelie's chest. "Would you like to wear it to visit your uncle?"

Aurelie had nodded, her wide green eyes tracking her mother's every move. Claudine wore simple dresses that were almost always covered by a smock or apron, because she spent most of her time working in her own laboratory or in the garden. Her hair, a few shades lighter than Aurelie's, was usually tied into a knot at the nape of her neck, though it was constantly slipping free.

Her father, Liam, came into the room then and smiled as Aurelie held up the dress for him.

"Mama says I can wear it to meet Uncle."

Her father, who was always easy with his smiles, had frowned, causing Aurelie to look to her mother, who gave a tight shake of her head. But by the time they were on their way to Wisteria University, her father was back to his usual, lighthearted self, and Aurelie chattered away between her mother and father about heaven only knew what. She'd been so indulged, so beloved, and she'd never appreciated it until they were gone.

The carriage had come to a stop, still in the countryside. Aurelie heard the driver say something, felt the shift as he stepped down from the carriage. Her father lifted the curtain and peered outside, ducking back in a second later, his face pale.

"What is it?" her mother had asked. By then, her father had removed a dagger from his pocket. Her parents began to argue, something they rarely did, and Aurelie had felt herself growing impatient. She remembered her father opening the door, against her mother's wishes, her mother's cry. "Liam!"

Only now, as she screwed her eyes tighter, the scene playing out in slow motion in her head, she realized it was possible she'd misheard her mother. Perhaps she hadn't screamed her father's name, but instead . . .

Demon!

Aurelie cried out, her eyes flying open, trying not to remember the next few moments but unable to stop herself. Her father, ripped from the carriage, his garbled scream. Aurelie pressed her hands to her ears as she had then, felt the weight of her mother's body over her, before she, too, was torn away. Aurelie somehow had the presence of mind to lift the seat and crawl into the boot beneath, where she was found later by a man she'd always believed to be a police officer.

Now, with the clarity of hindsight, she realized he was a member of the Iron Guard.

Aurelie swiped away the tears streaming down her cheeks. How could she have blocked out such important memories for so many years? Perhaps it was her mind's way of protecting her, but it had also kept her ignorant of so much. She had never seen the demon; that much she knew. The entry in Des's logbook had said it was a *verita* attack. Which meant someone like her had likely caused her parents' deaths.

Aurelie realized too late she was going to be sick. She only made it halfway to the garbage bin before she lost what little she'd eaten at the pub so many hours ago. Demons take her, she'd been such an absolute fool. She knew, if nothing else, that her own demons had never killed anyone. She'd never let them escape. But eventually, she would have conjured something beyond her capabilities, and then what? Had she truly expected someone else to risk their life to stop it? Her own selfishness brought up another bout of sick, though she managed to get this round into the bin.

When her stomach was empty, she cleaned up her mess and rinsed out her mouth, crawling under her blankets. How could Des possibly like her, knowing what she'd done? What she was continuing to do? What she still *wanted* to do, even knowing how dangerous it was. Why had she been cursed to love something so terrible? Her body was racked by violent shivers until she finally fell asleep, with Mephisto curled up by her head, keeping watch over its creator as though it knew, somehow, that it would not exist without her.

When Aurelie awoke to a single beam of sunlight through the boarded-up window, she immediately wished to be unconscious. Her head pounded, from the whiskey or the vomiting or the fever caused by her wounds, or perhaps a combination of all three. But she'd never go back to sleep now. She pushed the board aside far enough to let some light—and some very cold air—into the room.

Aurelie removed the bandage on her chest gingerly, wincing as she peeled it away from her skin. The angry red streaks were gone, but the wounds were still raw and gaping. She likely needed stitches, though that would require visiting a physician. She was going to have three jagged scars cutting above her left breast, but she deserved them for what she'd done to Willoughby. He had no family, as far as she knew, which was why he had been working during the holiday. But surely there were people who would miss him, who deserved to know what happened to him.

If it weren't for Uncle Leo, she would have turned herself in to Commander Yew. She made a new vow: if she managed to make it through this, she would. How could she live with herself otherwise?

With the new bandage in place, Aurelie dressed and steeled herself for the walk across campus to the cottage. Fortunately, the guards had removed Willoughby's body at some point last night, but the snow was still stained pink with his blood. Aurelie forced herself to bear witness to it, to not look away from what she'd done. Her tears froze on her cheeks as she passed.

Inside the cottage, she lit a fire in the library and another in the kitchen to make tea for the others. They had promised to come as soon as possible, but she had no idea when that would be. She sipped her tea in the library with the notes scattered before her on the floor. Her fever had left her lucid dreaming for most of the night, which meant she was still exhausted, but she'd also managed to translate several more runes in her altered state.

By the time the guards arrived, it was nearly noon. They let themselves in with the key they'd stolen, which meant Aurelie didn't hear them until they were tromping down her uncle's hallway in their heavy boots.

Aurelie rose and greeted them one by one, first Daisy, then Jasper. She noticed Gareth was missing and frowned. Des filed in last, and the moment their eyes met, she felt heat rush to her cheeks. It was impossible to tell what he was thinking when he acknowledged her with a curt nod.

Daisy proceeded directly to the tea service Aurelie had set out and helped herself to a cup of sugar with a splash of tea, while Jasper took an armchair. Des apparently intended to stand as far from Aurelie as possible. He leaned against a wall with his arms folded over his chest.

"Can I assume from your presence you've agreed to help me?" Aurelie asked.

"Gareth was the first to volunteer," Daisy said.

Des tore his gaze from Aurelie to look at Daisy. "And I forbade it."

"He tried to forbid me, too," Jasper added. "Unfortunately for him, he hasn't been promoted yet."

Aurelie nodded. "I see. So the three of you will help?"

"Yule is Thursday," Des said, as if they weren't all aware. "My promotion is scheduled for Wednesday. And as far as I understand it, you need to complete this portal by Friday."

"That's correct."

"We all have shifts in the coming days," Des said. "We have Yule off, but we have to work a twenty-four-hour shift starting tonight. We're on a skeleton crew this week."

"I'll take whatever help I can get," Aurelie said. "Thank you for being here."

Des and Jasper nodded. Daisy, bless her, smiled.

"Erm, right. I suppose I'm in charge of all this, aren't I?" Aurelie laughed awkwardly and gestured to the notes scattered on the floor. "These runes are, I believe, the key to activating the portal. I think my time is best spent trying to interpret the rest of them, since I have, at this point, at least some familiarity with Elder Vansion."

The only person who seemed to have any idea what she was talking about was Daisy, who nodded for her to continue. Perhaps she was simply being encouraging.

"For Jasper and Des, it would be extremely helpful if you'd begin placing the stones into the frame. They are quite heavy and I'm not sure Daisy or I will be of much use there. Though of course you are welcome to help them," she added hastily, nodding to Daisy.

"That's all right. Is there something else I can help with?"

"We need to affix the metal plates to the stones. I've tried out several methods and have found an adhesive that I believe will work best."

"Go on," Des said when she hesitated.

"Well, I tested a gelatin-based glue, but it's not particularly waterproof. Not that there will be water involved, necessarily, but one never knows. I've also been experimenting with my slug elixir, though I lack a large supply of slugs, so unfortunately, I will have to put that project on hold. Something to keep in mind for the future, though. Then there are the plant-based glues, of course. Pine pitch, which *is* waterproof. I've done some trials with a certain type of mistletoe. Oh! And there's a bacterium which I believe . . ."

Aurelie looked up to find all three guards staring at her.

She cleared her throat. "I believe acacia resin will work best."

"Acacia resin it is," Daisy said with a grin.

"Excellent." She glanced at Des to find him watching her intently, his brow furrowed, his arms still folded across his chest as though he were deliberately guarding his heart. She remembered the way his muscles had felt beneath her hands, reddened, and stooped to gather her papers. She'd tied the bow at her throat extra tight today, to make up for her utter lack of control yesterday. "Very well. I'll take you all to my workshop and let you get to it, then."

"Jasper knows the way," Des said, shooting a pointed look at the other guards. "I'd like to speak with Aurelie for a moment, if you don't mind getting started."

Jasper nodded, but not before Aurelie caught him and Daisy sharing a glance that seemed a little too knowing for her liking. Des wouldn't have told them about what happened last night, surely. He hardly communicated in anything other than grunts and commands. But when Daisy turned on the threshold and winked at Aurelie, she knew they at least had some inkling of what had transpired.

When the others were gone, Aurelie—her cheeks still burning with embarrassment—picked up the tea tray and headed toward the kitchen. She could feel Des behind her, his warm, looming presence. He followed silently until she'd placed the tray on the counter and began to fill the sink with water.

"Aurelie."

"Hm?"

"Turn around and look at me, please."

"I'd rather not."

She thought she heard him chuckle lightly. "Why not?"

"Because you'll see how flushed I am, and I would hate for you to think it has anything to do with you."

He made a low noise in his throat. "It has nothing to do with me, then?"

She fiddled with a dishcloth. "Nothing whatsoever."

When his hand skimmed her waist, she nearly dropped the teacup she was preparing to wash.

"What are you doing?" she whispered.

His voice was a murmur tickling her ear. "Nothing whatsoever."

This time she did drop the teacup. Fortunately, it landed in a sink full of soapy water, but Aurelie gasped anyway. The next thing she knew, Des had spun her around in his arms, and her soapy hands went to his chest to steady herself.

He must have seen the shock on her face because he started to step back. "I'm sorry. I don't know what came over me."

She gripped his shoulders, pulling him back to her. "Don't apologize. I just . . . I wasn't sure what today would be like." She bit her lip and dropped her gaze, only to feel his finger under her chin, lifting it.

"I wasn't either," he said gently. "I knew I should turn you in. If you were anyone else, I would have . . . I don't know, Aurelie. Something happens to me when I'm around you that I can't explain. I know that doesn't make any sense."

"It does," she insisted. "I feel it, too."

He lowered his face to hers, still tipping her chin up to him, but stopped when his lips were maddeningly close. "This is wrong, isn't it?"

She wanted to say no, but how could she, when she had put Des in an impossible situation? "Maybe."

"I can't think straight when I'm with you. I didn't sleep last night. I paid another guard to take my duty today. You've wrecked me, Aurelie."

Looking into his silver eyes, once as hard as iron but now soft and vulnerable, she had no choice but to take him at his word. This strong, focused, purpose-driven man was shirking responsibility, betraying the principles he was bound to uphold. If this didn't go as she'd promised, he would despise her for the rest of their lives. She would despise herself, for ruining him alongside her.

But she could not abandon her uncle for Des, no matter how much she was falling for him. It was cowardly, but she responded by bringing her mouth to his, hoping to convey her conflicting emotions without words, because they would never be adequate.

Des had always been gentle with her, but she could feel how taut his muscles were, how much restraint it took when he cupped the nape of her neck, his fingers tangled in her hair. She'd never kissed anyone before, but she knew intrinsically that no one would ever live up to Des, the way he claimed her mouth with his own, the way his touch had her melting against him.

He tugged on the ribbon at her throat, dragging his lips down her neck until he reached the hollow at the base of it. She found herself pulling her collar aside to grant him access, suddenly regretting her choice of dress, because he couldn't touch her as easily as he had last night. Even worse, she could hardly get to him beneath his leather breastplate, so she settled for his arms, his face, his hair, marveling at how her small hands could bend him to her will.

"We have to stop," he said between kisses, his breathing ragged as she arched against him. "Please, Aurelie. The portal . . ."

"Can wait a few more minutes. Can't it?"

He exhaled roughly as she trailed kisses over his jaw. "It's important."

"But this is so much more fun."

He laughed, a genuine, proper laugh that Aurelie felt in her soul. "Believe me, I know. Nothing has ever been this fun in all of history."

Now she laughed, forcing herself to pull away. "There will be more of this, won't there? Once we finish the portal and save the kingdom?"

He gazed down at her, her face cupped in his hands, his expression almost pained. "If we live? Absolutely." He kissed her again, so thoroughly she could barely stand by the time he pulled away.

"All right, I'm going. Just . . ."

She had begun to retie the ribbon at her throat, but she stopped when his voice trailed off. "What is it?"

"Just be careful, all right? You have your dagger?"

She patted her pocket. "Yes."

"Good. And if you accidentally conjure something, you'll tell me? You won't be foolish and try to handle it yourself?"

She smiled at his concern. "I've handled plenty of demons myself, Des."

“I know. But that was before I knew you existed. I’d never have allowed you to put yourself in harm’s way if I’d known.”

She cocked her head. “Allowed me?”

He ran one hand through his hair, clearly frustrated but doing his best to be diplomatic. “Just promise me, Aurelie.”

“All right, Des. I promise.”

He pressed a kiss to her forehead. “Good girl.”

She flushed at his murmured approval as though he were a professor giving her an excellent mark. She despised herself a little for how much she enjoyed it. “Go, before I change my mind.”

He straightened to his full height and saluted her. “Yes, ma’am.”

To her surprise, Aurelie found she quite liked that, too.

CHAPTER 31

DES

WHEN DES REACHED AURELIE'S LABORATORY, HE FOUND Jasper and Daisy staring at hard lumps of acacia resin, scratching their heads.

"Do you know how to make this into glue?" Jasper asked. "Because we have no idea."

Des held up a piece of parchment on a makeshift desk. "Instructions, right here. Aciano's beard, no wonder she thinks we're all daft."

"She didn't call us daft," Daisy said. "Did she?"

"Not in so many words, no." Des glanced around the room, trying to see it through Aurelie's eyes. It was dark and dingy, mostly empty aside from some wooden crates and the simple frame standing in the middle of the room. It was large, taller than Des and equally wide. He still didn't understand how a magical portal would somehow open up in this very room. Half of him didn't believe it would. And yet seeing Everard and his thrall, he knew that if anyone was capable of it, it was that gods-forsaken man.

Why had he chosen Aurelie? The question had plagued him last night as he lay in bed, his hands folded chastely on his chest to avoid temptation every time he closed his eyes and saw her, half-naked, kneeling on a desk in front of him. No boyhood fantasy could have ever conjured such a sight, especially not when the women he was surrounded by slept in the same tunics the men wore. Aurelie presented so many newly discovered desires, things Des could have never dreamed of for himself.

And the worst part was, he knew now what he had been missing. What he would continue to miss for the rest of his life. As much as he wanted to believe that this portal would do what she said it would—he believed *she* believed it, or else he never would have agreed to help her; at least if she conjured any demons, he'd be there to kill them—he had seen firsthand what happened when people messed with things they shouldn't. She was desperate to save her uncle. She'd do anything for him, Des now understood. Which was why he'd put his own plan in motion behind Aurelie's back.

Gareth had insisted on helping with the portal, and Des knew the kid would continue to pester him if he didn't have some other job. Even Daisy and Jasper didn't know about his "secret mission." Gareth was going to do some reconnaissance on Everard, learn if there was any way to get to Leopold Blake that didn't require Aurelie fulfilling this deal with the devil. If he was confident they could accomplish it, he would alert Commander Yew. Whatever Everard was capable of, Des could never accept he would be able to outsmart the entire Iron Guard.

Still, it pained him to betray Aurelie like this. He licked his lips absently, desperate for another taste of her. Demons take him, she was sweeter and softer than anything had a right to be. But it was her mind he'd fallen for, and the very idea was so ridiculous he almost laughed out loud to himself. He'd never met anyone more obstinate, more curious, more brilliant. He could have listened to her talk about adhesives until he grew old and feeble and died a happy man.

But Aurelie had an undeniable connection with demons, beyond her inventions. Everard had been able to exploit that somehow, spying on Aurelie with his own thrall, maybe even Mephisto. There had to be other inventors in Wisteria City. She claimed she'd killed every *verita* she created, but he'd faced *verita* many times, which meant there were other sources. Why *Aurelie*?

And why, in some twisted way, was he grateful? Because otherwise, they never would have met.

The entire time he and Jasper moved those blasted stones—which, they realized after their first three attempts, were not all perfectly even and therefore could only be slotted into the frame through a process of trial and error—he daydreamed of her delicate hands against his face, his chest, his abdominal muscles, as though she'd never felt anything more intriguing. He wanted to let her study him like one of her books, page by page, as slowly and thoroughly as she wanted to.

Blood and bones, he was jealous of her fucking books.

When she appeared in the room, he wondered for a moment if he'd conjured her, if his aching thoughts had somehow reached her across campus. At some point while they were working, Des had removed his breastplate, followed by his tunic, because despite the freezing temperatures outside, it had grown warm from the fire Daisy started in the massive fireplace to melt the acacia resin. And now Aurelie was here, staring at him with her front teeth absently pressed to her lower lip, her pale cheeks flushed pink, her hands idly fisted in her skirt.

If they'd been alone, he would have devoured her whole.

"Everything okay?" he asked, a smirk curling his lips.

"Yes, fine," she said, blinking. "I was going to run to the post office and wondered if I could pick up something on the way home to make for dinner."

The thought of her cooking for him was absurd, and yet he wanted nothing more than to have dinner with her in her uncle's cottage. All right, there were definitely *some* things he wanted more, but he wanted that, too. He wanted all of it. All of *her*.

"Des should go with you," Daisy said, before he could form a response. His initial instinct was to glare at her, but then he realized that he wanted to go to the post office with Aurelie. Anything if it meant more time with her.

"Oh, I'm perfectly capable—" Aurelie stopped herself, shook her head as if to clear it, and then nodded. "Yes, that would be nice."

Des thought he saw Jasper roll his eyes, but he couldn't blame him. He'd have done the same thing if anyone else was acting this moony.

While Des redonned his tunic and breastplate, Aurelie was telling Daisy something about the metal plates, and he watched in astonishment as the tiny demon, Mephisto, circled Daisy's ankle like a cat. A small, bizarre, entirely deranged cat. He had hated the creature on impulse, but if he hadn't known what it was, he might have found it . . . cute? And it didn't behave like any demon he'd ever seen. It was curious, almost playful, deceptively innocent. But he'd seen what its seeds produced. It was dangerous. And if it fell into the hands of Everard, they were all in serious trouble.

When he was ready, he and Aurelie walked into the chill afternoon. They had to leave tonight for their shift. They all did. But gods he liked the way she pressed into him as they crossed the main courtyard toward the front gates. As brave as she was, he had the impression she felt safe in his presence. That she knew intrinsically he would take care of her, no matter what. And she was right.

"So, the post office?" he asked.

"It's the runes," she said. "I think I have the correct sequencing, but there are still several I haven't translated yet." She opened the unsealed envelope and showed the piece of parchment within to Des. He read the words, but they meant little to him:

Spill ancient ___, ___ the fated thorn,
A quest for balance, through ___ reborn.
One ___ to extinguish destiny's might,
Renewal through ___, one soul to make right.
In the shadows lies the ancient ___,
Transformation, ___, to set ___ free.
At ___ dark, the portal will ___,
Creation from ___, the bond we shall break.

"What is a fated thorn?" he asked when he finished reading.

"I have no idea. The portal will *what*? It could be anything. I don't want to bother Professor Sheldrake on his holiday, but he might be the only person who can help." She pointed to a cluster of runes at the bottom. "I haven't translated these yet."

"Do you need to translate the runes to make the portal work?"

She bit her lip, distracting Des briefly. "I don't think so. But Professor Sheldrake said I'd be an utter fool not to translate them before activating the portal, and with everything Everard may be lying about . . . I may be irresponsible, but I'm not a total fool."

"When will your letter get to him?"

"Tomorrow, if we're lucky. But I'm afraid even if he responds right away, there will be no mail for the holiday. I should have written sooner."

"You're doing the best you can, Aurelie."

She turned to gaze up at him as they crossed the street to the post office. "It's not good enough. *I'm* not good enough."

Des had said the same thing about himself a thousand times, but to hear Aurelie say it about herself made something clench in his chest. "You are the smartest person I've ever met. You can do this."

Her eyes glittered when she looked up at him, as though he'd given her the greatest compliment imaginable. Truly, he'd never met anyone like her. If someone had asked him to design the perfect woman, he would have never been able to dream her up. And yet she was the most delightful thing he'd ever beheld. If only she weren't so cozy with demons.

They mailed the letter and stopped at the grocer's to buy carrots, potatoes, onions, and mushrooms for a stew Aurelie was fairly certain she knew how to make.

"Have you ever cooked?" he asked her as they headed back to campus.

"Not exactly. But I've watched our cook make stew at least a dozen times. How difficult can it be?"

Rather difficult, as it turned out. Fortunately, Daisy had learned to cook from her cousin, and she was able to salvage the stew into something semi-edible, though the carrots were hard, the potatoes were mushy, and the mushrooms had been abandoned entirely.

It was the first time Des had ever eaten in a proper home, at an actual dining table with real silver and crystal. Aurelie had insisted on serving, and as she'd ladled stew into his bowl, her hands trembling a little, he couldn't help smiling at her and whispering *good girl* under his breath just to watch the flush creep up her neck.

When they'd finished eating, Daisy helped Aurelie clear the dishes while Jasper and Des returned to the workshop to finish the second row of stones. Daisy had affixed a third of the metal plates to the stones in the order of Aurelie's diagram. Soon, she would be ready to engrave the runes. Just so long as she had everything translated.

Finally, around ten o'clock, Daisy yawned so wide Des heard her jaw creak.

"It's time to go," Jasper said. Aurelie had gone to her laboratory to feed Mephisto while they finished in her workshop. "I can't believe we have to work tonight."

"I know." Des wiped the sweat from his brow, astonished by how quickly the hours had passed. They were nearly finished with the stones. It had been a successful day's work. If he didn't think about it too hard, he could almost convince himself he hadn't abandoned his principles entirely.

"You're worried about her here alone, aren't you?" Jasper asked.

"Are you saying I shouldn't be?"

"I don't know," Daisy said. "She handled that demon pretty well yesterday. I think she can take care of herself."

"But she shouldn't have to," Des said.

"No. No one should." Daisy stretched up to pat him on the shoulder. "I'm proud of you."

He scoffed. "For what?"

"For being open-minded enough to listen to Aurelie, to understand that there's a different way of being in this world from the one you've always known." She handed him his breastplate. "Most of us didn't grow up in this. We got to see a world that wasn't only about demons. You didn't have that privilege."

"Serving in the Iron Guard—"

"Is a privilege," Jasper and Daisy said in unison.

"We know," Jasper added. "But Daisy is right. I'm not saying it was your best idea ever to fall for a girl who conjures demons. But it's nice to see you happy for a change."

Was that what this feeling was? Happiness? Des looked up to see Aurelie standing in the doorway, watching him. She may have heard what Jasper said, that he was falling for her. And for reasons beyond his comprehension, he wasn't humiliated at the thought. Maybe he'd never get to marry or have a family, but for the rest of his life, he would be able to say he knew what it felt like to lose his mind over a girl.

Pretty fucking fantastic.

CHAPTER 32
AURELIE

IN THE MORNING, AURELIE STRETCHED LANGUOROUSLY, having spent another night dreaming of Des. It was better than dwelling on her uncle in a cage, or Everard's demon sniffing about the university, or the trouble she could be getting the demon hunters into at this very moment.

Des hadn't said he was falling for her, but he also hadn't contradicted Jasper, and the look he'd given her had made heat pool in her chest and flow like molten lava to her core. If she could have found a way to manufacture and bottle that feeling, she'd be the wealthiest woman alive, no matter how many demons she spawned in the process.

She knew that demon hunters didn't marry. She knew that the odds of this portal working and demons being officially eradicated were so slim as to be negligible, because if it were possible, surely *someone* would have done it before. Which meant that she would likely die alongside her uncle, and Des should be the furthest thing from her mind. But she was eighteen. Her frontal lobe wasn't fully developed yet. And what was death compared to falling in love?

As she began to boil water for coffee, she noticed that Mephisto hadn't touched its dinner last night. She couldn't remember the last time it hadn't finished a meal; if anything, it generally demanded seconds. She pulled the jar of cockroaches out of the armoire, slowly unscrewing the lid, a sound that normally acted as a siren song for the demon. But there was still no sign of it.

Puzzled, Aurelie searched along the floorboards and even in the Load Lightener, but Mephisto wasn't here and likely hadn't been all night. A horrible feeling crept over her. What if Everard had taken it? Or used his link to demons to summon it? She'd known Everard wanted the creature for his own purposes, whatever those were. And she had been too busy living in a fantasy world—one where she had friends over for dinner; one where she had *friends*—to realize it was missing.

She swallowed her tears. If she completed the portal, Mephisto was going to be summoned back to the demonic realm. It might be happier there, where it belonged, among its own kind. But even as she had these thoughts, she knew they were untrue. Mephisto was happy here, with Aurelie. It was yet another sacrifice in her path to saving her uncle.

Until recently, she had thought of herself as someone curious and methodical, inquisitive and wise. But the painful reality was that deep down, she was a girl of hope and heartstrings, too. Love would break her as sure as it would any other girl, if she let it.

She finished her coffee and removed the bandage on her wound, relieved to see it was scabbing over. She let her shift fall to the floor and stood before the full-length mirror on her armoire door. The juxtaposition of her smooth, pale skin and the ragged scratches across her chest was jarring, ugly even. She'd never thought much on her physical appearance before, but now, imagining Des seeing her like this, she wondered if the scars would forever remind him of her traitorous actions.

Illegal inventor. Demon consorter. A brand she would carry with her the rest of her life.

—•—

She had known the demon hunters wouldn't come until well after nightfall, and yet she realized she'd been hoping Des would come earlier anyway by the disappointment she felt when he didn't. But there was no time to waste. Using a tool she'd found in Mr. Morel's workshop, she took a sheet of copper and began to practice engraving shapes in it.

It was so much harder than it looked. The burin, a tool with a round wooden handle and a metal shaft leading down to a diamond-shaped tip, was easy enough to hold. But it took years of practice for a skilled metalworker to wield it with strength and finesse, to create the curves and intricate details needed for Elder Vansion. Aurelie's first attempt looked like that of a child practicing their letters: wobbly, crooked, and unrecognizable.

Afraid she was going to ruin a noticeable amount of Mr. Morel's copper sheets, she decided to work on her own copper kettle, which she'd soon covered in dents and chicken scratches that were so embarrassing she knew she'd have to scrap the kettle altogether. This was impossible. What she needed was someone with excellent penmanship and strong forearms. Someone good at keeping secrets who wasn't busy today.

She needed Kiara.

Around lunchtime, Aurelie headed out into the city. The streets were crowded with last-minute shoppers, so blithely unaware of everything swirling through Aurelie's head that she resented them their trivial worries. If only finding the perfect gift for her uncle was her biggest concern.

The Morels lived in an apartment above a carpentry shop Mrs.

Morel managed. It was closed for the week, as were many businesses. Aurelie rang the bell, hoping that Kiara would be the one who answered, because it would lead to far fewer questions.

Unfortunately, it was Mr. Morel who came down the stairs and unlocked the shop door. "Aurelie! It's so lovely to see you. We were very disappointed when Kiara said you couldn't spend the week with us."

She ducked her head, hating to add another lie to her teetering pile. "I was, too. But I decided it was better for me to focus on my studies this week. I've gotten rather behind in everything this semester."

"I see. Is that what brings you here today? I assume you want to see Kiara?"

Aurelie nodded. "I was wondering if she could help me with something at school. Is she free?"

"Is she free? That girl hasn't lifted so much as a finger for a week! I'll send her down. Give us a few minutes. I think she might still be in her nightclothes."

Aurelie thanked him and stomped her feet to keep them warm while she waited. She was watching a family of five navigate an icy patch, laughing to herself behind her gloved hand, when she saw a familiar tall, spindly figure walking toward her.

Attached to Miles's arm was none other than Lavender Applebaum, pressed against him in a way that was clearly more than friendly.

"Hello, Aurelie!" Lavender said when she saw her. "We wondered if that was you! No one has seen you in ages."

Aurelie cringed and did her best to turn it into a smile. "Yes, it's been a busy few weeks. What are you doing this afternoon?"

"Shopping for Lavender's Yule present," Miles said, straightening his fogged glasses with his index finger. He didn't seem particularly pleased to see Aurelie *or* to be out shopping with Lavender.

"Oh," Aurelie said. "Are you two . . ."

"We're engaged!" Lavender exclaimed, pulling off her glove to thrust a massive diamond ring in Aurelie's face.

Aurelie could only blink in response.

"Well, congratulate us," Lavender prompted.

"Of course. Congratulations to you both."

Miles was watching Aurelie as though expecting . . . disappointment? Envy? Honestly, one would think he'd know her better than that by now. "And you?" he asked. "What are you doing at a . . ." He glanced up at the sign. "A closed carpentry shop."

"Just waiting on Kiara."

"Oh yes, the groundskeeper's daughter." Miles peered down at Lavender over the rim of his glasses. "Aurelie works with her. Don't you, Aurelie?"

"Yes, I do. We're both bricoleurs."

Lavender cocked her head as though the very idea was foreign to her. "I thought you said you were a student?"

"I am. People can work and study, you know."

Lavender laughed. "Well of course they *can*. I just can't imagine wanting to!"

Aurelie couldn't read Miles's expression behind his glasses, but his derisive tone of voice made it clear what he thought of her. "No one is as industrious as Aurelie Blake."

To her extreme relief, Kiara chose that moment to open the door to the shop and step outside. "True enough! And now she's forcing me to join her." Kiara twined her arm through Aurelie's and waved over her shoulder. "Happy Yule!" she called. Then, leaning into Aurelie, she said, "Now tell me what the hell we're doing today, oh industrious one."

"I will. As soon as we're back on campus." Aurelie wondered if she was *supposed* to be jealous of Miles so quickly turning his attention to another girl, but she only felt profound relief. He wasn't going to waste his time spreading rumors about her when he had found someone who clearly relished his attention.

"I'm surprised to see you," Kiara said as Aurelie unlocked the campus gate. "Does this mean things are going well?"

So much had happened that Aurelie wasn't sure where to begin, but she recounted as much as she could, including what had happened to poor Mr. Willoughby. Kiara didn't know the guards personally, but she welled up just the same. "Oh, Aurelie."

"I know. I've managed to make a mess of everything." Finally, she explained about the runes, though they seemed so trivial compared to Willoughby's death. "Do you think you can help?"

"I can certainly try," Kiara said as they settled on the sofa in Aurelie's lab. "But something tells me you left out a few details of your week so far."

"What details?"

"Details about you and Des."

Aurelie avoided Kiara's eyes. "I told you everything."

"Aurelie."

"Fine, almost everything."

A grin spread on Kiara's face. "You really like him, don't you?"

Aurelie had told Des as much, just the other night. But now *like* seemed much too simple of a word for what she felt. It wasn't *love*, of course. But she could imagine how easy it would be to fall into it, into him.

Her silence must have been all the confirmation Kiara needed, because she didn't press further. Instead, she began to practice engraving on a sheet of copper. She promised she'd replace them all without her father knowing.

Already, she was better than Aurelie. She felt terrible for dragging her best friend into this mess, but having Kiara here was grounding. In Des's presence, she was untethered; if she wasn't careful, she could float away altogether. But here, in the moment, was where she belonged. Nothing could matter more than saving her uncle. Nothing could matter more than this.

When Kiara was confident she could carve the runes, they made their way to Aurelie's other workshop. She spent a few minutes searching for Mephisto there, but the demon was still nowhere to be found.

"What is this made of, do you think?" Kiara asked as she studied a metal plate. "It's not gold or copper. I've never seen a metal like it, in fact."

"I know," Aurelie said, peering over her shoulder. "I couldn't find anything about it in the books I read, either. I suspect it's some type of alloy, electrum perhaps."

"Electrum?"

"Green gold. A gold-and-silver alloy." With the metal plates already affixed to the stone, Kiara had to work with them vertically. Some runes were far more complicated than others, and with thirty-six of them, it was going to be more than she could handle alone in one day. "I'll try one of the simpler runes," Aurelie said, glancing at her translation. "Hopefully we can get most of this done today, and then I can finish when Everard comes."

They worked for hours with painstaking slowness, lest they make a mistake and ruin a metal plate. There were no spares, and Aurelie knew Everard wouldn't accept failure, despite the impossible task he'd set before her.

By dinner, they'd finished all but the last of the runes. They stepped back to look at the portal, Kiara's chin on her fist, Aurelie pushing her magnifying spectacles up onto her forehead.

"It doesn't look magical, does it?" Kiara said. She was wearing coveralls and a kerchief to keep her hair out of her face.

"Of course it doesn't look magical yet," Aurelie countered, but inside, she'd been thinking the same thing. It was large, bulky, and it was rather evident which of the runes Aurelie had carved, because they looked like they'd been scrawled by a squirrel. "Once we finish the last rune, it will work. It has to."

"And you still don't have it translated?"

Aurelie shook her head no. She'd gone to the postbox by the front gate at midday to check, but Professor Sheldrake hadn't written. The mail wouldn't come again until after Yule.

"Aurelie, it's not too late to stop this, you know. Your uncle wouldn't want you to put yourself in harm's way for him."

Aurelie was exhausted from having this conversation, but she also knew that Kiara would want to have it at least one more time before she left today. "I know. But I refuse to let him die for me."

"And your parents?"

At that, Aurelie turned to look at Kiara, stung. "What about my parents?"

"Do you think this is what they would want for their only daughter?"

The words caught her off guard, stealing her breath. She didn't often consider what her parents would think of her life now, because she had always believed they would approve of it. She was a scientist, like them. She worked and studied hard, and she was a dutiful niece, aside from the whole illegal inventing bit.

But would they expect her to sacrifice Uncle Leo to save herself?

She knew the answer instinctively. They were her parents. Of course they would put their child above all else. That didn't mean it was right.

"I'm sorry," Kiara said when Aurelie didn't answer. "I'm just afraid you're being led into a trap."

"You'd do the same exact thing if your parents were in a cage in a madman's basement." To her surprise, she found her eyes filling with tears. "Wouldn't you?" she asked, her voice cracking.

Kiara sat down next to her, stroking her fringe away from her forehead. "I'm sorry. I know there's no easy answer here. I'm just worried."

"And I'm sorry I ever got you involved in any of this. But even if Everard didn't have Uncle Leo, there is clearly something going on with demons, Kiki. And Everard said that if the veil thins completely, it can't be put back. Ever."

She was quiet for a long moment. "Then I guess we'd better keep working."

Aurelie smiled through her tears, feeling indescribably fortunate to have such a loyal best friend. She had to believe she was doing the right thing, that Everard, who'd said himself that demons couldn't be trusted or controlled, had no interest in hurting anyone else. But deep down, she had a terrible feeling that Kiara was right. That this was a trap, and she was about to run headfirst into it, sacrificing far more than her uncle's life in the process.

CHAPTER 33
DES

GARETH, JASPER, DAISY, AND DES CLUSTERED AROUND A table for a late dinner, earning curious looks from the other guards. Des never ate with anyone but Daisy, and people were rightly confused by his sudden shift into sociability.

"What did you learn today?" Des asked Gareth.

"Very little," Gareth replied as he poked at his boiled peas. "Everard didn't leave the house once. The demon thrall left two separate times, but I don't know where it went."

Des was about to rebuke him when Daisy cut him off.

"You told him to watch the townhouse, not the demon," she murmured.

"Right. You're right. We need another set of eyes on the thrall."

"We're not dragging anyone else into this," Jasper hissed. "I was already forced to do an extra set of push-ups for being late this morning."

Daisy smiled and ruffled Jasper's hair. "Aw, sleepyhead. I'll make sure you're up on time tomorrow."

Jasper raised his lip in a silent snarl.

"I also went to the library," Gareth said, looking rather sheepish.

"The library?" Jasper and Des asked in unison.

"To do research on thralls," he explained as he pulled a piece of paper from his trouser pocket. "I found something that might be helpful."

Des skimmed the paper quickly: *Masters and thralls are tethered to each other; if one is harmed, the other is, too. While the master can see through the thrall's eyes, the thrall does not benefit reciprocally. Instead, it gains the weakness of its human master and none of its strengths.*

Des reread the words several times. "So Everard does have a weakness?" Aurelie had hinted at something along those lines, but he'd cut her off before she could finish.

Gareth nodded. "It seems so, insomuch as a demon can be considered a weakness. If you kill Kobal, Everard could also die."

The idea was intriguing, but exceedingly risky. It could alert Everard to their involvement, and Aurelie would never forgive Des if she suspected he was doing anything that might harm her uncle.

"Thank you, Gareth."

"I wish I could help more, but my family is expecting me for Yule," Daisy said. "I'll do as much as I can tonight."

Des was only half listening, because an idea was taking form in his mind. If he could trap Everard's thrall, he wouldn't only have potential leverage over Everard, but the perfect bargaining chip: the demon for Aurelie's uncle. And perhaps best of all, he'd also have the first known captive *verita* specimen. He could study its reaction to iron, prove that the veil really was thinning, which might be enough to convince Commander Yew that the king couldn't be trusted. Gods, it was treasonous even to think such things, but he couldn't deny that something dark was happening in Wisteria. And he couldn't sit back and watch it happen, either.

They finished dinner and headed back to their quarters to change, then left separately to avoid further suspicion. By a little after ten, they were letting themselves inside the university gates with Aurelie's key. Des still wore it on the leather thong around his neck. Every time he started to doubt what they were doing, he squeezed it in his fist, reminding himself that Aurelie was real. That she cared about him. That she knew what the Iron Guard meant to him and would never deliberately do something to compromise his position there.

She was in the workshop when they arrived, staring at the portal with her hands on her hips, her head cocked to the side. She was more disheveled than he'd ever seen her, her hair damp at the temples, a smudge of charcoal on her nose that made her look like an adorable, green-eyed rabbit.

Without thinking, he moved to wipe it away with his thumb, only stopping when he realized Jasper and Daisy were laughing. At him.

"Shut up," he growled, though it was so half-hearted that neither of them stopped giggling. Daisy had the gall to snort.

Aurelie, however, was still standing in front of him with her eyes closed, waiting for him to finish his ministrations, and it took all his self-control not to kiss the tip of her nose when he'd finished.

"How are you feeling about everything?" he asked her as they walked to the cottage to make tea—they were all going to need the extra energy tonight, and Daisy had complained of a headache due to lack of sugar consumption. What he really wanted to ask was, *How are you feeling about me?* But he'd never have dared.

"I don't know. I still have runes left to translate, and if we don't get this right . . ."

"We'll get it right," he said, ignoring the stab of guilt in his gut at the thought of going behind her back, of any of this going wrong.

"I hope so."

He worded his next question carefully, hoping to appeal to her scientific mind without arousing suspicion. "Have you ever tried to trap any of your demons, rather than kill them?"

"Other than Mephisto?" She shook her head. "No. Which isn't to say I haven't wanted to. I've collected as much data as possible about them, but I could never take the risk of keeping one alive. Even if they weren't hell-bent on eating me, it would put Uncle Leo in danger."

"You mean from the Iron Guard?"

She nodded.

"And what about you?"

She shrugged. "I don't know. I suppose I was overconfident in my abilities to kill the demons I created. None were faster or stronger than me. Not until the last one. It appeared so quickly." She considered for a moment. "Perhaps because the veil *is* thinning."

Inside the cottage, none of the gas lamps had been lit, but Aurelie knew the house well. Seemingly without thinking, she took Des's hand and guided him, and there was something in the gesture that made his chest ache.

"But if you were to trap one, how would you go about it?"

"Now this I have given some thought to," she admitted. "I suppose it would need to be composed of metal, though not pure iron necessarily. Perhaps an alloy metal with a high iron content to weaken the demon without killing it. It would need to be camouflaged in some way, most likely. And you'd need a lure."

"A lure?"

"Meat. Still alive, if possible. A small animal?" She shuddered. "Honestly, I would never be able to get past that part. I'd be more inclined to use myself as a lure than some hapless creature."

Of course she would. The thought was equal parts endearing and maddening.

When they reached the kitchen, he waited on the threshold while she lit a gas lamp and made a fire for the kettle. Her apron was untied in the back, revealing her slim waist and the flare of her hips, which he suddenly had the overwhelming desire to hold.

She squeaked when he came up behind her and began to tie the apron strings, which seemed less presumptuous than the other things he had in mind.

"What is it with you and the kitchen?" she asked, turning in his arms.

"I'll take any room I can get, so long as it's just the two of us."

She smirked up at him. "I've heard men are very simple creatures, but I didn't realize how true it was until now."

"Simple, huh?" He tucked a loose strand of hair behind her ear. "For what it's worth, there's nothing simple about my feelings for you."

"Now that I can believe," she said with a sigh. "This is far more complicated than I could have imagined."

"Really? I knew from the moment you shouted at me that this was going to be complicated." A lie, but a small one. He'd known from the moment he saved her from the runaway carriage. When the thought of harm befalling her was more frightening than any demon encounter.

"You liked me even then?" she whispered.

"Especially then," he said, leaning down to kiss her forehead. It was a deliberately chaste kiss. She was anxious tonight, her body tense. As badly as he wanted to lose himself in kissing her, he wasn't going to make any demands on her already limited time.

But when she pressed her hand to his check and tilted her mouth to meet his, he was so grateful he could have fallen to his knees.

Still, he tried to restrain himself, to kiss her slowly and deeply, not the frenzied rush of their first kiss, where he'd been as eager as a schoolboy. The kettle began to whistle, but Aurelie somehow managed to remove it from the flame without breaking away from him. It was such a deft move he pulled away himself.

"Have you done this before?" he asked her.

"This?"

"You know." He glanced down at their bodies.

She scoffed incredulously. "With whom?" she asked, as though the idea were absurd.

He shrugged. "Miles?"

She was caught so off guard she snorted, then covered her mouth in surprise, still laughing. "You're joking," she said. "Right?"

"Why would I be joking? You did go on a date with him, if I recall correctly."

"That was *not* a date. My uncle thought Miles Viridian would be a good match for me, simply because he's a dedicated student from a good family."

At that, a sliver of doubt wedged itself into Des's heart. He'd never even considered what Aurelie's uncle would think of him. Dr. Blake hadn't been present in the weeks Des had known her. But of course he wouldn't want his only niece to be with someone like Des. He had raised her since she was a small child to be just like him: smart, successful, devoted to her studies and academia.

"Hey, where'd you go?" she asked, reaching for him.

He shook his head, embarrassed. "It's nothing."

"It's not nothing." She forced him to look at her, and he resented her in that moment for not simply dropping the matter like Jasper or Aspen would have, for forcing him to confront his own insecurities. She and Daisy were too much alike in that way. "Listen, Miles Viridian is the most repugnant, sycophantic, self-absorbed man I've ever met."

He frowned, unconvinced.

"He was also recently engaged to Lavender Applebaum."

At that, the spark of hope relit in Des's chest, and he pulled her to him, kissing her greedily while she laughed. It was the most beautiful sound in the world, Aurelie's laughter.

Finally, he released her so she could finish making the tea. It quickly became apparent that Aurelie had hardly eaten today, so he went to the pantry to find whatever he could, determined that tomorrow he'd bring a fresh loaf of bread and cheese for her. The world needed more of Aurelie Blake in it, not less.

Just as they were about to head back toward the workshop, Aurelie set the tea tray on a console table and looked up at Des.

"What is it?" he asked.

"I just want you to know, if at any point you decide you can't be a part of this, I'll understand. You deserve to be promoted, Des. You deserve everything you want. And I'm not so naïve as to think you're going to change your entire life for me."

What was she doing? Letting him off the hook? Trying to tell him gently that they had no future together? Or was she simply trying to protect her own heart?

Instead of asking, he pulled her into his arms, holding her as tightly as when he'd pulled her away from the runaway carriage. And just like then, she didn't flinch at the stiffness of his armor or the unyielding grip of his muscles. Just like then, she melted into him, as though she knew that his armor, his muscles, were there to protect *her*, far more than they were for himself.

Because the thing he needed to protect most of all couldn't be safeguarded by armor or weapons, and the walls he'd built up around it had been reduced to rubble by this tiny, inimitable, wrecking ball of a girl.

CHAPTER 34
AURELIE

BY THURSDAY MORNING, THE PORTAL WAS NEARLY FINISHED. All of the stones were in place, the metal plates affixed with resin. Kiara had carved most of the runes on Wednesday while Aurelie continued to work on her translation. They were cutting it close—maybe too close. But she couldn't let herself think that way. She was like a horse in blinders, gaze narrowed to the hour, minutes, seconds ahead. If she widened her view at all, she started to feel the panic creep in—and that was the last thing she needed.

The fact that today was Yule was difficult to grasp. Aurelie had spent every Yule since her parents' death with Uncle Leo in his cottage. There was no pine tree this year, no presents beneath it, no dinner with other faculty members who lacked family or students who were stranded in town thanks to a freak snowstorm.

This year, there wasn't even Mephisto, who usually received an extra cockroach for Yule dinner. Years ago, Kiara had knit it a tiny stocking and hung it over a miniature mantel she'd carved out of wood in her father's shop. Since then, she would bring a diminutive gift for Mephisto, generally something completely useless, like a Mephisto-sized sweater with eight leg holes. Aurelie had given up attempting to wrangle the demon into it almost immediately for fear of losing a finger.

At noon, eyes blurring from her translation efforts, she went to the cottage to prepare another pitiful meal, feeling immensely sorry for herself. Of course, she knew Uncle Leo had it far worse, wasting away in a cage in a cellar. Perhaps they could celebrate a belated Yule once they were reunited. She would purchase something special for him. A new pocket watch or a fountain pen with a crystal inkwell. Anything he wanted, so long as they were together.

She started a fire and skimmed another crumbling tome on Elder Vansion, struggling to read it while her thoughts strayed in a thousand directions. The portal, Des, Uncle Leo. So many things had to go right for this to work, when only one wrong move would lead to utter ruin. When a knock sounded on the door, she dropped the book. Daisy was spending Yule with her cousin. Jasper and Gareth had friends they were going to visit. Des hadn't said if he had plans, but she hadn't dared hope he might choose to spend it with her.

But when she opened the door, there was Des, wearing his gray Iron Guard peacoat and holding a small, crooked pine tree.

"Happy Yule, Aurelie."

She could feel herself smiling overly wide, but she didn't even try to suppress it. It was astonishing how easily Des could make her forget all her other worries. "Happy Yule, Des." She ushered him in from the cold, holding the tree while he shrugged out of his coat and hung it on the coatrack.

"I didn't know if I'd see you today," she said as they walked into the library.

Des put the tree in a corner, far from the fireplace. "I hadn't planned to come," he said, looking sheepish. "But I knew it might be our last day together before . . ."

He didn't need to finish. "I'm so glad you're here." She glanced at the tree, which looked woefully naked without any decorations. "I have an idea," she said, taking his hand and leading him to the closet where Uncle Leo allowed Aurelie to keep one box of Yule trimmings.

Des picked it up and carried it back to the tree, and they spent the next hour placing baubles and tinsel on it, each being careful not to touch the other, as though they knew the moment they did, the tree would be forgotten, along with everything else.

When the box was empty, they stood back to admire their work.

"I've never had a Yule tree before," Des said. "It's pretty."

The thought that Des had never had a proper Yule made Aurelie want to cry. "Thank you, for bringing it. And for coming." Their eyes met. Aurelie's throat clogged with all the things she wanted to say. "Your promotion!" she blurted instead.

He blinked. "What about it?"

"I meant to say congratulations. How was the ceremony?"

He smiled, though Aurelie couldn't help feeling it didn't quite reach his eyes. "It was short but good. I'm officially Lieutenant Commander Whitlow." He leaned closer. "I expect you'll treat me with respect now, Miss Blake."

She grinned. "I expect you know me better than that by now, Destroyer."

They stared at each other for a long moment, both smiling like fools. She'd never felt anything like this. She was *giddy*, for crying out loud.

He opened his mouth to speak.

"Shall I make tea?" she asked, overly bright. She didn't know how long he planned to stay, but she'd do anything to drag their time out as long as possible.

"I'll help," he said, beginning to follow her.

She stopped him with a palm to his chest. "No, stay here. I'm afraid I'll never finish if you come with me."

He looked at her with such fondness she felt her heart might break. "Would that be so terrible?"

"Just, stay here, all right?"

He sat down in one of the wingback chairs, placing his hands on his knees obediently. "I'm not going anywhere."

Aurelie headed for the kitchen, put the kettle on, and then ran like a madwoman to her bedroom. She winced at the sheer volume of ruffles and bows, but it was absolutely not the time to redecorate. She stood in front of the mirror, assessing her appearance. She'd worn a green plaid dress today, the most festive thing she had, and put her hair in its usual braid for lack of anything else to do. She considered taking it down and then thought better of it. She'd let Des do it for her.

Even imagining it made her flush.

By the time she made it back to the kitchen, the kettle had been removed from the fire and the tea was steeping. She heard a rummaging from the pantry. A moment later, Des emerged.

"I told you to stay put!" she scolded.

For some reason, he smiled. "The kettle was screaming," he said as he placed a handful of items on the counter. "Where were you, anyhow?"

"That's none of your business." She glanced at the items on the counter and frowned. "What are you doing?"

"I'm baking you a cake. Daisy gave me a recipe." He held up a small piece of paper covered in flowery script. "Eggs, flour, butter, sugar, and milk. It seems simple enough."

Aurelie stared at him for a moment, wondering if she was going to melt into a mass of warm goo or spontaneously combust. Surely the feeling in her chest was a precursor to one or the other.

"Or not," Des said. "It was just a thought."

She stepped toward him. "My silence was not an indicator of a dislike for cake."

Ever so gently, he placed his hands on her hips. "What is it an indicator of, then?"

"Of how much I like you."

He closed his eyes for a moment, his grip tightening on her. "We could skip the cake."

She grinned, resting her head against his chest. "No. Let's have tea, and cake. Let's sit by the fire and talk. Let's do all of it, while we can."

He pressed a kiss to the top of her head. "That's a good thought, too."

When the cake was finished—burnt on the outside and somehow still runny on the inside—they sat down by the fire and ate it with their bare hands.

"It's terrible," Des said, wincing. He looked like he wanted to spit it out, but she shook her head.

"It was an experiment, that's all. Next time we'll turn the heat down and cook it for longer."

He swallowed and winced as though he immediately regretted it. "Is that how you handle your failed experiments?"

"Of course. What's the alternative?"

"Giving up? Accepting the fact that we're not good bakers?"

Aurelie smiled. "That's not how science works. And I'm guessing that's not how baking works, either. How many things in life do we get right the first time?"

Des was quiet for a moment. "The only thing I've ever tried to be was an Iron Guard. And I was good at it from the beginning."

"Hmm. I'm guessing you had a lot of failures along the way, though. Surely you didn't win every fight, especially when you were small."

"I told you, I was never small."

Aurelie knew that wasn't true. He may have felt big compared to others, but he'd been a child, once. Someone had held him, helped feed and dress him. Perhaps he couldn't remember it, but no one grew up all on their own.

Still, she wished he knew what it was like to be held. She scooted over to him, kneeled behind him, and draped herself over his back.

"What are you doing?" he asked, his face just inches from hers.

"Holding you."

He chuckled, a rumbling throughout his entire body. "Hardly. You're like a heavy blanket, at best. One that only covers a quarter of my body."

She sighed and sat back on her heels. "I'll have to think on this one. There has to be a way for me to make you feel as safe in my arms as I feel in yours."

He reached around and grabbed her by the waist, pulling her into his lap. Breathless, she looked up into his eyes, which were so warm in the glow of the firelight. How could she have ever thought them cold?

Gently, he brushed her hair out of her face. "Aurelie, you do make me feel safe."

"How?" she asked, genuinely confused.

"No one has ever put themselves in harm's way for me before. Not even when I was a child. From the time I could speak, it was my sworn duty to protect every citizen above myself. *I'm* the last line of defense, Aurelie."

She reached up to cup his jaw. "Not anymore, Des."

He kissed her with exquisite slowness, and when he finally pulled away, his eyes were gleaming in a way that suggested tears.

At the sight, her heart swelled until it burst, a sensation that felt a little like ecstasy and a little like dying. She kissed him again, her hand finding its way beneath his tunic to the smooth muscle above his heart. It beat wildly against her palm, an echo of her own.

Without thinking, she took his hand and held it to her own heart, so he would know how she felt. He sighed into her mouth, cupping her breast so tenderly that she pressed into him, craving more contact.

And then there was no more hesitancy, though the tenderness remained even as he untied the ribbon at her throat, laughing in frustration at the tiny buttons down the front of her dress, their lips never leaving each other's skin as she tugged at the hem of his tunic, eager to see more of him.

She sat back then to admire him, the way the firelight danced over his skin, highlighting the hard planes of muscle, the shadowed valleys formed by years of training, nothing soft about him save for the way he looked at her as she shrugged out of her dress. He looked hungry and a little desperate, as though he might starve without another taste of her.

"You're so beautiful," he said, rising to his feet.

"Then where are you going?"

Wordlessly, he picked her up and carried her to the sofa, setting her down as if she were as light as a feather. She attempted to pull him down to her, but he remained standing, one knee on the sofa next to her hip, gazing down at her as though attempting to memorize her.

She sat up and began to reach for the hem of her shift, but he stilled her with his hand.

"Let me, please."

She nodded as he lifted with agonizing slowness, drinking in the pale length of her legs, the curve of her hips, the swell of her breasts. Even the scratches across her chest received his full attention, and to her relief, he didn't recoil at the sight of them. Instead, he bent over her and pressed a kiss to the soft skin where her shoulder met her breast.

She gasped as he explored her with his lips, his tongue, his teeth. She wanted to give him the same pleasure, but the sensations were overwhelming, making it impossible to concentrate on anything other than this.

"Tell me what you like," he rasped against her ear, but all she could do was nod wordlessly and reach for his trousers.

He smiled against her throat and allowed her to undo his laces, helping her pull his trousers down his hips. When she saw him, actually saw him, she froze.

"Des," she whispered. "I don't think . . ."

Bracketing her between his forearms, he cupped her face until she looked at him. "It's like one of your experiments."

She hooded her gaze. "I assure you, this is *not* like my experiments."

He chuckled again, kissing her forehead. "We try things, find what works. Try again. If I'm doing my part right, this will be very successful. For both of us."

"Not like the cake, though," she whispered. "Right? Because that was truly terrible."

He smiled, but almost instantly his features settled into something more serious, nearly solemn. "Aurelie, above all things, I promise I will keep you safe. That includes from me, too. If at any point you want to stop, we stop. If you want to stop right now, we can go to the kitchen and bake ano—"

She pressed her fingers to his lips and put her mouth against his ear. "I don't want to stop, Des." To prove her point, she reached between them and took him in her hand.

His breath hitched. "*Aurelie.* If you do that, this may be over whether you like it or not."

"Oh," she said as realization dawned. "I'm sorry."

"Don't ever apologize for that," he breathed. "Now, tell me what you'd like from me."

She blushed, dropping her gaze. She wasn't sure how to voice what she liked. "It might be easier if I show you."

Where he'd once scowled at her as though she were an utter nuisance, Des gazed down at her now as though she were the most wonderful thing he'd ever beheld. That look alone was enough to undo her. But when he lowered his mouth to the hollow at the base of her throat and murmured against her skin, *good girl*, she knew she was lost completely.

CHAPTER 35
DES

AS DES LAY ON THE FLOOR—HOW HAD THEY ENDED UP ON the *floor*?—with Aurelie's head resting on his bare chest, he could only shake his head in disbelief. To think, he'd once doubted that she was good with her hands.

He hadn't come here today with this intention. The plan had been to bring Aurelie a Yule tree, to make her day a little less lonely—his too, if he was being fully honest—and put the first part of his plan into action. The fact that she was now lying next to him naked, her eyelashes fanned against her cheeks and her hair a mass of soft waves against his skin, was beyond anything he would have allowed himself to dream. In fact, he wasn't entirely sure this was real.

Her brow furrowed in her sleep, her lips curling in a small frown, and it took all his willpower not to pull her closer to him. She was so beautiful it was a physical pain in his chest, so sweet he could hardly breathe. And the way she had taken control, showed him exactly how to touch her . . . Demons take him, it was a fucking revelation. *She* was a revelation. And he knew, if only someone would grant him the chance, they could discover so much more together.

Her eyelashes fluttered as she began to wake, her hands instinctively reaching for him.

"Hey," he said, brushing her hair from her cheek. "How are you feeling?"

She made a small noise in her throat. "Sore." She turned her head to smile at him. "In a good way."

She was officially perfect. "It's nearly five," he said. "I was thinking we should get dressed, make some dinner?"

"That sounds lovely." She sat up and stretched, unselfconscious in a way he found unbearably attractive. His little buttoned-up schoolmarm was anything but.

After what they'd just shared, he almost couldn't bring himself to put his plan into action. But he was doing this for Aurelie, he reminded himself. "But first, maybe you could show me around campus?"

"I didn't know you had such an interest in the university," she said as she slipped into her shift and stockings. Watching her dress was almost as delightful as watching her undress.

"I didn't, before," he said as he reluctantly stopped admiring her to pull on his own tunic. "But it's where you've spent most of your life. I want to see your world, Aurelie."

She turned to smile at him over her shoulder. "That's maybe the nicest thing anyone has ever said to me."

He bowed and held his hand out to her. "Then lead the way, my lady."

As they finished dressing, Des was unable to resist helping himself to a few kisses in the process, and then Aurelie wrapped her hand around one of his fingers and led him outside into the lavender twilight. They walked past Easton Hall, through a small arboretum, and down a hill to an old cemetery, where the gravestones slanted in the soft earth like crooked teeth.

"Why is there a cemetery at a university?" Des asked, inching away from an aboveground tomb.

"There was a church here, around two hundred years ago. The clock tower is one of the only remaining parts. But no one was willing to build over the cemetery, so it remains." Aurelie ran her hands over a tombstone, apparently feeling none of Des's unease. "When I was little, I asked if my parents could be buried here, but Uncle Leopold explained that there was no room left. They were buried in our old village, or so I was told. I've never been back to see their graves."

"And what's this?" Des asked, pointing to the grotto.

"It used to be a fountain. It's mostly dried up now."

She opened the iron gate in front of it. "It's never locked anymore, but it would have been at some point, to keep out lusty students, I assume." She waggled her eyebrows and took a seat on the small stone bench, patting the seat next to her. "Join me?"

Des hesitated. "Here? It's somewhat . . . damp."

"Afraid of getting your trousers wet, are you?"

Des laughed. "Hardly." He took a seat next to her and she immediately snuggled in against him. He kissed the top of her head.

"Do you want to tell me about the ceremony?" she asked.

"It was dull. Military protocol, a lot of big words with very little said. But it did feel nice to be recognized for all the work I've put in over the years."

"Nice? I imagine you must be immensely proud, Des." She twined her fingers through his. "I know I am."

To hear her say she was proud of him was so bittersweet he had to clear his throat. "A few weeks ago, I was assigned to a new, elite unit, the Iron Swords."

She sat up to beam at him. "That's amazing, Des! Why didn't you tell me?"

"I thought you'd be upset."

"Upset?" She twisted her lips in a wry smile. "Des, I know what you do for a living, believe it or not."

"It's our mission to kill *verita* and capture their creators."

At that, Aurelie stiffened, and he wished he could take the words back. "Have you?"

"Last week was the first time." He angled his body so he could look her in the eyes. "I would never do that to you, though."

She furrowed her brow, looking entirely unconvinced. "Why? What's different about me?"

Aside from the fact that I'm utterly obsessed with you? "I know you're not trying to hurt anyone, for starters."

"*Now.* But you didn't know that before. If you'd arrested me the first time you met me, you'd think I was just as bad."

He wanted to protest, but he knew she wasn't wrong.

She forced a smile. "Well, when we finish the portal, there won't be any more *verita* for you to hunt, and inventing won't be illegal. So that should solve all our problems. Right?"

There was so much hope in her eyes, but he knew her well enough by now to know that there was doubt there, too. Just for tonight, he would hold on to her hope instead.

He nodded and gave in to the temptation to touch her, sliding one hand up her neck to cradle her cheek. "Can I kiss you?" he asked.

She rolled her eyes. "I would think the answer is rather ob—"

He kissed her before she could finish, but she didn't seem to mind. Before he knew it, she'd made her way onto his lap, and it was so simple to release her hair from its braid and drop the ribbon. He might have done it anyway, just to have his fingers tangled in her soft waves.

"You know," she said breathlessly, "we could go somewhere a little more comfortable."

"Gods, yes." He rose, still holding her.

"Des, I can walk!" She batted at his arm, but he only held her tighter.

"And risk soiling your dainty feet? I think not."

"My, Lieutenant Commander Whitlow, you certainly are a gentleman."

He started toward the cottage, but as they passed Easton Hall, she stilled him with a hand on his chest. "There," she said, and pointed to her laboratory.

"Are you sure?" he asked. "I was thinking a bed might be nice."

"You said you wanted to experience my world, Des. My lab is the very heart of it."

How could he deny her now? "Your wish is my command."

He proceeded up the steps, not even winded, and set her down at the top. When she pulled out her key, he touched it lightly. "Does that mean this is the key to your heart?" he asked, unable to keep a straight face.

She puffed a small laugh and moved the key aside so that his hand was resting on her chest. "*You* are, silly."

She dodged his next kiss, pulling him inside and practically skipping down the stairs to the long hallway. When they were in her laboratory and she was settled on the sofa, Des knelt in front of her and began to unlace her boots.

"What are you doing?" she asked.

"Helping you."

“I think I can manage that . . .” She reached up to her braid and frowned. “My ribbon. I must have left it behind.”

He hadn’t expected her to notice so quickly, wouldn’t have minded a few more minutes together, but this was always the plan. “That’s my fault,” Des said, rising. “Do you want me to go and get it?”

She hesitated. “Would you mind? Normally I wouldn’t care, but it was from my mother.”

“It’s fine. I’ll be back in two minutes,” he said, kissing her forehead. “In the meantime, you can get a head start on those boots. And whatever else you might want to remove.”

She grinned. “Presumptuous, aren’t you?”

“What can I say? You’ve turned me into something of an optimist.”

Des hated lying to Aurelie, and if he’d believed there were any other way to ensure they all came out of this alive, he would have moved mountains to see it done. But trapping Everard’s thrall was the only option.

He’d never meant to rope Gareth into it, either. The boy had caught him sneaking out of the armory yesterday with three iron spears, a length of chain, and a bundle of fake foliage.

For a moment, Des’s life had flashed before his eyes. He had no good excuse for what he was doing, no ready explanation. But Gareth had only asked how he could help, and wouldn’t be dissuaded. He was the one who discovered the grotto on a campus map.

It was always going to be a risk—but if they were successful, this could solve all of their problems. *So far, so good,* Des thought as he headed for the front gate. All except for the lying to Aurelie part. He could see Gareth's silhouette, shifting from one foot to the other. He jumped when Des hissed at him.

"Blood and bones, sir. You startled me."

"Any sign of the thrall?"

"Not yet," Gareth said. "But it's likely keeping to the shadows."

"All right." He opened the gate with a clang, hoping to alert the demon to their presence. "Come on, let's get to the grotto."

Leaving the gate open felt wrong, luring a demon onto campus even worse, but the thrall wasn't going to harm Aurelie. Des *should* be worrying about himself, or at the very least Gareth. They had such a short window to make this work. If he was gone for too long, Aurelie would undoubtedly grow suspicious. Worse, she might even come looking for him. He thought of her back in her laboratory, her hair unbound, her lips still swollen from earlier.

"Did you get her scent into the grotto?" Gareth asked.

"Yes," Des growled, not wanting to share any more details. "I left one of her ribbons there, too, and carried her back to her laboratory."

Gareth grinned, clearly about to say something suggestive, but thought better of it when he saw the look on Des's face.

The grotto was as they'd left it: the gate was still ajar, Aurelie's ribbon a dark tangle on the stone bench. They crouched in the shadows on either side of the grotto and waited.

Miraculously, it didn't take long before they heard the thrall's howl, sending shivers down Des's spine. This creature had been following Aurelie for weeks, possibly months, tracking her every move. *Everard* had been tracking her every move. This had to work, not least because he wanted to see that man rot in prison for what he'd put Aurelie through.

If Gareth's research on thralls was correct, Everard would be greatly weakened with the demon imprisoned behind iron bars. Tomorrow, Commander Yew would post a guard to Everard's house and arrest him the moment he stepped outside, if he could move at all. Des, Gareth, Daisy, and Jasper would come to the university to explain everything to Aurelie, and hopefully reveal the good news that her uncle was safe and sound.

Of all the difficult things Des had done in his life, telling Commander Yew the myriad ways he'd betrayed his trust was perhaps the hardest. He did it before his promotion ceremony, in case Yew changed his mind. But he'd heard Des out, which felt like a miracle in itself.

By the time he'd left Yew's office, Des knew he had utterly betrayed Aurelie. But Aurelie going to prison was better than her dying, even if the thought of her behind bars was unbearable. She should be free to learn, to love. To marry, though he knew it would never be him. Not once she knew what he'd done.

"I think I hear something," Gareth whispered.

Des had been so lost in his thoughts, he had missed the crunching of large paws in snow, but a moment later, the thrall's red eyes appeared in the dark. Its nose was low to the ground, tracking their scent. Des tensed in anticipation. They had only one chance to get this right. The chain was still coiled where he'd left it by the iron gate. He held his breath and said a silent prayer. This would work. This *had* to work.

"Now!" he shouted the moment the thrall entered the grotto. Gareth leapt on the gate, slamming it shut just seconds before the thrall's pointed snout was thrust through the bars. It yelped and leapt back at the close contact with the iron, giving Des enough time to wrap the chain around the gate and snap the padlock closed before its teeth snapped dangerously close to his fingers.

"We did it," Gareth breathed as they stood back, swords drawn, waiting for the creature to somehow break free of its cage.

Twice, it came close to the iron, growling as it sparked against its fur, tingeing the air with the smell of brimstone. It clawed at the stone at the back of the grotto but quickly gave up. It sat back on its haunches and released the most mournful howl Des had ever heard. It would be a miracle if Aurelie hadn't heard it. There was a strong temptation to kill it now, but he'd vowed to capture a *verita* alive. Besides, if they were wrong and killing it didn't injure Everard, then Aurelie's uncle could pay the ultimate price for his impatience.

"I have to get back," Des said to Gareth. "Come on."

Still astonished the plan had worked, they ran back to the university gate. Gareth was about to slip through when Des shocked them both by pulling the boy into a firm embrace.

"You did good, kid," he said, ruffling Gareth's hair.

And Gareth, bless him, smiled wider than Des had ever seen before.

"What will you tell Aurelie about the ribbon?" Gareth asked as Des closed the gate behind him.

"The ribbon is the least of my concerns right now. Tell Commander Yew we succeeded. I'll be back at the fort shortly."

Gareth started to go, then paused. "You're doing the right thing, you know."

Des had no idea if that was true, but it was too late to turn back. He could only hope that, someday, Aurelie would forgive him.

CHAPTER 36
AURELIE

AURELIE WOKE TO THE SOUND OF THE DOOR OPENING AND Des's large silhouette slipping through. Before she could say anything, he sat down on the ground next to the sofa and kissed her cheek.

"What took so long?" she asked, glancing at the clock. At least half an hour had passed since she fell asleep.

"I searched everywhere for your ribbon," he said, tucking a strand of hair behind her ear, his ice-cold fingers proof that he'd been outside all this time. "I'm so sorry I couldn't find it."

"That's okay," she said. "I'm sure I'll find it in the morning. Thank you for trying."

He nodded. "I should get back to the fort."

Suddenly, she was fully alert. "Already? What about . . . ?"

He smiled and kissed her so sweetly that Aurelie felt a curl of doubt in her stomach. "What's the matter?"

"Nothing," he said, his voice a soft rumble in the dark. "But you have a big day ahead of you tomorrow, and I think you should get your rest."

"I'll rest when I'm dead," she said, taking his face in her hands. "I want to spend tonight with you."

"Aurelie . . ."

She reached over to her nightstand to turn on her lamp. "What's going on? Everything was fine before you went to look for the ribbon, and now you're acting strangely."

Something passed behind his silver eyes, but it was a look she hadn't learned yet. Maybe that was why it elicited a sinking dread in her stomach. "I'm concerned about tomorrow, that's all."

"I wish you'd have a little more faith in me," she said, pulling him onto the sofa beside her.

"And I wish you'd have a little less faith in Everard." He ran his hands through his hair. "I know you don't want me here tomorrow—"

"It's not that I don't *want* you here, Des. It's that it wouldn't be safe for you. If Everard sees you, he'll think I've betrayed him in some way."

"What makes you think Everard isn't already well aware of me? If Kobal has seen me, I have to assume Everard has."

"If that were the case, he would have said something by now. Listen, I know it's difficult, but in twenty-four hours, this will all be over. Uncle Leo will be home, I'll be back to being a student, and if all goes well, you'll be searching for a new line of work."

To her relief, he smirked. "Seems a shame, when I just got a promotion."

"I've heard the Iron Guard has a good retirement program."

"I'm nineteen. A little young to retire, don't you think?"

She chewed her lip for a moment, and when she spoke again there was no teasing in her voice whatsoever. "Maybe it can be a fresh start. For both of us?"

He arched a brow. "What do you mean?"

"I mean, I'm going to give up inventing." She shook her head when he started to protest. "I've given it a lot of thought, and I can't in good conscience continue with it. Not after all the harm I've caused."

"But with the portal closed, you'll be able to invent without creating demons. It's hardly the time to retire."

She was grateful for his encouragement, when once he'd despised her for her inventing, but she'd made up her mind. "My uncle wants me to live a normal life. Even if inventing is legal again, there will be a stigma hanging over it for years to come. I'll finish university, earn my degree, get a proper job."

"But it's your passion, Aurelie. You can't just give it up."

"What about you? Have you thought about what you'll do next?"

He shrugged. "I haven't allowed myself to get that far, if I'm being honest."

Her heart sank. "Because you don't believe it will work."

She was grateful he didn't lie to her, that he had more respect for her than to offer false hope. "Even if it does. I never think beyond the immediate future. There's never been a point."

"Well," she said, leaning against him, "let's daydream for a minute. Close your eyes." She sat up a bit to make sure he was complying. "Good. Now, imagine yourself in ten years."

He shuddered. "I'll be nearly thirty."

"Exactly. Your life will just be beginning." Aurelie had never feared growing older. It was a privilege to live a long life, one her parents had been denied. "Now, you're a strong, handsome, *young* man. Where are you?"

He took in a deep breath through his nose and released it slowly. "I'm in a garden."

Aurelie shifted and Des cracked one eye open. "Really?"

"It's the first thing that came to mind."

"Hmm." Aurelie resettled. "All right, you're in a garden. Where is this garden?"

"Behind a cottage. *My* cottage, I think."

"Curiouser and curiouser. What time of year is it?"

"Early autumn. It's warm, but there's a hint of fall in the air. The first leaves are just beginning to turn."

"It sounds lovely."

"It is. You should join me." She could feel his heartbeat beneath her ear, slow and steady, content.

"Speaking of, is anyone with you?"

He was quiet for a long moment. "No, but I can hear someone moving around the cottage. Clattering, in fact."

She felt a grin tug at the corner of her mouth. "Clattering?"

"Yes, and giggling. It's the cutest sound in the world. There's a dog next to me. A very large, tough-looking dog, of course. And I can smell a cake baking. It's slightly burnt, but I'll eat it anyway."

She batted his arm, annoyed he wasn't taking this seriously, but also grateful that he had included her in this fantasy. "All right. When I'm not busy giggling and clattering, what am I doing?"

"You're in your laboratory. Right here, at the university. You're a science professor, and occasional inventor," he added, once again cracking an eye open to see her response. "And your uncle is so delighted you're nearby he doesn't say a word."

It was all so perfect, she felt the bittersweet sting of tears in the back of her eyes. "And Mephisto?"

"Here, in this very room, keeping it cockroach free. And preferably staying far away from our cottage."

She turned to look at Des.

He opened both eyes and stroked her cheek with the back of his hand. "What's wrong, love?"

"I want it. Everything you said. Why can't we have that?"

He leaned forward, resting his forehead against hers. "Who says we can't?"

Everyone, she thought. But she didn't respond, and when he finally brought his mouth to hers, she let herself believe, if only for a moment, that the future was theirs to create.

When the morning came, Aurelie found herself alone on her sofa, and the absence of both Des and Mephisto was a dull, throbbing ache she recognized as the deep loneliness she'd felt right after her parents died. Everard was supposed to arrive at ten for the completion of the portal. There was nothing left to do but get dressed and wait.

Aurelie put on her simplest dress, a plain black wool one that seemed fitting for today, which had the heavy, sobering atmosphere of a funeral. The temperature had dropped once again, refreezing all the melted snow into a treacherous sheet of ice. She nearly fell several times on the way to Uncle Leo's cottage. She lit a fire and prepared tea, but the warmth of both couldn't reach her today.

By nine, she was growing anxious, pacing up and down the halls with nothing to do. She wished Everard would hurry up and arrive so she could get this horrible day over with. She had forbidden anyone else from coming—had ensured it, in fact—and yet she couldn't help wishing that someone would rescue her from this terrible mess she'd made for herself. At nine thirty, when she couldn't stand sitting still anymore, she went outside to wait for Everard by the gates.

On a whim, she checked the postbox. A single letter was wedged inside, damp from snow but fortunately still legible. She was so relieved when she saw Professor Sheldrake's shaky handwriting that she nearly wept.

But as she scanned the words, her relief quickly turned to a thick, cloying horror that crawled up her throat like a scream.

Aurelie,

I can only pray this letter finds you in time. It's my fault, of course. I gave you free rein when I should have harnessed you like the reckless child you are. Please, if you are reading this, stop everything you've put into motion before it's too late.

You nearly translated the spell—I suppose you deserve some recognition for that—but I must have failed to fully impart how devious Elder Vansion can be. How reading it from the lens of a modern Wisterian could be ruinous, given how archaic the language is, how simplistic compared to New Vansion.

Aurelie skimmed the words beneath, her translation with the blanks filled in and corrected by Professor Sheldrake:

Spill ancient blood, seize the fated thorn,
A quest for balance, through treason reborn.
One flame to extinguish destiny's might,
Renewal through battle, one soul to make right.

In the shadows lies the ancient key,
Transformation, betrayal, to set forces free.
At crossroads dark, the portal will wake,
Creation from ruin, the bond we shall break.

Below that, Sheldrake had written, *"Shadow" is an archaic term for demon. I believe the "fated thorn" in question refers to King Aciano's hawthorn crown. Aurelie, this is a plot for treason. Whoever Everard is, he is not trying to send the demons back from where they came. He—*

"Good morning, Aurelie."

Aurelie thrust the letter into her pocket on instinct. Everard loomed above her like a gallows. "You're early," she blurted.

"Reading something interesting?"

She forced out a dry laugh. "Hardly. Just a note from one of my professors regarding a project proposal."

Everard's lips twitched. "Are you going to let me in, Aurelie?"

"Yes, of course." She fumbled with the latch, her cold fingers numb and useless. Finally, she managed to open the gate just wide enough for Everard and closed it behind him. She hadn't finished Sheldrake's letter, but what she had read was clear enough. This had all been a trap, and possibly one far worse than she could have imagined.

"This way," she said as they headed toward her workshop where the portal waited. Her mind raced for some sort of way out. Surely this wouldn't work. She hadn't translated everything properly—though she knew that likely didn't matter, since Everard had provided the actual runes and Kiara had copied them with exacting diligence. Well, she would simply have to transcribe the final rune incorrectly. If Everard were capable of doing it himself, he would have done so already.

Leading Everard down into the cold, dark basement, she had a terrible feeling that he was going to kill her as soon as she was finished. That he'd never meant to let her uncle go in the first place.

She turned at the bottom of the steps to find him standing so close to her she flinched. "Where is my uncle?"

"He's still in my basement," he said. "Here." He procured a key from his pocket and held it out. "This will free him. You have my word."

"I don't trust your word," she said, refusing to take the key.

He sighed and reached into the breast pocket of his coat, procuring a letter. "Go on, read it."

This she took, instantly recognizing Leo's handwriting.

My dearest Aurelie,

Whatever you're about to do, I beg you now not to. Everard cannot be trusted, and nothing he has planned is worth my life. I will die a willing sacrifice if only you'll call this off. I love you. All of you. Never doubt that.

Yours always,
Uncle Leopold

She looked up at Everard with fury burning in her eyes. "How is this possibly supposed to reassure me?"

"Well, he had to be alive to write it, didn't he?"

"He could have written it at any point. And he wants me to *stop* you."

Everard shrugged. "Of course. But I also know you won't."

Hot tears slipped down Aurelie's cheeks. "I despise you."

Everard sighed and stepped around her, approaching the portal. "I'm impressed," he said, as though she hadn't spoken. "I knew you were clever, resourceful. But I did not have faith that you'd pull it off."

"What choice did I have?" she demanded.

"You could have done it all by yourself, and then I have no doubt you wouldn't have finished."

Aurelie's stomach sank at the implication. "You know I had help."

"Of course I know. I already told you, child. I know everything. I was surprised when I realized the Iron Guards were helping you, though perhaps I shouldn't have been. There is something about you that I imagine people find appealing. Your single-mindedness is refreshing in a world of compromisers and settlers."

"Are you going to hurt them?" Aurelie asked, her voice shaking, her hands clenched in useless fists at her sides.

"There's no need." Everard glanced at the final metal plate waiting for its engraving. The one that looked something like an eye. The one that she now knew meant *wake*. "Now, am I going to have to force you to complete this, or are you going to comply like a good girl?"

Something about Everard's words struck a nerve deep inside Aurelie, the mocking echo of Des's very real praise, Everard's clear disregard for her humanity. She was a tool to him. Nothing more.

"Who are you, really?" she asked.

"I think you already know the answer to that, Aurelie."

It had nagged at her from the start, his flame-red hair, his in-depth knowledge of Wisterian history, his near-reverence for invention. "Prince Florian," she whispered, as the dread inside of her widened from a slowly creeping wormhole into a deep, unending chasm.

Before he could respond, a terrible howl split the silence, causing every hair on Aurelie's body to stand on end. "Is that . . . ?"

"Kobal. Yes. Your friends have grown desperate."

"What are you talking about?"

"Come, Aurelie," he said, taking her by the arm. "They won't get to you in time. Finish this, before they're all dead and you have nothing left to save."

"What have you done?" she asked, wrenching free of his grip.

He studied his fingernails with the callous detachment of a man without a soul. "How can I put this?" He looked up at her and smiled. "Well, let's just say your little demon friend has eaten well this week."

CHAPTER 37
DES

TO THINK, IT HAD ALL COME DOWN TO ONE FUCKING KEY.

Des hadn't slept last night, going over the rest of his plan detail by detail, convinced that if he imagined every possible outcome, he could somehow control the future. And he may well have, if it hadn't been for the damn key.

When had Aurelie swapped it? he wondered. It could have been at any point; he'd been so vulnerable around her, so trusting. Of course, he'd been so racked with guilt at all the ways he was betraying her that he hadn't stopped to think she might also betray him. Or worse, that she didn't trust him in the first place.

He had gone to the university gate as planned with Daisy, Jasper, and several Iron Swords. Commander Yew and the rest of the team had gone to Everard's house to arrest him, assuming they'd find him in a weakened condition given Kobal's entrapment.

But as soon as Des arrived, he knew something was wrong. There was a feeling in the air, a heavy foreboding that he didn't think was simply fear. They were early, and yet it felt as though he was far too late for whatever was about to happen next.

They had planned to go and check on Kobal first, before Everard's arrival. Des removed the key from his neck and tried to fit it in the lock. At first, he was sure he was inserting the key incorrectly. Daisy had even sighed in exasperation and tried it herself.

But after her third attempt, she had turned to look at Des with a pained expression.

"Des."

He swore, kicking the snow. "Why would she do this?"

"Because she knew you'd come," Daisy said. "She clearly wants to protect you."

"Of all the foolish, reckless, irresponsible things." He thrust his hands into his hair.

"There has to be another way in," Jasper said, eyeing the height of the gate in front of them.

Des blew out his breath, trying to regroup. "There's a tree at the back, near the clock tower. I think we can get over the gate that way. Jasper, with me. Daisy, I need you to wait here in case Everard comes." He started running, not checking behind him to be sure they were following orders. By the time he reached the back of the university, the bells were chiming a quarter till.

He was relieved to see Jasper right behind him. "You go first," he said. "I'm too heavy."

"On it." Jasper shimmied up the tree easily, followed by one of the other Iron Swords.

"Go and open the gate as quickly as you can," Des called.

"Where are you going?"

"To check on Kobal." With the other two guards already on the other side of the gate, Des climbed up the tree as fast as he could and crouched low as he walked along a thick branch over the fence. It was only a moment later that he heard the groan of a limb breaking, but by then, he was hanging below the branch and dropping to the ground.

Des's thoughts were racing as he hurried to the grotto, every fiber in him wishing he could check on Aurelie first. But something told him that whatever was happening to Kobal would inform every other decision he made from here on out.

To his surprise, the demon was lying on its side, breathing heavily, pressed to the back of the grotto. It tried to rouse itself when it saw Des, but immediately fell back again with a whimper. It was weakened, near death. He should have felt immense relief. And yet, he didn't.

"Des!"

He whirled around to see Jasper behind him, gripping a wound in his arm.

"What the hell happened?"

"It's bad. Demons at the gate. A dozen or more. They look like the one we killed here the other night. No word from Yew or the Iron Swords."

Des's stomach felt like it was in free fall, like the world was opening up beneath him. "Where's Daisy?"

"She's fighting with the others. We need you."

Swearing, Des broke into a run behind Jasper. "Your wound?"

"Not from a demon, thank goodness," Jasper said. "One of your Iron Swords threw me out of the way. I cut my arm on someone else's blade."

"Did you warn the others about the venom?"

Jasper nodded as they reached the gates.

It was utter chaos. There were demons everywhere, snarling and snapping at the guards, lashing out with their venom-tipped claws. To his relief, Daisy appeared unharmed and was fighting back-to-back with one of the Iron Swords. But as he pushed through the gate to get to her, a demon flew at him, knocking him aside and making a break for the open door.

Des caught its heel with his dagger, but as with the demon he and Aurelie had killed in the well, this one hardly seemed injured. "Decapitate them!" he bellowed as he pushed to his feet. "Cut off their heads!"

But before anyone could heed his command, the demons broke for the open gate in unison, nearly trampling Des as he dove out of their path onto campus.

The wind was knocked from his lungs as he hit the ground. He struggled for air, trying to get the other guards' attention, still unable to draw breath. Fortunately, Daisy saw what was happening and spread the order.

"Everard must have gotten here before us," she said as she helped him to his feet. "Did you find his thrall?"

Des nodded, managing a feeble wheeze. "Impaired but alive."

"Then Gareth was wrong about thralls?"

He shook his head. "I don't know." If the intel was wrong, Des would never forgive himself. Commander Yew should be back here by now, assuming he'd arrived at Everard's townhouse and found him gone. He could only hope they had rescued Dr. Blake in time.

As they raced across the campus toward the tower, his thoughts turned once again to Aurelie. She must have realized this was a trap by now. She wouldn't finish the portal, couldn't possibly fail to see how dire this had become. To his surprise, the door to the basement workshop was open, but the moment Des began to descend the steps, a demon flew at him, its claws missing him by inches.

He left it to the other guards to kill it as he dodged and barreled down the stairs to the workshop. He skidded to a stop the moment he hit the bottom step. Before him stood Everard, surrounded by six demons, the portal behind him. And in his arms, gagged, was Aurelie.

Des braced himself for the demons to attack, but they were as eerily still as the stone gargoyles they resembled. His mind raced. How was it possible that Everard had these creatures in his thrall as well? If Des killed one, would it harm Everard? Or would he only be endangering Aurelie?

"You must be Destrier Whitlow," Everard said, terrifyingly calm given the chaos around them. "Allow me to introduce myself."

"I know who you are," Des growled. "Let her go."

"You know me as Everard," the man continued calmly. "But my real name is Florian Hawthorn, rightful heir to the throne of Wisteria."

Des looked at Aurelie, wondering if he'd gone insane. But tears streamed down her cheeks, and if the most intelligent person he'd ever met believed this lunatic, it had to be true.

"What do you want?" Des asked. He could feel Daisy, Jasper, and the others behind him, weapons drawn, ready to help defend him should it come to that.

"Of you? Not a thing. Miss Blake was just about to finish my portal when you all decided to join us. I can see you're tempted to try to save her, but I assure you, there's no need. Once she completes the portal, she will be freed along with her uncle."

Aurelie mumbled something against the gag, shaking her head vehemently no. Des scanned Everard for some sign of a weapon, but all the man had was a small dagger strapped at his waist. He must be very sure of his demons to not even bother drawing the thing.

Everard turned Aurelie toward the portal and gave her a light shove, sending her stumbling forward. Des noticed there was a tool in her hand, the one she and Kiara had used for the engravings.

"Aurelie," he called, but she didn't turn. Something had happened since he last saw her, something that had convinced her that Everard—or Florian, or whoever he was—was a liar, that this plan would not go as he'd promised. Otherwise, she wouldn't have hesitated to finish the portal. "Whatever he's told you, don't believe him. We'll figure this all out together. I promise."

He knew she heard him by the stiffening of her spine, but despite it, she raised her hand to the metal plaque and began to inscribe the final rune. He started forward, as Everard must have known he would, because he released the demons in that moment.

Everything that followed was pandemonium. There were as many hunters as there were demons, but in this enclosed space, it was difficult to tell what was happening. Claws and teeth came at Des from all sides, and meanwhile there was a growing wind and a loud, distant roaring, like thunder.

"Aurelie!" he screamed as he stabbed a demon through the eye, but she couldn't hear him, or she chose not to. Behind him, he heard a woman shriek, and in a panic he turned to see a female guard—not Daisy, he thought with mingled relief and horror—eviscerated by one of the creatures. A moment later, Jasper cut the creature's head off at the shoulders, nearly choking them with a cloud of brimstone.

Des turned back to Aurelie just as she finished the last mark. The rune was wobbly and crude compared to the others, and a part of him was desperate to believe that she had some last-minute trick up her sleeve that could get them all out of this. He kept one eye on

Aurelie, the other on the demons as he continued to fight his way toward her.

As soon as she'd finished, Everard caught her under her arms and raised his blade to her back. Des screamed a warning, but Everard was only cutting through the gag tied at the back of her head. Aurelie immediately spat it from her mouth to scream.

He couldn't hear her over the roar, but he could see her calling his name. Telling him to run. As if he would possibly leave her now.

Everard then turned the knife on himself, slicing a deep wound in his palm. He pressed his hand to the center of the portal.

In that moment, there was only silence.

Des watched in horrified fascination as the metal plates began to whir and click, the metal channels on their sides locking into place, one after the other. This was what Aurelie had spent so long perfecting, and in any other circumstance, he would have marveled at it. But as realization dawned that she hadn't foiled Everard's plan after all, Des found himself numb. She'd said a dozen times that she wasn't going to let her uncle die. He should have believed her.

The runes began to glow, a soft blue at first that grew steadily brighter until it was a near-blinding shade of violet. The center stones receded backward, and in their place, a swirling purple vortex of light appeared. She'd really done it, had somehow taken Everard's stones and plates and wielded dark magic. He cast his glance at one of the nearby demons and jumped aside when he realized it was struggling, as though it were being pulled backward by a great force.

Blood and bones, the portal was sucking the demon in. The creature tore great gouges out of the stone floor with its claws in an effort to hold its ground, but a moment later, another demon crashed into it, and then they were both flying backward through the portal, disappearing into that brilliant, sickening light.

Everard laughed in delight. Aurelie was staring at Des, her face so pale he worried she might lose consciousness. Seizing the opportunity, he ran to her, gathering her in his arms before she could respond.

"I'm so sorry," he whispered, pressing a kiss to the top of her head. "I should never have gone behind your back."

Something changed in her then, and she pushed free of Des's arms with surprising strength. "Where's my uncle?" she demanded of Everard. "You promised he'd be safe. Where is my uncle?"

But the man wasn't listening. He was peering into the vortex as though he were waiting for something. And that was perhaps more frightening than anything else Des could have imagined.

CHAPTER 38
AURELIE

AURELIE WAS ABOUT TO ATTACK EVERARD FROM BEHIND with her bare hands, despite Des tugging at her waist to drag her from the portal, until she saw the figure looming on the other side of the vortex.

It was small at first, though its silhouette was monstrous. Horrified but unable to look away, she watched as the shape grew steadily larger.

No, not growing. Coming closer.

The portal was like a window to the other side of the veil, the demonic world that she'd relegated Mephisto and all its kind to. She knew intrinsically that it was something no human was ever supposed to see. The portal was like a vulnerable pane of glass in what should have been an impenetrable wall.

Everard had begun to whisper in a language she couldn't understand, though she suspected it was related to Elder Vansion. The runes pulsed, as though responding to his words, but the demon continued to move closer to the portal.

"Aurelie," Des growled in her ear. "Let's go, now, before it's too late." Behind him, several guards had already started backing up the stairs.

She turned to face Des, truly seeing him for the first time today. "What did you do?" she asked, her eyes taking in the dead female guard, the wound in Jasper's side.

His gaze was full of something Aurelie had never expected to see there: defeat. "I thought by capturing Kobal, we could take Everard. I'm so sorry. Gareth's research was wrong."

"It wasn't wrong," Everard said, still watching the portal intently. "Thralls and their human counterparts are connected when the human offers part of his soul to the demon in exchange for its powers."

"Then Kobal isn't your thrall," Aurelie breathed.

"No. He was the gatekeeper of the first portal, and mine to control as part of the bargain I made."

"And that?" Aurelie asked, turning to look at the demon and immediately recoiling in horror. It was twice the height of Everard but far larger, its shape shrouded in swirling black shadows. Aurelie could make out its glowing red eyes and the razor-sharp tips of two massive horns, but everything else was obscured, leaving her imagination to fill in all sorts of nightmares.

"Also under my control, should it enter this world."

"Come on," Jasper was urging behind them. "We need to get back to the Iron Fortress and warn the commander."

"What is your plan?" Aurelie shouted at Everard, because this might be her final chance to know. She had no idea if her uncle was alive or what came next for the Iron Guard, but she was bound for prison or death regardless.

Everard glanced over his shoulder at her. "To take back what is rightfully mine. To finally do what my father and brother failed to do. To make Wisteria the most powerful kingdom in the world."

"And the portal?" she spat. "It's not the mirror image of the one you told me about, is it? It's the original."

"Clever girl. Yes, Revenin destroyed the portal when he realized what my plans were. I killed him, which was admittedly shortsighted on my part. Without him, it took me decades to re-create his original plans."

"Des," came Daisy's urgent plea.

"Aurelie, please." She felt his hand on her shoulder, and a part of her was desperate to go with him, to turn herself in to the Iron Guard and allow someone else to clean up this horrible mess she'd made. But if the portal could be destroyed once, then surely it could be destroyed again. She was no mage, and yet she'd managed to re-create what Revenin had done. That had to count for something. Because otherwise, they were all done for.

Everard turned toward her then, as though reading her thoughts. He opened his mouth to speak and froze. Blood began to spill from his parted lips, and Aurelie looked down to see something dark and pointed protruding from his abdomen.

The demon from the portal. Its claws curled around Everard's torso, dragging him backward several feet. The damned creature was on *this* side of the door, and it was immediately clear that Everard did not have control over it as he'd thought he did.

Screams erupted behind Aurelie. Everard twitched as the demon shook him free of its horns, crumpling to the ground like a rag doll. Then the demon's entire head was through the portal, its shoulders barely restrained by the frame. Between the swirling shadows, Aurelie could make out mottled blue flesh straining against bulging muscles and a mouthful of fangs protruding from the demon's jaws like those of a lantern fish.

Everard looked up at her, and for the first time since Aurelie met him, he seemed afraid.

He mouthed a single word: *Run.*

Before she could comply, Des's hand found hers and she was being dragged out of the basement up into the main floor of the clock tower. They'd barely made it outside when they heard a roar behind them, one full of so much fury it made her blood run cold. She stumbled as her feet hit the ice, but Des was steady next to her. All she had to do was pump her legs to keep up with him.

But she faltered at the explosion of stone and rubble behind them. Aurelie turned to look over her shoulder and screamed. The demon had burst free of the building, shaking off dust and rocks as it roared again.

"What do we do?" Aurelie asked.

"We have to get back to the fort. Let's pray the iron gates are enough to hold this thing."

"We can't risk it! If iron isn't enough to contain the other demons, I don't see how this one can be controlled. And if it gets free in the city . . ."

Des reached the gate first. On the other side, Aurelie saw a battalion of Iron Guards standing behind someone who could only be Commander Yew.

And next to him, to her utter astonishment, was Uncle Leopold.

She shoved past everyone in her way to get to him, clutching the bars that separated them.

"You're alive," she sobbed. He was thin, so much frailer than when she'd last seen him.

"I'm all right," he said, taking her hands through the bars. "Everything is going to be all right."

"I'm so sorry," she managed, her entire body shaking with her tears. "I did so many things wrong. I know I let you down in every possible way."

"Aurelie, this isn't your fault. I prom—"

His words were cut off by another thunderous roar. Aurelie turned to see the demon standing on the other side of the courtyard, even more monstrous in the daylight. She pressed back against the gate, almost laughing at the absurdity of how she'd once thought she could contain this on her own. Everard was nowhere to be seen. The Iron Guards had their swords and spears drawn, Des among them. Aurelie's iron blade was in her hand, though she didn't remember reaching for it.

"Aurelie!" Uncle Leopold hissed from behind her. "Get through the gates, before it's too late."

"All injured guards and civilians are to get to the Iron Fortress immediately," a man shouted. It must have been Commander Yew, though Aurelie noticed none of the guards on this side of the gate obeyed his command.

Instead, one launched an iron-tipped arrow at the demon. It plinked uselessly off the monster's thick skin. All along its arms and back, its flesh glowed with strange symbols. Runes, Aurelie realized. Though the gates seemed to be holding it for now, Aurelie sensed it wouldn't be long before it discovered it could leap over them. They were not going to be able to kill this demon the usual way. Their best bet was to send it back through the portal somehow, and then destroy it, assuming the portal was even still standing.

"Come on, Aurelie," Uncle Leo said, his voice so full of fear Aurelie found herself wanting to comfort him.

She needed to talk to Des, to help him formulate a plan. "Go with the guards," she told her uncle.

"Not without you."

Aurelie risked turning her back on the demon to face her uncle. "I'm going to be all right. Please, just trust me. One last time."

Before he could respond, she squeezed his hands and ran to Des, whose face darkened when he saw her. "What are you still doing here? Commander Yew—"

They both turned at a commotion near the demon. One of the guards had foolishly approached it with an iron pike.

"NO!" Des roared, but it was too late. The pike was sharp enough to pierce the demon's skin, but not nearly strong enough to kill a demon this size. It seized the guard by his torso and latched its many teeth around his head, ripping it away before anyone could react.

And then all hell broke loose.

Guards who had previously been bravely facing the monster quailed. Several made a break for the gates, nearly shoving Aurelie off her feet in the process.

"Hold your ground!" Des commanded, but it was clear to Aurelie that he wasn't in charge here. She wasn't sure anyone was anymore.

"Come on," Aurelie said, grabbing Des's hand. "That demon is about to get even bigger. If we don't get it back through the portal now, we might never be able to."

Des searched her face with a look of desperation she'd never seen there. "Back through the portal? What are you talking about?"

"There are runes on its skin. I think we can control it that way."

Des shook his head in disbelief. "So you're saying you want to go back in there." It wasn't a question. Des knew her well enough by now. "Commander Yew will kill me."

Aurelie glanced back at the commander, who was busy yelling orders at his guards. "Then we'd better hurry," she said, pulling Des toward her laboratory while the demon continued to swat away guards like fleas.

"You said it yourself, if it eats anyone else . . ."

"Commander Yew knows how demons work, doesn't he? And I'm sure he's figured out by now that iron weapons aren't going to be enough."

Sure enough, Yew was calling off his guards, who were streaming through the gates now. Aurelie looked back at the demon, which had grown by at least another three feet since it fed.

"I can't just abandon my post, Aurelie."

"You won't be. We're going to help them." She tugged again, and was grateful that he didn't resist her this time. They began to run. "We need chalk and salt."

"I hardly think this is the time for one of your experiments," he hissed, but he followed her as she let them into Easton Hall.

"It's not for an experiment," she said, trying to catch her breath. "I need my Helping Hand. I have an idea, and you're just going to have to trust me."

Before she could go, Des stayed her with his hands on her shoulders. "What is it?" She looked up at him, at the sorrow and pain in his eyes.

"I'm so sorry, Aurelie."

Perhaps she should be angry with him for betraying her, but

then, she had done far worse. She had destroyed the life he worked so hard for. "I'm the one who should be apologizing. I'm so sorry, Des. I've done nothing but cause you trouble since the moment you met me."

He pulled her against him, so tight it hurt, but it was a reassuring hurt, the kind that meant they were still very much alive. "Turns out I like trouble," he said, resting his chin atop her head.

"I have to make this right, Des. I have to send the demon back and destroy the portal forever."

He squeezed her tighter. "And then we'll go find that cottage in the country and start our new life together. We could be happy, Aurelie."

Her heart hurt at his words, because as badly as she wanted to believe them, she couldn't. People like her, *criminals* like her, didn't get happy endings. But she nodded, and because she knew it was what he needed to hear, said, "I know we could, Des."

When they emerged from Easton Hall with their materials, the campus was deceptively quiet. Perhaps Aurelie had been too hasty and they should have waited to hear Commander Yew's plan. "Maybe it's already de—"

The demon landed with an earth-shuddering thud directly in front of them.

Aurelie screamed. Had it been on the roof? Could this thing fly? If so, they were doomed. They were caught on the steps. If they retreated to Easton Hall, they'd be as good as abandoning the city.

"What do we do?" Des asked, squeezing her hand so tightly she could feel her bones grinding together.

They braced themselves, but the demon was watching them, its head cocked in an almost curious way, and Aurelie wondered for a split second if it was hoping to communicate with her.

She was in no mood to talk to this demon.

"We're going to have to split up, Des. I don't think it will kill me."

"You don't think?"

"I'm going to lure it away from here. Go to Kobal, see if you can set it free. Then meet me at the tower."

"Aurelie . . ."

She turned her face toward him. "Please, Des."

She could see he was at war with himself, but finally, he nodded once. "All right."

Aurelie squeezed his hand one last time and then slowly moved down the first step. The demon didn't move. She took another, then another, until she was at the bottom of the stairs. The demon's eyes were fixed on her. In her peripheral vision she could see Des moving swiftly down the steps along the left side of the building. Aurelie walked right, away from the cemetery and the grotto. Skirting the edge of the courtyard, the demon followed her, but it kept the same distance between them.

Finally, she had to turn her back on the demon in order to make it to the tower. She was truly alone with it, and all she could do was take calm, measured steps, afraid if she sprinted the demon would chase her down and rip her head off as it had the guard's.

When she reached the clock tower, she looked back and gasped. The other Iron Guards were trying to engage the demon, which was still focused on Aurelie.

"Leave it!" she screamed, but they ignored her, instead darting forward and back, hoping to catch it with an iron blade while it was distracted. When one finally managed to slice across its heel, the demon roared and turned on the woman, tearing her in half with its massive fists.

Aurelie felt bile rising in her throat, did her best to choke it down. At least the demon was focused on her again. She crawled through the jagged hole it had left in the side of the building, praying it would continue to follow her.

Everard's body was where they'd left it, illuminated by the soft glow from the portal, which fortunately hadn't released anything else, though she could make out dark shapes in the distance. Perhaps they needed the gatekeeper's permission to enter, or perhaps they were just biding their time.

She stooped next to Everard and held her hand over his mouth to check if he was breathing. She wasn't sure if she was relieved or disgusted when she felt a puff of air.

A commotion from outside spurred her into action. Fortunately, they'd stashed bags of salt here as a precaution, and Aurelie tore a hole in one with her teeth as she walked around the portal, creating an open circle of salt. She could only pray it would be enough to hold the demon until she could enact her plan.

Aurelie startled when she heard footsteps on the stairs behind her. Des lumbered into the room, Kobal limp in his arms. He dropped the creature on the floor next to Everard.

"Where's the gatekeeper?" she asked, referring to the massive demon.

"It's right behind me," he panted, taking her by the arm. "What's the rest of your plan, Aurelie?"

“Lure it into the circle, leap out, and inscribe the banishment rune on the demon’s skin with the Helping Hand.”

Des stared at her blankly for a moment. “That’s ridiculous.”

Aurelie nodded curtly. “Why, thank you.”

“How do you know it will work?”

“That’s what Kobal is for.” She approached it cautiously, fairly certain it was too weak to hurt her but not sure enough to risk death. She poked it with the Helping Hand, moving a tuft of fur aside and smiling when she saw the faintly glowing runes on its skin. She had been right.

Now she needed to recall the rune for banishment.

She thought it was something like an upside-down *U* with a slash through it, but did the slash go left to right or right to left? It was also the rune for everlasting sleep—likely a euphemism for death—and destruction.

As if on cue, the demon roared again, closer this time.

“Aurelie,” Des urged.

She closed her eyes, steeling herself. She was just going to have to trust her instincts. Using the chalk, she drew an extremely crude rune on the demon’s skin, and waited.

Just when she was about to give up hope, the runes pulsed in time with the portal.

“It’s working,” Des breathed.

Before either of them could say another word, Kobal slid across the floor with horrifying speed, disappearing into the maw of the portal.

“It actually fucking worked,” Des said. “You are a genius.”

Aurelie wiped a bead of sweat from her brow and nodded. “All right, it’s time to get the gatekeeper.”

"Let me be the bait," Des said, taking her shoulders. "It's the very least I can do."

"No. You're much faster than me, and it doesn't seem to want to harm me. I need you to close off the circle and contain the demon. And I need your sword at the ready, should it break free."

He sighed but nodded. "All right."

Aurelie withdrew her dagger from her waist and hurried to the door, listening. "It's coming," she said. "Get—"

Before she could finish, the demon burst into the room, and Aurelie barely leapt back in time to avoid being crushed. The creature released an ear-splitting shriek, its breath fetid and foul as it moved toward her. It took all her strength to remain standing, her fear was so great, but she backed toward the portal slowly.

For a moment, the demon merely watched her, its strange fascination with her once more apparent. Or perhaps it sensed this was a trap. It scented the air, turning its massive head from side to side, clocking Des and Everard but making no moves forward. Unlike Aurelie's invention demons, it seemed self-possessed enough not to leap on its nearest food source. Its size was even more alarming after it fed, and she wasn't certain it would even fit through the portal now.

It took one step toward her, but Aurelie knew it wouldn't follow her into the salt circle without a little more temptation. Quickly, she drew the blade across her hand, eliciting a sharp inhale from Des. Fortunately, he remained in place, poised to complete the circle.

The blood was enough. The demon rushed toward her so fast she hardly had time to leap out of its path before its foot landed where she'd been standing only seconds ago. "Now!" she screamed, but Des was already on it, spilling the salt in an unbroken arc, completing the circle.

As soon as the demon realized what they'd done, it threw its head back and released another roar.

Aurelie picked up the Helping Hand. The demon was so large it took up most of the circle, which was fortunate, because it couldn't move away from her as she began to reach toward it.

It bellowed as the chalk touched its skin, turning toward Aurelie and bringing its face so close to the edge of the circle she was sure it wasn't going to hold.

"Over here!" Des ran to the other side of the circle, leaping about, trying to draw the demon's attention. But he, too, realized they needed a better lure. He cut his hand on his blade and squeezed his fist, dripping blood onto the ground just outside the circle.

Aurelie had to blink away her tears of sheer terror to complete the rune. It was as crude and childlike as all her other attempts, but as she drew the final slash, the portal began to glow again in earnest. Des joined Aurelie, pulling her against him, just as the demon began to shriek. Its muscles strained as it scrabbled for purchase, but there was nothing to hold on to save for the portal itself.

Inch by inch, the demon was dragged backward toward the vortex, roaring in fury as it realized it was being sent back to the hellscape on the other side. Aurelie was about to yell in triumph when she felt something heavy against the back of her head, and then everything was blackness.

CHAPTER 39

DES

ONE MINUTE DES WAS GRIPPING ONTO AURELIE'S WAIST, hardly daring to believe her plan had worked, and the next she was a dead weight in his arm, sagging to the floor.

Behind her was Everard, still holding the heavy wooden beam he'd used to knock Aurelie unconscious. He took another swing, aiming for Des, but he was too fast.

"What the hell are you doing?" Des shouted, leaping out of the way as Everard swung again.

But in his effort to avoid Everard, Des had made a foolish decision in leaving Aurelie's side. Everard threw the wooden beam aside and grabbed her, scooping her roughly into his arms and carrying her to the portal. The demon was on the other side now, but as far as Des could tell, there was nothing keeping it there. They needed to destroy the portal now, before it was too late.

For one sickening moment, Des was afraid Everard was going to toss Aurelie into the vortex, but instead, he stretched his palm wide, reopening the wound he'd cut earlier.

"Stop!" Des roared, his sword leveled at Everard's throat.

"I cannot control the portal without a soul," the man rasped. Though he'd survived the goring, he was still pale and bleeding, clearly wounded by the demon's attack. "And since I don't have one, it must be Aurelie's."

Cold horror spread over Des as he realized what had been staring him in the face all along. "You always knew you needed a soul to control the portal, didn't you?"

Everard gazed down at Aurelie almost reverently. "Of course I did. And who better to take it from than a girl who talks to demons? The *somnia*, even the *natia*. They tried to protect her from me. I learned more about demons by seeing them through Aurelie's eyes than I'd ever imagined. I think if anyone would want this, it is her."

"No!" Des stepped closer, his sword arm trembling. "She doesn't want this. She wants to be free, to learn, to grow, to change this undeserving world. Give her to me, before I slice your fucking head off."

"If I don't do this," Everard said, his voice pitched low, "then there is nothing stopping demons from entering our world. This portal is a doorway through the veil. It will remain open, no new creations required. Is that what you want?"

"I want to *destroy* this portal. If it was good enough the first time, it should work now. Let her go!"

"Revenin destroyed the first portal with magic, something neither you nor I have. Aurelie must make a bargain with the gatekeeper, as I did with Kobal, in order to control it."

"What were you hoping to do? Force Aurelie to use the new gatekeeper to do your bidding?"

"There will be no forcing once Aurelie has given away her soul. Power will be all she craves."

Des could feel his panic rising, something he had little experience with. There had to be some other way. But he wasn't like Aurelie, full of creative ideas and solutions. He was the sword, his actions dictated by strategists and tacticians, not the one who came up with battle plans. He had no doubt he could take Everard in a fight. The man may be able to heal from a hole in his chest, but he doubted he could regrow his damned head. But as long as Everard was holding Aurelie, he couldn't risk attacking.

Everard had to be wrong about her. It was impossible to imagine her no longer caring about others, turning into a monster like Everard. Impossible, and yet not something he would ever willingly risk.

"Then take mine," he said, laying down the sword slowly. "My soul will work as well as hers, won't it?"

Everard tutted in mock sympathy. "Oh, my dear boy. You're in love with her, aren't you?"

Des hadn't put words to his feelings for Aurelie. How could he, when he'd never experienced them before? But as soon as Everard said it, he knew it was true. Until he met Aurelie, he'd considered *love* a hyperbolic descriptor for an emotion that made humans act like animals, and perhaps it was. But that didn't make it any less true. He loved her, and he couldn't regret anything about their time together, even if it had led to this. His only regret was that he hadn't told her how he felt.

He blinked back the tears in his eyes. "Just tell me, will my soul work?"

Everard nodded. "Of course. One soul is as good as another."

"I'll die, then?"

"No more than I'm dead," Everard said.

Des's stomach hollowed out. Everard was as good as dead in

Des's eyes. He had no compassion, no conscience, no ability to care about anything beyond his own aims. But he would get to see Aurelie live, and that would be enough. It had to be enough.

"All right," he said. "Now please, just put her down."

Everard nodded and gently laid Aurelie at Des's feet. "Come here, boy."

Des took a single step over Aurelie, and then Everard's hand gripped his, his blade flashing so quickly Des had no chance to even cry out, his plans to grab Aurelie and run dissolving into smoke. Everard thrust Des's hand into the vortex of the portal. Wild with panic, Des tried to pull back, but then the gatekeeper was on the other side, its red eyes boring into his, and it ripped a hole in its own hand with its teeth, pressing its bloody palm to Des's within the space of a single breath.

Des knew the moment his soul left his body because of the white-hot pain that tore through him, searing him from the inside out. It was a pain that lasted a thousand years and yet only an instant, leaving him empty. Instead of pain, there was only a hollow, fathomless absence.

But it wasn't until he looked up into Everard's eyes that he realized what the man had truly done.

A small voice behind him said a single, plaintive word. "Des?"

And Des felt absolutely nothing.

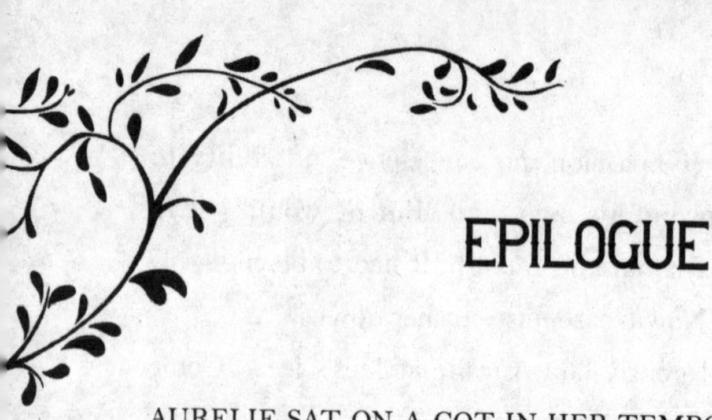

EPILOGUE

AURELIE SAT ON A COT IN HER TEMPORARY QUARTERS AT the Iron Fortress, cupping a now-tepid mug of tea in her numb hands. Uncle Leo's voice was a faraway drone in her head, in part thanks to her concussion, though she wasn't sure she'd be listening even if it weren't for the head wound she'd suffered at Everard's hands. Des was gone, or as good as, and it was all her fault.

"Aurelie, please. You must eat something."

She looked up from her mug to see Uncle Leo holding out a plate of unidentifiable meat, potatoes, and a vegetable that had probably once been green but was now a brownish gray. "I told you, I'm not hungry."

"I understand that. But sometimes we have to force ourselves to eat anyway."

There was an undercurrent of frustration in Leo's voice, which Aurelie could hardly blame him for. She'd ruined not only her own life, but his as well. The university had become its own fortress of sorts, their cottage commandeered by Everard, the entire campus surrounded by his thralls. No one would get near the portal as long as Everard lived. And beside him was the man who had once been Des.

Now, he was as much a shell as Everard. Or had been, the last time she saw him, after he bound himself to the gatekeeper demon, and, in a way she still didn't understand, to Everard himself. No one knew what his plan was yet. The veil was holding, though only by a thread, and demons had killed dozens of people before everyone started to realize that decapitation was now the only way to finish them off.

Fresh tears sprang up in her eyes, blurring her vision.

"Come now, don't cry," Leo said, setting the plate of food aside. "We're going to figure this out, my dear. The very best minds in the kingdom are working on it."

She couldn't help thinking that *she* had one of the very best minds in the kingdom, and instead of helping, she was here, imprisoned alongside her uncle, where she could be of no use to anyone. But then, what had she expected? She'd brought ruin upon Wisteria; of course no one would ask for her advice.

It had all happened so fast. One moment the monstrous portal demon had seemed to be passing back through, and the next she was on the ground with a splitting headache, Des standing beside Everard. She'd touched the back of her head, felt the blood congealing in her hair.

She had called to Des, hoping to make sense of what was happening, but when he looked at her, there was no recognition in his gray eyes. In that moment, she'd understood what he had given up to save her.

Now, as Aurelie and Uncle Leo awaited trial, there was little news of the world beyond the fortress gates. Their only sources of information were Daisy, Jasper, and Gareth, and they were forbidden from seeing them. Occasionally, Daisy would slip a note under their door. But the last one had been days ago, and Aurelie was left to imagine the worst.

Everard had complete control over the portal now, which he had never planned to destroy. He was using it to allow whichever demons he deemed useful through, though what his plans were beyond that remained a mystery to Aurelie. She'd heard rumors that King Gabor was in negotiations with him, or preparing to go to war, or was already dead.

"You know," her uncle said, placing a careful hand on her shoulder, "the entire time I was in Everard's basement, the only thing I prayed for was your safety."

Aurelie swiped at her tears bitterly. Better he had prayed for Aurelie's death. Uncle Leo had indeed gone to visit his friend—who, he finally shared, had been his lover many years ago—and waited until he died peacefully at home. On the way back to Wisteria City, Leo's train had broken down and he'd run into a tall, redheaded man at the station who was also returning to the city. Everard offered him a ride as a ruse for the kidnapping. He'd been told very little during his captivity, only enough to know that Aurelie had been lured into a dangerous scheme involving an invention.

Aurelie set her cold tea on the floor and was about to curl up on her cot when a knock sounded on the door of their quarters.

Uncle Leo called, "Come in," just as the door opened, revealing the hardened face of Commander Yew.

Aurelie had been interrogated by the man several times, so she assumed he was back for more questioning. She was already rising when he held up a hand. "Grab your belongings, Miss Blake. You won't be returning to this room."

She and Uncle Leo shared a startled look. Aurelie's mind

raced through all the possible scenarios, consistently returning to "hanged for treason."

"What's going on?" Leo demanded.

"The judges have conferred. They've finally decided on what to do with Aurelie."

She closed her eyes, bracing herself. *Courage, Aurelie.*

"What does that mean?" Leo pressed, standing beside her. He was still thin after his captivity, no more interested in the food provided by the Iron Guard than Aurelie, though he did a better job of choking it down.

Commander Yew took Aurelie by the upper arm and led her toward the door. She was sure he wouldn't tell them anything, but he must have taken some pity on Uncle Leopold, because he paused on the threshold and turned. "They've officially lost their minds, is what it means. They want her to join the Iron Swords."

End of Book One

ACKNOWLEDGMENTS

As always, first thanks go to my agent, Uwe Stender, and the team at TriadaUS. Your continued support is the one thing I can always count on in publishing, and I'm forever grateful.

Thank you to my editor, Clare Vaughn, for being such an enthusiastic supporter of Aurelie and Des, and for helping shape this book into something I'm truly proud of. Thanks also to the rest of the team at Harper: David Curtis, Erin DeSalvatore, Shona McCarthy, Danielle McClelland, Meghan Pettit, Andy Ball, Jenny Lu, and Matt Maguda.

Special thanks to Eleonor Piteira for the beautiful cover art. I'm honored to have your work gracing one of my books!

This book changed hands a few times before it finally found a place to land. Thank you to Bess Brasswell, Meghan McCullough, and the rest of the team at the late, great Inkyard Press for believing in me. I miss you all!

Thank you to Rebecca Ross for chatting with me about this story while it was still in its early stages, and for your friendship.

To the Echaniz family, thank you for letting me borrow Kiara's beautiful name. The character isn't based on her entirely, but I took inspiration from her kind heart and generous spirit. May her memory be a blessing.

To my siblings, thanks for the levity, the venting, and the understanding. I love our calls and hope they never end!

To Sarah, for the everything. And to Meep, Sarah's loyal companion, who inspired Mephisto. You were scrappy, sassy, snappy, and adorable. A little demonic, some might even say. But your love—like your eyebrows—was unparalleled. You are missed, smol dog.

Jack and Will, you guys continue to amaze me with your resilience, your open minds, your willingness to embrace the new, the scary, the absurd. Thank you for putting up with this crazy life. We promise to pay for the therapy.

To John, for two decades and counting of this wild ride. I love you.

And finally, to the readers, whether this is your first or seventh (!) of my books. There are so many stories out there, and it means the world that you picked up one of mine. I hope you like it. And I hope you'll forgive me for the ending.